John O'Hara's HOLLYWOOD

John O'Hara's HOLLYWOOD

STORIES BY
JOHN O'HARA

EDITED BY
MATTHEW J. BRUCCOLI

CARROLL & GRAF PUBLISHERS
NEW YORK

JOHN O'HARA'S HOLLYWOOD

Carroll & Graf Publishers
An Imprint of Avalon Publishing Group, Inc.
245 West 17th Street, 11th Floor
New York, NY 10011

First Carroll & Graf edition 2007

Library of Congress Cataloging-in-Publication Data is available.

ISBN-10: 0-7867-1872-2
ISBN-13: 978-0-78671-872-6

9 8 7 6 5 4 3 2 1

Printed in the United States of America

DESIGNED BY PAULINE NEUWIRTH, NEUWIRTH & ASSOCIATES, INC.

Distributed by Publishers Group West

Contents

This collection is dedicated to

the editor's friend Budd Schulberg,

who was John O'Hara's friend.

The United States in this Century is what I know, and it is my business to write about it to the best of my ability, with the sometimes special knowledge I have. The Twenties, the Thirties, and the Forties are already history, but I cannot be content to leave their story in the hands of the historians and the editors of picture books. I want to record the way people talked and thought and felt, and do it with complete honesty and variety.

—John O'Hara, Foreword to *Sermons and Soda-Water*

Introduction
Matthew J. Bruccoli

JOHN O'HARA WENT to Hollywood in the summer of 1934—before publication of his first novel, *Appointment in Samarra*—as a dialogue writer at Paramount. He had previously worked as a publicist for Warner Bros. in New York. His first movie-related story—which is set in New York—"Mr. Sidney Gainsborough: Quality Pictures," was published by *The New Yorker* in December 1932.

Between 1934 and 1955 O'Hara worked for Goldwyn, MGM, RKO, and United Artists, but mainly for Twentieth Century-Fox. He welcomed what he regarded as easy money but did not take the work seriously. In the Thirties he was paid $750 per week—a lot of money during the Depression—and his salary was raised to $1,000 and $1,250 during the Forties.

O'Hara received five screen credits, four of them shared with other writers. His only movie that pleased him was *Moontide* (1941), for which he received sole credit; but his screenplay based on Willard Robinson's novel was revised by Nunnally Johnson and producer Mark Hellinger. *Moontide,* Jean Gabin's first American movie, was expected to launch him as a Hollywood star. It was a major production with Thomas Mitchell, Ida Lupino, and Claude Rains; and it had two top directors, Fritz Lang and Archie Mayo. This atmospheric, quasi-tragic movie received good reviews but was not a box-office success.

O'Hara enjoyed the company of his transplanted writer friends from the East—including Robert Benchley, Dorothy Parker, and F. Scott Fitzgerald—and he formed close new friendships with Budd Schulberg and Clifford Odets. Many of O'Hara's Hollywood writer friends were committed leftists. Although his political ideas in the Thirties were liberal, he never became a party-line writer. His visits to Communist Party "study sessions" bored him. He made his only screen appearance in a bit part as a corrupt newspaperman in *The General Died at Dawn* (Paramount, 1936)—written by Odets and directed by Lewis Milestone—in which he had three lines. O'Hara enjoyed the Hollywood night-life and was a regular at the Vendome, Ciro's, the Trocadero, the Brown Derby, Al Levey's, and the Coconut Grove. Divorced since 1933, he steadily dated actress Zita Johann in 1934.

In Spring 1936 O'Hara met Belle Wylie—who was not in the movies—at a dinner party in Hollywood. They were married in December 1937.

O'Hara's last job in Hollywood came in 1955, when he wrote the original story—but not the screenplay—for *The Best Things in Life Are Free,* a biographical musical based on the song-writing team of DeSylva, Brown, and Henderson. At the same time he was writing *Ten North Frederick* at night. O'Hara's name appeared over the title on the movie. He subsequently wrote unproduced original screen stories for Twentieth Century-Fox at his home in Princeton. Five of his books—*Pal Joey* (1957), *Ten North Frederick* (1958), *Butterfield 8* (1960), *From the Terrace* (1960), and *A Rage to Live* (1965)—were made into more-or-less successful movies; but O'Hara did not work on the screenplays. *Appointment in Samarra* was never sold to the movies because he held out for a million-dollar fee.

John O'Hara wrote major stories about movie people, but he did not write a major Hollywood novel. O'Hara's third novel, *Hope of Heaven* (1938), is a Los Angeles or California novel; but it is not a Hollywood novel. The hero, screenwriter Jimmy Malloy, a stand-in for O'Hara, is not seen working. O'Hara did not write a Hollywood novel until *The Big Laugh* (1962), twenty-eight years after his first Hollywood writing job. Despite the popularity of what amounts to a sub-genre, American literature has only three major Hollywood novels: *What Makes Sammy Run?* and *The Disenchanted,* both written by insider F. Scott Fitzgerald; and *The Love of the Last Tycoon: A Western,* an unfinished masterpiece by Budd Schulberg, an outsider. Nathanael West's *The Day of the Locust* possibly qualifies for the shortlist.

O'Hara's Hollywood stories are about movie people—actors, actresses, producers, directors, agents, writers—not about the motion-picture industry. Despite his defining concern with the inside dope for his material, none of these stories examines the actual making of movies. The two long stories—O'Hara made a distinction between novellas and novelettes, but it is unclear to which category "Natica Jackson" and "James Francis and The Star" belong—are primarily character stories. "Natica Jackson" apparently draws on Euripides's *Medea.* O'Hara consistently examines the sexual opportunities provided by stardom or celebrity. A sense of borrowed time runs through most of the stories; the stars worry about how long their fame and money will last. In "The Way to Majorca" and "Yucca Knolls" second-rank actresses marry homosexual men who take care of them. "Saffercisco," written in 1936 during his second Hollywood stint, is an exemplary O'Hara story.

John O'Hara was a moralist. He was concerned with the effects of money and fame on movie people, many of whom are accidental and temporary celebrities. Despite the good times he had there, his Hollywood stories establish his disapproval of the industry's power to damage or destroy the people it uses and discards. He also indicates that there was something corrupt about some of his characters that made them susceptible to self-destruction before they ever set foot in a movie studio. As the literary master of the American class structure, O'Hara found abundant Hollywood material for his examination of social stratification. These stories document the professional standing of movie people in terms of how they live and spend money. In John O'Hara's time movie money had a built-in ostentation or conspicuous vulgarity, for which he details the nuances.

I am indebted to Herman Graf for persevering in the publication of this book.

Mr. Sidney Gainsborough: Quality Pictures

MR. GAINSBOROUGH'S ENTRANCE was important. As vice-president and sales manager of Quality Pictures, it is his duty to sell, to theaters in the East and South, the films which Q. P. makes in Hollywood. Mr. Gainsborough himself is important.

He swung wide the door of his secretary's office. He slackened his pace—actually he halted, although he seemed to be moving—long enough to say: "Good morning, Miss Garvin. Any calls?"

"No A calls, Mr. Gainsborough. Some B's and C's."

"The hell with them," he said. "Don't bother me for a minute or two, unless it's important."

He entered his own office and threw his coat and hat on a deep, leather-cushioned chair. He walked to his desk, but then went back and picked up the hat and coat. He hung the coat on a hanger in a maple closet, and he smoothed out the indentations of the cream-colored hat until it lost all individuality.

He sat down at the massive desk and laid his head in his hands. Then he opened the carafe and poured some water into an enamelled, monogrammed glass. He took a sip of the water, then spat it out in the tall brass cuspidor which was at his side but was hidden from possible occupants of any other chairs in the office. He began to read one of three piles of letters. He read the first letter through, but he barely glanced at the others. He took a gold pencil from his pocket and wrote on a Florentine leather-bound pad: "Wash., Atlanta, New Orl., Memphis, St. Louis, Chi." He made a check mark beside each entry. He gazed out the window and rubbed his beard, caressing the cleft in his chin. He looked at the large photograph of his wife and two daughters and made a face at it. Then he turned to stare at a photograph of a young woman, which hung on the opposite wall. The photograph was one of many: some of the subjects were men, some were women. Some were in costume: cowboy costume, flying suits, military uniform. Some of the men were wearing polo coats with upturned collars. Some of the comedians wore the imbecile expressions which had made them famous. The young woman who had his attention was wearing a white top hat, black panties and stockings, and a mess jacket with nothing underneath. She was pointing a white stick at some invisible object. Her photograph bore the written inscription: "To Sidney Gainsborough, with Affection and Esteem." The other photographs bore either the same inscription or a variant: "To Sidney Gainsborough, with Esteem and Affection."

Mr. Gainsborough pushed one of a series of six buttons on the desk. Miss Garvin appeared, with her notebook in hand.

"Well, it looks like I'm going to take a trip South," said Mr. Gainsborough. "I just checked over Washington, Atlanta, New Orleans, Memphis, St. Louis, and Chicago. All these muggs have the same story. They say they're doing swell business, considering, but only a couple gave me any real figures. Chicago's all right, but I don't know about the rest of them. I guess I better plan to be gone about a month. I don't know how long I'll stay in each place. Probably a week. Now, uh, I'll leave Friday for Washington. Make the arrangements, will you please? And then tell that What's-His-Name, in the publicity department—"

"Mr. Frank?"

"Him. Tell him I want to see him."

Miss Garvin left, and Mr. Gainsborough poured another glass of water, and spat it out. He lit a cigarette and awaited Mr. Frank. The signal buzzed, and Mr. Gainsborough said into the telephone: "If that's Frank, send him in." He busied himself with a letter and fountain pen.

"Good morning, Mr. Gainsborough," said Frank.

"Sit down. I have a story for you. Get it in all the trade papers. Patsy Vane is going to make personal appearances all over the South—in the key cities, that is—in connection with the opening of 'Strange Virgin.' Take this down. She opens in Washington this weekend and stays there a week, then jumps to Atlanta, Georgia; New Orleans; Memphis, Tennessee; and probably St. Louis. A week at each place. You want to mention that this is the first time Miss Vane is appearing in her native South, the first time since she was given a long-term contract with the company. You know. Hoke it up. She's from some place down South."

"New Orleans," said Mr. Frank. "They all come from New Orleans."

"What?"

"I said I understand she comes from New Orleans."

"Well, that's for you to find out. Anyhow, I want all that in the trade papers, and be sure the theatres on her route have plenty of advance stuff, see?"

"Yes, sir, we'll take care of that," said Mr. Frank.

"And get that out today. You can go now. Oh, wait a minute. Come in and see me in a day or two. I may have to go on a business trip to some of our branches, and I may want some kind of a story about that. But I'll tell you about that later. O.K."

"Thank you," said Mr. Frank.

Mr. Gainsborough watched Mr. Frank leave the office. He poured another glass of water and spat in the cuspidor. "Wise guy, eh?" he said, and began to write a memo to the publicity department regarding Mr. Frank.

Saffercisco

WHILE JACK GRANT is not the world's most famous movie actor, it can be truthfully said that he has been; and even today his name on the marquee of the Paramount in Palm Beach or the Majestic in Tamaqua, Pa., means box office. But it is not with his power as a draw that this little anecdote is concerned. Maybe it would be better to say that among his four or five wives (many persons are vague as to whether he ever actually was married to one of the ladies) are two of the, say, fifteen most popular movie actresses. And among those fifteen at least two more have been his mistress. That score more or less establishes the fact that Jack got around, and when he fell for Maude Hislip it was as much of a surprise to him as it was to anyone.

She came out to Hollywood on the crest. That is, she had been in one hit, one forced-run play, and several turkeys. Shortly after she came to Hollywood, she married Bobby Waterman, the writer. (He is the kind of writer whose name is inevitably followed by the appositional "the writer.") They got veiled up and were together about two years when Jack met Maudie.

Well, he fell in love. He had met her at parties, but then suddenly one day he really saw her, and loved her dearly. He also liked Bobby Waterman. Jack thought it over and thought it over and talked with a friend (an old girl friend) about it, and he made up his mind that he had to marry Maudie. So he called her up and asked her if he might come to dinner the following Friday, and Maudie said she'd be delighted. What Jack wanted to do was to lay his cards on the table; say to Bobby, "Bobby, I love Maudie and I want to marry her." Open and aboveboard. Honest. Decent. Civilized. He could hardly wait till Friday. He consulted his old girl friend about what clothes to wear: whether to wear the tweed jacket and flannel slacks, or dinner coat, or tails. The girl friend said he would be wise to wear tails; it was a momentous occasion, and besides he was at his handsomest in tails.

So that Friday Jack was dressed and ready at seven, and he had a couple of drinks and drove out to Santa Monica, arriving at Maudie and Bob's around eight o'clock. Bob was in riding breeches and coat, with a scarf around his neck, and he greeted Jack pleasurably and obviously sincerely. They had a drink together and a few more, and no sign of Maudie, but Jack didn't want to be hasty or gauche or anything like that, so he did not say anything. They had a lot of drinks, fast, and nine o'clock came and no sign of Maudie and no sign of dinner. And they were getting stewed. Jack read a lot, and they covered the world's literature, then they talked movie politics and exchanged funny stories about producers and things that had happened to them on location and all about horses and dogs, and Jack thought he never had met a more charming guy, and Bobby not only thought so, but in time came to the point of telling Jack so. "I didn't know you were such a nice guy," Bobby said. "You know, I *like* you. I thought you were more or less of a heel at first, but you're all right. O.K. You ought to do this oftener—drop in for dinner."

"Drop in?" said Jack. "I didn't drop in. Wuddia mean drop in? Maude knew I was coming."

"Did she? Didn't say anything to me about it. Oh, well, I don't care. Here you are, so let's have a powder, one more little powder, then we'll go in and graze. Wunnia say?"

"Sure, but what about Maude? Don't you think we oughta wait for Maudie?"

"Oh." Bobby began to laugh quietly. He looked down into his drink and shook his head, signifying nothing. He kept it up until he exasperated Jack.

"What is this?" said Jack. "Didn't Maudie expect me?"

"Don't think so. If she did, she didn't tell me, Jack." Bobby cleared his throat and changed his tone. "You know where she is, don't you? You don't mean to tell me that you don't *know* where Maudie *went.* Don't you know where Maudie is?"

"No, of course I don't. I had a dinner engagement right here in this house. Right *here.*" He made a gesture like an umpire indicating Strike One. "Where is she?"

"Saffercisco."

"Sa' Fra'cisco?"

"S-a-n Fran-*cisco.*"

"You mean on location, or what? A personal appearance?"

"No, no. No, no, no, no, no. Maudie is up in Saffercisco spending the weekend with Harry Lotterman, her director."

"What do you mean?" said Jack.

"What do you mean, what do I mean? You know what I mean. She went away with Harry Lotterman for the weekend. Wunnia think I mean? Jack, you're not dumb. You're a big boy now. Wunnia mean, what do I mean? What kinda talk is that, Jack?"

"You mean to sit here and tell me your wife goes to Sa' Fra'cisco with a louse like that and you just sit here?"

Bobby looked at him a long time, wet his lips a couple of times, getting ready to talk, and then he gazed at his cigarette until he began to get cross-eyed. Then he said, "Well, Jack, I'll tell you. I wanna tell you something. Listen to me, Jack, while I tell you this. Maudie, the first time she did this I just coudn't stand it. It hurt me. It hurt me, Jack. And then the second time. That hurt me, too. Really did. Bu-u-ut then, you know you can only stand so much, Jack. Only so much. Then you begin to get used to it. I had to get used to it, Jack. And let me tell you something"—he leaned over and tapped Jack's knee—"Jack, old boy, you might as well get used to it, too."

Brother

THERE WERE A lot of voices; there was one authorized voice singing "I'm Putting All My Eggs in One Bas-ket"; there was a fine jazz orchestra wasting its arrangements on three hundred and fifty unheeding persons; seltzer bottles squawked their bottom drops into highball glasses. At the moment there was no conversation at one table, around which were seated four persons, three ugly men and a pretty girl. The girl was sitting so she could see the dancers, and the men were characteristically looking over their shoulders at the dancers, at people at other tables, at people entering the place. This was Hollywood.

"Hello."

The four persons glanced at one tall, thin young man, pale of face, blond of hair, and garbed in a gun-club-check jacket and dark-blue flannel slacks. Around his neck a silk scarf.

"Hello, Leonard," said the pretty girl.

"Can I sit down with you?" said Leonard.

"Sit down," said one of the men.

"How's Ruthie?" said the pretty girl.

"Fine," said Leonard.

"Yeah, how's Ruthie?" said one of the men.

"She's fine," said Leonard.

"How's your mother?" said another of the men.

"Fine. I just left her," said Leonard.

"Have a drink, Leonard?" said the third man.

"I'll have a beer," said Leonard. "I'll pay for it, though."

"Naah," said the first man. "Waiter, give him a beer."

"I'm only drinking beer," said Leonard.

"Fattening," said one of the men.

"He can use it," said another.

"Yes," said Leonard. "I want to put on some weight."

"Where's Ruthie tonight?" said a man.

"I don't know. I thought she'd be here."

"That's for me, that Ruthie," said another man.

"Yeah, I go for that. I'm glad she's not my sister."

They all laughed.

"I bet Leonard's glad she's *his* sister," said a man. The men laughed.

"Shut up, wise guy," said the pretty girl. "All of you."

"They can't kid me," said Leonard. "I got plenty of that even before I came out here. Where I used to work they'd always try to kid me about me being Ruthie's brother. They used to call me that, Mr. Ruth Rugby."

"Where'd she ever get that name, Rugby?"

"Rogowicz," said Leonard. "Rugby is a school in England, also a game."

"I heard of the game," said a man.

"Well, what's with you, Leonard?"

"How do you mean, what's with me?" said Leonard.

"You gettin' much?"

"Oh, shut up, you guys," said the pretty girl. "Leonard's a nice kid. Leave him alone."

"Oh, they can't kid me," said Leonard. "I got a letter from a friend of mine back in New York Monday. He said I suppose you're right in there with those chorus girls for Ruthie's next picture. I wouldn't do that. Wouldn't that be a smart thing if Ruthie's brother got mixed up with some chorine?"

"Cho*rine,* is it?" said a man. "Say. The gaberoo."

"He knows from nothin'," said another man.

"Don't pay any attention to them, Leonard. Did they start shooting yet on Ruthie's new picture?"

"Yes. Yesterday. I'm glad," said Leonard.

"What the hell, she gets paid anyway," said a man.

"I'll slap your face, Louis Harrow," said the pretty girl. "Why are you glad, Leonard?"

"Oh, gives me more to do. I get tired of doing nothing. When she's working at the studio I drive her to work every morning. I do it for something to do."

"Why don't you go to college? U.C.L.A. *That's* a big college," said the girl.

"Well, I don't know. I never finished high school," said Leonard.

"They hadda burn down the school to get him outa the freshman class," said a man.

"Oh, geezes. With Cantor they'll have you next," said another.

"Why don't you go home, wise guy?" said the girl.

"Some people haven't got anything else to do but make cracks. Agents," said Leonard.

"Who ast you to sit here if you don't like it?" said the man.

"Parasites that live on their ten per cent that they didn't earn," said Leonard.

"Don't answer him, Leonard. Don't give him that much satisfaction," said the pretty girl.

"Go out and call up Ruthie," said another man.

"I would, only I don't know where she is," said Leonard.

"I could tell you," said another man.

The others snickered.

"You only think you could," said Leonard. "I went by there and her car isn't there."

"Oh, he knows," said a man.

"Dirty, evil-minded bastards, all of you," said the pretty girl. "Don't mind them, Leonard."

"Certain people try to get somewhere and they don't, so they get sore. You know, Peggy," said Leonard.

"She knows, all right," said a man. "Nobody's sore at Peggy."

"Wade a minute," said another man.

"Oh, all right," said the man who had made the crack.

"Well," said the man who had resented the crack.

"Of course it's all right what she calls me because I want to rib this punk. Sure. I'm a bastard because I rib Leonard."

"He's right," said Peggy's defender. "You oughtn't of called him that."

"Then what right does he have to say things like that about Leonard's sister?" said Peggy.

"It ain't for you to insult your friends, though. Nobody ast Leonard to come to this table. Not even you. So don't call your friends names like that. I don't like it. You owe Louis an apology."

"I'll owe it to him," said Peggy. "I guess you better go sit with some other people, Leonard."

"I was just going to," said Leonard. "Good night, Peggy."

"Good night, Leonard," said Peggy.

"Gi' my regards to Ruthie," said a man.

"She wouldn't even know your name," said Leonard, going.

"That's what *you* think," said the man. "I have a notion to give him a punch in the nose. Punk."

They watched Leonard. A few people spoke to him, with that expression in which there is full recognition, achieved without a nod and with only an almost imperceptible movement of the lips. It so uncompromisingly means, Don't sit down. Then he was gone out of sight.

Richard Wagner: Public Domain?

SILENCE DID NOT hang over this huge room. Silence punched its way through what sound there was, and finally came to a little group of disconsolate people. The disconsolate people were sitting with their legs over the arms of the folding camp chairs, or they were smoking cigarettes half-way down and stamping on them and looking down at the butts and shaking their heads at the crushed butts. In one way or another they were all saying "God-damit," and worrying. High above these people, and at an angle, were men in undershirts, not worrying. The men who controlled the lights did not worry much about the people down below; the men with the lights, and the extras, got their dough, and it was up to the disconsolate people to figure out some way to finish the picture. Meanwhile the undershirts and the extras were earning their pay.

A fat man with an Anglo-Irish name and a nose that was strictly from Rivington Street scratched the full growth of hair between his shoulder blades. He shook his head. A skimpy little Irishman shook his. Director, and assistant director.

"I know! Ask Mischa. That's what he gets paid for, writing songs," said the skimpy little Irishman.

"What I was thinking of!" said the director. "Ask 'im."

The little Irishman began calling out, "Mischa, Mischa," and a few moments later one of the extras said to him, "Over there. Over where the card game is going on."

"Why didn't you say so?" said the Irishman. He went over where the card game was going on. "Mischa, we're in a spot," he said.

"Away," said a little man with a waxed mustache. "I bump," he said to another little man at the table. Someone else said, "It's up to you," and then there was more talk of bumping. "This here sounds like 'A Yank at Oxford,' " Mischa said. "Pay me. I go to the head of the river. Now what the hell do you want, jerk?"

"Mischa, we're in a spot," said the little Irishman.

"Who?"

"Arch wants to ask you something," said the Irishman.

"I do anything for Arch," said Mischa. "Tell 'im to come over."

"Aw, now, Mischa," said the Irishman.

"Oh, all right. Deal me out," said Mischa.

"Well, anyway, leave some of the matches," said one of the men at the table.

"Sure. I'm in you for like roughly—I'll settle for a deuceroo each. Now what is it, dear? What does Arch want?"

"He—"

"I'll talk to Arch," said Mischa. He got up and went to the director. "What is it, Arch?"

The man with the nose scratched the hair again. "We got all these people here. If we could, I do' know, what's use shooting around people if you got all these people here, but the script don't call—"

"Now listen, Arch," said Mischa. "What do you want and if I can I'll do it. What is it?"

"Music. We're four days behind schedule, and here that means but plenty. If we had something we could fill in, wit' all these people. Like a night-club sequence."

"A night-club sequence," repeated Mischa. "With what you own—you don't want me to write a little number."

"No. I just thought. I don't know what the hell I thought."

"Lit's sit down a minute," said Mischa. "Night club. Night club. Of course I could *write* something. I better sit down a minute." He sat down, in Arch's folding camp chair, and scratched his chin with one finger. "I know! 'Smile, Brother'!"

" 'Smile, Brother'?"

"Sure," said Mischa. " 'Smile, brother, smile, brother, let's con-grat-u-late each other.' You don't know it? Well, Bing used to sing it with the Rhythm Boys. Eleven years ago. 'It won't be long now.' Bing, Barris—I forget who was with them. You could get it for hay. Buttons. You could get it for buttons."

"Yeah, but we don't want to pay buttons. We don't want to pay anything, Mischa. This, we only want to fill in this night-club sequence."

"Mm. Maybe you own it. Maybe Paramount owns it. But anyway, let me think. I'll play it for you." Mischa, a trumpet player, went to a piano and played it for Arch. Arch liked it. He especially liked it when Mischa and one of the poker players did an imitation of the Rhythm Boys. It was easy to see he wanted it, but it was easy to see he was thinking of the shooting schedule and the budget on this picture. It was so easy to see it that Mischa looked sad, and then Mischa began to think. He asked Arch to wait a minute, and Arch waited more than a minute while Mischa fumbled around the unfamiliar piano. Arch went back to his chair and was almost dozing away when Mischa yelled out, "Is Wagner in the public domain?"

"I think so," said Arch.

"Send somebody out and find out. Call up. If Wagner is in the public domain we got it."

Arch sent the Irishman to call up and find out if R. Wagner was in the public domain, and turned back to Mischa. He said, "But, Mischa, I don't get it. Even if Wagner is in the public domain what good does that do us?"

"Arch, for cry sweet sake," said Mischa. "Listen here. Jevver hear the Fire Music? Well, listen." He fooled around with the piano, not going above middle C.

"No," said Arch.

"Well, now listen," said Mischa. He played some more.

"Oh," said Arch. "Can we do it?"

"We can if Wagner's in the public domain," said Mischa. "And even if he isn't, for God's sake." Mischa unbuckled his belt and half turned to Arch. "Geez, Arch, if I'd of only stayed in school I cudda done the lyrics too. I'm not gunna wait for that donkey. 'Smile, brother. . . .' "

Reunion Over Lightly

THE FAT MAN in the dark-blue loose-fitting suit danced over to the table where the three men were sitting and separated from his partner but kept his right arm part way around her waist.

"I beg your pardon, Mr. Prentiss," said the fat man.

"Yes?" said Prentiss, with a smile, all teeth and face muscles.

"I don't want to be a visiting fireman, but I did meet you, two years ago on the *Normandie.* You wouldn't remember."

"N-no, but I probably will. Won't you sit down?" Prentiss stood up and with a nice little gesture he indicated the two vacant chairs at his table.

"No thanks. The only reason I came over like this, I told this lady, my sister-in-law, I said I met you once on the *Normandie,* and of course she said Bert Prentiss was one of the few movie stars that wasn't high-hat."

Prentiss bowed slightly and smiled at the woman. "I hope I deserve that at any rate. *Please* sit down."

"Well—" said the fat man.

"Oh, sure," said the woman.

"Well, first of all, my name is Stenton. I was travelling with Professor Norman. Taught you at Cornell?"

"Of course! I *do* remember. We played bridge together," said Prentiss.

"That's right," said Stenton.

"I told you," said his sister-in-law.

"Well, Mr. Prentiss, I want you to meet Mrs. Olforth."

"It's a great pleasure to meet you, and very nice to see you again, Mr. Stenton. Of course I remember now. You took some money away from me."

The fat man gave a quick, fat chuckle. "Thirty-some dollars," he said. He and Mrs. Olforth sat down.

"How's Normie? Are you at Cornell, too, Mr. Stenton? Or is it Dr. Stenton?" Prentiss wrinkled his brow, trying to recall.

"Yes, I'm afraid it is."

"So sorry," said Prentiss. "Mrs. Walford, may I present Mr. Cohen—and Mr. O'Byrne. Dr. Stenton: Mr. Cohen, Mr. O'Byrne. You ought to know each other, gentlemen. O'Byrne and Cohen make a lifework of taking money away from me, Dr. Stenton. O'Byrne's my lawyer and Cohen's my agent. Now, what would you like to drink, Mrs. Walford?"

"Well, I've *been* drinking gin fizzes."

"Then another gin fizz? And Doctor?"

"I'm having Bass's, thanks," said Stenton.

Prentiss looked at the hovering waiter to see if he got that. He got it and went away.

"Well, well, we meet again," said Prentiss. "Did you say you are at Cornell, Doctor, or not?"

"No, I'm at a much smaller place, my alma mater, little college called Kenyon, in Ohio. I'm out here on a visit. Mrs. Olforth lives here in Los Angeles, and with things the way they are in Europe I decided I'd see California this year instead of going abroad."

"Yes, I seem to recall your saying you went abroad every year."

"That's right. Normie and I managed to get abroad together every year the last five years except this one. My wife went, though."

"Oh, really?" said Prentiss.

"Yes, she's Mrs. Olforth's sister. You couldn't stop *her.* She and my daughter. I have a daughter a junior at Mount Holyoke, and she and Mrs. Stenton wouldn't let a little thing like a war stop them. I had a letter from them the other day. Tuesday." He halted and looked at Prentiss, then at Cohen, then permanently at O'Byrne. "They're travelling with gas masks in their bags."

"Well, I'll be a son of a bitch," said O'Byrne.

Stenton looked away from him and back at Prentiss. "I didn't get across in the last one and I guess I'm too old now, but—" Whatever he was going to say never was said, because the drinks arrived. Prentiss helped the waiter put the drinks at the right places.

"You ready for some more, Mr. Prentiss?" said the waiter.

Dr. Stenton looked at the two glasses in front of Prentiss. One glass was quite full, and beside it was a Coca-Cola bottle not quite empty. The other was a water glass with a stem, and there was ice in it. That glass was about half full.

"Not yet, thanks, Manuelo," said Prentiss.

"Coca-Cola?" said Dr. Stenton. "As I recall, Mr. Prentiss, when we were on shipboard you—"

Cohen spoke to Prentiss. "Bert, for God's sake, who do you think you're kidding wit' that prop coke?" He turned to Stenton. He picked up the stem glass and thrust it forward under Stenton's nose. "Get an inhale of that," he said.

Stenton smelled it. "Gin?" he said.

"Straight gin, unless you wanta count the ice. That coke, he has that in front of him all night. Twice I hadda take a sippa the goddamn stuff myself, to make it look authentic. Straight gin in this glass. This fella's a bad boy, Doctor."

Prentiss smiled sadly.

"I *tell* you," Cohen continued. "Over there, the little fella wit' the blonde against the wall, that's Bert's producer and Bert ain't suppose to be drinking. So who knows he is drinking? Only the entire population of Los Angeles County, including Pomona, Oxnard, Van Nuys, Long Beach, everybody."

"Oxnard?" said O'Byrne.

"So he orders a prop coke when he sees Levitt come in. The prop coke, then the water glass he fills up with the straight gin and a little ice to make it authentic. Bert, *you're* not fooling Levitt."

"Oxnard isn't in Los Angeles County," said O'Byrne. "Is it?" He asked Mrs. Olforth.

"No, I don't think so," she said.

"Any damn fool would know that," said O'Byrne.

"Doctor, the guy's drunk as a monkey this minute," said Cohen. "He couldn't walk across the floor if I asked him. He'd fall right flat on his face. You see what I'm up against, and he makes a crack like that when you sat down. I *protect* him." Cohen bit the end off a cigar and spat it into his cupped hand. "Any time he isn't satisfied with his representation, all he's got to do is call up and say so, or if I'm not in, tell my secretary and he'll have his release within twenty-four hours by registered mail. I admit he's one of the most valuable properties in the industry. I admit that, but don't ever get the idea I don't earn my fee. Say, isn't that *Paula?* What's she doing gout with that jerk?"

"Is Paula here?" said Prentiss.

"Paula who?" said O'Byrne.

"Oh, you know, Paula that Bert had out the ranch Saturday. She came with Joe Friday night."

"No, she's still up at the ranch," said O'Byrne.

No one noticed it going, but the gin was gone from the water glass. "Manuelo," said Prentiss.

"Yes, sir?" said the waiter.

Prentiss touched the glass with a finger.

"Yes, sir," said the waiter.

"I'm not sure that's Paula, but I will say she does resemble Paula," said Cohen. "Bert, that ain't Paula rover there, is it? Paula, from last Saturday at the ranch?"

"Where?" said Prentiss.

"Striped skirt, dancing with that jerk," said Cohen.

"Definitely not Paula," said Prentiss. "Say, I think it is Paula."

"Where?" said O'Byrne.

"Dancing, with the striped skirt on, over with that jerk rumbaring."

"I don't see her," said O'Byrne.

"There's somebody between her now," said Cohen.

"It's Paula all right," said Prentiss. He grinned. "Who's that with her?"

Cohen looked at Prentiss and frowned, and then it almost seemed as though he were about to cry. "Now, Bert, please! For me, Bert." He turned to Mrs. Olforth. "Lady, you forgive me if I sound rude and impolite, but if she comes over here, you won't like it, so to spare yourself embarrassing moments—Bert, now, don't get up. Just wait till she comes over this way. She'll be over."

"That's perfectly all right," said Mrs. Olforth. She and her brother-in-law stood up.

"What's this? What's this?" said Prentiss.

"We've got to get back to our own party," said Mrs. Olforth.

"I'm so sorry, but I will be seeing you Saturday, won't I?" said Prentiss.

"Sa—" hissed Stenton.

"Thanks again," said Mrs. Olforth. She took Stenton's hand, the one he was offering to Prentiss, and pulled him away.

"Look at Paula," said Prentiss. "Isn't she cute? Ed, isn't she the one, though? That's my she, that Paula."

"I wish I was back somewhere," said Cohen.

The Magical Numbers

GREGORY PAULSEN, THE director, tossed his Alpine hat upon the white, deep-cushioned chair. It teetered, and fell. "The hell with it," he said. He took off his African bush coat and tossed it upon the chair. It stayed. He removed his bandanna neckerchief and stuffed it in his pocket and looked at his wife.

She was sitting in another white, deep-cushioned chair near the fireplace. Both legs were on the seat, curled under her, and she was staring at the newspaper. "Hello," he said.

"Hello," she said.

"Well, what are you reading so intently?"

She raised her eyes to the top of the paper and read aloud, "The *Herald Express.*"

"God, you look as if you were studying a problem in math."

"In what?" she said, looking at him for the first time.

"In math. Mathematics. Arithmetic. Algebra."

"I am," she said.

He sat down and lit a cigarette. "Oh, I see. Well, I always thought they'd come to that."

"Who?"

"The *Herald Express.* I always used to say it's only a question of time, matter of months or weeks, then they'll have to turn it into an arithmetic book." Paulsen rang for the butler. "Nobody cares about murder or rape any more. The American people—"

"Shut up. I'm trying to remember something."

"Can you remember what happened to Harry? Why doesn't he answer the bell? I want a drink." He got up and rang a second, a third time.

"I was born in 1917. That's true," she said.

"Harry, get me a Scotch-and-soda and *put some Scotch* in it. Gladys? Drink?"

She shook her head no. "I have to concentrate. Liquor makes me not concentrate." To Harry she said, "Harry, get me a pencil and a piece of paper. Some old paper, not the engraved."

"Yes, Ma'am." Harry went on his errands. "I can't do this in my head, but I think they're right," said Gladys. "Here. I might as well show it to you." She held out the paper.

"Read it to me. I won't move out of this chair till I get a drink."

"Well, it's an article in the *Herald* and it says, this is the headline, 'Gladys Gray's Lucky Numbers.' That's the headline. Then it says, underneath, 'The magical numbers seven and eleven have played an important part in the life of lovely Gladys Gray, Twentieth Century-fox featured player now appearing in "Strange President," the story of the life of John Tyler, the Darryl F. Zanuck production which is now showing at Grauman's Chinese.' I wonder how it's doing."

"Sensational. . . . Thanks, Harry," said Paulsen.

"Thank you, Harry. Anyway, then it goes on to say, 'Grauman's Chinese. Miss Gray, who laughingly denies being a slave to superstition, nevertheless admits that if she were so inclined she would be influenced by the numbers so dear to the devotees of the "galloping ivories." ' I wish they didn't put that in. I don't want people going around thinking I'm a crap-shooter."

"They wouldn't if they ever saw you," said Paulsen.

"Do you want me to read this or will you stop interrupting?"

"Continue, continue," said Paulsen.

"Just remember you're not my director. When you come home, you leave that stuff at the studio and don't keep directing, directing, directing. That's the—"

"The numbers seven and eleven," said Paulsen.

"Well. Just remember. 'Miss Gray was born on July 11, 1917; July is the seventh month, and she was born on the eleventh day of that month.' That's right. 'Also there is an eleven and a seven in 1917. She has appeared in eleven pictures.' That's not counting shorts, I guess. 'She was married to Gregory Paulsen, the director, on April 7, 1937, which not only has two sevens, but also April is the fourth month and four plus seven equals eleven. Prominent in the activities of the Tail-waggers, Miss Gray has owned seven dogs; there is an eleven in her licence plates and a seven in the street address of her Roxbury Drive home.' Jeepers Creepers! It's uncanny."

"Is it?"

"Of course it is. It's *definitely* uncanny, especially because I never noticed it before. It's been going on ever since I was born and I never noticed it. Where do you think they got it?"

"The publicity department, naturally."

"Kline?"

"Not Kline. He couldn't be bothered with that. Somebody you never heard of. Probably some office boy. They do it all the time."

"I never heard of it before. Anyway, how would they know all that?"

"Listen, lovely Gladys Gray, if I had a buck for every time that gag has been used, I'd—I could buy you seven hundred and eleven diamonds, at least. When I was with *F.B.O.* for God's sake they were doing it. The first time I was with *Universal* they were doing it."

"But it's true."

"All right, so it's true. As far as that goes, I have seven letters in my first name and seven in my last. There are seven days in a week. I am thirty-eight years old. Eight and three's eleven. It's a gag. And not a very good gag, either."

"You can't sit there and tell me it doesn't work out more with me than it does with you. Why look, from the day I was born. Your birthday isn't anything like mine. I'll bet it works out in thousands of ways. Ring for Harry."

"Gladly," said Paulsen.

Harry appeared. "Yes, Ma'am?"

"Harry, how old are you?" said Gladys.

"Forty-one, Ma'am."

"How old is Elsie?"

"I think she's thirty-six, Ma'am."

"Thirty-six. Six and three. Are you sure she isn't thirty-eight?"

"Pretty sure, Ma'am. I ain't even sure she's thirty-six yet."

"Maybe she's thirty-four."

"I don't think she's thirty-four, Ma'am. I'm pretty sure of that," said Harry.

"Maybe she could be seventy-seven," said Paulsen. "Harry, I'm about ready for another one."

"Yes, sir," said Harry.

"My mother!" said Gladys.

"Ma'am?" said Harry.

"Not you, Harry. You can get Mr. Paulsen's drink."

"No, not you, Harry. I have to have six more drinks. Or maybe ten," said Paulsen.

". . . October, *November.* Eleven. I know it was November. Do you remember Ma's birthday?"

"Very well," said Paulsen.

"It was in November, and that's eleven. See?"

"That's right. I should have given her eleven hundred dollars instead of a lousy old even grand," said Paulsen.

"I gave part of it, don't forget."

"I remember you were *going* to give part of it. But Christmas, new fur coat, one thing or another. Those things naturally slip one's mind. I know how it is. Easy come, easy go. What are we having for dinner?"

"That's all right. You lose that much playing poker."

"I'll have you know I'm ahead of that game. I'm over two thousand bucks ahead of that game."

"Highball, sir," said Harry. "Elsie says she's thirty-five, Ma'am. She'll be thirty-six next birthday. She says you have a record of it in some insurance papers."

"Thirty-five. Oh, well, she was thirty-four when we hired her," said Gladys.

"Mrs. Paulsen's interested in numerology, Harry. That's all, thanks."

"Yes, sir," said Harry.

When he had left the room, Paulsen got up and went to see for sure that Harry wasn't listening outside. "You damn fool," said Paulsen. "They'll walk out on us. They think you're crazy, and the best damn couple in Hollywood."

"You're making a mountain out of a molehill," she said. "Anyway, maybe we ought to let him go. He isn't either one, seven, or eleven. At least she was seven when she came here, but he never was. Oh, I know. How do you spell O'Neill?"

"What's that got to do with it?"

"That's Harry's name. How do you spell it?"

Paulsen thought a moment, moving his lips slightly and counting on fingers that he held behind his back. "O'Neill? Why, 'o-n-e-i-double-l.' "

"You sure?"

"Positive. There's no other way to spell it. Eugene O'Neill. Look in the bookcase. The plays of Eugene O'Neill. See for yourself."

"Six! Six and five, eleven! Jeepers Creepers! Harry O'Neill, eleven. See?"

"You're right, Gladys. You're certainly right. Yes sir."

She looked at him with hostility and suspicion. "I don't know. I'm not so sure."

"Now what?"

"A minute ago you were saying it was a gag, and now suddenly you're all enthusiastic. Are you trying to shut me up by babying me?"

"Oh, now honey, don't misjudge me," said Paulsen.

"Well," said Gladys. She picked up the paper again. He watched her nervously until she said, "For God's sake, who do you think they gave Claudette's dressing room to?"

Adventure on the Set

DEAR HAL:

Well, stupid, my latest epic is in the can and in a couple more weeks Broadway and Main St. will have the opportunity of sitting through 95 minutes of looking at my kisser. "Strange Courage" they finally decided on as the name of the latest epic and in it I play this young doctor that gets out of medical college and goes to work in a small town in the middle west or west but not the far west. It is more a modern picture than horse opera. I get out of medical college and full of ideals and pretty soon my ideals take a terrific pasting around because I no sooner unpack my trunk and hang up my "shingle" than there is some kind of an epidemic and I tangle with the water company as the epidemic turns out to be typhoid fever (very good scene where I say it is typhoid fever and the old doctor in the pay of the water company says it is not typhoid). So then I burn and go to the head of the water company and start raising hell (very good lines here where I talk about ideals but not too high hat). This head of the w.c. is not what you think. Not a regular heavy but just ignorant. It seems he likes the working man and poor people like that all right but he didn't have the time to examine the water and see if there was any typhoid bacteria in it but of course I do not find that out till later. I have this scene bawling him out and in comes his neice in the middle of the scene and slaps my face because she likes the old duck and does not know I am there to protest against the typhoid bacteria in the water. It is love at first sight on both parts although we do not know it till later. She thinks I am just a boore and does not know I am the new young doctor in this town. Well finally I straiten out the epidemic and it turns out the old doc was the owner of the land where the typhoid bacteria was coming from and the only thing he can do when I expose him is shoot himself which he does. There is a lot of other stuff in between but you can catch the picture and let me know what you think of it. They previewed it in Glendale last Friday and from the applause and the cards the audience sent in giving the audience reaction it looks like my best to date. It is a good part and not strictly hameroo where I do nothing but show the good side of my kisser all the time. I got damn sick of those parts and I told the studio last summer I wanted a dramatic part where I could act and so they dug up this book and made a story out of it, although I guess not much of the book is left. Anyway they like me in it, both audience & studio and I wish the old man was alive so he could see I can act. From now on it looks like acting parts for your freind Don and no more of those pretty boy parts that made me sick to my stomach. It is all very well to say the women like those parts but you ought to see some of the letters I would get from husbands and boy freinds like I was a nance. A funny thing about those guys is why would the women go for me if I was a nance? I could never figure that out. I use to read some of those letters and think, well you heel if you think I am a nance I would just like to have an hr. with your wife and you would change your mind. The only trouble is the wife would probably turn out to be a Edna May Oliver or Beulah Bondi type and no Ginger Rogers or glamor girl type.

Well we had a few adventures while shooting "Courage" and I know you are always interested in them. I sure wish you could get set out here some time although I guess you would rather stick to your rehearsal classes and maybe get a chance to carry a spear in "Macbeth." Not that I dont often envy you because as I told you when I first came out here you miss the audience when you are working in pictures. Not that I ever had much of an audience while on Bway but sometimes I did and I missed it when I first came out here but got use to it. We work like hell when we work but a lot of times when they are setting up the cameras etc. preparatory to shooting a scene we have nothing to do but read. The extras knit and we read although some of the female principles knit as well. When I first came out here I use to have fun giving guys the hot foot but it is in my contract now that I get 50% billing and that means I have to stop having fun because the extras don't act natural with you when you are featured and you want to act natural with them. So mostly I park myself in my private dressing room on the set and read.

Well I was in there reading while we were shooting "Courage" and it was very tedeous. I could not get intrested in my book and I was just sitting there waiting for my man to bring my tea (everybody has tea every afternoon) and I looked up and there was this new number, what they call a starlet, and she was standing there and I said hello. Her name was Barbara Bradshaw. She was one of those thousands of little beauty contest winners that gets $75 a week the first six months and seven years options. She said, "Can I join you Mr. Page?" I said sure. She had a bit in "Courage" and plays a young nurse that faints during the epidemic. If you want to see her dont stoop over to tie your shoe or you wont. She is in one of the hospital scenes and I pick her up bodily and take her off the floor and put her on the bed and she dies. I get very sore about this and it is one of the things that make me so mad I go in and bawl out the water company president.

Well she comes in and I start making conversation to put her at her ease and she sits down and just then my man comes in with my tea and she joins me. I asked her how she enjoyed working in pictures and she said she enjoyed them o.k. but she was afraid Fenway was jealous of her. Well of course Fenway plays the niece, the big woman's part and I guess you never met Fenway. Fenway is o.k. if you know how to handle her, but a young kid like this Bradshaw is too unexpereinced to know how to handle Fenway. "Nonesense," I said. "You just have to know how to handle Miss Fenway." Fenway got where she is by being a picture stealer and so naturally she is on the lookout for anyone else doing the same thing. "You are a pretty girl," I said to Bradshaw and she said, "Oh, do you really think so Mr. Page?" I said she wouldnt be in pictures if she wasnt and at this her eyes clouded over a bit because I knew she wanted me to put the compliment on a personal basis but I am too wise for that. I know Fenway as you will see. Well we chatted a while and then Bradshaw asked me if I wanted to rehearse our scene and to humor her I said I would be glad to. So we began rehearsing the scene where she does the pass-out and I pick her up and put her on the bed. I have a cot in my dressing room where I lie down sometimes and I put her on the cot.

Well who should walk in while we were rehearsing but Fenway? She often comes to my dressing room and I often go to hers and so that was how it was. I was just putting little Bradshaw on the cot when in walks Fenway. "O, I beg your pardon," says Fenway and storms out. Bradshaw was not half as embarrased as I was because (strictly Masonic) I was having a quick touch with Fenway because that is one way to get along with her while making a picture as a lot of the boys have found out. So I was embarrased but so was Bradshaw as she was afraid Fenway would have her kicked off the lot, contract or no contract. Then I began to see the humor of the situation, me innocent as a new born babe but Fenway thinking I have moved in on Bradshaw. I told Bradshaw not to worry and she went out and then Miles the director said no more shooting that day and we could go home.

Well I was use to taking Fenway home in my car or going in hers but when I looked around for her she was gone and the next day she asked Miles to shoot around her as she was frightfully ill of a headache. I know those headaches. When she gets one of those headaches its everybody else that gets them too, the way she screams and yells and curses everybody out. So when she came back to work two days later it was very amusing to watch her, especially where she and I have a couple of love scenes. We were rehearsing a love scene and we would be in a passionate clinch and she would say "rehearsing, eh?" Sore as hell. So when Bradshaw and I were doing our scene where I pick her up off the floor I suddenly saw Fenway sitting there staring at me as if she wanted to put a knife in my back and the humor of the situation got the better of me and I burst out laughing and I was so weak from laughing I had to drop Bradshaw. It damn near had everybody in hystarics. All but Bradshaw. Not that she was really hurt but it came as a surprise to her of course. Miles didnt know what the hell was going on but it must of looked very funny because he laughed and all the others on the set. I had a hard time concentrating before we could do the scene over again good enough to print it.

Well later I told Miles what happened and so for a gag he waited till the picture was in the can and then he made up a story saying we would have retakes and to tantleize Fenway he would make me do retakes of the scene with Bradshaw. We had Fenway crazy. She tried to take it out on Bradshaw but Bradshaw's contract has two more months to run. I had to take Fenway to the preview of "Courage" at Glendale last week and when we come to that scene with Bradshaw and I I suddenly got the worst kick in the shin I ever got from Fenway. "You and your rehearsing" she said.

Well, boy, when you see the picture I hope you get a laugh out of it, only dont laugh too hard out loud as it is one of the most tender scenes in the whole picture. It was tender for poor Bradshaw when I dropped her. Write when you get a chance.

YRS.
DON

Fire!

MULLINS WAS PUFFING when he rang the doorbell. It was not a steep hill by automobile standards and from the boulevard it was only a matter of four blocks, but the most walking Mullins ever did was to go from his office to the studio commissary twice a day; the first time at lunch and again at four-thirty for a coke. Once, back in the early Thirties, he had played pretty good golf and strong tennis and had done a lot of swimming. That, however, was at a time when he had a house with a wife and a pool and a tennis court. At the hotel where he had lived for ten years or more there was only a more or less continual crap game; no pool, no tennis court, and, happily, no wife.

Even before he was halfway up the short driveway a bunch of dogs gave tongue. Their non-appearance did not serve to put him any more at his ease. He did not love dogs, and dogs did not like him. When the door opened he did not look his best and he knew it. The maid did not recognize him. "Yess-s-s?" she said.

"Miss Carter at home, Gretta?" he said.

"Oh, it's Mr. Moolinss," she said. She smiled. She was a perfect maid, and she had to be; she was an enemy alien. "Miss Carrtuh iss igspecting you. I tell her."

He followed Gretta to the library, a comfortable room adorned with beautifully bound classics, a good many of the war correspondents' volumes and all the popular novels of the last dozen years, as well as snaffle bits, harness monograms made of brass, a ship's model under glass, photographs of H. G. Wells, Willkie, and Lin Yutang, among others. There were also six or seven derringers and a cigarette lighter resembling a derringer, four silver loving cups, a cold blue by Rockwell Kent, a large globe that lit up, a portable bar, a profusion of leather chairs and coffee tables, and on the desk the petrified phallus of a bear. Alta Carter was fond of telling people that this room she had done herself, just filled it up with the things she loved and junk and stuff. If anybody wanted to be formal, she would say, that was okay. Billy Haines had done the rest of the house, but in this room you could take off your shoes and relax. Mullins knew the room and its contents, but with a sudden curiosity he went over to the bar merely to see how completely stocked it was. When he saw a bottle of Falernum and one of Calvados he was satisfied. He turned away, and there was Alta Carter, standing at the doorway. She smiled in mock sadness and shook her head slowly from side to side.

"Go ahead, darling. Have one," she said.

"Hello, Alta. No thanks, I don't really want one."

She went to him and gave her cheek to be kissed. "But you've finished the play. You can drink as much as you want to now."

"Listen, that was always your idea," said Mullins. "I didn't stop drinking while I was writing it. I've never stopped in my life, not since I started. Why should I?"

"Because everybody should. You know what it's done to people out here, Paul. You've seen what it's done to so many of our friends, the old gang. Whitey, Fred."

"I know, but it never did me any harm, you know that. It never cost me jobs and it's never done anything to my constitution."

"Maybe," she said. "Sit there."

They faced each other from twin love seats. "Why are you worried about booze all of a sudden?"

"I'm not. I just saw you standing there as though you were resisting temptation, don't you know? I thought you were going through some kind of a struggle."

"Not me," he said. "You didn't used to worry about drinking when I first knew you, in the old days in New York."

"I know, I know, I know. I'm silly, but I don't want anything to go wrong with. . . ." She looked pointedly at the briefcase in his lap. "I want this to be right, everything about it. It'll soon be fourteen years since I did a play. Fourteen years! I've been away from the theater longer than I was in it."

"I'll say you have. You only *ever* did two plays on Broadway."

"Yes, that's right. But I want it to be right for both our sakes, yours and mine. Mine first, but don't forget, you son of a bitch, you never had anything on Broadway. What were you when you came out here? A lousy newspaper reporter. I don't see how you ever got here in the first place. At least I made a hit in 'Face Backward.' "

"It's a long story and anyway I told it to you," he said. "How's the major?"

"Oh, he hates Washington. I talked to him last night. He's trying to wangle a trip out here but everybody knows he's married to me and he hates to try too hard. You know, people saying how convenient for Logan, wangling a trip to the coast and married to Alta Carter. Oh, I guess he does all right."

"Yeah," said Mullins.

"Don't say yeah like that. Don't agree so quickly. At least try to—oh, Paul, shall I do it? Is it good? The hell with Logan and everything else. *Do you want me to do your play?*"

"That's a goddam silly question to ask after I've been working on it for eight months. Wrote it for you."

"You know what I mean? Just look at me—"

"I am looking at you. I didn't take my eyes off you."

"Look at me and—yes, I can see," she said. "It is good, isn't it?"

"I think it is or I wouldn't be here."

"That's all I want to know," she said. "Give it to me. How long will it take me to read it?"

"I don't know. It's 165 pages if that'll give you any idea. Do you read fast?"

"I'm a quick study," she said.

"Not the same thing," he said. "Why, do you want to read it now, in front of me? Read it tonight when I'm not here. I don't want to sit here watching your expression and waiting for laughs."

"If you think I'm going to wait till tonight. I can read it in two hours, can't I?"

"I imagine so."

"All right. You go for a ride and come back at, uh, seven o'clock, and I'll tell you how much I love it." She clutched the brief-case to her famous bosom.

"All right, but I forgot. I can't go for a ride. I ain't got no chariot."

"Why, what's the matter?" she asked.

"Nothing. I came out on the bus to save gas."

"That's ridiculous. Take one of my cars and go for a ride. Go to a movie or something, but don't get drunk now. Can you drive a Fiat, one of the little baby ones?"

"Why don't you stop with that drunk stuff? Yes, I can drive a Fiat."

"All right, then, run along. The garage door's open. I'll see you at seven o'clock. Bye-ee." Still clutching the brief-case to her chest she ran out of the room.

Mullins went out and lowered himself into the car. He drove to the business district of Santa Monica, found a movie house that was showing a Pine & Thomas western, and joined the audience of California kiddies. He saw the picture through, had a bourbon Old Fashioned, and reached Alta's house at 6:55.

He was surprised when Alta herself answered the door. "What's the matter?" he said. "Gretta quit? Play lousy? Everything collapse all at once?" For she was solemn in contrast to his good spirits.

"It's Gretta's night off," she said. She let him close the door. He followed her to the library. She walked to the fireplace and stood with her back to him for a count of fifteen before she turned around. Then she threw back her head the way she did to denote gallantry on the screen.

"Paul," she said. "I am not—going—to do—your—play. It's-notforme, Paul. I am not—going—todoit."

He sat in the huge davenport that faced the fireplace. "I see," he said. "Would you mind telling me why not?"

She stared over the top of his head. "I told you. It's not for me."

He lit a cigarette. "I see. But would you mind going into a little detail. You know, Alta. Eight months work. Passed up some awfully good picture jobs. A guy'd kinda like to know what's wrong with it."

"Yes, I know," she said, nodding slowly.

Now she looked at him in a way that seemed to order him to continue telling what the play had cost him. "I never wrote a play before, at least never finished one. There're a lot of things I don't know. Granted. But this little opus. I can't defend it from attack when I don't know where it's being attacked from. I told you the story it's based on last Spring and you agreed with me it was a natural. People were real because they had to be real, taken out of life. The dialogue, well, I'm not apologizing for that. The construction—I never wrote a produced play, but I've seen a lot of them and read everything good that's been produced in New York during the last twenty years or more. And don't forget in the stuff I've done out here I've done scripts based on a dozen or more hit plays, and when you take them apart you're bound to find out how they were put together. I think I know construction pretty well. What *is* it, Alta?"

"All that you say is true," she said. She clasped her hands behind her back and gave him her three-quarter face. "I read it avidly, punct—conscientiously, fascinatedly. The doctor is fine, strong. The rabbi—you will kill intolerance wherever your play is shown."

"I see. Then you think—"

"Please let me finish, Paul. The mother? I cried. I couldn't help it. The little midget? Beautiful, beautiful. He was beautifully done, Paul, and never too much of him. The girl, my part, I—oh, don't you see, Paul, don't you see? *It's us!*" She threw out her hands and he thought he saw a tear in her right eye.

"I'm sorry," he said.

"The characters are all there, the dialogue, construction, everything. But the fire isn't there! The fire! It's us! It's this goddam place that's eaten us alive. Oh, Paul, if you'd written this play ten years ago there'd be nothing wrong with it, not a single thing. There's nothing wrong with it now, but it lacks something, I can't tell you where or how. Fire, that's all I can say." She threw herself on the davenport beside him and put her face in her hands. "And ten years ago, ten years ago I'd of played it and we'd of run a year. But now—oh, I'm so ashamed to say this, but Paul, now I'm afraid. Do you see that, Paul? I'm afraid. I'm not sure of it and that makes me afraid. Or maybe I'd be afraid no matter whose play it was or what play. It isn't only your play. It's us. God help us, it's us." She turned and put her hand on his cheek. She smiled tenderly. "And I've hurt you and we've always been such friends and we mustn't hurt each other, Paul. Say something nice to me, darling."

He smiled. "I think you're a bitch but you're awful pretty," he said.

"Yes, that's nice," she said. "It's exactly what you ought to say right this minute." She took his face in her hands and kissed him. She stood up suddenly. "Wait here till I see if Gretta's still hanging around."

"I'll wait," he said.

Everything Satisfactory

THE STATUS OF Dan Schecter was such that he was as welcome, or was made as welcome, in a Hollywood night club when he came in alone as when he brought with him a party of twenty. Not that he ever had brought a party of twenty to the Klub Kilocycle. The Klub, which has been called the little club without charm, is a late spot chiefly inhabited by musicians and radio characters, and visited by picture people only when broadcasts draw them to the vicinity of Sunset and Vine. No such thing had brought Dan to the Klub initially. He dropped in that first night without quite knowing where he was; it was during the time when he was carrying that torch for Sandra Sardou, and he'd been drinking.

"Good evening, Mr. Schecter," the headwaiter said.

"Good evening," said Dan. "Why, it's Paul. Where the hell've you been, Paul?"

"Right here, Mr. Schecter. Five years. I own a little piece of the joint. You alone, sir?"

"Uh-huh. Didn't you use to be at the Troc?"

"No, sir. The Victor Hugo and Lamaze, remember?"

"That's right. Paul, I wanta sit down."

"Yes, sir." Paul took Dan to a table, transmitted the drink order—double brandy and soda—to a waiter, and, with his native tact, left Dan before either man got bored with the other. When Dan woke up the next morning he was in his own bed, alone, and his car was in the driveway, intact. This latter was a pleasant discovery, for he was fully clothed, and it was a matter of fairly common knowledge that when Dan woke up with his clothes on there was usually a wrinkled car downstairs, or no car at all. His lawyer had told him that it was becoming more and more difficult to square these motoring lapses. He examined the match books in his pockets, which vaguely recalled to him his visit, or the early part of his visit, to the Klub Kilocycle, and he remembered Paul.

Later that day he telephoned Paul, who told him that one of the boys had driven him home on orders from Paul. "You always used to take care of me, Mr. Schecter. It was nothing. Glad to do it, Mr. Schecter."

"How much do I owe you?"

"You signed a small tab, sir. Eleven or twelve dollars," said Paul. "And I gave the waiter five dollars to take you home. You understand I had to take the waiter off his station, so I had to give him something."

"I'll be in tonight or tomorrow, Paul. That was very decent of you."

It was three or four nights later that Dan went to the Klub for the second time, again alone. Sandra still would not leave the little nobody she was married to, although Isabel Schecter had walked out on Dan. Never had Dan managed such things so badly, and he was in the paradoxical situation of carrying a torch and losing his grip. He began to think of Paul as his only friend. He shook hands with him and in his hand was a fifty-dollar bill, which Paul glanced at as he led Dan to a table.

At that time the entertainment at the Klub was rather special but of a kind that Dan, who had owned a four-hundred-dollar set of drums in college, could appreciate. The eight-piece combination was for your listening pleasure and not intended to be danced to; the guitar, double-bass, and piano trio had made several recondite records; the blonde who sang with the band was known to every habitué, and Dan, watching her go to work, became aware that she was also known to him. He realized he must have been too drunk to notice her during his first visit.

"Paul," he said, summoning Paul. "Isn't that Mimi Walker?"

"That's right," said Paul, smiling.

"She looks wonderful," said Dan. "Tell her I'd like to buy her a drink."

Paul nodded, and when Mimi finished her songs he spoke to her. She turned in Dan's general direction and nodded, and in about five minutes she presented herself at Dan's table.

"Hello," she said. She seemed not to see that he had offered his hand and that his whole manner was of the friendliest. She sat beside him. "I'll have a bourbon and ginger ale."

"I didn't know you were here," said Dan.

"Come on, Dan. You didn't know I was anywhere. How phony can you get?"

"Do you think I'm a phony? I don't. A lot of things, but not a phony."

"Then don't start out as if you'd been—as if you had the Missing Persons Bureau out looking for me. I see where Sandra's still with her husband."

"Do you know her?"

"I was in a show with her. Oh, she's a lot younger than I am, but I used to know her, all right. She was always a lot smarter than I am. In fact, she still owes me some money on the Louis-Schmeling fight, and you know how long ago that was."

"She told me she was twenty-six."

"She could have been," said Mimi. "I mean she could have

been sixteen when I knew her. That would make me thirty. O.K. I'm thirty. But you know better if you stop to think."

"You look wonderful," said Dan.

"Thanks."

"How long have you been here?"

"Five years," she said. "Since it opened."

"Oh."

"What do you mean, 'oh'?"

"I seem to remember Paul told me he's been here five years and owns a piece of the place. Is that how it is, Mimi?"

"For your information, I own a little piece of the joint myself. *Now* where are you?"

"Nowhere," said Dan.

"And that's exactly where you're going to get, Dan, so if you like the way I look, O.K., but just don't start thinking of a return engagement."

"You're a little ahead of me, but I guess that's what I *was* thinking."

"No!" She called the waiter. "Now I'll buy *you* a drink so you won't worry about the eighty cents it cost you to find out what you just found out. Give Mr. Schecter a double whatever he's having."

The waiter bowed respectfully. "The party on Five asked if you'll come over and have a drink with them, Miss Walker," said the waiter. "The one fella said he's a friend of Nat Wolff's."

"I'll be over," said Mimi.

"I know Nat, too, so don't go right away," said Dan, trying to be pleasant.

"Terribly sorry, chum, but I have to do another number."

"So soon? Well, I'll wait," said Dan.

She started to sing, "It'll be a long, long time." She got up and went to Table Five and spoke to the people but did not sit down. She went to the bandstand and sang a number and when she finished she went back and sat with the people on Five. Dan had a few drinks. He became aware of Paul standing near his table. How long Paul had been there, Dan had no way of knowing; he had been staring at the back of Mimi's head.

"Everything satisfactory, sir?" said Paul.

"I wouldn't go so far as to say that, Paul." He was on the point of asking Paul a question or two but decided against it for the time being. "We'll see how things work out."

Paul smiled. "Yes, sir."

The time passed. Dan clocked Mimi for six minutes at Table Five, and then when he thought it was six minutes more, it was over an hour more. Mimi would get up now and then and do a number and always rejoin the people at Five, and Paul would come around to Dan's table and smile and ask if everything was satisfactory. Dan's answers varied with the readiness of his wit. Somewhere along the line his drinks were being served in coffee cups, which, Paul felt he had to explain, was on account of The Law. The drinks went just as fast from coffee cups as they did from highball glasses, and they didn't have as much soda in them. On returning from a trip to the men's room, Dan hovered over his table unsteadily, glancing at the empty chairs and then at Mimi, laughing and talking at Table Five. Dan started to sit down, and if it had not been for Paul's help he would have missed the chair. "Thanks, Paul," said Dan.

"Everything satisfactory, Mr. Schecter?"

Dan laughed. "Goddam unsatisfactory, but I said I'd wait and that's what I'm gonna do."

"Yes, sir," said Paul. "Tom, bring Mr. Schecter another drink." Dan and Paul grinned at each other.

The music stopped, had stopped without Dan's noticing, or noticing that he was the only customer in the place. He studied his watch without succeeding in concentrating on the position of the hands. "Paul!"

"Yes, sir."

"Am I the last one here? Where's Miss Walker?"

"She went home, sir," said Paul.

"Where does she live? Foolish question number five thousand two hundred and eighty." He gulped his drink and reached in his pocket and took out a money clip. He put two twenties on the table. "I'll give you twenty dollars more if you tell me where—no, *you* wouldn't tell me, you son of a bitch." He stood up and staggered to the street. Paul came up behind him and said to the doorman, "Mr. Schecter's car."

In a moment or two a boy drove the car around from the parking lot, and Paul went back inside the Klub and leaned against the bar. Mimi was standing there, and they both watched Dan getting into the driver's seat. She was frowning.

"I can't let him go like that," she said.

"You stay where you are," said Paul. "We'll read about him in the papers." The car roared away.

Drawing Room B

NOBODY BIG HAD taken Leda Pentleigh to the train, and the young man from the publicity department who had taken her was not authorized to hire the Rolls or Packard that used to be provided for her New York visits. Nor had they taken their brief ride from the Waldorf to Grand Central. This time, she was riding west on the Broadway and not the Century, had come to the station in an ordinary taxicab, from a good but unspectacular hotel north of Sixtieth Street. Mr. Egan, it is true, was dead, but his successor at Penn Station, if any, did not personally escort Leda to the train. She just went along with the pleasant young hundred-and-fifty-a-week man from the publicity department, her eyes cast down in the manner which, after eighteen years, was second nature to her in railroad stations and hotel lobbies, at tennis matches and football games. Nobody stopped her for her autograph, or to swipe the corsage which the publicity young man's boss had sent instead of attending her himself. Pounding her Delman heels on the Penn Station floor, she recalled a remark which she was almost sure she had originated, something about the autograph hounds not bothering her: it was when they didn't bother you that they bothered you. Of course, it was Will Rogers or John Boles or Bill Powell or somebody who first uttered the thought, but Leda preferred her way of putting it. The thought, after all, had been thought by thousands of people, but she noticed it was the way *she* expressed it that was popular among the recent johnny-come-latelies when they were interviewed by the fan magazines. Well, whoever had said it first could have it; she wouldn't quarrel over it. At the moment of marching across Penn Station, there seemed to be mighty few travellers who would take sides for or against her in a controversy over the origin of one of her routine wisecracks; far from saying, "There goes Leda Pentleigh, who first said . . ." the travellers were not even saying, "There goes Leda Pentleigh—period." The few times she permitted her gaze to rise to the height of her fellow-man were unsatisfactory; one of the older porters raised his hat and smiled and bowed; two or three nice-appearing men recognized her—but they probably were Philadelphians in their thirties or forties, who would go home and tell their wives that they had seen Leda Pentleigh in Penn Station, and their wives would say, "Oh, yes. I remember her," or "Oh, yes. She was in Katie Hepburn's picture. She played the society bitch, and I'll bet she's qualified." Katie Hepburn, indeed! It wasn't as if Katie Hepburn hadn't been in pictures fifteen years. But no use getting sore at Katie Hepburn because Katie was a few years younger and still a star. At this thought, Leda permitted herself a glance at a Philadelphia-type man, a man who had that look of just about getting into or out of riding togs, as Leda called them. He frowned a little, then raised his hat, and because he was so obviously baffled, she gave him almost the complete Pentleigh smile. Even then he was baffled, had not the faintest idea who she was. A real huntin'-shootin' dope, and she knew what he was thinking—that here was a woman either from Philadelphia or going to Philadelphia and therefore someone he must know. The gate was opened, and Leda and Publicity went down to her car. Publicity saw that she was, as he said, all squared away, and she thanked him and he left, assuring her that "somebody" from the Chicago office would meet her at Chicago, in case she needed anything. Her car was one of the through cars, which meant she did not have to change trains at Chicago, but just in case she needed anything. (Like what, she said to herself. Like getting up at seven-thirty in the morning to be ready to pose for photographs in the station? Oh, yes? And let every son of a bitch in the Pump Room know that Leda Pentleigh no longer rated the star treatment?)

In her drawing room, Leda decided to leave the door open. There might, after all, be a Coast friend on the train. If she wanted to play gin with him—or her—she could do it, or if she wanted to give her—or him—the brush, she knew how to do that, too. Her window was on the wrong side of the car to watch people on the platform, and she sat in a corner where she could get a good look at the passengers going by her door. She opened a high-class book and watched the public (no longer so completely hers) going by. They all had that beaten look of people trying to find their space; bent over—surely not from the weight of their jewelry boxes and briefcases—and then peering up at the initial on her drawing room, although they could plainly see that the room was occupied by a striking, stunning, chic, glamorous, sophisticated woman, who had spent most of the past week in New York City, wishing she were dead.

She drove that little thought out of her mind. It would do no good now to dwell on that visit, ending now as the train began to pull out—her first visit to New York in four years, and the unhappiest in all her life. What the hell was the use of thinking back to the young punk from one of the dailies who had got her confused with Renée Adorée? What difference the wrong tables in restaurants and the inconveniently timed appointments at hairdressers and the night of sitting alone in her hotel room while a forty-dollar pair of theatre tickets went to waste? The benefit in Union City, New Jersey. The standup by Ken Englander, the aging architect, who had been glad enough in other days to get once around the floor with her at the Mayfair dances. The being made to wait on the telephone by the New York office of her agent, her own agent. The ruined Sophie dress and the lost earring at that South American's apartment. Why think of those things? Why not think of the pleasanter details of her visit?

Think, for instance, of the nice things that had been said about her on that morning radio program. Her appearance had been for free, but the publicity was said to be valuable, covering the entire metropolitan area and sometimes heard in Pennsylvania. Then there was the swell chat with Ike Bord, publicity man for a company she had once been under contract to. *"Whenner you coming back to us, Leda?* . . . Anything I can do for you while you're in town, only too glad, you know. I didn't even know you were here. Those bums where you are now, they never get anything in the papers." And it was comforting to know she could still charge things at Hattie's, where she had not bought anything in four years. And the amusing taxidriver: "Lady, I made you right away. I siss, 'Lydia Penley. Gay me an autograft fa Harry.' Harry's my kid was killed in the U.S. Marines. Guadalcanal. *Sure, I remember you.*" And, of course, her brother, who had come down all the way from Bridgeport with his wife, bringing Leda *a pair of nylons and a bona-fide cash offer* in case she had a clean car she wasn't using. The telephone service at her hotel had been something extra special because one of the operators formerly had been president of Leda's Brooklyn fan club. Through it all was the knowledge that her train fare and hotel bill were paid for by the company because she obligingly posed for fashion stills for the young-matron departments of the women's magazines, so the whole trip was not costing her more than eight or nine hundred dollars, including the visit to Hattie's. There were some nice things to remember, and she remembered them.

• • •

The train rolled through Lancaster County, and it was new country to Leda. It reminded her of the English countryside and of American primitives.

She got up and closed her door once, before washing her hands, but reopened it when she was comfortable. Traffic in the passageway had become light. The train conductor and the Pullman conductor came to collect her tickets and asked for her last name. "Leda Pentleigh," she said. This signified nothing to the representative of the Pennsylvania Railroad, but the Pullman conductor said, "Oh, yes, Miss Pentleigh. Hope you have an enjoyable trip," and Leda thanked him and said she was sure she would, lying in her beautiful teeth. She was thinking about sending the porter for a menu when the huntin'-shootin' type stood himself in her doorway and knocked.

"Yes?" she said.

"Could a member of Actors' Equity speak to you for a moment, Miss Pentleigh?" he said. He didn't so much say the line as read it. She knew that much—that rehearsal was behind the words and the way he spoke them.

"To be sure," she said. "Sit down, won't you?"

"Let me introduce myself. My name is Kenyon Littlejohn, which of course doesn't mean anything to you, unless you've seen me?"

"I confess I did see you in the station, Mr. Littlejohn. In fact, I almost spoke to you. I thought I recognized you."

He smiled, showing teeth that were a challenge to her own. He took a long gold case out of his inside coat pocket and she took a cigarette. "That can mean two things," he said. "Either you've seen me—I've been around a rather long time, never any terribly good parts. I've usually got the sort of part where I come on and say, 'Hullo, thuh, what's for tea? Oh, crom-pits! How jolly!'" She laughed and he laughed. "Or else you know my almost-double. Man called Crosby? Very Back Bay–Louisburg Square chap from

Boston. Whenever I've played Boston, people are always coming up to me and saying, 'Hello, Francis.'"

"Oh, I've met Francis Crosby. He used to come to Santa Barbara and Midwick for the polo."

"That's the chap," said Kenyon Littlejohn, in his gray flannel Brooks suit, Brooks shirt, Peal shoes, Players Club tie, and signet ring. "No wonder you thought you knew me, although I'm a bit disappointed it was Crosby you knew and not me."

"Perhaps I did know you, though. Let me see—"

"No. Please don't. On second thought, the things I've been in—well, the things I've been in have been all right, mostly, but as I said before, the parts I've had weren't anything I particularly care to remember. Please let me start our acquaintance from scratch."

"All right," she said.

He took a long drag of his cigarette before going on. "I hope you don't think I'm pushy or anything of that sort, Miss Pentleigh, but the fact is I came to ask your advice."

"You mean about acting?" She spoke coldly, so that this insipid hambo wouldn't think he was pulling any age stuff on her.

"Well, hardly that," he said. He spoke as coldly as he dared. "I've very seldom been without work and I've lived quite nicely. My simple needs and wants. No, you see, I've just signed my first picture contract—or, rather, it's almost signed. I'm going out to California to make tests for the older-brother part in 'Strange Virgin.'"

"Oh, yes. David's doing that, isn't he?"

"Uh—yes. They're paying my expenses and a flat sum to make the test, and, if they like me, a contract. I was wondering, do you think I ought to have an agent out there? I've never had one, you know. Gilbert and Vinton and Brock and the other managers, they usually engage me themselves, a season ahead of time, and I've never *needed* an agent, but everybody tells me out there I ought to have one. Do you agree that that's true?"

"Well, of course, to some extent that depends on how good you are at reading contracts."

"I had a year at law school, Miss Pentleigh. That part doesn't bother me. It's the haggling over money that goes on out there, and I understand none of the important people deal directly with the producers."

"Oh, you're planning on staying?"

"Well . . ."

"New York actors come out just for one picture, or, at least, that's what they say. Of course, they have to protect themselves in case they're floperoos in Hollywood. Then they can always say they never planned to stay out there, and come back to New York and pan pictures till the next offer comes along, if it ever does."

"Yes, that's true," said Mr. Littlejohn.

" '*That* place,' they say. 'They put caps on your teeth and some fat Czechoslovakian that can't speak English tries to tell you how to act in a horse opera,' forgetting that the fat Czechoslovakian knows more about acting in his little finger than half the hamboes in New York. Nothing *personal,* of course, Mr. Little."

"Thank you," said Mr. Littlejohn.

"But I've got a bellyful of two-hundred-dollar-a-week Warfields coming out and trying to high-hat us, trying to steal scenes and finding themselves on the cutting-room floor because they don't know the first thing about picture technique, and it serves them right when they find themselves out on their duffs and on the way back to their Algonquins and their truck-garden patches in Jackson Heights or wherever they live. God damn it to hell, making pictures is work!"

"I realize—"

"Don't give me any of that I-realize. Wait'll you've got up at five and sweated out a scene all day and gone to the desert on location and had to chase rattlesnakes before you could go to bed. Find out what it's like and then go back and tell the boys at the Lambs Club. Do that for twenty or fifteen years." She stopped, partly for breath and partly because she didn't know what was making her go on like this.

"But we're not all like that, Miss Pentleigh," said Littlejohn when she did not go on.

His talking reminded her that she had been talking to a human being and not merely voicing her hatred of New York. His being there to hear it all (and to repeat it later, first chance he got) made her angry at him in particular. "I happen to think you are, eef you don't mind. I don't care if you're Lunt and Fontanne or Helen Hayes or Joe Blow from Kokomo—if you don't click in Hollywood, it's because you're not good enough. And, oh, boy, don't those managers come out begging for us people that can't act to do a part in their new show. When they want a name, they want a movie name. Why, in less than a week, I had chances to do a half a dozen plays, including a piece of the shows. What good can New York do me, I ask you."

"The satisfaction of a live audience," he said, answering what was not a question. "Playing before a—"

"A live audience! On a big set you play to as many people as some of the turkeys on Broadway. Live audience! Go to a premiere at Graumann's Chinese or the Cathay Circle and you have people, thousands, waiting there since two o'clock in the afternoon just to get a look at you and hear you say a few words into the microphone. In New York, they think if they have three hundred people and two cops on horses, they have a crowd. On the Coast, we have better than that at a preview. A *sneak* preview! But of course you wouldn't know what that is."

"Really, Miss Pentleigh, I'm very glad to be going to Hollywood. I didn't have to go if I didn't want to."

"That wasn't your attitude. You sat down here as if you were patronizing me, *me!* And started in talking about agents and producers as if Hollywood people were pinheads from Mars. Take a good gander at some of the swishes and chisellers on Broadway."

"Oh, I know a lot about them."

"Well, then, what are you asking me for advice for?"

"I'm terribly sorry," he said, and got up and left.

"Yes, and I think you're a bit of a swish yourself," said Leda to the closed door. She got a bottle of Bourbon out of her bag and poured herself a few drinks into doubled paper cups and rang for the porter.

Presently, a waiter brought a menu, and by that time Leda was feeling fine, with New York a couple of hundred miles and a week and a lifetime behind her. Dinner was served, and she ate everything put before her. She had a few more shots and agreed with her conscience that perhaps she had been a little rough on the actor, but she had to take it out on somebody. He wasn't really too bad, and she forgave him and decided to go out of her way to be nice to him the next time she saw him. She thereupon rang for the porter.

"Yes, Ma'am?" said the porter.

"There's a Mr. Entwhistle—no, that's not his name. Littlefield. That's it. Littlefield. Mr. Littlefield is on the train. He's going to California. Do you think you could find 'im and ask 'im that I'd tell 'im I'd like to speak to him, please?"

"The gentleman just in here before you had your dinner, Ma'am?"

"Yes, that's the one."

"Mr. Littlejohn. He's in this same car, PA29. I'll give him your message, Ma'am."

"Do that," she said, handing the waiter a ten-dollar bill.

She straightened her hair, which needed just a little straightening, and assumed her position—languor with dignity—on the Pullman seat, gazed with something between approval and enchantment at the darkening Pennsylvania countryside, and looked forward to home, California, and the friends she loved. She could be a help to Mr. Littlejohn (*that* name would have to be changed). She *would* be a help to Mr. Littlejohn. "That I will, that I will," she said.

Eileen

All morning the flowers had been arriving, and the telegrams, and some of them had been there when Joe Stone appeared at his office, at twenty past nine. The messages all made little jokes on his completing his first year as a producer, the jokes not always in direct ratio of intimacy to the cordiality of his relationship with the senders. Some of the agents, for example, seemed to think that if they called Joe their pal, that meant he was their pal. Some of those people knew better, and still others would never, never know better, and for them he felt a little pity. They were the ones who could not really afford to send anything—not even telegrams—and sent large baskets of flowers. His fellow-producers on the lot likewise sent baskets of flowers, but their cards said things like "Nice going," or made gags of a complimentary nature based on the titles of Joe's two enormously successful pictures or the one that was at the moment in work.

He did not wonder long how so many people had hit the anniversary right on the nose. Joe was not yet in *Who's Who*, and hardly anyone had remembered his birthday a month ago, but his first anniversary as a producer was a date that got remembered; and of course there was Elsie, his secretary, who knew her way around the studio. Elsie would expect other secretaries to remind her of their producers' anniversaries (unless their producers happened to be on the way out), and so she had reminded them of this big milestone in Joe's career.

Elsie had put the flowers in his private office, and she followed him in. He turned around to her and smiled. "How do you think it looks? You know all that stuff. Am I on the way out, or is it just the right number? Not too many, or not too few?"

"Just exactly the right number. Pile of telegrams on the desk," said Elsie. "I've started a list of telegrams and another list for flowers."

"Good girl. Thank you."

"That's part of my job. I didn't send you anything."

"If you had, we couldn't have kept a straight face."

"That's more or less what I figured," said Elsie.

"How about a kiss to celebrate?"

"Stop. If you ever wanted a kiss from me, you wouldn't have to ask for it."

"Well, in that case . . ." he said.

"No, now. Don't put on an act. It's an insult when we both know it's an act. The square basket's from Mrs. Stone. I'd better not tell you what the flowers are, because she'd know I told you."

Joe took off his lapel-less jacket and hung it in his bathroom closet. He replaced his sunglasses with his reading glasses and went through the telegrams rapidly. "You say you have a list of who sent flowers?"

"The name you'd be looking for isn't on the list, so far," said Elsie.

"You could be wrong, you know."

"I don't think so. The big boss's name heads the list. The other name isn't on it. Am I wrong?"

"Never," said Joe.

"The young lady'll be here in person at three-thirty, you know—or how dull can I get?"

"Where do you think I ought to send these things—Cedars of Lebanon?"

"Send some to Los Angeles General. I'll take care of it. I'll call Transportation just before I go home, and get a studio truck."

"Why not before that? This'll be like trying to work in Forest Lawn."

"Look, Mr. Stone, I can't help it if the young lady's going to be embarrassed because she didn't send you flowers. There'll be people that did send flowers coming in and out of here all day and they'll expect you—"

"All right, all right."

"And you *have* to be here at six, because they're planning a little surprise for you in the executives' dining room. The big boss'll be there."

"How to start the day wrong," said Stone.

"How to end it wrong, if you're not in the execs' dining room at six."

"When *have* I been off the lot at six? I'll be on hand."

"Well, it's a living," said Elsie. She flipped open her notebook. "Forrest Bedford wants thirty-five hundred and a ten weeks' guarantee or he won't leave the Cape. He says he's working on his play, and he also wants the studio to get him a house at Malibu. No? . . . The table at Romanoff's is O.K. for eight-thirty. . . . Research says you were right and they didn't wear spiral puttees at the Mexican border in 1916. . . . Washington says it's no use trying to talk to General Pershing. . . . General Funston died in 1917. . . . I'll get it." She answered the telephone. Joe Stone was in his second year.

AT THREE-TWENTY, ELSIE spoke to Joe over the intercom. "Miss Eileen Clancy is here."

"Ask her to come in, please," said Joe.

He stood up when she came in, and held out his hand. "Nice to see you, and always punctual."

She shook hands. "That's the way I was brought up, and I want to get ahead."

"You will," he said.

"What's the big occasion? Is it your birthday?"

"The one that counts around here. One year ago, I became a producer."

"Well, if what everybody says is right, you'll be spending a lot more of them around here. Congratulations. At least I could have sent you a telegram. I will when I go home."

He knew, because he often had waited for other people's decisions governing his own career, what she must be going through, and yet she seemed to be enduring no anxiety. She seated herself at the left side of his desk, in a large, comfortable chair—large enough to rate its own little table, cigarette box, lighter, and ashtray. The afternoon sun came in on her, but she had nothing to fear from it, even though nobody's hair could be genuinely that color. It was almost the color of her skin. But, at least for a while, no one would want her to change it. Her features were of such regularity as to be next to uninteresting, and they were interesting because they were perfect. Her mother and father had been in show business and they had taught her makeup; they knew, and she knew, that she could use that much lip paint, which on anyone else would have been too much. She was wearing a good, plain white dress, left unbuttoned in a frank display of her breasts. The only jewelry she wore was a tiny wristwatch with a heavy gold snake band.

"Well, I wanted to tell you myself, Eileen. I have good news for you." Joe could not resist making her wait a few seconds. The corners of her mouth showed the beginnings of a childish smile, but her eyes showed something far from childish, which had shown up in her last picture, a bit that had been cut out and that he had seen before the picture was cut. "In fact, a lot of it," he said.

"Tell it to me slowly," she said.

He picked up a paper knife, held it by the forefinger of his right hand and the forefinger of his left hand. He spoke slowly. "You are getting a new contract," he said.

She lit a cigarette and inhaled faster than a worried horse-player. "Uh-huh." She nodded twice.

"You're being tested for Sara Duval," he said.

"Yes," she said. She could tell from his inflection that there was more.

"And a very good break. I persuaded Franklin Ames to make the test with you. He never makes tests with anybody—not since he's been a star."

She looked at him in a way that at first was difficult to understand. He had no feeling that she was seeing him—and then he recognized the expression. He had seen it before, on a few women with whom passion took the form of sadness. There are those who cry. He was witness to the end of the life she had led until now and watching the beginning of the new life, as a star, that she had always wanted. It was probably more intense than any passion she ever had experienced, and she was helpless. And he was closer to her now than he ever had been before. All he had to do was touch her, yet if ever there was a time not to touch her, this was the time. Now, this minute, it wouldn't have made any difference who touched her, but it would be better to have her remember later that he had not.

The moment passed and her expression changed. "I think you cut your finger," she said. She stood up.

"Why, God damn it, I did," he said. "I'm bleeding to death."

She put her handkerchief over the two tiny drops of blood where the paper knife had pricked him. "May I keep the handkerchief?" he said.

She nodded. "Do you always have that much self-control?"

He looked up and saw that he could hide nothing from her. "I've never had to before."

"Then the more thanks for having it now." She sat down. "I

didn't have any of my own, but I have now. Joe, I'm in love with somebody, or I think I am. He isn't anybody you know. He isn't even in pictures. I guess I'd better get off this lot. I wouldn't be any good to you, and you've been good to me."

"I wouldn't bother you."

"No. I could count on that, but I know I bother you. If they want me that much here, I can get work someplace else. You can get me my release."

"I could, but I couldn't stand it with you not here. Let's try it and see how it works out," he said.

"You know what's sensible? It's for me to shake hands and say thanks and goodbye."

"That wouldn't have been the case if you hadn't read my mind. Try it, Eileen. See how it works out."

"I have my car. I think I'll go for a long ride." She stood up.

"I'm sorry if I spoiled your big day."

"I'm sorry if I spoiled yours, Joe."

"You didn't."

"Shall I come in Monday?"

He smiled. "Same time, same station."

She went out.

THERE WAS SOMEONE else waiting to see him, and someone after that. It was a little past five-thirty and he was alone when Elsie came in and laid a telegram on his desk. It was from West Los Angeles and it said: "I have thought it over and have decided it will work out all right." It was signed "E.C."

"Any answer?" said Elsie.

"No," he said. The answer was not up to him, but he could not tell that to Elsie—any more than he could tell her that the future looked bright.

The Industry and the Professor

A FINE BLACK 1947 Cadillac limousine was waiting first in line at the curb when McCrosland came out of the hotel. The doorman and a chauffeur were chatting. McCrosland, blinking in the California sun, stopped at the curb, and the doorman said, "Taxi, sir?"

"No thanks," said McCrosland. "I'm supposed to be—uh, there's a car supposed to be picking me up."

"What is it—a Tanner?" said the doorman.

"It might be. I don't know what a Tanner is. This car is from the Kurtz studio," said McCrosland.

"Oh," said the doorman. "This is your car, right here." He notified the chauffeur, who had been leaning against the marquee post during the doorman's conversation with McCrosland. The chauffeur immediately became courteous and efficient, held the rear door open for McCrosland, and drove him expertly to the Kurtz studio. McCrosland, sitting so far away from the chauffeur, made no attempt at conversation during the drive, and the

only statement the chauffeur made was at the entrance to a building inside the studio gates. "I'll be here whenever you want me, sir," he said. "My name's Fenstermacher, or Ed."

"Oh, you don't have to wait," said McCrosland.

"Yes, I do," said Ed. "I'm assigned to you all the time you're here."

"Oh," said McCrosland.

He entered the building and was greeted with a big smile from a man in a policeman's uniform, who was sitting behind a window. "Yes, sir?" said the man.

"My name is McCrosland—"

"Professor McCrosland? Yes, *sir!* We're expecting you. Just have a seat, Professor." The policeman spun the dial three times and mumbled into the mouthpiece. He had hardly returned the apparatus to its cradle before a short young man in a bright-blue suit opened the door beside the policeman's window and introduced himself to McCrosland.

"My name is Tom Mitchell—no relation to the actor. We often got our mail mixed up when he was on this lot, but we're no relation. In fact, I never even met him when he was here. It's funny, but I just never happened to. Will you come with me, Professor, down to my office, and we can sort of map out a program."

McCrosland followed Mitchell to an office with a hanging sign with the painted words "Special Services—Tom Mitchell." McCrosland took a seat in a very low chair, declined cigar and cigarette, and was silent while Mitchell told an intercom instrument that he was not to be disturbed. A girl's voice cackled back, "O.K."

"Well, did you have a nice trip out? Everything satisfactory at the hotel?" Mitchell asked. "If you want your room changed, we can arrange that."

"I'm very comfortable, thank you."

"Good. Excellent. Um—ah, Mr. Kurtz is all tied up with a producers' meeting today and he's only sorry he wasn't able to take you around himself, but I'm at your service, and I understand you're going there for dinner tonight."

"Yes. I wanted to ask you. Is that black tie?"

"Oh, no. No, no. The ladies are wearing long dresses, but the men aren't dressing. Just an informal little dinner, and I suppose they'll run a picture after. Uh, now—uh, was there anything in particular you were interested in seeing, Professor?"

"I don't think so. It's my first trip to California, and I dropped a line to Irving—"

"Oh, yes. Yes, yes. Irving. Mr. Kurtz's eldest. Oh, *that's* a real talent. You know Irving, too?"

"Not too, Mr. Mitchell. Only. I've never met his father, Mr. Kurtz. Irving was in classes of mine."

"Oh, I see. You *taught* him. I see. You teach at Dartmouth. Oh. *Mm-hmm.* Irving was one of your pupils. I—uh, should have thought of that. I don't know why I didn't. You know, I thought you possibly were out here on some kind of a survey, or some such thing. Well, then, you're just—uh, you'd just like to have a quick kind of a résumé."

"No, I simply thought I'd like to see the inside of a studio," said McCrosland. "My vacation, you know. I wrote Irving, and that's how Mr. Kurtz happened to put me up at the hotel and so forth. Just a tourist."

"That's what I meant. I guess résumé isn't the word I should have used in that connection. You're not planning—well, what I'm getting at is you don't plan to write anything, or anything like that."

"Well, no, I suppose not. I teach sociology, but I'd hardly expect to—"

"Of course not—not like some of them come out here for a couple of days and think they could run a studio. I took sociology."

"Is that so?" said McCrosland. "Where?"

"At S.C."

"Oh, yes," said McCrosland. *"Oh, Southern California.* That reminds me, are we anywhere near the U.C.L.A.? The driver said he was at my disposal, so I thought if it wasn't too far I have a friend there."

"Whatever your wishes dictate, Professor." He smiled. "You're getting what we call the full-A treatment. I'm not permitted to take you to the executives' private dining room, but outside of that you get the same identical courtesy as ex-President Hoover. Anywhere you want to go, anyone you want to talk to, any questions you want to ask . . ."

"Where's Irving?"

"Irving's up North."

"Alaska?"

"Oh, no. Marin County. On location. Northern part of the state. We could fly you up there tomorrow, if that suits your convenience. Irving's working as assistant director on *Strange Virgin.* Temporary title. You could pick up a nice piece of change if you could dream up another title, by the way. The novel was *Strange Virgin,* but we can't use that."

"No, I guess not. I can see where there'd be some objection to that. I'd like very much to see Irving, but I promised my wife I wouldn't fly, so I guess I'll have to wait till he comes East again."

"Married man, Professor?"

"Yes. Close to twenty years. Why?"

"Well, I make all kinds of arrangements in my job, and those parties at the Kurtz residence—week nights he's off to bed at eleven o'clock on the dot, so if you wanted to see the night life, that's part of my job."

"That include getting me a girl?"

"Oho, that's for sure. Did you have somebody in mind?"

"Well, I've always wanted to meet Mary Bates," said McCrosland.

MITCHELL SNAPPED THE intercom and said into it, "Get me Mary Bates."

"What?" said McCrosland.

"I just told my secretary to get Mary Bates on the wire."

"It's as simple as that?"

"It is *now,*" said Mitchell. "Mr. Kurtz isn't being rude when he goes to bed early, but he's one of the early risers in this business. His car's always out here when I come to work in the morning and still here when I leave, around six P.M. There isn't a harder worker in the business than—excuse me." The intercom signal light was on. "I'll talk to her," said Mitchell into the instrument. "Mary? I have a friend of Mr. K.'s here, and he's having dinner there tonight but he figures to get away around eleven-thirty. . . . But you can break that, sure. I'd appreciate it. We'll pick you up at your house around eleven-thirty, quarter to twelve. Goo'bye, now." Mitchell hung up.

"As simple as that?" said McCrosland. "Good Lord, I've been wanting to meet her for ten years. It's a family joke."

"Well, you got the last laugh. Or will have. It's up to you."

"Well, it's up to her, too, if you mean what I think you mean," said McCrosland, laughing. "Seriously, you mean I could sleep with her tonight?"

"Oh, I don't say that. I don't guarantee it. But on the other hand, I don't know why not."

"Does everybody?"

"Mary? No."

"Well, now, for instance, our Mr. Kurtz? Could he just call up like that and be reasonably certain that before the night's over, he'd have slept with Mary Bates?"

"I can give you the answer to that right away. He'd never call her up."

"Why not? She's a handsome woman, about thirty to the best of my knowledge and belief, and wasn't it his magic name that made her break a date, to meet me?"

"I have to explain that. You see, Mr. Kurtz—well, let's take somebody else. Some other producer, not on this lot. Say—uh, Jones. I don't know any producer named Jones, but let's say he's as important in the industry as Mr. Kurtz, or next in importance. Now, Jones would very seldom get mixed up with anybody in between. Jones would have either some absolutely top star or else kids you never heard of. But not the in-betweens. The in-betweens—they're a headache for a man like Mr. Jones. Maybe they're still young enough to be ambitious and make trouble, or they're old enough to be desperate and make trouble, figuring what have they got to lose. Whereas, with you or I the in-betweener might figure we could help her get one picture. Jones, though, he might have to go for a contract. You notice Mary didn't try to get invited to the Kurtzes' tonight. That's because, in the first place, she couldn't have got invited and, second, because she'd have a lousy time. If they had a party for three hundred people, she'd be invited, but not an intimate affair."

"Interesting. Interesting." McCrosland nodded.

"Well, where would you like to go first, Professor?" said Mitchell.

"Well, I guess I'd like to see them shooting."

"O.K. On Stage Eight—no, that's Boone Crockett. I don't think so, unless you insist."

"Boone Crockett? Say, he's one I kid my wife about. When she kids me about Mary Bates, I can always come back at her with Boone Crockett. Why don't you want to go there?"

"Uh—he's being difficult."

"Temperamental?" said McCrosland.

"No, not yet. He hasn't been temperamental yet. These days, I don't care how big a star is, if he gets temperamental, that cooks him. He might as well start taking television lessons. If a star gets the reputation of being called temperamental, there isn't a producer in town'll touch him. Not a one."

"Oh. I think I know what you're hinting at. Mr. Crockett's got a little hangover."

"No, no, no. Boone's been off the sauce for fourteen months, close to fifteen. He's A.A.—Alcoholics Anonymous."

"Then what *is* the matter? I'm only pursuing this because you told me I could ask any question I wanted to."

"Difficult. He told them to make some changes in the script. He has script approval in his contract. But yesterday he found out they didn't make all the changes, so he acted up. That was yesterday. Today, he's down there on Stage Eight and won't come out of his dressing room. That's difficult. Tomorrow, if he still holds up shooting, he better look out or Bob Swenson'll say he's temperamental. Bob'll give him one warning, and if he doesn't straighten out, Publicity'll tip off one of the columnists, Boone'll be marked temperamental, and he's cooked."

"But what I don't see is if he has the right to approve of the script—"

"Listen, Professor. Crockett's one of our biggest stars, and he gets paid a big bundle fifty-two weeks a year, with over a year to run on his present contract. He has something else in his contract. It stipulates now that if the studio doesn't have a script ready by such-and-such a date, he can make an outside picture—a picture at another studio. But what this studio can do is mark him temperamental and let him die. No other studio'll have him if he's marked temperamental, these days. We have to go on paying him, but what's that? Buttons. When the time comes where we're supposed to have a script ready for him, we can say we don't have one ready, and he's free to go out and try to get an outside picture. But the other studios'll say no, sir, Crockett's temperamental—no part of the son of a bitch. What happens then? He crawls back here, and he knows that *we* know he can't *get* an outside picture. The result? Next picture, he's a good boy. Next picture, he won't even be difficult."

"Does everybody know this?"

"Everybody but Crockett. He thinks it's 1945, when every picture made money, no matter how much of a dog it was. Not now. This is 1949, when you gotta give them the assassination of Lincoln with the original cast. Anyway, Crockett's a Commie."

"He *is*?"

"Well, not a Commie. But he came out verrrrry, verrrrry strong for Truman. He didn't have to come out that strong. If he wanted to come out for him, all right. That's enough. He didn't have to shoot off his face. I'll bet you'd have a hard time convincing people like Bob Montgomery and George Murphy he isn't a Commie."

"And Jeanette MacDonald?"

"And Jeanette MacDonald. And top producers. Mr. Kurtz won't ever have him in his house again."

"Well, I guess if he's just sulking, I won't see him making a picture," said McCrosland.

"We could go and watch Takso Myckit. She's on Stage Seven. You know, she's the new Swedish importation."

"Is she new? I've seen her name, haven't I?"

"Well, you've seen her name. Lew Kalem has her under personal contract. He brought her over from Sweden two years ago and taught her diction and English and all that. She's here on a loan-out from Lew's studio. Sixty-five."

"Thousand dollars?"

"Uh-huh," said Mitchell. "Her first picture."

"Well, that's a nice, respectable sum for a first picture, isn't it?"

"Well, of course she doesn't get that."

"What *does* she get?"

"Now? I think she gets seven-fifty. It may be five, or maybe it's a thousand. But I think right now it's seven-fifty, depending on what option phase she's in. See, Lew paid her while she was learning diction and English. He'll be there tonight. You'll see him. Mrs. Kurtz is his sister, you know."

"No, I didn't."

"Sure. Then when Takso finishes here, she goes to Warners' on a one-shot deal. I think that's for eighty or eighty-five. The word is when this one's released—the one she's doing here—they'll just forget Bergman, Garbo, all of them."

"But she'll never make the money Garbo made, for instance."

"You mean because Lew has her under contract? But he took the risks. She's making more than she'd ever make in Sweden."

"Very likely," said McCrosland. "You mentioned television. I understand Hollywood's rather worried about that."

"Who worries about television? Radio actors that don't have any more ability than to sit at a table and read a script—*they* worry about television."

"No, I mean the people like Mr. Kurtz."

"Listen, Professor, what can they lose by television? If it's home television on film, are you and your wife going to tune in on a dog-and-pony act, or Boone Crockett and Takso Myckit? Well, who has them under contract? People like Mr. Kurtz. And if it's television in theaters, who owns the theaters? Picture people. And are they going to throw away a billion dollars of movie investments to let television compete in their own theaters? They own the stars, they own the theaters, they own the studios, they own the literary properties. And you're getting the A treatment, so maybe I can get them to show you some television stuff this studio owns right this minute—stuff this studio shot."

Mitchell clicked the intercom, but there was no answer. "God damn it, my secretary's probably taking dictation from the guy I share her with. They let about forty secretaries go, so I have to double up with this one. Anyway, these people are smart apples. They knew about television long ago, and it's in nearly all their old contracts, when people thought it was a joke to talk about. No, these people will land on top. All television did so far, as far as I can see, was give the studios an excuse to get rid of some overpaid cousins. Associate producers that were making a hundred or two hundred thousand a year for nothing. You knock off two hundred Gs off your budget at the beginning—that's a nice start. You get rid of a cousin and maybe take care of your story cost."

"Well, well," said McCrosland. "Mr. Mitchell, could I use your phone?"

"Certainly."

"It's a West Los Angeles number. I have it here."

"Dial O and give the operator the number."

McCrosland did so. "Hello, is this the residence of Professor Titus?"

"Yes," said a woman's voice.

"Martha, this is Ben McCrosland."

"Ben! Where are you? Is Ruth with you?"

"I'm not very far away. In Los Angeles. Ruth is at Columbia getting some credits—on that Master's degree, you remember. I'll tell you when I see you. I was wondering if you had room for me for one night. Tonight."

"Well, I should say we have. Walter's at the lab, but he'll be free this afternoon. Where are you? Can I come and get you?"

"I wish to God you would. I'm at the Kurtz studio."

"I'll be there in no time. I'll meet you at the main gate."

"Thank you, Martha. Thank you." He hung up and turned to Mitchell. "Mr. Mitchell, I don't want to seem ungrateful to you or to Mr. Kurtz. But I don't think I really want to see any more."

"See any more? You haven't seen *anything.*"

"Well, yes and no," said McCrosland. "This friend of mine is going to pick me up at the gate, so I won't need the Cadillac. Then I'll ask my friend to take me to the hotel and I'll check out of there. I'll pay my own bill, if you don't mind. And I'll write a note to Mrs. Kurtz and one to Mr. Kurtz telling him how helpful you were, and—"

"But for Christ's sake—"

"Now, don't you worry about a single thing. I can write a very diplomatic letter when I want to," said McCrosland. "I'm sorry I didn't get a chance to see Irving, but I'll write him, too."

"Well, suit yourself. What about Mary Bates?"

"I'm *very* sorry I won't see *her,* but I suppose she'll forgive me."

"Yeah, you'd probably never make your train tomorrow." He leaned back in his chair and tucked his thumb under his chin.

"Well, good day, Mr. Mitchell."

"Right," said Mitchell. "Oh, I just remembered—you'll have to be cleared at the main gate. You came in an executive car. I'll phone the gate, and they'll let you out."

"Thank you."

McCROSLAND LEFT THE building and walked to the main gate, where a cop stopped him. "My name is McCrosland, I—"

"O.K.," said the cop.

McCrosland passed through the gate and waited for Martha Titus. At first, the cop paid no attention to him, but McCrosland, standing just outside the gate, became fascinated by the policeman and his equipment. He wore a black shirt, trousers, and cap, and a plaited black leather belt, plaited black leather holster containing a .38 Police Positive revolver, a smaller plaited black leather holster for chain twisters, and, in his hip pocket, a black leather-bound truncheon. The man also wore steel-rimmed spectacles, and, facially, looked more like a night cashier in a cheap restaurant than a cop. He grew restive under McCrosland's prolonged study of him. "Well, what are *you* lookin' at?" he said.

"Hmm?" said McCrosland.

"Nuts," said the cop.

McCrosland turned away and saw a Crosley convertible approaching the gate, and almost immediately he recognized Martha. She was waving and grinning, and she called to him, "I'll turn around."

McCrosland nodded and turned to the cop. "Say, Officer," he said, "if somebody tried to get Margaret O'Brien's autograph, would you shoot him?"

"What are you—a wise guy?" said the cop. He started toward McCrosland. "Let me see some identification." He was moving close, and fast, and McCrosland suddenly ran. Martha Titus, now on her way back, sped up the car and opened the door; McCrosland jumped in, and the cop gave up.

"Ben, what on earth?"

"Tell you when I get my breath," said McCrosland, laughing.

In a Grove

In this obscure little California town, far away from Hollywood and not even very close to the Saroyan-Steinbeck country, William Grant once again encountered Richard Warner, as he had always known he would.

Johnstown—to give it a name—was one of those towns that vaudevillians used to describe as "a wide place in the road" and that had owed its earliest existence to the gold strikes of more than a century ago. But in the intervening years it had been all but abandoned until irrigation began to help agriculture, and Johnstown got a second life; unspectacular, unromantic, unexciting, and obviously unprofitable—the last place Grant would expect to find Warner, and yet, since his disappearance had been so complete, the kind of place that was just made for a man who wanted to leave the world in which he had once been widely known.

Grant stopped his car at a filling station. "Fill it up, will you please? The oil is okay, but will you check the water and tires?"

"Right. What do you carry, twenty-six pounds, the tires?" said the attendant.

"Twenty-six, right."

"You been driving a distance, they'll all be a little high, you know. You want me to deflate to twenty-six?"

"Yes."

"Some don't, you know."

"Well, I'm one of those that do," said Grant. "What's the name of this town?"

"Johnstown. Johnstown, California."

"Is that a cigarette machine in there?"

"It's a cigarette machine that's out of order. The nearest place is the supermarket. You can see it there on the edge of town. They call it a supermarket, but nothing very super about it. It's only what used to be the Buick agency, that's all it is."

"But they have cigarettes there."

"Oh, they have cigarettes. They have most everything you find in a supermarket, but I don't know who they think they're kidding, calling it a supermarket. It's no bigger than when it was the Buick agency."

"What happened to the Buick agency?"

"What happened to it? This was never a town for Buicks. You wait here a few minutes and you'll see a couple Model-A Fords, still chugging away. Maybe some International trucks, been through various hands, one rancher to the other. Way back, when I was a kid, one family had a Locomobile. You ever hear of the Locomobile?"

"Yes."

"Another rancher had a big old Pierce-Arrow. Those big ritzy cars, but I'll tell you something. You look on the running-board of those cars and every one of them carried canteens. Ed Hughes, that owned the Locomobile, I remember he had like a saddle holster he had strapped to the right-hand door, to carry a 30-30 rifle in. They didn't buy those cars for show. They bought them because they stood up. That was before they thought up this planned obsolence."

"Planned obsolence. Uh-huh."

"You know, 'Here's this year's piece of junk, come back and see what I allow you on it two years from now.' That's where all the trouble lies. Now what you got here is a foreign car, and it aint even broke in at forty-five thousand miles. This is an automobile. You don't mind if I take a look under the hood? I know, you said you don't need oil, but—"

"That, that just went by. That was no Model-A," said Grant.

The attendant had missed the passing Jaguar, but now waved to it. He smiled. "No, that was Dick Warner. He's a fellow lives here. You ever hear of the expression, as queer as Dick's hatband? I think that's who it originated with, Dick Warner."

"Dick Warner? How long has he lived here?"

"Oh—I guess fifteen, maybe twenty years by now. Why, do you know him?"

"Possibly. Where did this fellow come from?"

"Oh, well I'm not even sure about that."

"Is he a tall thin fellow? Brown hair? About my age?"

"Well, I guess he'd answer that description. What are you, the F.B.I. or something like that?"

"Hell, no. If I were the F.B.I. I'd go looking for the deputy sheriff, wouldn't I?"

"You found him. *I'm* the deputy sheriff, and I never had any bad reports on Dick, bad or good for that matter. He pays his bills, don't owe nobody, and his fingerprint's on his driver's license. Well, now he's making a U-turn. Maybe he recognized you."

"I doubt it."

"Heading back this way. Yeah. Moving slowly. Wants to get a good look at you. Mister, are you armed? You got a gun on you?"

"No."

"Well, Dick has, so get behind something. I am."

"There's not going to be anything like that."

"All the same I'm getting out of the way till I make sure. I'm going in and put my badge on. And my gun."

"Go ahead. I'll stand right here."

The Jaguar drove past slowly, the driver staring at William Grant. After the Jaguar had gone past the filling station it stopped, then backed up into the parking area. Dick Warner got out.

He was tall and thin and wore a planter's Panama with a band of feathers, a safari jacket with the sleeves rolled up, sun-tan slacks and leather sandals. "Is it you, Grant?"

"Yes it's me. Hello, Dick."

"Christ Almighty," said Warner. He put out his hand, and Grant shook it.

"No, just me," said Grant.

"What the hell are you doing here?"

"I was looking for a good place to hide out from the law."

"Then get going. There isn't room for two of us. Well, God damn it, Bill. Hey, Smitty, come on out and meet a friend of mine. This is Mr. Grant, Mr. Smith. See that you give him four quarts to the gallon."

"Now, Dick. Now, now."

"Mr. Smith thought you might be going to shoot me," said Grant.

"Now why'd you have to tell him that? I didn't know but you were somebody snooping around and Dick didn't want to see you."

"I hear you carry a gun, Dick," said Grant.

"Smitty, whose side are you on? You talk too much."

"This fellow stard asking me questions. He's the one with the big mouth. That'll be four-eighty, Mister, and the next time you come here there's another filling station the other end of town."

"You decided not to check the air for me?"

"I decided if you wanted to check the air you can do it yourself, and there's the hose if you need water."

"All right, Sheriff. You owe me twenty cents," said Grant, handing Smitty a five-dollar bill.

"Mr. Grant's a nice fellow, Smitty. You shouldn't take that attitude."

"I know what attitude to take without any advice from you, Dick."

"I know. Your gums are bothering you again," said Warner. "Smitty has a new upper plate, and he won't give his gums a chance to get used to it."

"I don't think it's his gums. I think he's just a disagreeable guy."

"Move on, Mister, or I'll give you a ticket."

"What for?" said Grant.

"Obstructing traffic. Failure to pay for parking on my lot. I'll think of a few things."

"He will, too, and his brother-in-law's the mayor," said Warner. "Smitty, this is no way to treat a visitor to our fair city."

"We don't encourage tourists. If this fellow's a friend of yours, Dick, you get him off my property pronto."

"All right. Follow me, Bill. And don't go through any stop-signs."

"I'll get out of here as quickly as I can."

"Thirty-mile zone," said Smitty.

"I think that dentist gave you the wrong plate, Smitty," said Warner. "Come on, Bill."

The built-up section was four blocks of one-story white stucco business buildings, which changed abruptly to a stretch of one-story frame dwellings, all badly in need of paint, and then there was country, bare in the rolling hills where the irrigation was not effective. Grant followed Warner for about a mile, until Warner blew his horn, slowed down, and made a right turn into a dirt road. A few hundred yards along that road Warner again slowed down and entered a dirt driveway that ended in a grove of various trees, in the center of which was a ranchhouse. Two horses in a small corral looked up as the cars approached, and a collie ignored Warner's car to run along beside Grant's, barking ferociously. Warner signaled to Grant to drive up alongside him.

"Stay in your car till I put Sonny away. He's liable to take a piece out of your leg," said Warner. He got out and the dog came to him, and he grasped the dog's collar and snapped a leash to it and attached the leash to a length of wire that ran between two trees. The dog could run only between the trees. "You're safe now."

"What do you feed this dog? People?"

"I don't have to. He helps himself. Particularly fond of Mexicans. Itinerant workers. Salesmen. Hollywood writers, he hasn't had any but I can tell he's willing to have a taste of you."

"I can tell that myself."

"Well, just stay out of reach."

"All right, Lassie," said Grant. "Maybe if I gave him a good swift kick."

"You'd never leave here alive if you did. Even if I let you get away with it my wife wouldn't."

"Oh, you're married."

"Good God, do you think I could live here if I wasn't?"

"Well, what the hell. Itinerant workers, Mexicans."

"Lay off the Mexican angle. My wife is half Mexican."

"What else do I have to look out for?"

"Well, at certain times of the day, down there near the ditch, rattlesnakes, but they don't come up here much. I've done a pretty good job of exterminating them around the house. Anyway, you won't be here that long. You're on your way somewhere, obviously. Come on in and meet my bride and have a cooling drink."

"And I forgot to get some cigarettes."

"We have plenty. The señora's a heavy smoker. There she is."

A girl, not readily identifiable as Mexican but wearing a multicolored peasant blouse and skirt and huaraches, opened the door of a screened porch. "Hi," she said.

"I brought somebody out of my past. This is Bill Grant, used to be with me at Paramount. Bill, this is the present Mrs. Warner, Rita by name."

"Hi," she said. "And what's with that present Mrs. Warner bit?"

"We can only wait and see."

"You wait and see. Come on in, Bill. What would you like to drink? I got some cold beer."

"Thank you, that's just perfect."

"Where did the great Warner run across you? Or you across him? He never has any company. From Hollywood, anyway. Dick, you get the beer."

"All right," said Warner, and went to the kitchen.

"I'm working for TV now, and I came up this way scouting locations. Have you been in pictures?"

"No, but I know what scouting locations means. I went to high school in L.A. Fairfax."

"How did you stay out of pictures?"

"You think I'm pretty enough? I guess I'm prettier than some of those dogs, but I was never discovered. Except by his majesty."

"Where did he discover you?"

"You better ask him, he has a different story for everybody. He told a couple people in Johnstown I was his daughter. The son of a bitch. I *am* married to him though. You married?"

"Sure. I have a daughter around your age."

"Well, so has Dick, although I never saw her."

"I know. She lives back East."

"And he has a son. You don't have to be cagey about that side of him. Three ex-wives, a daughter and a son. A brother, a sister, a mother—all that I know. Did you know him a long time?"

"A long time ago I knew him pretty well. Then we had a falling-out. I can't remember what about."

"Well I remember," said Warner, bringing in a tray of bottles and glasses. "I fired you because you went on a three-day bender and never let me know where you were."

"I guess that was it."

"You made me look bad on my second picture as a producer."

"Yeah. You behaved like a jerk producer, that's right."

"Why do you say jerk producer? What other kind is there? You're one now, only in a worse medium. I've seen your name in the paper once in a while. The hell with that. What are you up here for?"

"What are you?"

"I asked you."

"I'm scouting locations."

"Stay away, will you? Go on up to Marin County. I don't want a bunch of those bastards coming to Johnstown. I went to a lot of trouble to get away from them, so don't spoil it for me, will you?"

"I won't promise. Anyway, I might make you a few dollars. I could rent this place for a couple of weeks."

"I don't need the money."

"Hey! Who don't need the money?" said Rita. "I could use a few bucks."

"On what? We have enough."

"I was wondering about that," said Grant. "You do have enough? This is a nice place and all that, but I remember when you were playing polo."

"I could still play polo if I wanted to, but who plays polo these days? For that matter, who makes pictures these days?"

"His majesty thinks the movies stink," said Rita. "That's why he never goes to them, and that's why he knows all about them."

"You don't smell with your eyes. The beautiful odor is wafted all the way from Culver City," said Warner.

"Culver City is where I work. I shoot a lot of stuff on the Metro lot," said Grant.

"Speaking of shooting, what was that conversation with Smitty?"

"He told me you carried a gun. Apparently he doesn't know anything about you, your background, where you came from."

"I've seen to that."

"But this is the strange part. He was willing to believe that you were ready to shoot it out with the first stranger that asked about you. That's an odd impression to leave after living here fifteen years."

"I've told Smitty what you might call conflicting stories. It's nobody's business what I did before I came here, or what I do now, if I stay within the law."

"What *do* you do now?"

Warner pointed to a wall that was completely covered with bookshelves containing paperback books and old magazines; western stories, detective stories, science fiction, popular delvings into the human mind.

"You write them?" said Grant.

"I steal from them and then write my own. I have five bylines, and I make anywhere from five to fifteen thousand a year, turning out stories. I'm what we used to call a pulp writer."

"It must keep you busy, but do you need the money? I thought you left Hollywood with plenty of glue."

"Don't give this greedy little Mexican the wrong idea," said Warner. "We live on what I earn."

"Except when you want to buy a Jaguar, or send away to New York for some clothes," said Rita.

"My extravagances, my spirit-raising expenditures, they come out of my capital, the money I took out of Hollywood," said Warner.

"You let him get away with this, Rita?"

"She's devoted to me, you can see that. Sit on his lap," said Warner. "He's wondering if he can make you, so let him have a try at it."

"You want me to sit on your lap, Grant?"

"Of course. He's right."

She put down her glass and sat on Grant's lap. Grant took her in his arms and kissed her and felt her breasts.

"Cut!" said Warner. "Now go back to your chair."

The girl returned to her chair and picked up her glass.

"How do you feel, Chiquita? Would you have gone on?"

"What do you think, king? Of course I'd have gone on."

"Then why didn't you?"

"Because I knew you were going to say 'Cut.' "

"That isn't the answer you're supposed to give."

"That's the answer I gave, though. I told you I have a lot to learn."

"She has spirit, this girl," said Warner.

"Plenty."

"Oh, not only what you mean. She still has a mind of her own."

"I always will have. His majesty thinks he rules me, but he doesn't tell me to do anything I don't want to do. You can't hypnotize somebody against their will."

"Yes you can," said Grant. "But there's some theory that while they're under hypnosis they won't do anything they don't want to."

"I guess that's what I meant."

"Let me remind both of you that this has nothing to do with hypnosis. I am not a hypnotist."

"Maybe not, but you like to think you have hypnotic powers," said Grant.

"There you're perfectly correct."

"I'd like to know why you said 'Cut'? It wasn't just to show your power. It was because you were afraid."

"Nonsense," said Warner. "Afraid of what?"

"Ho! Afraid that Rita and I would get in the hay. She was willing to stop because she was getting embarrassed."

Warner gave a short laugh. "Embarrassed? Rita? Tell the man what you used to do for a living."

"I was a hooker," said the girl.

"A fifty-dollar girl that got tired of the grind," said Warner.

"And several other things," said Rita. "You don't only get tired of the grind."

"My wife doesn't embarrass easily, Grant."

"I guess not," he said.

"The complexities and deviations are all old stuff to her. What did you think of Grant when you first laid eyes on him?"

"Well, I knew by the car that he was probably some Hollywood friend of yours."

"Yes, but what else?"

"Well, he'd make a pass at me if he had a chance."

"So far nothing very complex," said Grant.

"Well, I knew he didn't like you."

"Now we're getting somewhere. Do you know why you thought that?" said Warner.

"That I couldn't tell you."

"All right, never mind. Tell us some other first impressions and reactions."

"I thought I wouldn't mind getting in bed with him."

"She doesn't see many men here," said Warner.

"Let her tell it," said Grant.

"But he wouldn't be much fun after a while. You're still the most fun, king."

"Why is he so much fun, Rita? Not just sex," said Grant.

"Don't knock sex. And it is sex. With this character everything is sex. Want to ask you a question, Grant. Did he lay all those picture stars?"

"He had his share, but not many of the big ones. He was afraid to go after the big ones. He was afraid he'd get a turndown and it would get around that he'd made a pitch and was unsuccessful. In Hollywood, honey, that's losing face. No, your husband didn't score with the big ones."

"I knew you were lying about that," said Rita to Warner.

"Grant is only telling what he knows. There's a hell of a lot he doesn't know."

"What Academy Award winner did you ever lay? Now don't give me any best-supporting actress. I mean the Number One. Or what star that got top billing, her name over the main title? Or a hundred percent of the main title."

"What's that?"

"Your name in letters as big as the title of the picture," said

Grant. "The only one was Ernesta Travers, and she was giving it out to projectionists. She actually laid a projectionist while he was running a picture for her."

"You've got the story wrong, but no matter. I even forgot about Ernesta."

"I didn't know she was ever a big star," said Rita. "Have some more beer, Grant."

"All right, fine," said Grant.

"You, king? You want another?"

"If you get it, yes," said Warner.

She left them.

"Yes, what you're wondering is true. She was a hooker."

"Well she was a damn pretty one. Is. I have to be careful of my tenses. Is damn pretty, whatever she was."

"Would you give her a hundred dollars now?"

"Sure."

In a loud voice Warner called out: "I've got you lined up for a fast hundred dollars."

"With Grant?" she responded from the kitchen.

"Yeah."

"All right," she said. She brought in three bottles of beer, clutching them by the neck. She put a bottle in front of Warner, then sat herself beside Grant and poured beer into his glass. "Do I get to keep the whole C-note?"

"Certainly," said Warner.

"Do I get shot in the back?" said Grant.

"That's the chance you take."

"Just so you don't shoot him while he's in the kip with me."

"That's the chance *you* take, señora."

She looked at her husband. "Listen, how much of this is kidding and how much is kidding on the square?"

"I'm not kidding at all. If you'd like to make yourself a quick hundred dollars, Grant and I made a deal. Ask Grant if I'm kidding."

"Just like old times, back in the Thirties," said Grant.

"I don't know," said the girl.

"What don't you know?" said Warner.

"Well, what the hell?" she said.

"It's how you used to earn your living," said her husband.

"I don't deny that. But the first friend of yours ever came to the house and you promote him into a party with me," she said.

"Don't you want the hundred dollars?" said Warner.

"I always want a hundred dollars."

"Well, you necked him, you let him give you a little feel."

"Yeah, but I thought that was—I was just playing along with the gag."

"Grant wasn't playing along with any gag, were you, Grant?"

"To tell you the truth I guess I wasn't."

"And it was no gag when you said you'd give her a hundred bucks."

"No, I'd give her a hundred bucks."

"Well, you son of a bitch, if you meant it, I'll level, too," said the girl to her husband. She reached out her hand. "Come on, Grant."

Grant stood up. "You'll excuse us, I'm sure," said Grant.

The girl looked at her husband. "You can't be on the level," she said.

"Why not?" said Warner.

"God damn you. God damn you!" She ripped off the peasant blouse and, naked to the waist, put her arms around Grant and kissed him. "Come on," she said, and led him by the hand.

She lay on the oversize bed, and Grant shed his clothes and got down beside her. She looked at him. "Don't worry, I won't welsh on it now," she said. She put her arms around him and began running her little hands up and down his spine, slowly, caressingly.

"Perfect." Warner's voice was cold and calm.

The girl saw her husband in the doorway, then she screamed. "No! No!" The first shots struck Grant in the spine, he shuddered and died. The girl tried to hide behind his body, but Warner grasped his hand and pulled him aside and took his time firing the remaining four shots. Then he went to the telephone and dialed.

"Smitty, come on out here. I've got something for you," he said.

The Glendale People

NO PLACE IN Florida is very highly situated, but from Dale Connell's cottage it is possible to see the Gulf of Mexico while seated on the screened porch. It is a somewhat obstructed view; between the cottage and the water there is a busy highway, and across the highway a row of cottages not unlike Dale Connell's, and in back of them is the narrow beachfront. But the Gulf of Mexico is there, flashes of it between the cottages, and above the cottages a thin blue arc that is the horizon. When the traffic is momentarily halted by the red light, you can even hear the surf sometimes during the day, and late at night and early in the morning the small attacks of the waves upon the sand are continually audible and very helpful in producing sleep.

The cottage is the best he could do for the money, and Dale Connell is reasonably content. He has a livingroom, bedroom, bath and kitchen. Some of his neighbors use their livingroom as a bedroom, but Dale Connell is alone and does not need a second bedroom. Some of his neighbors envy him the luxury of the livingroom that is a real livingroom and not a part-time bedroom with a convertible couch. Dale Connell has room for what he calls his stuff—his souvenirs and framed photographs of movie actors and actresses—and when the weather is not at its best he can entertain indoors. Having a nice place to receive guests, being a bachelor, and always wearing a jacket when he goes for a walk—these items set Dale Connell apart from his neighbors. It is also known that he is writing a book, and his neighbors are a little envious of that, too. It would be wonderful to have the knack of writing a book, or doing *something*.

The neighbors look upon Dale Connell as a very lucky man, and because they do, so does he, and he has made friends with dozens of people whom in the past he would have ignored, the kind of people he spent most of his life avoiding. They are what he used to call Glendale people, married couples from the Middle West who had come to California to save money on overcoats and tire chains, bought small bungalows in Glendale and Burbank and less well known places like Watts and Anaheim. They could truthfully write home and say they picked their own oranges in their own backyards, that there were hummingbirds outside their bedroom windows. They went, with a hundred thousand like them, to the annual Iowa get-togethers in Griffith Park; they queued up at the radio stations to attend the Breakfast at Sardi's and Queen for a Day programs. Some of them became Townsendites, some of them went in for food fads, some were devoted to Aimee Semple McPherson. They all had false teeth and took high colonics. And about once a week they would provide the Los Angeles newspapers with a murder; about once a quarter they would commit a murder that showed imagination, like the man who killed his wife by forcing her leg into a box of rattlesnakes. Dale Connell had given them the name Glendale people, although they could have been described as Culver City people, Santa Monica people, Santa Ana people. He just happened to have spent more time at the Warner Brothers studio and had passed through Glendale on his way to work, month after week after day. The appellation had nothing to do with his own name, which in any event was a name he had adopted along the way.

His present-day friends, those he would once have called Glendale people, are his own age. That is, they are anywhere from the middle fifties to the middle seventies. He is not unmindful of the fact that he is more tolerant of Glendale people since he became their contemporary. He does not mind living in the midst of Glendale people so long as he does not have to live with them in Glendale.

Most of the men he used to know are dead, and those who survive have lost touch with Dale Connell, do not even know that he is alive. When he dies, and the highlights of his career appear in his obituary, there will be people who will say that they thought he was dead; others who will wonder why they never heard of him; others who have heard of him and will say they wish they never had; and a few who will laugh and say unkind things not unkindly. Dale Connell is aware of all that. In the morning, when he has finished with the breakfast dishes and put on his double-breasted blazer and wrinkled Panama, and walks the eight blocks to the out-of-town newspaper stand, he opens his New York papers to the obituary pages before turning to the entertainment and book sections. He is precisely fair in his personal epitaphs of old acquaintances; he knows what they would say about him, and his thoughts of them are measure-for-measure gentle and severe, plus the embarrassing triumph of having for a while outlived men who lived better lives than his own. But there is never any severity in his judgments of women whose death notices he reads. He has forgiven every woman who ever gave him a bad time, and all the numerous women he has known are now creatures of equal rank in a company formed by his memory. No matter how unique and individualistic each of them may have been at the time, they all are banded together now, rather like a bundle of love letters tied in red ribbon, resting in the bottom drawer of his bureau under his New York shirts.

On his way home from the newsstand he carries his Panama, gripped by the brim, in one swinging hand, and tucked under the other arm are the newspapers and his stick. Many of his friends carry canes, not tucked under their arms but used for support, and they are cheap, despised pieces of wood. Dale Connell is fond of his Malacca, with its initialed brass ferrule, bought for him at Swaine, Adeney's by an Englishwoman from whom he had expected at least an Asprey cigarette case. Another Englishwoman, who could not really afford a walking stick, had given him a Dunhill gold lighter with a watch in it. The Malacca makes him think of the second woman's generosity, even though the lighter has long since been pawned; but the giver of the Malacca had been generous in her way, too, and Dale Connell will have something to say about the unpredictability of Englishwomen when he comes to that part of his book.

He works on his book in the mornings, after he has read the newspapers, made his bed, and prepared the instant coffee. The actual writing is not as easy as he thought it was going to be. He has been at it for five years, and he has taken twenty-five hundred dollars from a New York publisher who will not advance any more money until Dale Connell shows him some manuscript. Any publisher would be glad to bring out the memoirs of Dale Connell, and Carson Burroughs was extremely enthusiastic when Connell wrote and told him that he had started a book. "You realize, of course," Burroughs had replied, "that even today we may have to tone it down. However, I promise you that we will do our utmost to retain the validity of your memoirs. Meanwhile, when do you think you will be able to show us the first five hundred pages?" Six months passed, and Dale Connell had got nothing down on paper. "I have torn up everything I have written so far and am off to a new start with an entirely fresh approach," he wrote Burroughs. "Could you see your way clear to advancing me another thousand?" He got no immediate answer to this letter; instead he got a surprise visit from Burroughs.

It was more than a surprise; it was something of a shock. He came home one morning and an enormous Cadillac convertible was parked in front of his cottage. It had Florida licenses plates, but Dale Connell knew no one who owned a Cadillac. Most of his Florida Glendale people owned no car at all. The shock came when he opened the screendoor of his front porch and was greeted by Burroughs.

"Hello, Dale," said Burroughs. "I thought I'd drop in and see how you were coming along."

"Drop in? Are you in town?"

"Palm Beach. I flew over this morning."

"Is that your car?"

"Hired. Your letter was forwarded to me, I guess my secretary didn't know you were on the West Coast and Palm Beach is on the East Coast. Anyway, she thought she was using her head. And she was."

"Of course. Will you have a drink, or would you like some coffee?"

"I'll have a cup of coffee with you, but don't go to any trouble. I'm chiefly interested in your memoirs. How're they coming?"

"Well, as I told you in my letter, I've got a whole new fresh approach. I wasted a couple of years trying to lick it, but it wasn't altogether waste. I learned how it *shouldn't* be done. You see, I was never a writer before. I used to dictate everything to a secretary, or into a Dictaphone."

"When you were in Hollywood? You have quite a few screen credits. Didn't you write those scripts?"

"Original-story credits, they were. I used to dictate them, and I could always get a secretary to put them in shape. All they cared about was the story line. Very different from sitting down and writing a book, I found out."

"Well, why don't you get yourself a tape recorder and get going that way? I can always find somebody to whip it into shape, once we have the stuff. I'm perfectly willing to advance you another thousand dollars if I have something to show for it, but I have to convince my partners. That's why I came over to see you personally. Hell, if you just sit down and tell the story of your checkered career, Dale, you'd have a real blockbuster. I admit that. Married what? Four times?"

"Five. The first one nobody knows about. That was back in Ohio, when I was twenty years old. I married my piano teacher, she was twenty-eight."

"You didn't stay married to her very long."

"It was annulled. I blew town and joined the Canadian army. Then right after the war I married—"

"Gaby Perrier? Right?"

"Right. She divorced me to marry the Bolivian, and I married Valerie Vale."

"Beautiful. I always thought the most beautiful girl Ziegfeld ever had. Tragic, of course."

"Yes, at least it turned out that way. You knew what her trouble was?"

"Booze, I always heard," said Burroughs.

"No. That's what everybody thought. No, it wasn't booze."

"What was it? Dope?"

"Not dope, either."

"Well, come on, give. What was it?"

"Wait till my book comes out," said Dale Connell.

"You son of a bitch, what kind of a come-on is that? All right. Then you married Sylvia Rumson and you divorced her because she put you in a novel while you were still married to her."

"Is that the way it was, Carson?"

"Well, wasn't it? She did put you in a novel."

"Was that me, or was it somebody else? Everybody said it was me, but was it?"

"Wasn't it?"

"If I told you who the guy really was in that book, you'd call me a liar. I divorced Sylvia, but I didn't have to pay her any alimony. I didn't even have to pay for the lawyers. If you think back a minute, the next two years I lived like a prince, a maharajah. Not bad for a young guy from Ohio that didn't have a job or anything.

No, the guy in that book wasn't me. I won't tell you who it was, but I'll tell you this much. He was a banker. Wall Street. Sylvia disguised the character in the book to make him look like me, but all those details were the banker, not me. In other words, Sylvia pulled a fast one on both of us. Oh, she was quite an operator, Sylvia. You ought to know."

"Not me."

"Oh, yes. You. She told me about you, Carson. Some kind of a convention in Chicago, and you drove back together in your car. I think you had a Marmon."

"Well, that was before she was married to you, so you can't hold that against me. Then you married Kitty Romaine."

"Married Kitty Romaine, was divorced by Kitty Romaine, married her again two weeks after the divorce, and was with her when she died."

"And she was the real love of your life."

"No. Not that I didn't love Kitty, because I did. But she wasn't the real one, my big number, as we used to say then. No, you wouldn't know who that was even if I told you."

"Is that going to be in the book?"

"Yes, without mentioning her name."

"Oh, happily married?"

"No. She's a nun."

"A nun? You were in love with a girl that became a nun? What was she before that?"

"Nothing. A schoolgirl. I used to walk home from school with her. Carry her books. We used to talk. Her father was a doctor, the greatest man I ever knew, although he had no use for me. Coached the high school football team, and he'd scrimmage with us in his street clothes. He could do anything. Box. Shoot. Play the piano. Sing. Serve Mass. And keep up his practice. Had the first automobile in town. But he only had one child, a daughter. Dark brown hair and blue eyes. Everybody said Doctor Callaghan should have had a son, but he had only this one daughter and I guess no young guy ever measured up to her father. Oh, she was pretty. She could have been the belle of the ball, but she never went out on dates. I'd walk home with her during the winter and spring, when there was no football practice, and we'd stand and talk at their front gate. How I was going to be a big song-writer, and have my own orchestra, and travel all over. Or else maybe I'd go to Western Reserve and study medicine. She never believed that, but she'd pretend to. I always wanted to *talk* to *her,* and I did. By the hour. She really didn't have very much to say, but she had intelligent eyes and I always knew she was listening. They sent her East to school, and that was the year I ran off with the music teacher. I never saw Agnes again after she went away to school. Never heard from her. Never heard from her to this day, not that I expected to after the big scandal. And yet I guess I did expect to hear from her. I wanted her to forgive me. I haven't been inside of a confessional since I was nineteen years old. I never went to confession when I was in the army, when the chaplain would come around the night before we were moving up. Agnes was the one I wanted to forgive me, not some Canuck priest." He was silent.

"This is a new side of you, Dale," said Burroughs.

"No it isn't."

"No, I guess maybe it isn't," said Burroughs. "If you get this down the way you tell it, it sure would surprise a lot of people."

"It sure would," said Dale Connell. "It would spoil my reputation. Maybe America isn't ready for that."

"Maybe not. But if I advance you another thousand dollars will you spend some of it on a tape recorder?"

"Make it fifteen hundred and I'll promise to buy one."

"That's more like the Dale Connell I know. All right. Fifteen hundred, but that'll be all until I get five hundred pages of manuscript."

"How much is that in tape?"

"I have no idea. You send me the tape and I'll have it transcribed, and when you have five hundred pages I'll advance you another thousand. Making thirty-five hundred advance royalties."

A few days later a tape recorder arrived from Miami, with it a Carson Burroughs calling card on which was written, "Start talking—good luck—C.B."

During the next few days Dale Connell studied the instructions and learned to operate the apparatus. As a toy it was amusing. He sang into it, and did his parlor imitations of actors he had known, but when he began to dictate his life story he froze. "I was born on the fifteenth of January, 1897, in the town of High Ridge, Ohio. I was the youngest son of Mr. and Mrs. Daniel J. Connelley and I was named after my father. I attended the public school and graduated from high school in 1915." At that point he always stopped. It took him weeks to discover why he always stopped there: it was that the next autobiographical fact was his elopement, and speaking into the apparatus made him sound to himself like a boy telling his sins to a priest. That he would not do; he was not a boy, the apparatus was not a priest, and every time he approached the apparatus to begin again, Agnes Callaghan became more real and alive to him than she had been in almost fifty years. He could visualize her in her nun's habit; the face he had last seen in 1915, the features unchanged but the cheeks framed in white linen, the forehead almost hidden by white linen, and he could imagine her fingering a crucifix as he had seen other nuns do. Soon the apparatus was so inextricably identified with the calm face of a young girl that he did not like to go near it. He stayed away from it, until one night after some visitors went home he decided to exorcise the spirit of the apparatus, and he did so by turning on the microphone and speaking to it of women he had known. He had had more than his usual two cocktails and a brandy, and he described in detail their bodies and their passions. He played the recording back, and the nastiness of his performance so disgusted him that he pulled the tape from the spools and dropped the machine on the floor. He did not have it fixed. He put the broken apparatus in a closet and left it there. It is there now, much the worse for five years in the air that circulates over the Gulf of Mexico. The air is damp and salty, but the sun shines nearly every day and a man does not have to stay cooped up in a closet, like a broken tape recorder.

In the afternoon, after he has had his soup and pie, Dale Connell changes into cotton slacks and polo shirt and blue rope-soled espadrilles and goes to the beach. He takes a book with him, in case he sees no one he knows, but most days he is joined by some of his Glendale people, who love to hear him talk. "You must bear in mind," he says, "that anything can happen in the movie business, and anything can happen in Southern California. So when I tell you a story that sounds insane, just remember that combination."

"Tell us about the party at Lew Cody's," someone will say.

"The Lew Cody party? Well, he was having his house moved from Hollywood to Beverly. The men came to move the house, and Lew had a party going on. So he told them he didn't want to interrupt the party. Just disconnect the electricity and the water lines, he told them. And they put the house on rollers and moved it, but the party went right on, all the way out Wilshire Boulevard, for two days and nights. Lew, and Norman Kerry, and Fatty Arbuckle. Plenty of booze. A jazz band. Girls. Quite a party."

It is all new to his Glendale people, and when he has told them a story he makes a mental note to include it in his book. The trouble is there are so many stories. His Glendale people remember those stars, and they want to hear about their favorites. (Theda is just an anagram for death, Bara is Arab spelt backwards.) The Glendale people care not a whit about London or Paris or Rome and the people he knew during the frequent and sometimes lengthy sojourns he made in Europe. He wanted to say to his Glendale people, "You are missing a lot by not showing more interest in my European days." He has tried them out on stories of gambling in Monte Carlo, racing at Cowes, horse races at Ascot, the extravagances of nobility when they are sowing their wild oats, the practical jokes and the freak bets in the London clubs. But he has noticed that the Glendale people have a way of looking at him, when he tells foreign stories, that is a mixture of polite skepticism and a lack of curiosity. Some of the stories are partially provable; he has trinkets to show for some of his adventures, a half-filled scrapbook—started late, neglected early—that would substantiate some others. Nevertheless the Glendale people do not encourage those overseas reminiscences, and at first he blamed their Middle Western isolationism. But it isn't that, really; not in the usual sense of corn-belt insularity. It is something more personal.

They like it when he talks about his Hollywood experiences, because they know he came from Ohio, and what happened to him in Hollywood could have happened to them. (Fat chance; but that's what they think.) He retains his Ohio twang, in spite of a few Englishisms (stick for cane, jacket for coat), and their ears tell them that he is one of them. It is stupid of them not to realize that what sets him apart from them is not his livingroom, or being a bachelor, or his manner of dress. In the matter of clothes, for instance, they see only a blazer, and everybody wears blazers today. If they had a little more curiosity they would examine the buttons on his blazer and he would gladly inform them that the crest was that of a dinner club he belonged to in London in the mid-Twenties: a duke was honorary secretary, a member of the royal family paid his three guineas annual dues, a theatrical producer, as famous abroad as Ziegfeld at home, was honorary steward. The Glensdale people see only a cane, and some of the Glendale women as well as the men carry canes—could not take two steps without one. They never ask about his Malacca, and he has not created the opportunity to tell them that the lady who gave it to him was indeed a Lady. But they eat up everything he sees fit to tell them about Kitty Romaine. They all remember that Kitty Romaine was almost as famous as Pearl White.

Now and then Dale Connell begins to get a sensation of being overwhelmed by the Glendale people, of being irresistibly sucked back into the Middle West. He has never been back, he has had no communication with anyone in High Ridge since cabling the money for his mother's funeral in 1935. In 1934 he could not have sent the money; he was broke and in debt. In 1936 his sister would not have known how to reach him; he was in Calcutta, trying to promote a motion picture company. But in 1935 his sister telephoned a columnist on the Cleveland *Plain Dealer,* who obligingly gave her the address of Alexander Korda, Dale's most recent London employer. When Ursula Connelley died, in 1943, no one notified Dale. He could not have done much in any case; he was in Scotland in an O.S.S. film unit, with his major's pay and nothing more. Ursula was always a whiner, anyway, and in her rare letters to him through the years seemed compelled to say how awful his first wife looked, as though taking him to task for seducing a woman who in fact had seduced him. High Ridge, Ohio, was not small enough to be obliterated by progress, like the pretty little villages that are bulldozed out of existence to make way for super-highways, or inundated for the construction of dams. But there was nothing—and no one—in High Ridge that tugged at Dale Connell's heartstrings. Forty-five, almost fifty years, a long time, and in that time nothing that happened in High Ridge had happened to him. Nevertheless the town is still there, and in his moments of suspecting that his Glendale people have captured him, High Ridge becomes the Middle West, and he wonders if it has ever let him go.

So far there has been no one from High Ridge among the Glendale people. Roberta Wagner's granddaughter is a Pi Phi at State and has visited Tom Cookson's granddaughter in High Ridge. Dale Connell remembers Tom Cookson as an earnest boy who clerked in J. J. Cookson's grocery store and didn't get—or seem to want—much fun out of life. "We never knew each other very well," said Dale, when Roberta mentioned the Cooksons.

"They all remember you, though," said Roberta. "As Dan Connelley. All the girls were crazy about you, is what I hear."

"Now, now, Roberta. You only heard about one."

"Well—one was enough. Imagine running away with your music teacher. There was a case like that in Marion, Indiana, where I come from, only they stayed married. They moved away, but they kept on being married. It just goes to show, all that funny business isn't just confined to Hollywood."

Roberta's husband, Sam Wagner, is a mean little bastard. He has won the Senior Citizens' putting championship for three years running, and he is one of the few Glendale people to have a car. He has a way of listening during a conversation as though he were not listening, staring to his right three or four minutes, then suddenly staring to his left for another three or four, and back again to his right, and then he will make some remark that shows he has not missed a word. "Dale, I can't figure you out," he once said.

"How's that, Sam?" said Dale.

"Well, I listen to these stories of yours, and I never been able to figure out where you been all the time. One minute it's Hollywood, California. Then the next minute you're in London, England."

"That's just about the way it was, too," said Dale.

"Writing scenarios. But didn't you tell us you wrote songs?"

"I wrote a lot of songs. Probably a hundred, but only a few of them got published, and only four made a hit. That's how I live. I get a little income from ASCAP. No income from the scenarios."

"Then why don't you knock out some more songs, if that's where the money is."

"Not my kind of songs, not today. 'Wackity-Doo.' 'Little Chapel on the Lake.' They don't go for my songs any more. 'Moana Moon.' 'Let's Tarry in Tallahassee.' "

"Jevver hear of those songs, Roberta?" said Sam.

"Oh, yes. I used to play 'Little Chapel on the Lake.' "

"That was my biggest hit," said Dale. "You still hear it once in a while on the radio. 'Wackity-Doo' when they revived the Charleston, although I wrote that before the Charleston was popular."

"What were you doing in Europe all that time?" said Sam.

"You name it. I wrote scenarios. Some songs. Acted in a couple of plays. Co-produced several shows on Broadway that I brought over from London."

"You certainly were a jack-of-all-trades, all right."

"I had fun," said Dale.

"Is that a picture of you?" said Sam. "You had a waxed moustache?"

"And a full head of hair. Yes, that's me."

"Look at that collar. It's a wonder it didn't choke you. It looks like it was cutting your ear lobes."

"We all wore them then."

"I didn't."

"That was London."

"You look to me like you had lipstick on," said Sam.

"I did. Theatrical makeup. The girl was Jocelyn Candee, a very big name in the London theater."

"Maybe in London, but they wouldn't have given her a second look in Hollywood," said Sam Wagner.

"No, but she managed to become Lady Medlock, the wife of one of the richest men in the United Kingdom. I visited their—"

"They always left me cold, Englishwomen. I couldn't understand half of what they were saying. We were there in '28, year before the crash. I said I was never going back there, and I never did. And the men were no better."

"Some of the men," said Roberta Wagner.

"Aah," said Sam Wagner. "You know what Napoleon Bonaparte called them, don't you? A nation of small shopkeepers."

"Pretty good shops, though," said Dale Connell.

"No. You order a suit there, and it takes a couple months to have it ready. But that's not what I object to. What I object to, they do everything on credit there, you see. Cons'quently, *you're* paying for the deadbeats. I'd rather do business on a cash basis and get what I pay for, not making up their losses on bad debts. You put that in your book, warn the American tourists what they're paying for."

"It won't be that kind of a book."

"Oh, you could put it in somewhere. Are you gonna have that picture in it?"

"I might."

"You better put some of the others in, too, or everybody'll think you're a pansy. That lipstick. Boy! That oughta go big in England. Is this you in the uniform? Doesn't look like the same person."

"I've never been the same person I was in that picture," said Dale Connell.

"Do you think a person changes that much?" said Roberta. "I think we stay the same."

"Of course we do," said her husband. "I'm the same, you're the same, and Dale's the same. You know the old saying, you can take the boy out of Ohio but you can't take Ohio out of the boy."

Dale Connell shook his head. "That young fellow in the Canadian uniform—I'd have nothing in common with him today."

"Don't you believe it," said Sam Wagner. "Our characters are formed by the time we're eighteen, and we stay that way the rest of our lives."

"I'd hate to think so," said Dale Connell. "I certainly don't want to believe that all the places I've been and the people I've met, the things I've done—all that had no effect on me. I was twenty-one when that picture was taken. Now have a look at this one, taken when I was about thirty-five. You don't see any difference?"

"Of course there's a difference," said Sam Wagner. "In this one you're wearing a gray high hat and a swallowtail, and it looks to me like you have a waxed moustache. Field glasses. Some race track in England, I imagine."

"Yes, and who do you think the other men are? Well, this man on my right. You may not recognize him, but you'd recognize his brother."

"I doubt it."

"His brother was the Prince of Wales. Now the Duke of Windsor."

"Oh, let me see that," said Roberta.

"That may well be," said Sam Wagner. "All the same, underneath the swallowtail and the high hat, it's still you."

"I don't even look the same," said Dale Connell. "Here, do you recognize this man?"

"Sure, that's the writer—Ernest Hemingway. One writer I would recognize. I'd know him, even without the gun. But what are you trying to prove? I admit you must have known all those people. But I can show you some pictures I have at home. One of me shaking hands with Bob Taft. I have one of me and Benny Oosterbaan. And Roberta has one of her congratulating Tommy Milton."

"It's lost," said Roberta. "I don't know what happened to it."

"You lost that picture of you and Tommy Milton? It must be somewhere, in storage."

"No, it's gone," said Roberta.

"Well, anyway, me, Sam Wagner, and my wife, Roberta, we had our pictures taken with famous people, but I don't claim that changed us. I claim just the opposite. Like that time I sat up and talked half the night, going East on the Broadway Limited, this fellow and I. He seemed familiar, but I couldn't place him and I couldn't place him. Turned out to be Al Jolson, only he didn't have his makeup on. Now there was a fellow I would of liked to get to know him."

"If you had, you would have changed. I knew Joley."

"I'll never forget him in *The Jazz Singer,*" said Roberta. "Where did we see that, Sam?"

"You saw it twice. We saw it together in New York, but you saw it in Chicago when it played there."

"No, I think I saw it in Indianapolis. I went with Mary Jane Strohmyer. She didn't like it as much as I did. Al married a girl named Keller."

"Keeler. Ruby Keeler."

"Was it Keeler? I always pronounced it Keller, but you knew them. It's funny, I always pronounced her name Keller. Cute little thing. She used to do a tap dance with a cane. Keeler, huh?"

"But she wasn't in *The Jazz Singer,* "said Sam.

"May McAvoy," said Dale Connell. "But I just happened to think, Roberta. Jolson's *first* wife was named Keller, although I don't know how you'd know that."

"I don't either. I'm not sure I did."

"Don't be so modest," said Sam Wagner. "You used to follow those movie stars. Probably know as much about them as Dale does, without knowing them personally. You ask her something sometime."

"Oh, heavens, I have a terrible memory, and it's getting worse. I can remember what I wore to a party when I was fifteen, but don't ask me where I was last Thursday."

"Just for the hell of it, where were you last Thursday?" said Dale Connell.

"Thursday?" she said.

"That ought to be easy," said her husband.

"Is that a hint? Oh, I know. You were putting against Cy Runstadt."

"Bet your sweet life I was, and beating him three and two. See, you remembered."

Dale Connell has seen snapshots of Roberta in her girlhood, but they tell him very little, much less than he has been able to imagine from having seen her granddaughter in person. Although Roberta's hair is white, and she is rather tall for a woman, it is not impossible, from looking at her, to conjecture some similarities between her and the present Agnes, Mother Callaghan, of the Sacred Heart nuns, that do not depend on mere physical resemblance. It may come down to no resemblance at all, but rather a gentleness in common, and Dale Connell's strong belief that for the Wagners sexual activity is a thing of the past. He could be wrong about that; among his Glendale people he sees signs of erotic consciousness—fierce jealousies, hand-holding, flirtatiousness—but Sam Wagner is seventy, interested only in his capital and in beating other men on the putting green. He is generally disagreeable, and it is a commonplace among the Glendale people that Roberta is the only person in the world that could put up with him (although the principals in that commonplace are, so to speak, interchangeable; Sam Wagner says the same thing about his friends Cy and Lillian Runstadt). Roberta has the same sweetness that Agnes Callaghan would have today, and she is the first woman he has known in forty years that he likes to talk to—when he gets the chance—as he once talked to Agnes. In an odd way she is less sophisticated than Agnes. Simpler. During all those long conversations with Agnes he had never been given an inkling that she was mulling over in her mind a major problem, coming to a decision that would determine the course of her life. Roberta Wagner could not be so reticent. A certain kind of guile was essential to maintain that kind of reticence, and Agnes possessed it; Roberta said everything that came into her mind, and with an innocence that he had not discovered—or looked for—in any woman since those long conversations at the Callaghans' gate.

There is no manuscript of Dale Connell's memoirs, in the sense of a narrative that has continuity; there is only a stack of notes and a long list of names of once-famous actors and actresses, of big-game hunters and polo players, playwrights and theatrical managers, movie producers and directors, orchestra leaders and torch singers, restaurateurs and ballroom dancers, English novelists and American heiresses—and men like himself, who had minor talents in the arts or in sports, who had suites at Claridge's when they were in the money or stopped at the Cavendish when they were not. Carson Burroughs is quite right when he says that Dale Connell's memoirs would be a blockbuster, but it is a manuscript that Burroughs will never see. Dale Connell is trying to be conscientious. Every day he adds a name to his already long list; but he cannot bring himself to put down on paper the true stories of all those women. Once it was the face of Agnes Callaghan in a nun's habit, that made him smash a tape recorder. But now it is Roberta Wagner, a real presence, who intrudes. "I am dying to see your book," she says. But she would be repelled by the book he wants to write. She believes in Mary Miles Minter.

Yucca Knolls

IT IS NOT a colony they have, and the circumstances of their choosing Yucca Knolls were different in all three cases, but for twenty years now Cissie Brandon, George W. ("Pop") Jameson, and Sid Raleigh have been, as they say, more or less neighbors. Weeks often go by without any two of them seeing each other, and as for the three getting together, it only happens at Christmastime every year and at much greater intervals when a picture magazine or a television program rediscovers Cissie or Pop or Sid and, quite by accident, learns that the other two also live in Yucca Knolls. But any time Cissie, or Pop, or Sid is in any kind of trouble, she, or he, lets the others know about it right away. They have never expressed it in so many words, but when the chips are down you go to your own people, and your own people are not your neighbors, or your family, or friends you have made in recent years. They are the people who were stars when *you* were a star. Well, if not quite a star, a featured player. Cissie was starred, Sid was starred; Pop never quite made it, his name above the title of the picture. On the other hand he lasted a little longer than Cissie and Sid. In fact, Pop still gets work in TV westerns. Cissie and Sid will not take such work; they don't need the money—nor, for that matter, does Pop. Cissie and Sid would consider it undignified of Pop to take those dirty-old-men parts in TV if he had been a star; but since he was always a character actor, they don't hold it against him now when he goes unshaven for four or five days and goes without a haircut and, six months later, appears on The Box. He is never on for very long. His longest scene usually shows him lying behind a rock, an arrow through his chest, and he is saying, "Think they got me this time, consarn it. But don't you wait around, Jeff boy. You still got time to head them off 'fore they reach the stockade," and *quick* his head falls and he dies with a smile on his face.

A few hours after seeing Pop die in prime time, the television audience can see Cissie or Sid in full-length films; Cissie, for instance, in *The Humperdinks Abroad,* in which she played Jane Humperdink from Mountain Falls, Iowa, and had those hilarious sequences when she and Ezra Humperdink were invited to go on a fox hunt in England. That was the one in which it turned out that Lord Chesterton had always hated fox hunting and was delighted with Cissie's antics, so much so that he willingly gave his blessing to the marriage of Barbara Humperdink and young Eric Chesterton, who wanted nothing better than to go to Iowa and raise Poland Chinas.

Sid Raleigh was not a comedian. In his starring vehicles, visible on the late shows, he is a World War One aviator, an infantry lieutenant in the same war, a district attorney with a younger brother who has become a gangster, an idealistic architect, a peacetime test pilot, a bandleader, a forest ranger and, three times, a newspaper reporter. A Sid Raleigh picture seldom ran longer than seventy-five minutes, but with the insertion of commercials and station breaks followed by commercials Sid may be back and forth from one A.M. to two-forty-five, shooting down Fokkers, putting the ax to beer vats, making speeches to aroused taxpayers about the inferior materials in the new high school, and kissing June Wentworth, the former Mrs. Sid Raleigh, who is now married to a chiropractor in Redondo Beach.

Sid is not often recognized these days. The curly locks, that even thirty years ago were augmented by hair-pieces, have entirely gone, and there was nothing that could be done about the wattles. Nose jobs were still very much in the experimental stage in the early Thirties, and Sid could not resist legal imported beer and liverwurst sandwiches. "All of a sudden I was thirty-five years of age and looking like my Uncle Max," he says. "This is fine if I am making my living in the poultry business, a better-than-average living Uncle Max was making. But I am suppose to be the poor man's Ronnie Colman, a B-picture Warner Baxter, if you prefer. What the hell? I had a few bucks, some various income-producing properties out in the Valley. So a couple friends and I got together and started Yucca Knolls. Who needed Warner Brothers, and anyway they had Flynn. I don't have to care any more now how I look, a forty-two-inch waistline, and at six o'clock in the morning I'm getting my best sleep, instead of driving out to Corrigan's Ranch and monking around with some bronco that hates all human beings but particularly Jews. I swear to you, I seen more anti-Semitic horses than the Czar with the Cossacks. I made one picture where I was a big Mexican landowner, Don Something or Other, and I had this pure white steed that was suppose to come when I whistled, untie knots when I was bound with rope. You wanta know something? I have to have a double just for patting that horse on the neck. The first time I ever went near that animal he tried to chew my arm off. Ripped the sleeve off my costume, and they had to shoot around me till they got a new one. I said to Roy Risman, Roy was directing, I said, 'Roy, that horse don't like me. Already he don't like me, and before I had a chance to do anything to him. But if he can read my mind, what I'm thinking about him, tomorrow he's going to kill me. So you get another white horse or another actor.' Well, they solved it by having my double ride the horse in the long shots, and close shots and medium close shots they put the saddle on a white dummy. You couldn't tell the difference. But *I* could!"

Cissie Brandon's pictures are action-filled, as much so as Sid Raleigh's, but the action is directed to the task of creating laughs. Her pictures contain even more close-ups of her face than Sid's of his. The Cissie Brandon Burn and the Cissie Brandon Slow Burn were famous in the profession, often imitated but never equaled. It is impossible for any television comedienne to copy the Cissie Brandon Slow Burn because none of today's comediennes (or any other day's) has the Cissie Brandon face or the Cissie Brandon timing. One of the New York critics observed that Cissie Brandon always looked as though she had her hat on crooked even when she was not wearing a hat. Her hats, incidentally, were all sight gags, always good for an entrance laugh. But sight gags were surplus, laugh-getting insurance; the Cissie Brandon face, doing a takem or a double takem, a burn or a slow burn or a fig bar, registering sadness or any other emotion the situation called for—that face was always the focal point of the scene, always better than the material they gave Cissie. She never had to be afraid to have a dog or a child in a scene with her, and no human performer, co-star or bit player, was allowed to do or say or wear anything that would divert attention from Cissie. If a performer attempted to steal a scene and the attempt escaped the notice of the director, Cissie would go through the scene uncomplaining, apparently unaware. But when the scene was finished and the satisfied director said, "Print that," Cissie would say loud enough for everyone on the set to hear, "No you don't. No—you—don't. That son of a bitch in the policeman suit. When did he develop a tic in his face? He doesn't have a tic in the long shots." The director would order the scene reshot, and the man in the policeman suit would behave himself. Cissie Brandon's pictures were family-type comedies, made on low budgets, and retakes cost money. An habitual offender, a performer who kept trying to steal a little of a scene from Cissie Brandon, would find himself on her personal blacklist; and yet it was an impersonal war that she carried on with bit players. She fought them, protected herself, but it was a game that minor actors played with stars, stars with minor actors, on every set in Hollywood. Some of Cissie's friends among the bit players were guilty of trying to steal scenes, and if they got away with it, that was part of the game. No hard feelings, but if they did it too often Cissie could keep them out of work. She could also pull a few tricks of her own; she could tramp on their lines without saying a word, merely by making a moue. Or she could raise her hand to her head, pretending to smooth out her hair, and get her elbow in front of the actor's face, between him and the camera, and blot him out completely just as he was reading the only lines he had in the picture.

She could also use her powers to help a friend, and the bit players knew about that, too. She had what amounted to her personal stock company as well as a personal blacklist, and since Cissie Brandon made a minimum of two pictures a year, it was practically guaranteed income to be one of her favorites. Cissie Brandon's films were the studio's bread-and-butter pictures, cheaply made, making use of old sets, written by five-hundred-dollar writers. They never played the Radio City Music Hall, but they were box office all over the world, year after year after year. She did eight Humperdink pictures with Carl Buntley as her husband, Ezra Humperdink. When Carl died, the studio decided to take no more chances on the fragility of actors; the Humperdink series was abandoned, and Cissie had a new husband in every picture that had a story-line which called for a husband. There were not many; the studio preferred stories that had her unmarried or with a husband who was not seen. It was not studio policy to give an actor the buildup that he would get as husband of Cissie Brandon, and Cissie most heartily concurred. She was as firmly opposed to one writer's suggestion that she be given a female co-star. The studio tried teaming her up in one picture, and it was the only Cissie Brandon film that ever lost money. Audiences in Manchester, England, and McKeesport, Pa., resented the intrusion of Ruth Chalmers, her co-star, who was well enough known from other pictures. The trouble with Ruth Chalmers was that Cissie Brandon's fans came to see Cissie Brandon, and felt cheated when given so much of Ruth Chalmers. Thereafter Cissie went it alone, using the same catalogue of facial expressions in every picture, whether she played a housewife, a boarding-house mistress, the proprietress of a grocery, or the owner of a beauty parlor.

The people understood her, and made her the "well loved." She would step out of her rented limousine at movie premieres, bejewelled and beminked, and a roar would go up. "It's Cissie! Cissie Brandon!" The people would cheer her, and she would reassure them as to her appearance in the accouterments of wealth; she would stare at her Cadillac, as though surprised, and wink at her fans. She would take hold of her gown in the middle and hitch it up. She would pretend to stumble on the red carpet. The people knew that in spite of the limousine and the diamonds and the evening gown, she was their Cissie.

And she was nothing of the kind.

She would clown it up for the benefit of the crowd outside Graumann's Chinese, but at the party after the premiere she would be herself. Newcomers to the industry and non-professional guests would see her at these parties and ask incredulously if that could be Cissie Brandon. She had dignity and good manners, and she just missed being beautiful. As it was, she was a handsome woman, and if she had not been a star comedienne, she could have made a more modest living, in Hollywood terms, as a dress extra, one of those creatures who provide the human background at the embassy ball, the hunt breakfast, the society wedding. The face that she contorted to make the people laugh was, at rest, the face of an aristocrat. The facts were played down in her publicity, but she had attended a young ladies' Episcopal seminary in the Middle West and was the daughter of a Kansas City physician who drank himself into bankruptcy and death. She worked in stock companies and repertory theaters across the country, and eventually as a bit player in silent films. At twenty-five she was playing old maid schoolteachers and taking pies in the face. But no matter how degrading the slapstick action or the descriptions of her on the sub-titles, some trace of dignity was always left, and because of it she escaped from the custard pies and got into character acting. Earl Fenway Evans, an early director who was one of the first to see artistic possibilities in the motion picture medium, put Cissie in a straight part. He cast her as Doris Arlington's jealous older sister in a society melodrama. He thought that having Cissie's aristocratic face in the picture would provide authenticity to the fiction of Doris Arlington as a society girl. His theory did not work. The vast movie public were willing to accept Doris Arlington as a society girl, and Cissie Brandon, from long habit, could not overcome the temptation to make funny faces. Nevertheless Evans became Cissie's biggest fan among industry people, and for years he told his colleagues that some day he would find the right story for her and Hollywood would have a great dramatic actress. As a direct result of Earl Fenway Evans's enthusiasm for Cissie, she was given the part as Carl Buntley's wife in the first Humperdink story. She stole every scene from Carl Buntley, and he meekly shared star billing with her in the next Humperdink and the subsequent Humperdinks. Carl Buntley knew a gold mine when he saw one, and he had never heard about Art. He had hardly heard of Earl Fenway Evans.

The friendship between Earl Evans and Cissie Brandon was a perplexing relationship for Hollywood. He was a perplexing man all by himself. He was given to violent outbursts and many men were physically afraid of him. He had a smashed nose and the scars of cuts that had been stitched above his eyes and on his mouth. Four of his fingers had been broken. On several occasions he had beaten up men who did not realize that an argument had reached the violent stage. When he fought he would not stop until he was beaten insensible or pulled away by at least two men. He fought to kill, and he would fight anyone: smaller and weaker men, bigger and tougher men. Whatever the odds, he would wade in with both fists, heedless of what was happening to his face. It was generally (and hopefully) agreed that some night Earl Fenway Evans would come up against a man who would kill him.

He was a drinker, but he got into fights sometimes while he was perfectly sober. A man's attire, his gait, his voice, the way he ordered a meal—any small thing could annoy Earl Evans to such a degree that he would goad the man into a fight. In any other community, in any other industry, people would not have put up with him; in Hollywood, however, men who loathed and feared him gave him jobs because he made money for them. He was known as a woman's director. Other directors knew how to photograph women to their best advantage, but Earl Fenway Evans was one of the very few who would have long discussions with a female star well in advance of the first day's shooting. He would tell her things about the character she was to play that could never, never be hinted at on the screen or described in the script. He would analyze the character so thoroughly that some actresses would wish they had not signed for the part. But Evans knew what he was doing: he was directing the star even before the picture was in production. Once he had implanted the suggestion that the character was, for example, a nymphomaniac, no actress of any intelligence would be able to dismiss the thought entirely, and Earl Evans and the camera would get at least a little of that thought on the screen. With some of the more stupid actresses, he would wait until a scene was about to be shot, and the assistant director had called out, "Quiet please! This is a take. Shut the hell up back there, we're rolling." Then Earl Fenway Evans would suddenly get up out of his chair and go to the actress and whisper something naughty in her ear. She might be confused, irritated, or amused, but in some cases, with some actresses, the tactic worked. There was no denying that he had earned his reputation for putting animation and sex appeal into some of the most wooden women in the industry, and he did it without the help of tight sweaters and deep décolletage.

He had come originally from a small town in Nebraska, joined the Navy in time for service in one of Sims's destroyers in World War One, and bummed his way across the country to San Francisco. He had two or three fights as a middleweight, losing them all, and got interested in sculpture as a model. From sculpture he went into painting. For a while he lived with a woman who had a studio in San Francisco and taught him a few basic elementals of painting. He married her, or he did not marry her; his stories of his early years did not always check out. In any event he moved to Los Angeles and got a job as assistant to a vaudeville actor who was directing two-reel comedies. In Southern California he had his own bungalow, all the women a man could wish for, and time to read. He had graduated from dime novels to Rex Beach and Jack London, to Stephen Crane and Galsworthy and Bennett and the Russians, Maugham and Mann and Anatole France, Conrad and Anderson and Sinclair Lewis, Cather and Dos Passes and Mencken. He read only for entertainment; the men and women with whom he earned his living and had his fun were not bookish—or if they were they were as reticent about it as he. He was about twenty-seven years old and earning two hundred dollars a week when he discovered Havelock Ellis and Sigmund Freud, and the shock of discovering himself through them was almost too much for him. He was so fearful of turning up in one of Ellis's case histories that he wanted to kill Ellis. He was never again able to take a long look at a human being without wondering what she—mostly she—would confess to Ellis. In time he forgave Ellis for giving him a shock; indeed, he was grateful to the bearded old men for having lived at the wrong time in the wrong place, for keeping their prying eyes and irresistible questions out of his life. But he was also grateful for their having shown him that he was not alone in the world with his troubles, and that his troubles were not unique. Even men who had been to Eton and Oxford, lords and ladies who stood beside the king. . . . As never before, he met the world with self-confidence. In less than a year he was directing a six-reeler.

He married three times in the movie industry, in addition to his yes-or-no marriage to the San Francisco painter. His actress wives ran to type: they were top stars, they were tall and slender, and in a community that was not renowned for quality, they were ladies. He once said, "I married three out of the four ladies in this business. I would have married the fourth, too, but she wouldn't spit in my eye." He would never identify the woman whom he considered to be the fourth lady; it was fun to let people guess, and one guess was that the fourth woman did not exist. The marriages, as well as the wives, ran to type: a brief, urgent love affair; an elopement; an exchange of extravagant presents; a reconciliation between public quarrels, and a friendly divorce. Once safely parted from him the women became genuinely fond of Earl Fenway Evans. He boasted that all three would take him back—for one night every six months or so. Only one of the three admitted there was any truth in his boast, but all three remained on fairly good terms with him and were unanimous in describing their marriages as an experience, if a nightmare.

In all three instances he had been the one to insist on the legal ceremony. Regina Knight, the second of his actress wives, said that Earl admitted to her that he was creating a public, formidable record of interest in women to offset his true feeling for them, which was contempt. "Well, I have no contempt for Reggie," he replied. "She used to come home from the studio so tired that she wished she was married to a fairy. And now she's convinced I was. Reggie can say what she pleases about me, just as long as I can go back there every six months or so for a re-take."

His first actress wife, Helena McCord, returned to her first love, the theater, and thereafter did only an occasional film. Whenever a studio approached her to do a picture in Hollywood she would telephone Earl for information and advice. She was a serious-minded woman who did not permit any references to their conjugal past. "I get a feeling that her husband is listening in on the extension," said Earl. "Maybe not, but I don't give him anything to complain about. She was a right guy, Helena."

Marietta Van Dyke, the third actress wife of Earl Fenway Evans, was a Southern California society girl who had been East to school. She started her movie career at the top because there was no other way that she could be induced to go into films at all. Her father was rich, her mother was rich, and Marietta Van Dyke, known to her friends as Van or Vannie, had accepted the movie offers to spite her Eastern schoolmates, who had been somewhat condescending to the rich and beautiful Californian. Almost overnight she became the most famous alumna of her school, and she got letters that began, "I don't know whether you will remember me . . ." from girls who would sometimes have trouble remembering her when they saw her at college parties and in New York restaurants, a year or so earlier. Having put those Eastern girls in their place, she set out to put the movie stars in theirs. They had resented her unearned stardom and were very outspoken about it. To them she represented the society type that the Eastern society types, her schoolmates, said she was not. She hired a dramatic coach, an English actress who had played Shakespeare and Noel Coward; a personal press agent; and a German gymnast who conducted her daily calisthenics. She undoubtedly would have cultivated Earl Fenway Evans, but it was not necessary; he saw her first, and with a few well-chosen insults he cut her down to size, seduced her, married her, and left her. She was the only one of his three Hollywood wives who hurt him financially. Although she did not need his money, she retained the Van Dyke family lawyer, who hated all picture people and got every cent that the law would allow. Earl did not call Marietta a right guy; she had not, in fact, played the game. The other women had not asked for money. But since it was part of his own pose to care nothing about money, he made jokes about the financial arrangements. "According to my figures, it comes to about fifteen hundred dollars a night," he said. "That's pretty high when you think of how much you can get free."

"You'd better stop saying those things," said Marietta, when his comment reached her. "I could tell a few stories about what kind of a man you are—or are not."

"Too late. Everybody knows by this time," he said.

"I didn't," she said.

"You didn't know *anything*."

"Well, I do now. I certainly do now."

"But you're not sore at me, Van."

"No, not a bit. When I was a little girl I had a broken arm and appendicitis at the same time. Everything all at once, and that's what it was like being married to you."

"Well, at least you won't have to have your appendix out again," he said.

"Exactly," she said.

"Although you could break your arm again."

"I'll try not to. I'll be more careful from now on."

He saw little of Cissie Brandon during his seven marrying years. She invited him to her own wedding; he accepted the invitation, then forgot to attend. He was too busy with the details of the divorce from Regina Knight, a new picture he was directing for Goldwyn, and the early curiosity about Marietta Van Dyke. His secretary picked out a nice pair of silver pheasants, six hundred dollars at Brock's, and it was the present of which Cissie was most proud. The silver birds adorned her dinner table on all important occasions, and Cissie could be coldly scornful of anyone who suggested that they had been a gift from Pathé, which had a chanticleer as a trade mark.

It was two years before Earl Fenway Evans saw his wedding present on Cissie Brandon's dinner table. By that time she had come up in the Hollywood society world. She was, in fact, more firmly established in that world than Earl himself. He was fully qualified as a director who had imagination and taste, and to whom pictures with high budgets and top stars were intrusted; but there were some homes to which he was not invited. Movie moguls, as they were then called, who had come from the garment industry, food products, wholesale jewelry, or the real-estate side of picture business, were afraid of Earl Fenway Evans. He had never actually struck one of them, but the threat was there; and they had good reason to be afraid of his outspoken comments on their value to the movie business. His sarcastic labels had a way of sticking. To one producer he said, "Joe, I hear you got the Last Supper in your new picture. Why? Because you want to do the catering?" To another he said: "Well, now you can put your whole family to work, Harry. All those Levinsons, all that scrap iron in the one picture." This was a reference to a Levinson version of the currently popular railroad epics. The movie magnates could sit in sullen silence, or they could pretend to laugh off the insults, but they were afraid of a man who cared so little about the consequences *to himself* of the ill will he was creating. He knew they hated him; they knew that he knew they were waiting for him to begin slipping. But his pictures made money, and there were four or five of the biggest female stars who wanted no one else as their director.

It was impossible to deal with a man who was not afraid of scandal, who could not be threatened or blackmailed by bad publicity. The peculiarities of his sexual relations with women could not be exploited to his disadvantage without damage to his former wives and to the female stars of his pictures. "You dirty little bastard," he said to one producer. "You'd like to get at me through Reggie Knight, but you won't hurt me. You'll only ruin Reggie." He was totally lacking in the instinct for serf-preservation, and when one producer hinted at evidence of homosexuality, Earl Fenway Evans destroyed the effectiveness of the threat by supplying names of his accomplices in all-male orgies. "Unless I'm very much mistaken, one of those boys is a nephew of your wife's," said Earl Fenway Evans. "He's going to be very cross if he isn't invited any more." He offered to notify the producer of the time and place of the next orgy, so that the police could be informed. "But if there's a raid, you can just push the whole damn picture business into Santa Monica Bay," he said. "Your wife's nephew is such small change he won't even get his name in the papers. But, oh boy, the names that *will* get in!"

His enemies could only hope that he would die, or, failing that, that his pictures would lose money. Meanwhile he was left out of parties to which his professional standing entitled him to invitations. But he came anyhow. "You didn't invite me, but here I am," he would say. "You can either try to throw me out, or you can make the best of it. Suit yourself." Hostesses slowly learned that if they made the best of it, he would behave himself and, even better, put a kind of hazardous life into routinely dull parties. There was always the danger that he would start a fight, but apart from that danger, he would often provide the only entertainment for a gathering of men and women who made their living in the entertainment business. He had a bitchy wit, he had a lifetime of unconventional behavior to draw from, and his lack of self-preservational instinct enabled him to tell stories on himself that a cautious man would keep secret. "I wish I could write like Jim Tully," he once said. "He's not the best writer in the English language, but he knows how to write the kind of things that happened to me. I was an errand-boy in a whorehouse in Omaha, Nebraska. . . ." He was not bothered by fact, but he told his stories with an intensity that momentarily supplied the element of truth, and in all his stories that concerned women, the men were villains or chumps, the women no worse than sympathetic figures. "We were in Queenstown, or Cobh, they called it, and you could tell by the amount of stuff they were putting aboard that we were going to be gone at least a month. So another fellow and I smuggled this little Irish hooker aboard the *Smithfield.* That was the destroyer we were on. If you've ever been on a four-piper, you know there isn't room for an extra pair of socks, let alone a fat little Irish girl. Nevertheless. . . ." Women liked to listen to his stories. He seemed to be their friend, and in the film business even the vainest, stupidest women would sometimes become aware of how much like cattle they were. (There was, in fact, one producer who referred to all performers, male or female, as his livestock.)

Cissie Brandon, increasingly famous through the Humperdink series and growing richer by the minute, brought her dignity to most of the parties that Earl Fenway Evans, invited or not, attended. A sense of gratitude to him, a sentimental belief that she owed it all to him, kept her in awe of him after she had ceased to be in awe of anyone else in the industry. She was secretly distressed to see him make a fool of himself, piling up scores of ill will that he would have to pay the moment he showed an inability to pay. The men and women he offended were not the only ones who were waiting to tear him to pieces: he was thoroughly hated by others, whom he had not specifically attacked, but who had not dared to defy the powerful and by their timidity had made tacit admission of their inferiority of talent and spirit. These, the uninsulted, were potentially his worst enemies, since he could not identify them and they did not identify themselves.

As time went on, and Earl Fenway Evans, invited or not, became a party entertainer, Cissie Brandon observed that her hero was enjoying himself in the role. She knew that hostesses frequently refrained from inviting him to their parties but carefully saw to it that he was informed that a party was to take place. "He's really more fun if he crashes than if you invite him," they said. "If you do invite him, half the time he doesn't show up." The men called him a nuisance, a pest, but the women were usually delighted when he appeared, and butlers were instructed not to turn him away.

He liked to show up while the guests were still at the dinner table. He would be dressed in jacket, breeches and boots, or in a yachting costume (although he owned neither horse nor boat); for Sunday luncheon he would come in a Tuxedo, as though he had not been to bed the night before; and at other times he had been known to come to dinner in white flannels and blue blazer, with an Old Etonian scarf about his neck. He would go to the hostess, kiss her hand, and pull up a chair beside her. "Bring me a plate of food, and a bottle of wine," he would say to the butler. If the guests included strangers to the movie business and one of them was seated on the hostess's right, he would watch for indications of the stranger's reaction. "Don't look goggle-eyed at me, Mister," he would say. "This kid happens to be my mistress." In most cases the stranger had been warned that Earl Fenway Evans, the eccentric genius, would most likely show up; one of the idiosyncrasies of Hollywood social life; pay no attention if he gets a little out of hand. First-time visitors from the East were delighted with this proof of the Hollywood legend of strange behavior among its geniuses. "There was this Earl Fenway Evans, the famous director, or at least we were told he was famous. Actually he was quite a good story-teller, if you don't mind hearing someone come right out with the real words. You know, the words you're not supposed to know till you ask your husband. I looked around the room and the only woman that seemed at all shocked was Cissie Brandon. Oh, she was there. And wait'll I tell you about *her.* Mrs. Schuyler Van Astorbilt. *Yes!* Cissie Brandon, no less. I don't suppose she's more than thirty-five, but she's the one they all sort of not exactly look *up* to, but *sort of* look up to."

Cissie Brandon's reaction to Earl Fenway Evans's stories was not lost on him. "Cissie, you don't even fake a polite laugh," he said. "What am I doing wrong? Punching my lines too soon?"

"No, not at all, Earl. You're the best story-teller I ever heard, bar none."

"Nobody'd guess that to watch your face."

"Come to dinner next Saturday. Just you and Lester and I. You can leave early, if you don't want to waste a Saturday night."

"All right," he said.

He arrived at her house on Beverly Drive at a few minutes past eight, dressed in a blue suit and black shoes. He was met at the door by Lester Long in a velveteen smoking jacket and black bow tie. "Well, how nice to have you at last, Earl. Cissie's been looking forward to this ever since we've been married, she's so proud of the silver pheasants. You remember the silver pheasants?"

"I sure do. How've *you* been, Lester?"

"Oh, I'm all right. I keep about the same. Outside of my sinus condition, but Cissie only has another week shooting and then we go to the desert for a month. That always does wonders, but it really isn't so bad. Cissie's out in the kitchen, but we're not supposed to go out there. What can I get you? I was just opening a bottle of champagne, but you don't have to have that."

"All right, I'll have a glass of champagne."

"It's the only thing I like with my sinus. I have to explain now, Earl, but I'm only going to sit with you through dinner. Then I'm going up to my room. So don't be surprised if I leave you two alone. I have a terrible lot of things to do that I have to finish up before we go to the desert. You know, I take care of everything. The ordering. The bills. You wouldn't think there'd be much with just two, but we have three servants and a chauffeur and a gardener, and it's quite a household. Just between you and I, we're getting ready to fire the couple. The butler and his wife. He thinks he's some kind of a Romeo and they fight all the time. The night before last he came home late and they went at it hammer and tongs, and Cissie has to get her sleep. So we're not taking them to the desert. Too bad, because as far as the work goes he's topnotch. He does all the silverware, takes care of my wardrobe. Serves beautifully, beautifully. But he gets a lot of personal phone calls. The maids in the neighborhood all have hot pants for him, and Irma, his wife, she shows her age much more than he does. He has a marvelous physique, Earl. I'll tell you who he resembles quite a lot—"

"Hel-lo, boys. Who resembles who?" Cissie Brandon Long made her entrance while raising her apron over her head.

"Hello, Cissie."

"Hamish, he resembles Tom Meighan."

"Not a bit. The dimple in the chin, otherwise no. Lester, pour me a glass of champagne too, will you, dear? Well, Earl, at last we've got you here in person. How do you like Humperdink Hall? That's what we ought to call it. We bought it because it was the only house in Beverly that looked anything like the house I was brought up in, in Kansas City, Missouri. They could have been done by the same architect, although this house is only about fifteen years old, if that. Do you remember houses like this back in Nebraska?"

"Yeah, but I never got inside of them."

"How do you like your steak, Earl? That's what you're getting. Good old Kansas City cut. We like ours rare."

"So do I."

"Swell. Then I won't have that to worry about. All three the same. Lester, how about if you put them on, dear? Everything else is ready. The potatoes are in the oven. String beans in the double boiler. You call us when the steaks are ready."

"All right, but you're wrong about Hamish. He does so resemble Tom Meighan. I saw Tom Meighan every day for years when I was with Mr. Lasky."

"If you want my opinion, I think he looks more like Mr. Lasky, but he doesn't really look like either one of them. Now go put the steaks on like a good boy, will you please? And call as soon as they're ready."

"Oh, don't hurry me, Cissie. I'll be so glad when we go to the desert. The last week of shooting she's always so bossy, it's a wonder I have the patience to put up with her." He left.

"That's the dearest, sweetest little fellow. I just love him. I finally got the studio to put him on the payroll, so now he has quite a nice income of his own. Of course he wants to spend it all on me, but I refuse to let him."

"How did you ever happen to marry him?"

"Oh, I don't know. Two lonely people, I guess. He took care of things for me at the Stern office, my bank account, my investments. And I don't exactly know when we got on a more personal basis. I didn't think I'd ever get married, and I don't have to tell *you,* Lester wasn't interested in me as a woman. But his sister died and left him all alone in the world, and I was the one that I guess you'd call it proposed. I'll say this, I've never regretted it, not for one second. And having him has probably kept me from making some very serious mistakes. I know it. When I have nightmares he comes in and gets in bed with me. He babies me, and that's what I need sometimes. But that's all we ever were to each other. Maybe *I* could want something more, but I don't miss it, and he more or less told me that he couldn't live with me if I made any demands on him."

"Would he care if you slept with another man?"

"That hasn't come up, and I don't guess it will. I'm not romantically inclined, and when I was I always had some kind of a sixth sense that warned me away from men. That's our protection, we plain Janes. I'll tell you later, if you want to hear about it. Oh, I like my little fellow, glad to see me when I come home from the studio, gets me into a hot tub—not that he ever sees me naked. And we have our dinner together in my room. Sometimes he reads to me, sometimes not. But I fall asleep knowing he's there, and if I have a nightmare he comes in and wakes me out of it and gets me back to sleep. When we reach a certain amount I'm not going to do any more Humperdinks. One picture a year, and the rest of the time travel."

"Glad to hear it. Maybe you and I'll do that one picture a year."

"I'll talk to you about that after dinner. Les told you he was going to leave us, didn't he?"

"Yes."

They hurried through the meal, the diffident Lester not wishing to keep the others from their conversation. "I may not see you again, Earl, but it was a pleasure having you," said Lester.

"The steaks were just right," said Earl Fenway Evans.

"Were they? I hope they were. Well, goodnight, kids. Not goodnight to you, Cissie. I'll come tuck you in."

The silence was heavy after he left. "Where do we start?" said Earl. "What kind of pictures do you want to do when you quit the Humperdinks?"

"I don't want to talk about that, Earl," said Cissie Brandon. "All this, this house and everything in it, I wouldn't have if it hadn't been for you. So let's talk about you."

"Don't start licking my hand, Cissie."

"I would never do that, and anyhow I wouldn't know how to any more. I'm a big star. I say that because I have to. I have to remind myself that I'm a star so I can give you a good talking-to."

"What about?"

"I need a writer for my next line," she said.

"You're a big star, don't forget."

"All right," she said. "Earl, why don't you quit going to those parties? Why don't you save your energy for your work?"

"I have plenty left over, that's why I go to those parties."

"That's not why you go."

"Why do I go, then?"

"I'm not sure. Loneliness, partly. But whatever it is, you aren't doing yourself any good. You're making yourself into a comic, an entertainer, and all those bastards are just waiting for you to stub your toe, then look out."

"I know that."

"Is it true that you went to Zimmy and Sylvia's in drag?"

"I didn't go there in drag, but I guess I spent most of the evening in one of Sylvia's dresses."

"And made a play for Eddie Blaine. Pretended to make a play—or was it pretending?"

"Half-pretending, I guess."

"There's no such thing as half-pretending in things like that."

"Maybe not."

"But you don't *like* Eddie Blaine. Did you do it to embarrass him?"

"Those kind of Arrow-collar looks annoy me."

"Eddie can't help how he looks," she said. "It used to be that you got in fights, then you changed into being a story-teller. But lately I hear it's the fag act. If you want boys, have them, but what's the use of flaunting it in people's faces? Nobody's going to hold it against you if that's the way you are. But the fighting, and crashing parties, and camping all over the place—you're just going out of your way to make enemies every way you can. Earl, you're not that good."

"Yes I am. Have you seen the figures on *Desperate Love?*"

"I have. But *Desperate Love* has Doris Arlington in it, and had four top writers doing the script. Don't take all the bows for *Desperate Love,* Earl. I could name you three other directors that could have done just as well as you did. There was nothing in that picture that had any particular Earl-Fenway-Evans stamp to it."

"Oh, come on, Cissie. You're not talking to Lubitsch."

"I wasn't talking about those little touches. I was thinking more of whole scenes, where in your best pictures you can get a girl like Doris to do two whole minutes without a cut."

"Who notices that but a few people in the business? If you can get the same effect in short takes, do it in short takes. That's what cutting is for."

"But you *didn't* get the same effect. You're getting lazy."

"Maybe I am. Not lazy, but I admit I'm not as interested as I used to be. I know exactly where you meant in *Desperate Love.* Where Doris doesn't know whether her husband is dead or alive, after the explosion. Is that where you meant?"

"No."

"It wasn't?"

"No."

"Where did you mean, then?"

"Long before that."

"Long before that? Oh."

"Where they're first married, and she realizes how much she loves him. Long before any explosion or any of that. The kind of thing you could always get out of Doris and girls like that. In this picture you skipped it. You dodged it. And it wasn't fair to Doris, because you could have made her a much more sympathetic person."

"See this? I don't hear any complaints from Doris," he said, and slipped off a gold wristwatch with a gold mesh band. "With 'Desperate Love,' Doris."

"Very original. And very expensive. But Doris gives presents to everybody. And I'm not impressed by the grosses on *Desperate Love,* either. I'm merely telling you that I can see you getting lazy, or indifferent, or blasé. Whatever you want to call it. I'll have it engraved on a gold wristwatch, if that makes more of an impression on you, Earl."

"I forgot to wind this. What time is it?"

"Twenty after nine."

"Well, at least you didn't say it's later than you think." He set the watch and put it back on his wrist.

"I didn't think of it or I would have."

"Or that you're telling me all this for my own good," he said. "You should have married me instead of Lester."

"Well, I would have."

"Maybe you ought to now."

"No thanks—if that was a proposal."

"Not exactly a proposal. I was just being agreeable. I thought maybe it was what you wanted."

"Would you tuck me in at night? Would you wake me when I had a nightmare?"

"What do you have nightmares about? You're all set."

"Well, you don't believe that, either," she said. "You know what my trouble is."

"No, I was never sure. I used to think you were a Lez, but if you were you kept it pretty quiet."

"I went through that. But it was only because I had to have somebody. It wasn't what I wanted, though. If I'd stayed home in Kansas City I probably would have married somebody, but I went in show business and then pictures, and when you're not pretty and you play the kind of parts I got, it isn't like being in one place all the time. You know. The less attractive men in a small town, they give up trying to marry the prettier girls and finally settle for girls like me. But then when I began making money in pictures it was an entirely different story. The gigolo types, men that wanted me to support them. They were always so surprised when they saw me without any clothes on, but that didn't flatter me. It infuriated me. It showed that they'd never really thought of me as a woman, but only a meal ticket. Then for a while I had a friend, she was a biologist. Older. The physical part wasn't very satisfactory to me, and therefore not very satisfactory to her. She said I was holding back, and maybe I was, and she introduced me to a friend of hers, a quite beautiful woman. Married. Wife of a musician, fascinating-looking, and any woman that had an affair with her was supposed to be through with men forever."

"Oh, I know who you're talking about. First name Naomi?"

"Yes."

"You were really getting into the inner circle."

"I didn't though. I shook like a leaf whenever she came near me. I made the mistake of going away with her for a weekend, but I was so nervous that she gave up in disgust. She slapped me in the face and sent me home. She was wrong about me, though. I was fascinated by her, and if she hadn't sent me home so soon, lost patience with me, I would have been in the inner circle. Once in a while I see her at parties and she glares at me."

"And you didn't go back to the biologist?"

"No. I would have liked to have her as a friend, but I think she was afraid of Naomi."

"They're all afraid of Naomi. She has them all hypnotized."

"Exactly."

"Is she the cause of your nightmares?"

"Some of them."

"Do you want me to speak to Naomi? I know her."

"What about?"

"Well—you could get rid of some of your nightmares."

Cissie shook her head. "They're not so bad. And I'd rather have the nightmares than be dominated by her all the time. I don't get them very often, and they're not all about her."

"Do you ever get them about me?"

"No. I used to have dreams about you, but never any nightmares."

"Used to have. Not any more?"

"No. At least not the same kind."

"Who do you dream about now? What man?"

"I wouldn't think of telling you."

"O.K. That means it's somebody I know."

"Know of. I don't think you know him personally."

"An actor, it must be."

"Yes, an actor. It's so ridiculous that you'd kid me about him, and it's too personal a thing. Some day you might say something to him. I don't trust your discretion, not in things like that."

"I think it's time I went home, Cissie."

"You're not cross because I said that?"

"Hell, no. No, it's because I feel like making a pass at you, and I don't think I'd get anywhere. Or would I?"

"You mean here, in this room?"

"Yes."

"No, Earl, not here. And not now. Some other time, and some other place, maybe. But not now. And never in this house."

"Because of the little guy upstairs?"

"I guess that's why. He's not really my husband, but I don't think he'd like it and I owe him that. He has his troubles, too."

"He sure has."

"I've seen him look at Hamish, the butler. And yet I know he'd never do anything while Hamish was working for us, in this house."

"Well, then I think I'll go home, Cissie. Would you ever come to my place?"

"I don't know. Maybe when I have time to think it over I'll decide against it. You have what you want, and maybe I want what I have. Not bad. You have what you want, and maybe I want what I have."

"But what you have is nothing."

"I know, or just about nothing. But what have I *ever* had? And I wouldn't want to lose my little fellow upstairs."

"You really love him, don't you?"

"He loves me, Earl. That's a hell of a lot, to me."

Earl Fenway Evans rose. "I have a feeling, Cissie, that I'm not going to see you any more. I don't mean that I'm going out and drive my car madly over some cliff."

"No, don't do that."

"Although damn little difference it would make to anybody if I did just that. But you and I have come close a couple of times and never got anywhere, and maybe we're not intended to."

"We're pretty close, considering. I've never talked to anyone the way I have with you tonight. That's pretty close."

"And I had a good time, regardless of your bawling me out."

"I'm glad."

"Will you kiss me goodnight?"

"No. I'm not used to that. That's all I'd need. Did you have a coat?"

"I never wear them."

"Not even when it rains?"

"It never rains here, in sunny California, you ought to know that."

"I forgot. I'll see you to the door. Where will you go now, not that it's any of my business?"

"I have no idea. Is anybody having a party that I could crash?"

"Do you want me to look in my book? I keep a record of all invitations, even when I'm not going."

"The old story. Hollywood. No matter how hot it gets in the daytime, there's no place to go at night."

"Never heard that one. If you really want to crash a dinner party. . . ."

"No, I think I'll just drive around a while, and maybe end up losing some money at roulette. Or pay a call on Miss Francis. Always run into somebody there. Goodnight, Cissie. And say goodnight to the little fellow."

Cissie Brandon heard two nights later that Earl Fenway Evans had dropped twenty thousand dollars at roulette. He thereby became the heavy loser of that week, and while he could afford to lose twenty thousand dollars, she heard a few days later that he had gone back to the gambling joint and lost heavily again. This time the loss was said to be thirty thousand dollars, and he had had to go to the studio for an advance on salary to cover it. The very next night he returned to the roulette wheel, lost again, and the studio refused to advance any more money unless he renewed his contract for two years at no raise in pay. He refused to sign the new contract on those terms, and Cissie Brandon knew that they were beginning to close in on him. She telephoned him.

"How much do you need?" she said.

"Where did you hear about it?" he said.

"Several places," she said. "Earl, you must let me give you the money, and if not give it, lend it. Lester and I can lend you fifty thousand, and you can pay it back any way you like."

"Cissie, you're a good girl, but I can't take your dough."

"But those gangsters—"

"Oh, they're not talking tough yet. They know I can raise the money. And I have a year to go on the old contract. I'm not broke, in spite of Miss Van Dyke. But I'll never forget this, you and Lester. You two, and Doris, and one or two others have come through for me."

"Earl, this is Cissie. Don't lie to me. I won't lie to you. Do you know what I heard?"

"I'm not lying to you."

"I hear your studio has you just where they want you—"

"Over a barrel," he said. "Yes, in a way they have. They want me to renew for two years at the same money I'm getting now."

"I heard it's worse than that," she said. "Maybe you haven't heard this, and maybe it isn't true. But someone told me that they're not going to let you work for anyone else until you do the picture you owe them. And they're not going to give you a picture. Can they do that to you?"

"Yes, unfortunately they can. I haven't got a time clause in my contract, a starting date. I didn't want one when I signed the contract, and now it turns out I was a damn fool. I didn't have a lawyer on that contract. I thought I knew it all and was getting what I wanted. I have the right to turn down stories, but they don't have to start paying me till I accept one. I guess a smart lawyer could fight them, but right now the smart lawyers aren't in when I phone them."

"Maybe the studio's just trying to teach you some kind of a lesson. Have you thought of that?"

"I've thought of it. That's looking on the bright side."

"You think they'll offer you nothing but junk?"

"I'm sure of it."

"Why don't you fool them? Why don't you take the junk, and make a good picture out of it?"

"Cissie, have you ever tried to buck a studio when they're out to ruin you? No, of course not. But you must know what they can do."

"I've heard. But it doesn't make any sense to ruin you. You're still one of the five or six best."

"Cissie, they did it to Griffith."

"Well—I don't know what else to say."

"You've already said some beautiful things. You and Lester. Doris. Two or three others. I'm going to sell my house, and that'll be more than enough to pay off the gamblers and enough to live on for a year or two."

"Please don't do any more gambling."

"That's easy. I have no more credit, and just now very little cash."

"How little?"

"Oh, five or six thousand, I guess."

"How much do you owe the gamblers?"

"Now, Cissie. Don't you go near them."

"I'd be willing to pay them, if they agreed to stop your credit."

"Thanks very much, but it's better this way. I was never much of a gambler. I never played for such high stakes before. I don't know how I got started now. But I've had a ninety-thousand-dollar lesson."

"That much? I thought it was less than that."

"No, this was one time when Hollywood didn't exaggerate. I lost thirty the first night, and I paid that. Thirty the second night, and the studio advanced me that. And the third night the gamblers took my marker, my I.O.U. So what it comes down to is that I owe the studio thirty, and the gamblers thirty. When I sell my house I'll pay the gamblers, and then I think I'll leave town for a while. I ought to get around seventy-five for my house. More than that, furnished. I'll be all right, old girl. I've been thinking I'd like to rent a little house down at the beach and try to paint some pretty pictures. It's what I've been wanting to do, and now it's forced on me."

"Do you think you can?"

"Paint? No, not well enough to earn my living at it."

"I didn't mean paint. I meant do you think you can leave town, and stay away for a while?"

"God, yes."

His house, she heard, was put on the market and in a quick cash sale brought sixty thousand dollars. "They say he had rugs worth almost that much," said Lester. "He should have waited."

"No, it's better for him to get away. Frankly I was afraid he'd hang around, crashing parties and so on. And I know he wasn't going to be allowed to crash. They weren't going to let him in, and if he tried to force his way, they were going to have him arrested."

"Who?"

"Practically all the people that give parties. I wonder where he went to?"

He vanished, and was not seen or heard of for a year. Someone had seen him, or a man who looked very much like him, coming out of a grocery store in Balboa, carrying a large paper sackful of provisions. He—if it was he—was dark brown from the sun, wearing a striped Basque shirt and blue jeans, and he did not return the wave or answer to the call of his name. He got in a yellow Ford roadster driven by a young man of college age. Someone else reported seeing him in an elevator in the Westlake medical building. Lester Long showed Cissie an eight-column newspaper photograph of the crowd at a movie premiere on which he had drawn a circle around one face. "Who does that look like?" said Lester.

"I see what you mean, but it couldn't be Earl. It says that these people had been waiting since six o'clock in the morning. Can you imagine Earl doing that?"

"Sure I can. He'd love it. And hope people would see his picture. You know, ironic sense of humor."

"Maybe," she said. "But I have a hunch that the Balboa rumor was correct. You may be right though. This picture, it doesn't look very much like him, but he has this wide-eyed exaggerated grin, just like the people that start lining up at six o'clock in the morning. If he did it, that's the kind of face he'd make. It might be Earl, at that."

"It's just the kind of thing would strike his sense of humor," said Lester.

"Well, at least he has that, if nothing else," she said.

One day the studio had made too many Humperdinks. It was almost possible to fix the exact date; it was a year or so after Cissie and Lester had seen Earl Evans's picture in the premiere crowd. Three Humperdinks had been released that year, and the confused public finally had had enough of them. The third of the three made money, but so little money compared to the anticipated profits that the studio considered the picture a loser. "Cissie, we're gonna have to think of a new format for you," said Arnold Bass, production head of the studio.

"So I gather," she said.

"You got any ideas of your own?"

"I have, but you wouldn't go for them."

"Like for instance? Try me," said Arnold Bass.

"Put me in a straight part. The kind of thing Aline MacMahon does, or Agnes Moorhead. I started out as an actress, you know."

"They'd never stand for it. It'd be a dreg on the market."

"Who wouldn't stand for it? Put me in a big picture, in the supporting cast. It'd be a year before you released the picture, and I'd be getting a whole new start."

"Do you have anything in mind?"

"No, but I have a director in mind. Earl Fenway Evans."

"Earl Fenway Evans. A long time since I heard that name. Where is he?"

"I haven't the faintest idea, but the studio can find anybody if they want to."

"The problem here being, do we want to? As far as I know he's still under contract to Metro, and they don't make it a practice to loan out anybody unless you give them the moon. No, there's too many complications to it, Cissie. And anyway we don't even know if he's alive."

"That's one of the things I'd like to find out."

"Well, there's nothing stopping *you* from hiring a private eye, Cissie. Give me one reason why the studio should bear the brunt of that expense."

"The studio is richer than I am, that's all."

"No, I guess we better forget about that scheme. But I'll mull it over you doing a straight part. I'll take it up with New York. We want to use you."

"I know you do, Arnold."

"Why do you say it with that sweet smile?"

"Because I know Paramount's been making inquiries."

"Oh, you heard. I should go to more parties."

"You would go, if you were invited, Arnold."

"So I don't move in Hollywood society circles."

"That's right, you don't. Now the question is, do you find a straight part for me, or do you loan me out to Paramount, or do you just go on paying me till my next option comes up?"

"That's three questions, and I don't have the answer. That will be up to New York to make the decision."

"Well, you looked pretty good while the Humperdinks were making all that money. You ought to have some influence."

"I have the influence, but don't you look for any gratitude, if that's what you were thinking."

"No, I could tell that when you said I could hire my own private eye to find Earl Evans. A year ago a little thing like that wouldn't have taken you two minutes. What's next, Arnold? Am I going to have to pay my own secretary, or is it going to be the park-off-the-lot routine?"

"Those things are in your contract, and you got two more years to run, almost. However, since you bring it up, Lester is off the payroll as of now. He was only part of the Humperdink unit, and there is no more Humperdink unit. Still, at twenty-five hundred a week, that's a hundred and twenty thousand a year. That's pretty nice for you."

"Not if I don't work. You know that. My salary will be charged off against the budget on the next picture I do, and the longer I'm idle the bigger that gets. If you put me in a picture now, my salary goes on that budget now. I could be in two pictures and split the charge against the two budgets."

"The voice is the voice of Cissie Brandon, but the words are the words of Lester Long. I can't promise you anything, Cissie. It's up to New York."

"Then is it all right if Lester and I plan a trip abroad?"

"What do you want to go *there* for? They're getting ready to have a war."

"Going abroad doesn't necessarily mean Europe."

"If you want my advice, this is a good time to stay home."

"Don't send me a bill for that advice, because I won't pay it," she said.

"Cissie, you shouldn't high-horse me that way. I been your friend a long time, and I'll do what I can to put you in a straight part. But don't expect me to enthuse if you start high-horsing me. All these things take time."

"What on earth has that got to do with it?"

"I don't follow you," said Arnold Bass.

"Exactly," she said.

No one underestimated the shrewdness of little Lester Long, no matter what jokes they made about his virility. He now proceeded to prove to Cissie, who needed no proof, that his devotion to her had its practical side. "What do we do now?" she said, after the conversation with Arnold Moss.

He pulled his feet up on the chair and sat tailor-fashion and grasped his ankle with both hands, rocking back and forth. He was grinning with delight at being in action again. "Why, we just fool them. We just outsmart them," he said.

"How? You mean get Paramount to put on some pressure?"

"Heavens no, Cissie. That's what they expect us to do," he said. "If we go to Paramount and ask them to put on the pressure, they will. No, sweetheart, what we do is I go to Paramount tomorrow and tell them that Arnold and the studio are being mean to us. They don't want to loan you out."

"What does that accomplish? I know it accomplishes something, or you wouldn't say it. But what?"

"It accomplishes as follows. First, it shows Paramount that the studio is afraid to loan you out. That makes Paramount want you the more. Second, it makes Paramount sore at Arnold and the studio. Puts us and Paramount in the same boat, we're allies."

"I see."

"The Humperdinks are all through, a thing of the past. So just sit tight and do nothing except draw your salary for seventeen more months."

"You mean I don't do a picture for seventeen months?"

"Not a thing. And all that time Paramount will be sizzling. And of course we'll get it around that Arnold is being a bitch, Arnold is the one we want to make the heavy in all this. Nobody likes him much anyway, and my Cissie will be known as a martyr. In and out of the industry people will hear about how Cissie Brandon is being kept out of pictures because Arnold Moss is a bitch. So when the seventeen months are up, you'll be in demand."

"Let's hope so. And what do we do in the meantime? I'm not so sure I want to leave the country."

"We're not going to leave the country. We'll stay right here in California, but we're going to move. I have some news for you. We're going in the real-estate business."

"Oh, Les. Stop teasing me."

"Sid Raleigh is starting a development out in the Valley. He's calling it Yucca Knolls, and we're in it. He's raised close to a million, of which a hundred and fifty thousand is ours. Do you know how much we pay out in servants every month?"

"I have a pretty good idea."

"Well, we're going to get rid of that headache. The houses at Yucca Knolls are going to be one-story, modern type, that you can get along with one servant. They're not going to be your Altadena type, little Glendale bungalows at all. Nothing cheap about them. But the day of the big house like this, where you need at least three servants, that's passé. The minimum at Yucca Knolls is going to be forty-five thousand that you can spend on a house, so it isn't going to be cheap at all. But all the domestics are starting to get jobs in new airplane plants, and the others are asking outrageous salaries."

"What do we do with this house?"

"We hold on to it and rent it."

"Furnished?"

He nodded. "All but things we care the most for. Most of our things wouldn't go in a modern type house, anyway."

"When did you start thinking about all this?"

"When they previewed the last Humperdink. Remember, they sneaked it in Westwood. You didn't go, but I did, and they were laughing at the wrong places."

"That's a college audience."

"No. No it isn't. The college is there, but the bulk of their audience is mostly young couples that live around there. And then I happened to run into Sid and he got me interested."

"Sid Raleigh. I never knew he had that much brains."

"He started out as a runner in Wall Street. A very good business head on his shoulders, Sid."

"I always thought of him as just a bedroom athlete."

"Well, that. But he never let it interfere. And he's worked steady ever since he came out here. He part-owns a chain of hamburger stands, and he has money in several other things. Did you ever notice that furniture storage on Santa Monica near Hacienda? Big white building? He owned that and sold it to go into this Yucca Knolls development."

"Is he going to live at Yucca Knolls? Will we have him for a neighbor?"

"Yes. But I'll bet you wouldn't know him if you saw him now. Don't worry about Sid. He's very conservative. The only other picture people will be George Jameson."

"Pop? That's a combination, Sid and Pop Jameson and us."

"Pop wouldn't be in it but for the fact that he and Sid were in the hamburger stands together. Sid doesn't want any of the so-called glamour crowd. Mostly business men in the twenty-five thousand and up bracket, but no divorcees or picture people. Only people he figures will stay. And it's a little out of the way, so we'll have seclusion. And yet only twenty minutes from downtown L.A. Or, if you want to go through Cahuenga Pass, maybe a little less than that from Beverly, when you want to go to a party."

"Are you retiring me, Les?"

"In a way I am. But it's what you want. These last couple years, it was the same thing over and over for you. Work hard, go to the desert for a rest. Back to work. A few parties, with always the same people. It's time you got what you wanted out of life."

"And what is that?"

"Kansas City, without going back there. You could never live there again, I know that, but you'll like Yucca Knolls. I got an architect coming here Sunday, and you can have fun planning your new house."

"Our new house. Never forget that, Les. Now tell me the truth, Mister Man. Is all this because you were worried about me and the studio? Did you think I was upset over my so-called career?"

"No. Yes."

"Which?"

"Well, you're not used to long stretches without working, and you have to have something to do. But I don't think you care much for acting, and I don't blame you. Maybe if you and Earl could have got together it would have been a different story, but the Humperdinks were drudgery, irregardless of the financial security."

"I was getting so I could do them in my sleep," she said.

He paused before speaking. "Maybe you did do them in your sleep. All those nightmares."

"No, they were never about the Humperdinks."

"I know that much, sweetheart. You didn't have nightmares about the Humperdinks, but half the time you'd go to the studio so tired that you were only partly awake."

"Now I see what you're doing," she said.

"Do you mind?"

"Lord, no. I want you to take care of me. Who else have I got to?"

"We're well off, Cissie. Very well off. You never have to work again unless you want to."

The house at Yucca Knolls was a great success, both as a place to live and as a means of occupying her time and energy. It was situated high enough above the floor of the Valley so that the only sounds that reached them were the shrill cries of locomotives, softened by the intervening distances, the scornful laughter of transport planes on takeoff, the droning of airliners coming over the mountains on their way to a landing. At night they could look down on the lights of Glendale and Burbank and the continuous beams of automobile headlights, all equally impersonal and remote. It became harder to get Cissie Brandon to leave her house for a party in Beverly, and she put off her own housewarming until her friends stopped asking her about it. "It's Kansas City, all right," she said.

"Only more so," said Lester. "I understand Kansas City is pretty wild."

"Yes, I suppose it was, even while I was there. I didn't see much of that side of it. My father did."

"What was your father like, Cissie?"

"If you want to see my father all over again, take a good look at Pop Jameson."

"On or off screen?"

"Either. Both. When I first started working in pictures I had such a crush on Pop that I was ashamed to talk about it. The other girls were trying to get to meet Valentino, or Jack Holt, or Wally Reid. Not me. I was dying for Pop Jameson."

"Good grief, if I'd known that I never would have bought in here."

"That's all past and done with."

"How did you get over it? Don't tell me you had an affair with Pop Jameson."

"No. It was about as unromantic as anything you could imagine, how I got over Pop. I'm almost embarrassed to tell you."

"Oh, *tell* me, Cissie."

"Well, I was working for Universal. That was when they were still in Hollywood, but we were on location for a week. Horse opera. Two other girls and I were living in a tent, and there was one tent they used for the ladies and another for the men, only they weren't very far apart. And every morning for a week I could hear Pop Jameson going to the can. He had the noisiest bowel movements you ever heard, and he'd come out of there pulling up his suspenders and looking as if he'd just won the Academy statue. That cured me of my romantic notions about Pop Jameson. He was too much like my father in that respect, I guess. My father made a lot of noise in the bathroom, too. So you don't have to worry about me and Pop Jameson. Or anyone else."

"The only thing I ever worry about is because there *is* no one else."

"If I don't worry about that, why should you? I'm the neuter gender, I guess."

"No. I am, but you're not. You could always fall for some man."

"Not any more. Maybe once I could have, but not any more."

"Didn't you ever want children, Cissie?"

"No, I never did. Children never liked me when I was a young girl. Babies never liked me. My face is too big, probably. After they got used to seeing me in pictures they weren't so afraid of me, but before that I used to frighten them, when I was just Cecilia Brandon, nobody. That had its effect on me. I got so I didn't like kids any more than they liked me, and the thought of having one of my own, in my tummy—well, you can imagine. I would have been a lousy mother, even if I'd been married. One time I thought I was knocked up, and all I could think of was what I would do with the baby."

"You mean like—drown it?"

"Yes! Or do away with it somehow. It wasn't only the disgrace I was afraid of. It was the thought of having a child and not caring for it, and especially if it was a girl that looked like me."

"But people love you, all over the world."

"Mm-hmm. Or at least they love Jane. But Jane isn't me, and I'm not Jane. How much would they love me if they knew I went away with Naomi Sobleff? Or that I was Virginia Dimming's girl friend?"

"The people that love you, or Jane, don't know that people like Naomi and Virge exist."

"Or me. They don't even know that people like me exist."

"Well, if they do, they'd rather not. The secret of the

Humperdinks' popularity isn't because they're home folks. Every damn one of those families have their own troubles. Little Johnny won't stop playing with himself, and Cousin Judy does naughty things to the iceman. The old man probably gets drunk every payday, and Mom can't do without her patent medicine. My own sister used to take Bromo-Seltzer four times a day, if not more. When I was a kid and one of the other kids showed up with a nickel ice cream cone we used to holler at him what did he have to do to get a nickel cone. Mr. Thompson upstairs from us, every Saturday night he used to beat the hell out of Mrs. Thompson, as regularly as clockwork. And how do you think *I* got started? You know that story. No, the people that love the Humperdinks like to pretend that that's the way *they* are. It's the same way with the rich society people that go to see those plays by Philip Barry. You can't tell me that society people talk as witty as that."

"Well, not Kansas City society."

"No, and not Newport, Rhode Island, either. Or Pasadena, for that matter. But the average person goes to see a Humperdink, and they see you in an apron and Carl Buntley, dear old Carl, smoking his pipe and can't find the sports section, and then there's a couple of sight gags and you do the famous Cissie Brandon Burn. Home folks. They can't go home pretending they're rich society people, but they can pretend they're Jane and Ezra and life isn't so bad after all. That is, till they have to get up the next morning and *he* looks at *her* and *she* at *him,* and they think good God! Only they don't really look at one another, do you know that? They don't have to. Only too well they know what's there, her with her bosoms flopping down on her big fat belly, and him blowing on his coffee to cool it off but if it wasn't hot he'd hit her with his lunch pail."

"My public?" She chuckled.

"Sure it is," he said. "I wouldn't of said this if you were going to make any more Humperdinks, but now the Humperdinks are all washed up, and I don't want you to miss them. The home folks will miss them, but don't you, Cissie. You made a lot of money out of them, you earned every damn cent and more."

"Well, it's over a year since I put on that apron," she said.

"Just don't brood over it."

"Do I?"

"Oh, now and then."

"It's the ham, I guess," she said.

"Save the ham for when you sign to do a straight part. And that won't be long, now." He rolled back in his chair, and the momentum as he rolled forward carried him to his feet. He looked down at her. "Pop Jameson, eh?"

"Uh-huh."

"I used to think it was Earl."

"Well, it isn't anybody any more. I haven't had a nightmare since practically since we moved here. Have I?"

"No. No."

"There's one too many no's there, Les." She reached for his hand and held the back of it against her cheek. "You're a sweet, sweet man. You are. A sweet man."

"Often a sweet man, but never a sweetheart," he said. "I'm going out and have a look at the glads. Mr. Yokohoma says they're dying. Personally I think he put a curse on them. Maybe I ought to just fire Mr. Yokohoma, and I'll bet the place would be overrun with glads."

He was spared the trouble of firing the part-time gardener, Mr. Yokohoma, when Mr. Yokohoma's compatriots dropped their high explosives on Pearl Harbor. Mr. Yokohoma vanished completely, not even bothering to collect a day's wages that were owed to him, and presumably was placed in an internment camp. The outbreak of war at first made remarkably little difference in the daily lives of Cissie and Lester. They owned three cars—Lester's Buick coupe, a Dodge station wagon, and a Cadillac limousine-sedan—and gas rationing, in Southern California where nearly everyone used an automobile, was loosely enforced. "Any time you run short, I guess I can take care of you," said Sid Raleigh, who was on the local gas-rationing board. Cissie and Lester never ran short. They would use their cars to drive in to Los Angeles or Beverly Hills, park the car, and take taxicabs; and on special occasions they would hire a Tanner limousine. The special occasions became more special because they were fewer in number, and during the first year after Pearl Harbor Cissie could not make up her mind what to do in the war effort. She did a few shows at army camps and naval installations, and the young service men were politely appreciative, but they saved their roaring enthusiasm for the glamour girls. "If I were a soldier I'd be the same way," she told Lester.

"Maybe we ought to put you there in an evening gown. You have the shape."

"No, that's not my forte. They don't know I have a shape and it's not what they're looking for from me. Not that the shape is that good anyway, although thanks for saying so. I'm not competing with Rita Hayworth, Lana Turner, those girls. I want to find something else, not these little sketches at the camps and the defense plants. And what the hell are we doing, entertaining those jerks in the airplane factories? Who gives a damn about their morale? I'd like to go overseas with the Red Cross."

Lester took a job with the Red Cross, investigating the wants and needs of service men's families, and he was conscientious and made to feel useful. He was sympathetic, but after his years in the motion picture business, not easily fooled. He enjoyed the work, and he forgot that Cissie was not accustomed to being home alone. She grew bored and restive when he tried to tell her that she would find something she really wanted to do. At this stage Earl Fenway Evans re-entered her life.

She answered the doorbell one day, and there he was, tacky in a cheap double-breasted suit and a plaid shirt without a necktie. "Why, Earl! It's you, come in," she said.

He was half grinning, in a way that could quickly change to a real smile or to no smile at all. "Hello, Cis," he said. "Long time."

"Forever. Where have you been keeping yourself?"

"Oh—what I have been doing? Well, I was walking hots at Santa Anita, the last job I had."

"You were what? Come in. What did you say you were doing?"

"Oh, what the hell difference does it make? Got any cigarettes?"

"Yes, we have some. What kind do you smoke? You know I don't smoke and Les doesn't very much, but they save us a couple of cartons a week at the market. Sid—Sid Raleigh—owns the market."

"If you can spare a pack or two of Philip Morris."

"Of course. We may have a carton. Yes, here's a carton. Les smokes Chesterfields, but sometimes the market is out of them and they send us another brand. How about a cup of coffee? I was just going to have one."

"With sugar and cream?"

"You have sugar and cream. I take saccharin. A sandwich. Would you like a sandwich?"

"What kind?"

"Well—fried egg?"

"You wouldn't have a steak sandwich on the bill of fare?"

"Not today. We had a steak but we ate it last night for dinner. There was enough for three, too, darn it. Let's go out in the kitchen."

"Where's the little man?"

"Has a job with the Red Cross. He's gone from seven in the morning till sometimes eight or nine o'clock in the evening. How did you know where we were?"

"Oh, once in a while I read the papers. I guess it must have been about a year ago I saw where you were living out here. You all shook free of Arnold Bass?"

"Oh, yes, long ago."

"You haven't quit pictures, have you?"

"No. But I haven't been offered anything I wanted to do. Sit down and I'll make you an egg sandwich."

"Why don't you ask me to stay to lunch?"

"All right, will you? It's only half past ten. You could still have a sandwich."

"Yes, and I guess I look as if I needed one."

"Now *I* didn't say that, Earl."

"No, you didn't have to. I can read you like a book. Well, all right, I'll have a sandwich, and I'll fill you in on what I've been doing."

"We often wondered about you. Les cut a picture out of the paper that he thought was you. Some opening at the Chinese, I think it was. Was he right? Was it you?"

"Christ, I forgot about that. Yes, I did that for a gag. I went and sat with all the hyenas, and I thought it would be a laugh if I got my picture in there with all the rest of the boobs."

"I didn't think it was you, but Les was positive. Then I think somebody said they saw you down in the Westlake medical building."

"They could have. I was in there quite a lot."

"Oh, were you sick? Why didn't you let us know?"

"I was getting rid of a dose of clap. It hung on for quite a while."

"Sorry to hear it."

"Well, it could have been worse. At least I didn't get Big Casino."

"Is that syphilis?"

"Yes."

"Then I guess another report we got wasn't true."

"What was that?"

"That you were living in Balboa with a young boy. Somebody thought they saw you, but they weren't sure."

"That was true. That was before I picked up my dose. You know me. I'll take on anybody, if I'm in the mood. Sometimes when I'm *not* in the mood. I wasn't in the mood when I took on the little girl from Olvera Street, so I ended up with my dong in a sling for six months."

"Where have you been living all this time? Balboa. Santa Anita. And we also heard you were up north, Carmel or some place."

"Say, they kept pretty good track of me. Yes, I was up there for a while, trying to paint. But *they* wanted to talk about Hollywood, and I *didn't,* so I came down here again."

"Has your money held out?"

"What do *you* think?"

"Well—you didn't get that suit at Eddie Schmidt's."

"Leo Sunshine Fonarow. Eighteen dollars. Do you ever listen to Jack the Bellboy, on the radio?"

"I have, when I have trouble sleeping. But you had a lot of money, Earl, for the kind of life you seem to've led. Where did it all go, if it's any of my business?"

"That's a good question. When it's all going out and none coming in, you'd be surprised how fast it can go. And in addition to that, I went down to Tia Juana a couple of times with Duane, that was the young boy I was seen with. He could go through a bankroll very fast. Anybody can, at roulette, but he had it down to a science."

"And what have you been living on since? I'm surprised they haven't drafted you."

"When that happens, we've lost the war. . . . What have I been living on? Haven't you heard of the manpower shortage? It isn't hard to get jobs. Do you know how much they pay an undertaker's assistant these days?"

"Have you done that?"

"No, but that's a sure thing. And you can walk into any restaurant in L. A. and get a job as a waiter. Plenty of jobs, especially if you're slightly decrepit and don't look as if you're going to be drafted."

"Egg sandwich. Some ketchup?"

"Sure."

"So you're all right for money?"

"I didn't say that. I said there were plenty of jobs. But I only work when I have to."

"And where do you live?"

"Everywhere. A couple of years ago I would have been picked

up for vagrancy, but now the cops are so used to seeing people with no place to sleep that they don't bother you. Stay out of fights, don't get caught committing a crime, and the law pays no attention to you."

"You. Have you committed any crimes?"

"I haven't been caught."

"What kind of crimes do you commit?"

"Well, when things get tough I can usually pick up a few bucks as a lush-roller."

"A lush-roller. That means you roll lushes. Take money away from drunks? Is that it?"

"Yes."

"I should think you might get killed that way."

"You forget that I can throw a pretty good punch with either hand."

"Oh. You beat them up first?"

"No. I pick a soldier or a sailor, preferably an officer because they usually have more money. I follow them to see if they're soused, and then I usually tap them on the chin to make sure. My best customers are the fly-boys, the aviators. They like to get stewed, and they collect flight pay."

"I'm surprised at you, Earl. I would have thought you'd be more patriotic. You were in the Navy yourself."

"I certainly was. And when I see an ensign or a j.g. with aviator's wings, it all comes back to me how I used to hate those ninety-day wonders, in '17 and '18."

"Won't it be nice if you get caught?"

"You mean I'll be disgraced? Famous film director a lush-roller? Can you imagine how much sleep I lose over that? If I ever get pinched I'm gonna make damn sure the papers know who I am. Damn sure."

"Oh, then this is sort of your way of getting even?"

"It'll be some consolation if I have to go to jail. I don't want to go to jail, but if I do, the movie business will have to take part of the rap with me."

"I never knew you hated us that much."

"Us? What the hell is this us? It's two years since you did a picture, and you got a screwing."

"Maybe, but I can't help thinking that it was the movie business that paid for that sandwich you're eating, this coffee I'm drinking."

"Well, I'll be a son of a bitch. You *are* a chump, Cissie."

"Oh, I don't know. Maybe you're a chump, too," she said. "Tell me, why did you want to come see me?"

"Well, I tell you. This morning I woke up and I don't know how I got to thinking about you, but I did."

"Where was this?"

"A flophouse downtown. A kind of a luxury flophouse. A dollar and a half a night. Not exactly a room, but your bed is partitioned off. The walls don't go all the way up to the ceiling or down to the floor. It isn't the Beverly-Wilshire, but you don't have to be afraid somebody'll steal your shoes while you're asleep."

"Would anybody steal *those* shoes?"

"I did. So anyway, I woke up and I didn't feel so damn good, and I got to thinking about a lot of these bastards that weren't even awake yet. In the flophouse you have to be out of your room by eight o'clock, and this was about ha' past six. These no-talented bastards that I made millions for. The butler would come and bring them their cup of coffee and orange juice, and they could have a steak if they wanted it. And here I am, getting close to fifty years old, and the only thing I can make a good living at, they prevent me. And living in a flophouse. It's no-smoking in the flophouse and I like a cigarette the first thing when I get awake, but I couldn't even have a drag on a cigarette because that's one thing they're strict about. If they catch you smoking they kick you right out and don't let you come back. So I had to get all dressed and go outside before I could even smoke a lousy cigarette. And believe me, it was a lousy cigarette. Some wartime brand I never heard of till recently.

"So I checked out my hotel and went to the hamburger stand for a cup of coffee and a roll. Seven cents. Nickel for the coffee, two cents for the roll. Then I started walking up towards Pershing Square, you know, where the rest of the bums hang out, near the Biltmore."

"Uh-huh." She noticed now that while he was speaking, telling a story as vividly and with the same enjoyment he always got out of telling a story, his right hand was not still. It moved continually, back and forth, slowly, as though he were trying a key in a lock. He was not at all conscious of his spastic condition, and Cissie could also safely observe in detail other marks of time and dissipation that had been less obvious during the early minutes of his visit. His eyelids were heavy, slumberous even while he told his story, and he could not breathe through his nose. He seemed to reach for air with his mouth, like a fox terrier that had learned to catch tossed morsels of food.

"I go there every so often," he continued. "I almost expect to see Percy Marmont turn up there some day. You know, *The Street of Forgotten Men*. They don't know who I am or anything about me except what I tell them, and I've told them some beauts. No worse than some *they've* told *me*. One guy there that claims to be a Harvard graduate. About my age or a little older. He told me to call him Larry Lowell. Said it wasn't his name, but it would do. He knows me as Spike Evans, which was what they called me in the Navy. He only has one eye. Says he lost the other in a street fight in Paris, but I doubt it. He does speak French. He and another guy, a White Russian known as the count, talk French together when they want to say something about me. I don't know any French but it's easy to tell when they're talking about me. I called them on it one day and they didn't deny it. The count said it was all very complimentary, and offered to tell me what they'd been saying. So I said all right, if they told me separately, so I got the count off to one side and he told me what they'd been saying, and then I got Lowell alone and he told me the same story. They didn't have any chance to get together on a story, so what I got was the truth."

"What were they saying?"

"That I was either a writer or a painter, and that if I told them my real name they'd probably both recognize it. So I said they were right, I was a painter, but I was on the lam, and didn't trust them with my real name because they'd turn me in for the reward. They knew that was crap, that part of it. Nobody on the lam would ever sit in Pershing Square. The flycops go there every day to have a look around, and I never knew them to make an important pinch there. The first thing you think of when one of the regulars doesn't show up for a couple of days is that he's either dead or in trouble with the law. If you sit in the Square it's pretty certain that your conscience is clear, at least as far as breaking the law. In a big way, that is. I'm *always* there when I've lifted somebody's bankroll the night before, and on those days I usually let Lowell buy me a bowl of soup."

"You *like* that kind of life."

"The hell I do. But I make the most of it. I get a few laughs, and that's why I came to see you."

"To give me a few laughs?"

"No, no, for Christ's sake. I want to make some money. I want to make some big money. You always said you owed everything to me, didn't you?"

"Yes, I did," she said.

"Well, that was an exaggeration, but still there was *some* truth in it. Through me you got out of the slapstick two-reelers and the bit parts, and so forth and so on. Right?"

"Absolutely."

"All right. Now *you* can do something for *me.* You still have an in with the big shots. At least you can get to see them. I can't. Or anyway, I don't want to. The last couple of years I did a few things that I more or less got away with because nobody knew who I was. But if I got back into pictures and started getting some publicity, some people that are sore at me would say, 'Hey, isn't that the son of a bitch that did this and that?' And I'd be in for a couple of lawsuits. As far as that goes, Marietta Van Dyke could attach any money I got from a studio. I owed her thirty or forty thousand bucks when I blew town. That's why I was so anxious to get out quick, with the cash, before her lawyer could get wise. There's another matter, too. I'm still in hock to the gamblers, and they have long memories. If I collected any money from a studio, the boys with the black shirts and white ties would be around calling on me. In other words Cissie, with Marietta and the mob and the income tax people, and not to mention those other creeps that would come up out of the ground, it could easily take me a half a million dollars to get in the clear. And then I'd only be in the clear. I wouldn't have any money."

"That much?"

"I beat up a guy in San Diego. He was a fag that was after my friend Duane. He didn't know who I was, so he was willing to settle for six hundred dollars I paid for the hospital and the doctor bills. But if I suddenly made some money from some studio, he'd sue me for sure. And I had a little trouble with a young girl in Pedro."

"What kind of trouble?"

"Rape. Whether it was rape or not, she was fifteen years old and Duane and I had her down at the shack for about three weeks. That was going to be real trouble. I didn't wait around to pay off her old man. I just blew. But can you imagine if they found out who I was and saw in the paper that I sold a story to a studio?"

"*That's* what you want to do? Sell a story."

"Not me. You. I'll write the damn thing. I'll write an original and a treatment, and give it to you and Lester to peddle to the studios. You can tell them it was written by your nephew, back in Kansas City, or some unknown novelist. They don't have to know who wrote it. You can say you wrote it in collaboration with Ernest Hemingway, if you think you can get away with it. You can say it was written by somebody that doesn't want to have his name on the picture. Tell them you stole the idea from some Nazi. I don't give a God damn, just as long as we sell the story and don't get me any publicity."

"And the story is about your friends down in the Square."

"More or less. I'd give anything if I could direct the God damn thing. There's a woman in it that you could play, if you have the guts. I can cast the whole picture, sitting here."

"How much have you got written?"

"On paper? None. It's all up here," he said, tapping his forehead with a quivering hand.

"How long would it take you to write a six-page original?"

"Two weeks, maybe three. Then I'd do about a thirty-page treatment. So—wuddia say?"

"Well of course I'll do it. I'll talk about it when he gets home this evening, but I know what his answer will be."

"I'll know what it better be, the little son of a bitch. I don't owe Les anything. I don't owe *you* anything, as far as that goes, but if you swing this for me I'll call it square. We'll be even."

"Do you need some money now?"

"Sure I need some money. I want to get a shack somewhere, get away from Skid Row and write this thing. Let me have five hundred dollars. Do you have that much in the house?"

"Yes, most likely. If not I can get it quickly enough."

"Give me whatever you have."

"It's in the wall safe," she said. She rose, indicating that he should follow her. "Do you know what would be wonderful? If you sold this story and they wanted more, and then maybe we could take the studio into our confidence and somehow work it out so that you could be back in pictures."

"Be wonderful, all right, but it'll never happen."

She moved the sliding panel in the wall and turned the dial of the safe. "Do you want to tell me any more about the story? I mean, it's a dramatic story, isn't it? Not a comedy."

"It's a murder story. Not a murder mystery, but there's a murder in it. It's not a whodunit, and it's not a Mr. Moto. Not that we're going to see many Mr. Moto's from now on. Bogart would be the man I'd want to see in it, so maybe we better try Warners first."

"Not a war story?"

"I wouldn't waste my time on one. Propaganda slop. Did you ever see *The Kaiser: the Beast of Berlin?* Irene Castle, in *Patria.* And there was one by Hudson Maxim, the inventor of the Maxim silencer. I was an ignorant, unsophisticated kid from Nebraska then, but I didn't go for that crap."

"Here you are," she said. "Five hundred."

"Thanks. Do you want a receipt?"

"A receipt? Oh, come on, Earl."

"I wish it wasn't all in hundred-dollar bills."

"Do you want me to take it down to the bank and have it broken into smaller?"

"No, never mind," he said. He folded the banknotes and stuffed them in his pants pocket.

"More coffee?" she said.

"No, I was just looking around at the setup you have here. For you it's kind of—modest. Don't you have any servants?"

"Right now, a woman that comes in three days a week. Les and I manage."

"That's not what you should be doing. I always said you were an artist, one of the few real ones."

"Oh, I don't mind the housework."

"The hell you don't."

"Well, I won't say I like it, but it's wartime."

"There's a part in this picture for you," he said.

"So you said."

"The wife of one of the principal characters. If they buy it I know who they'll think of right away. ZaSu. But don't you let them put her in it. Maybe you ought to make the sale conditional on you playing it."

"That might hold up the sale."

"On the other hand, it would explain why you were trying to sell the story."

"Yes, that's true."

"We don't want them asking too many questions."

"Les will know how to handle it," she said.

"Les. Les. You and I should have teamed up. If I'd had any sense I would have married you instead of those three long-stem beauties. I could have made you into one of the real greats."

"Well, it's too late now."

"Not for you. If you play the wife in this picture, and maybe Tod Browning to direct, this could be a whole new start for you."

"Tod Browning? That's a long way from anything you or I ever did. Tod shoots everything in the dark."

"The longer away the better. And he *doesn't* shoot everything in the dark. Nobody uses lighting better. Tod Browning. Bill Howard. Tay Garnett. Either one of those fellows would be almost as good as me. Where I'd be good is getting you to forget Mrs. Humperdink."

"Stop talking that way, Earl," she said. "You're making me miserable." She smiled, to show how miserable she was not, but she convinced neither herself nor Earl.

"How do you think *I* feel, giving my picture to some other director?"

"It's kind of exciting, though, isn't it? To be getting back to work again. To be doing something."

"Write down your number, in case I have to call you. You know, I may run out of money before I finish the original. This should last me for five weeks, easily, the scale I've been living at. But I may want to call you about something. I sure as hell will. I'll want to call you tomorrow, to hear what you and the little man are going to do."

"I'd like it better if you stopped calling him the little man. He's my husband, and you know his name."

"Your husband. You know damn well you could get this thing annulled any time you felt like it."

"But I never will feel like it."

"How about you and me trying a little experiment?"

"What kind of an experiment?"

"You start by taking your clothes off."

"Don't be silly, Earl."

"I could take mine off and where would you be?" he said.

She looked at him steadily for a count of four or five. "Earl, what if I *did* take my clothes off?"

"Then we'd have some fun," he said.

"No we wouldn't," she said. "You wouldn't get any pleasure out of looking at me. I wouldn't get any pleasure out of looking at you."

"Are you trying to talk me out of raping you?"

"Oh, cut it out. If I had any real desire for you, or you had any for me, there's nothing to stop us. Nothing or nobody, and you know it. You insult me. The last time you were in our house you insulted me the same way. You always get around to insulting me. Does it make you feel big when you do that? When you call Les the little man? You come here wanting money and wanting us to help you sell a story, and when I show you I'm willing to help you, you insult me because you think that makes you a big man. Asserting your independence. Listen, why don't you just take your five hundred dollars and your carton of cigarettes and go away? I really don't want to see you any more. You bore me."

"I don't bore you. Maybe I scare you, but I don't bore you."

"No, you don't scare me," she said.

On an impulse, but acting slowly, he picked up a heavy crystal ash tray and hurled it through a picture window. He hardly bothered to observe the damage, but he watched keenly the effect on her.

"What was the point of that?" she said.

"What was the point of it? I'll tell you what was the point of it. Don't start treating me like some bum that you just gave a sandwich and a cup of coffee. I don't have to be grateful for your lousy handouts. That's the point of it."

"I think you'd better go now, and don't come back."

"What about my story?"

"I've lost interest. Keep the five hundred dollars, but just go away."

"You don't seem to realize."

"What don't I seem to realize? All I realize is that I don't want to see you any more."

"God damn it, you don't seem to realize, I'm dangerous. Do you realize I could take a butcher knife and hack you up?"

"You could, but you won't."

"You're bluffing," he said. He then went about the room, systematically breaking small and large objects of glass, porcelain, jade and earthenware. After each act of destruction he would look at her before going on to the next. She watched him, but said nothing. His tour of depredation took him finally to the dining alcove, where, on the table, rested the silver pheasants he had given her as a wedding present. "These are mine," he said.

"Yes, they're yours," she said.

"I'm gonna take them with me."

"All right, take them."

"The hell I will. Do you think I'm gonna walk down the street with them under my arm? The first time a cop saw me. And don't you phone them when I leave, or do you know what I'll do? I'll give out a story that will be in every newspaper in town. All over the country. I'll ruin you."

"That's if anybody would believe you," she said.

"They wouldn't have to believe me. They'd print it anyhow. Where did I put those cigarettes?"

"Right there in front of you," she said.

He tucked the carton of cigarettes under his arm. "Don't you give anybody my idea," he said. "I'm going to watch the papers, and if I read anything about you selling my idea, you'll be sorry. You won't get away with it."

He left the house then, and she watched him walk down the road. He was laughing, and she was almost sure he was talking to himself. Her first telephone call was to Pop Jameson, but he was working at RKO. She tried Sid Raleigh and after several calls she reached him. He promised to come right out to her house.

"No police," she said, when she finished her account of the visit.

"I don't know if you're doing the right thing, Cissie," said Sid. "On humanitarian grounds he ought to be put away."

"Not through me, though," she said.

"But when I survey all this damage, just look at the destruction. I would say he's downright demented. Are you gonna feel safe, alone here so much?"

"I don't think he'll ever be back."

"Hard to say."

"I wish there was some way I could keep it from Les, but unfortunately most of the things he broke were things Les bought."

"Oh, you can't keep it from Les."

"He'll want to quit his job with the Red Cross, and he mustn't do that."

"Well, we'll find some solution. Like if you say checked in with my office ten o'clock every morning, three o'clock every afternoon. If my operator didn't receive a call from you she'd send someone out to investigate."

"That could get to be an awful nuisance for all concerned," she said.

"Well, I'll take it up with Les and maybe he'll have some ideas," said Sid. "You'll be home this evening?"

"Oh, sure."

"Meanwhile anything I can do? You could spend the rest of the day at my home. Bitsy would enjoy your company I'm sure."

"Oh, thanks, Sid, but I'll be all right, I know I will. You and Bitsy come out this evening. Les is usually home by nine."

"We'll do that," said Sid Raleigh. "Take care."

In the evening Bitsy Raleigh and Cissie Brandon stayed in the kitchen while their husbands conferred. "So's to put your mind at ease, Les," said Sid Raleigh. "I didn't say anything in front of Cissie, but Earl's gonna be picked up. What happened today isn't gonna figure in it. I simply thought it over and picked up my phone and called this friend of mine I happen to know in the L.A. Police Department. Lew Berger. I knew him from ten, fifteen years or more, and I did him a lot of favors. So I presented him with the whole picture of what occurred today and said we didn't want any publicity or nothing like that, but I said if he wanted to pass the word along that this party was a lush-roller, not to mention a fag, not to mention what sounded to me like an advanced case of the syph, and Lew said yes, they had several reports of service men getting rolled and it tallied with Earl. Somebody that knew how to throw a punch, and mostly young officers. Now they have a full description, and it's only a question whether he gets picked up by the cops or the M.P.'s or the Shore Patrol. As soon as he blows the five hundred he got from Cissie he'll be back to his old habits. Lew called me back and said Earl didn't check in at the fleabag up till about an hour ago, but now they knew where to look for him. There, and Pershing Square."

"Well, that finishes Earl Fenway Evans, I guess," said Les. "A pity."

"Well, yes and no, He didn't work any harder than the rest of us, and he made a hell of a lot more money. Don't feel too sorry for him."

"Oh, I don't. I really hated him. He put some sort of a spell over Cissie. I wish he'd taken those silver pheasants with him. Still, he was a good director."

"Now there's where I differ with you, Les. I never considered him topnotch, considering the calibre of people he had to work with."

"You better not say that to Cissie. She worshiped him. And very likely still does, regardless of today."

"Very possibly. But he couldn't have bought his way into Yucca Knolls if he came to me with a certified check for a half a million dollars. As the fellow says, I never liked him and I always will. It's all right to have talent, mind you, but you don't have to go around insulting people."

"We sound as if we were talking about a dead person."

"Well, maybe that's only a question of time, too," said Sid Raleigh. "While I'm here, Les, we're thinking of taking an option on a hundred acres just this side of the fire break. For after the war, that is. Would you and Cissie be interested? We can get it for practically nothing now, whereas if we wait till later somebody else may beat us to it. It's for protection as much as anything else. We want to keep Yucca Knolls the way it is."

"Well, I was gonna suggest that, Sid. You mean and keep out the Hollywood riffraff?"

"Strictly, Les. Strictly. That's what we wanted to get away from."

"It sounds like it might be a good investment, if the price is right."

"We can't miss. I have a lot of faith in Southern California real-estate values," said Sid Raleigh.

The Answer Depends

THEY WONDER HOW we can sit and watch ourselves in those old movies on television. Doesn't it embarrass us to be reminded of the awfulness of the bad pictures, and embarrass us in a different way to see the inferior quality of our pictures that were supposed to be good? Our makeup was so awful, the lighting was so unprofessional, the cutting so jumpy, the direction so unimaginative when it was not artily intrusive, the dialog so dated, the stories so untrue to life. They laugh, the younger ones, and kid the clichés and ask us why we don't buy up those old pictures and burn the negatives. One of them said to me last week, "Come on, Bobby, you have enough money stashed away. You can afford to buy back a thing like *MacKenzie of the Royal Rifles.*" Well, I have not got enough money to buy back *MacKenzie,* but even if I had, I wouldn't buy it. Yes, I am momentarily uncomfortable when my grandson sees me as a gallant young subaltern—wearing too much lipstick and too much eye-shadow. Only too well do I know what he is thinking: his grandfather must have been a swish. His manners are just good enough to keep him from coming out and saying so, but he looks at me on the TV screen and then at me, there in my den, and in his mind are serious doubts of my virility. I, on the other hand, cannot banish those thoughts by revealing to him that at the time I was making *MacKenzie of the Royal Rifles,* his grandmother was sulking in our North Canon Drive mansion because I was away on location with Doris Arlington. I cannot tell the boy that his grandmother had every good reason to sulk. I would not tell him that I very nearly did not go back to his grandmother, that Doris Arlington and I went from the High Sierras location to a cruise in a borrowed yacht that had nothing to do with the making of *MacKenzie of the Royal Rifles.* "My boy," I could but cannot say to him, "if Doris Arlington had been a better sailor, you would not be alive today, and neither would your father."

We don't see what *they* see in those old movies. The news and sports and the weather are finished, and the night's movie comes on. Sometimes it is a picture I never heard of, sometimes it is a picture in which I had the male lead. Most often it is a film that stars men and women I used to know, and frequently I am able to recall the giant première at the Chinese or the Egyptian or the Carthay Circle. The pra-meer, they pronounced it. That was the year I had my first Duesenberg. That was the year I had my first Rolls. That was the opening that Lowell Sherman came to in a broken-down flivver—but there I am confusing fact with scenario. Lowell Sherman did that in a film called *What Price Hollywood?* Someone else did it in real life. Who was it, who *was* it that came to a world pra-meer in a broken-down flivver? I remember Connie Bennett in *What Price Hollywood?,* the Brown Derby waitress in a starched, ballooning-out skirt. It was a good, good picture. Gutsy, with a suicide ending. But who actually did drive the flivver to a grande luxe opening? I can remember Connie singing "Parlez moi d'amour" in the film, but why can't I recall the actual driver of the actual flivver? I make a note to telephone Bill Powell in Palm Springs. He'll remember. But by the time the night's picture is finished I forget to telephone Bill.

Oh, we would never do anything to keep those old films off TV. It would be like burning a diary. It would be worse than burning a diary. I did burn a diary before I went to the hospital a few years ago. No one else knew that I had kept the diary, no one in the world. It contained no written-out names, but there were a few people who would have been able to make pretty good guesses as to identities and events, and their guesses would not have made anyone happy. The doctor said my operation would be merely exploratory, which is what it turned out to be, but he was quite pleased that I seemed to be so calm. "Most men your age put on a good act, but you're not a bit worried," he said. I told him I had great confidence in him and let it go at that. I didn't want to tell him that I had prepared for the operation by burning a diary. Surgeons are such hams, every bit as bad as we are, every bit as hungry for a little applause. And at my age my doctor is almost a companion, if not exactly a friend. I have no friends who are also companions. Bill Powell is in Palm Springs, Dick Barthelmess was until recently in Southampton, Ned Revere has his farm in upstate New York, Jack Paisley has returned to England. They are all far removed from my little ranch in the San Fernando Valley. But I don't really miss them. I could move to New York and join the actors' clubs, take up bridge and pool, and sit in the club bars with men who would do to me what I would do to them—interrupt my reminiscences with questions of fact or because I had been talking too long. I know those clubs, I used to belong to them in my movie-star days because membership in them spruced up my biography in *Who's Who;* but I seldom went near them, and when I did I always came away depressed and re-determined never to end my days in them. I don't need clubs, and I certainly don't want my recollections to be interrupted by other retired actors who think their memory is more accurate than mine.

I get very good reception on my TV set at my ranch. Day or night I can go to my little den and sit alone. My family and my neighbors know that my doctor has told me to stay out of the sun, and they think I am "making the best of it." Well, I am, but not in the way they believe. I am having a very good time. Every old movie, whether it was a super production or what we used to call a program picture, takes me right back to the exciting days when I was on my way up, or to those later days when (according to one magazine writer) my face was on some screen in some part of the world every hour of every day, when I was making fifteen thousand a week and spending at least half that. I bought suits twenty at a time, ordering them from swatches, and many of them I gave away without having worn them a single time. I once owned a speedboat that I never even saw because I was too busy to go to Catalina. Now, of course, I am limited to a stationwagon and a black sedan, neither of them in the five-thousand class, but a couple of weeks ago I was watching an old film about a monarch in a mythical kingdom, played by Jack Paisley. There was a scene in which Jack is riding through a village in the royal town car. The car runs over a child, and a revolution starts. I had forgotten about that film, but I recognized the car. It was my car, a Rolls with a Barker body, and I had lent it to Sidney Gainsborough, of Gainsborough Pictures, as a personal favor, for that picture. I think he paid me a thousand dollars a day, although I had not asked him for any money. They kept the car on the Gainsborough lot for three or four weeks while making the picture, and I recall that the money they paid me was more than the car had cost me new. That was how we did things in those days, too. The strange thing was that it made sense, according to Sidney, to rent my car instead of waiting a whole year while the Rolls and the Barker people built a car new. That was how we thought in those days, too. We who remember those days are not mystified by the cost of making pictures, even forty-million-dollar pictures. I was never paid a million to make a picture, but I made a million a year for six or seven straight years, and Tom Mix made much more than I did. This Taylor girl, by the time she gets through paying her taxes, will wind up with a lot less than Mary Pickford put away, and don't you forget it. In fact, I wouldn't be surprised if when she reaches my age, she has less than I have now. I spent it freely, but I didn't spend it all. Ronnie Colman, Warner Baxter, Bill Powell, Dick Barthelmess, Jack Paisley, Ned Revere and I held on to enough to give us security. Even Ned Revere, with five ex-wives, won't die broke on that farm of his up near Cooperstown, N.Y.

Good old Ned, the rascal. This present wife of his was an acquisition of his post-Hollywood days, and I don't know very much about her, but she must be a pretty good sort. Ned had that automobile accident ten years ago that left him rather badly crippled, just when he seemed about to be embarking on a new career on Broadway. He got those excellent notices in one play that folded after three weeks, and some young fellow who had never seen him in those comedy movies wrote a play especially for Ned. I would never have thought that Ned would strike anyone as the type to play a broken-down old politician in a Southern town. I had known Ned so well that the ravages of time had not been particularly noticeable; to me he was a good light comedian who was getting older, as I was getting older. But to the young playwright, seeing him for the first time, he was the perfect actor to play an unprincipled old buzzard who had always been able to get by on his charm. To some extent that was true of Ned himself, in real life, but it had never occurred to me that anyone would get that impression of Ned so strongly as to want to write a play about it. Ned understood it, though, and he told me when he went into rehearsal that it was going to be very difficult to overcome the temptation to play himself instead of the character as written. It was especially difficult, he said, because he was a native Southerner and after all those years of stifling his accent, he was being encouraged to lay it on thick. He was genuinely apprehensive, and for the first time in his life he was thinking of someone else, in this case, the young playwright who had such confidence in him. He wanted to be good for the playwright's sake. Well, as everyone knows, he was. The notices were unanimously favorable and there was praise for all concerned; for Ned, for the playwright, for the supporting cast, the director. Then Ned was injured in that smash-up of his taxi and a mail truck, and the only luck Ned had was that he came out of it alive, plus the fact that he met the lady who eventually became Number 6. She was in the hospital at the same time, and they would meet in their wheelchairs in the sun room. She was a widow, fully aware of Ned's matrimonial record, and inclined to be moralistic about it. But besides being moralistic she was sympathetic toward the afflicted, as moralistic people are sometimes apt to be, and Ned was at his lowest ebb. He had a good deal of pain during a series of operations, and was pessimistic as to his future. His old ebullience was gone, and she began to think of him more as a discouraged invalid than as a much-married movie actor. He in turn began to realize that she never said a word about her own illness, which was cancer, and that she was giving him a lesson in courage. She invited him to visit her at her farm near Cooperstown, repeated the invitation when she was leaving the hospital, and he found after she left that he missed her companionship so much that when it came time for him to leave the hospital, he went to Cooperstown and stayed.

I hear from him once in a while. He has one of those golf carts that enables him to get around in good weather. I have a standing invitation to visit him, but it is one I shall never accept. It isn't only that Cooperstown is too far away. In fact, in a manner of speaking it is much too near. Ned Revere, dependent on a golf cart to get him around, is not Ned Revere in a Stutz Bearcat or a Mercer Raceabout, as he always was when we were making silent films. When the talkies came in we bought the newer cars; Ned persuaded me to buy my first Duesenberg. He doesn't even remember that, and I will not go all the way to Cooperstown to get into an argument over it. He wrote to me a couple of months ago, and I saved his letter, although I don't know why I did. It is so full of misinformation that it is practically a classic.

Dear Bobby [he wrote]: I suppose you saw in the papers that

Dick Barthelmess has passed on. The ranks are getting thin. I had not seen Dick in recent years. He spent most of his time on Long Island. Am told he had seven operations and was down to 110 lbs when he died. Was always fond of Dick in the old days. Sent me a wire on opening night of *The Blighted Magnolia* & had tickets for the night after I had my accident with the taxi and the mail truck. He was one of the first to send me flowers to the hospital. Dear old Dick, a real gentleman & a fine actor.

I caught you on TV the other night, the late show. It was *Lord of the Forest* the one in which you played a civil engineer who wants to build a big dam & the girl threatens to shoot you when she sees you surveying the timberland. If they show it in California don't look at it. You will want to cut your throat. It wouldn't be hard, either, as you go around in all kinds of weather with your collar open and your chest showing as if you were a sweater girl. It is not the worst picture I ever saw but it will do till a worse one comes along. All I could think of watching that picture was you and Edna Blaine, who played the girl. My wife was watching the picture with me & she said you seemed to be really in love with the heroine. "I'll say he was," I said to her. I told her about how you and Edna sneaked away after the shooting was finished and went off on a cruise in Sid Gainsborough's yacht. But you were seasick from the minute the yacht left the dock and Edna got so fed up that she made the captain turn back after you were only gone two days. Still, you were quite a chaser as long as you stayed on dry land. I saw another of your pictures *MacGregor of the Royal Rifles* with you and Doris Arlington. She was just a kid at the time, everybody was after her, including yours truly, but she was really stuck on you. I was always surprised you didn't marry Doris. I guess you would have if you had to. Then some new kid came along & you palmed Doris off on Jack Paisley, a lousy trick to pull on any girl. I don't watch TV very much. They are always reviving our old pictures & there ought to be some kind of a law like invasion of privacy to keep them from digging into our past. I guess one good thing is that the young people today think we are all dead. The young fellow who manages our farm, a young Cornell graduate, worked for us two years before he discovered that Edward J. Revere was the Ned Revere he saw on the late show. I guess if the truth be told I always hated Hollywood. They kept me doing those damn comedies till I could never get a decent part in anything serious. I was in my late fifties before I ever got a chance to show I could act & then it was Broadway, not Hollywood, that gave me the chance. I was never cut out to be a comedian. I should of left Hollywood thirty years ago and concentrated on the legitimate stage, maybe doing a comedy now & then like Alfred Lunt but mostly sticking to dramatic roles. Well, it is too late now and there is no use being bitter. . . .

No use being bitter, he says. Poor Ned. I see him on the late movies, and it is true that those comedies were not worth remembering (although they made money for everyone connected with them). But I pay so little attention to the dramatic content of our old pictures. I don't try to follow the plot lines of Ned Revere's films. In a few minutes after one of his pictures has begun to roll, I am in a daze of recollection, of remembering Ned as a gay companion; irresponsible, Quixotic, romantic, attractive to men as well as to women, and with no illusions then as to his stature as an artist. He himself often said that his pictures were all the same picture, based on the foolproof formula of boy meets girl, boy loses girl, boy gets girl. I confess that I may have envied him a little in those days. I had to work so hard to create a new character in every new picture, whereas Ned, with his perennially youthful countenance and those sure-fire parts, could show up at the studio with absolutely no preparation and let the director do the thinking when any was necessary. I remember a discussion with Jack Quinlan, who directed so many of Ned's films, silents and talkies. Ned's mind, Jack said, was like an old-fashioned schoolboy's slate. You wrote something on it, then you rubbed it out and wrote something else. Ned was never bothered by subtleties or nuances, and I don't suppose he had ever read a book in his life. He had a perfect light-comedy face, as Jack pointed out to me. Regular features, a small straight nose, a fine head of hair with a widow's peak, and an awkward grace that was natural and could not be copied by anyone else in the business. There was absolutely no difference between Ned on-screen and off, and the smart directors like Jack Quinlan never tried to make Ned do anything or say anything that required discipline or invention on Ned's part. It was his naïveté that got him into so many marriages. He might just as reasonably have married five other girls instead of the five he did marry. He merely happened to have proposed to five girls who accepted his proposals. He had a daughter by his second wife, his only child, but she grew up with her stepfather, took her stepfather's name, and probably has not heard from Ned in more than thirty years. I doubt if Ned ever gives her a thought. Certainly he never used to mention her to any of us. Come to think of it, I can't recall his ever mentioning his mother either. I suppose you would call him a man with no emotional ties, who never inflicted his problems on us because he had none. His lack of them, of course, made him an ideal companion for the rest of us, who may have had a tendency to exaggerate our emotional involvements. You could tell him anything, he would listen, nod at the right places, and forget what you said. I told him, for instance, that Doris Arlington had been seasick on Morris Spitzer's yacht, but he will believe to his dying day that I was with Edna Blaine on Sid Gainsborough's yacht. Sid never had a yacht, but he did have Edna Blaine. I don't know who is better off: me at my TV, with memories as fresh as the news in the morning paper; or Ned, scornful of those pleasant and profitable days, and with the lingering bitter taste of that one success on Broadway. Who is better off? Why I am, of course, unless you put the same question to Ned Revere.

James Francis and The Star

JAMES FRANCIS HATTER, the writer, having eaten his usual large breakfast and finished with the Los Angeles newspapers, took a second cup of coffee and the Hollywood trade papers out on the terrace, and inside of two minutes the day that had started so well—well, it was utterly ruined for him. All because of one little item in one of the chatter columns. "Town buzzing over chic dinner party tossed by Rod Fulton to celebrate his return to local scene. Rod just back from three years abroad and three pix in Italy and London. His new Holmby Hills manse a real smasher," said the item, and followed with a dozen names of Fulton's guests. The names were old and new, but all big.

James Francis Hatter knew, of course, that Rod was back. That news, accompanied by photographs taken at the airport, had been in all the papers. Not too long ago James Francis Hatter would have been at the airport to greet him. A very long time ago James Francis would have been at the Pasadena station when Rod came in on the Super-Chief. And still longer ago Rod Fulton would have been at the station to meet James Francis, helping James Francis with his luggage and leading the way to James Francis's car. Rod would have got the girls and reserved the table at the Troc for James Francis's first night home. He would have washed James Francis's Packard convertible, and on the ride down from Pasadena to Beverly Hills, Rod would have read off a complete and accurate list of the important telephone calls that had come in during James Francis's absence.

Things had changed, as they were bound to change, as James Francis had often said they would change. "Don't *worry* about it, fella," he would say to Rod. "You need two good pictures, one right after the other, and you're in, I tell you. Then the dough you're in me for can come out of your first week's salary."

"I wish *I* thought so," Rod had said. "I'm about ready to go back and start hitting the managers' offices in New York."

"Not till you click here," said James Francis. "I won't let you. These muzzlers out here gave Gable the same kind of a run-around. Tracy. Astaire. I could name you a dozen. With a dame it's different. A dame can make it on her back, whereas there aren't many producers that are fairies. So be patient a little while longer."

"I owe you eighteen hundred dollars, not to mention what I'd owe you if you charged me for board and room."

"The money you will pay me back, I know that. The rest, I lived off friends of mine before I began hitting the *Post.* Twenty-two stories I sent them before they finally accepted one. Then things began to happen fast, and they will for you, too. I know when people have something and when they haven't, and you have, Rod. I'll try to get you the gangster's brother in this one I'm working on now. Then you'll need something else good, not necessarily big, right after that. Meanwhile, keep yourself in good condition. The people in makeup can always make you look dissipated if the part calls for it, but if you *are* dissipated they can't make you look healthy. So watch the booze, and the rich food. Not only for now but for later. You don't want to have to take character parts when you're forty, just because you made a pig of yourself when you were thirty."

"Well, fortunately I like to take exercise, and if I never had another drink I wouldn't miss it."

"Fortunately for me, my living doesn't depend on how I look."

"You do all right with the dames."

"*Some* dames," said James Francis. "If you can't make a score in this town, the next stop is Tahiti. Or Port Said. Or maybe a lamasery in Thibet."

"What do they have there?" said Rod.

"What they don't have is dames."

"Oh," said Rod. "What did you say that was?"

"A lamasery. The same as a monastery."

"Do you think I ought to read more, Jimmy?"

"Well, it wouldn't hurt you to try. But you don't have to. Some directors would rather you didn't. But some of *them* don't read any more than they have to."

"I wish I could have been a writer."

"I wish I could have been a good one," said James Francis. "But failing that, I can be a fat one."

"Well, you're getting there, slowly by degrees. You're the one ought to start taking the exercise, Jimmy. I mean it."

"Oh, one of these days I'm going to buy a fly swatter."

"A fly swatter? You mean a tennis racket?"

"No, I mean a fly swatter."

"You bastard, I never know when you're ribbing me," said Rod Fulton.

The cash debt had mounted to three thousand before Rod was able to start repaying it, and it took three pictures rather than two for his career to get in high gear. But thereafter there never was any doubt about it. He was a star, a big, dumb, youthful man whom women wanted to go to bed with and men wanted to go fishing with or to give him a good punch in the mouth. He bought a house of his own on North Roxbury, quite a distance from James Francis Hatter's house high above the Sunset Strip, but he did not cease to be grateful to James Francis. "This is the guy, this is the *one* guy that had confidence in me when I didn't have it in myself," he would say. And he would express it in other ways than words.

If James Francis happened to be working on the same lot, he and Rod would have lunch together every day. When James Francis was working somewhere else Rod would call him on the telephone just to chin, or to talk about getting a couple of broads. James Francis went along for the ride when Rod took a trip to Oregon to fish for steelheads, and at Rod's request, his studio paid all of James Francis's expenses on Rod's first visit to Europe. It was only James Francis's second, but Rod had the studio believing that James Francis had traveled as much as Lowell Thomas. Actually the studio was relieved that Rod had not insisted on taking some broad. He was at the moment having a secret romance with a waitress at the Beverly Derby as well as a widely publicized affair with Doris Arlington, and the studio wanted the European public to think of him as unattached.

The only unpleasantness of the trip occurred when an Englishwoman of title invited Rod to her house for the weekend, and Rod said he would have to ask Jimmy. "Jimmy? Is that Hatter?" she asked. "But surely you don't take your orders from your secretary?"

"He's not my secretary."

"Oh, I *see.*"

"He's my friend."

"Yes, exactly. Well, in that case that does change things, doesn't it?"

"He happens to be one of the highest-paid writers in Hollywood. He got me started in pictures."

"Oh, yes. Well, you see I hadn't really counted on having an extra man. I thought it would be just you and I and another couple, friends of mine. Mr. Hatter being there would complicate things, wouldn't it?"

"I don't know. Would it?"

"Yes, rather. My friends aren't married, to each other, that is. *She* has to be awfully careful, and I'm afraid she'd back out if a total stranger—"

"*I'm* a total stranger," said Rod.

"Not to me."

"Well, no," said Rod. "Get another girl for Jimmy."

"A *girl?*"

"Well of course a girl. He may be getting fat, but he's one of the greatest swordsmen in Hollywood."

"He *is?* You couldn't be mistaken about that, of course."

"What the hell are you hinting at? You don't think Jimmy is a fag, do you?"

"As a mattrafact I did."

"Then what does that make me?"

"Oh, now, Rodney, don't put me in the spot."

"*On* the spot. In the spot is lighting. On the spot is what you're trying to say."

"I don't know *what* I'm trying to say," she said. "Yes I do! I'm just afraid that as we can't possibly have Mr. Hatter, and I've promised Sybil—she has to be *so* careful now—I'm going to have to disinvite you, dear boy."

"Six, two, and even Sybil would end up in the kip with Jimmy, whoever Sybil is."

"If only you knew, you'd be bloody well impressed, Mr. Fulton."

"Not me. I don't know these English broads. Jimmy does, but I don't."

"Then all the more reason for not having your Jimmy person. No, you and I must make other plans."

"We don't *have* to. Anyway, I don't like you inferring about Jimmy and I."

"My fault, really. I should have known. He doesn't *look* like a secretary." She was talking to herself. "Darling, you will have lunch with me Tuesday. At my flat? One-ish?"

"No can do. All day Tuesday I'll be at Elstree."

"You and Jimmy?"

"That's right, me and Jimmy," he said.

The countess's suspicions of James Francis were as natural to her, as automatic and unthinking as Rod's defense of him. Nevertheless now that someone had come right out and said it, thus showing that someone else had thought it, Rod admitted to himself that he had wondered a little about James Francis. Various kinds of homo were nothing new to Rod, particularly after he had got his first job as a chorus boy in the road company of a Broadway musical. On several occasions, when the money was low, he had allowed them to seduce him, and at the beginning of his friendship with James Francis he had half expected more of the same. But when weeks passed and James Francis had continued to treat him as half-brother, half-servant, and unemployed friend, Rod stopped waiting for that other shoe to drop. The actor who had told Rod to look up James Francis was an older, fortyish, hard-drinking, saloon-brawling man, who had a speaking part in the road show. His tastes, like James Francis's, were for women and booze. He completely ignored the queens among the chorus boys. If Rod had had no show business experience he might never have had the slightest suspicion of James Francis, and such as he had soon vanished. James Francis had never married and he was often content to sit alone and listen to highbrow music on the phonograph. He read a lot. But he was a writer, the first successful writer Rod had ever become acquainted with, and writers were *supposed* to be intellectual. One of the best things about James Francis was that regardless of how successful a writer he was, he did not look down on people who couldn't even write a good letter. He wore expensive cashmere jackets and doeskin slacks, and horn-rim glasses, and looked more like a writer than a bank clerk; but directors and cameramen and high-priced film cutters dressed the same way. For a man making the kind of money he made, James Francis Hatter was God damn democratic. And a great sense of humor. He kept the whores laughing for hours at a time, just by the things he said. He was a great guy.

And the countess was a bitch, twenty-four karat, to revive those forgotten suspicions. She was something new for Rod. In her taking for granted that he and James Francis were sweethearts she had shown not the slightest bit of surprise or censure. Her only concern was for the Sybil broad, who did not want to get caught with her boy friend. (They had some divorce law in England which they nicknamed the Decree Nazi.) She trusted Rod, because he was a prominent film star, but she did not have sense enough to trust James Francis. She was a bitch, and he kept thinking about her long after he returned to Hollywood. He was determined that nothing she had said would affect his gratitude and friendship for James Francis; he saw Jimmy as much as ever. As Rod's fame expanded and his pictures made more money, there were inevitable changes in their relationship. Publicly, Jimmy became the uncaptioned companion of the big movie star; in the industry, he was the man you had to talk to if you wanted to get to Rod Fulton; privately, he was the only person whom Rod could rely on to tell him the truth. Hollywood, after John Barrymore's memorable performance as Svengali, applied the nickname Trilby to Rod Fulton, but not within his hearing. He had got too big for that; the only person who could talk that way to Rod Fulton was Svengali Hatter. Moreover, even Hollywood, which enjoyed its moments of sentimentality, was aware that this was a remarkable friendship. It gave the lie to the charge that movie stars are ungrateful.

Then in 1942 the alert Public Relations men of the Air Force beat the Marine Corps to it with a firm offer of a captaincy to Rod Fulton. The Navy ran a poor third. There was a certain amount of apprehensive discussion among the Air Force brass. Jimmy Stewart was a fully qualified peacetime pilot and properly belonged in the Air Force. Clark Gable was not a pilot and had no better education than Rod Fulton, but was given a commission.

What then if all three big movie stars got killed? What would be the effect on military and civilian morale? It was decided that the chance was worth taking on the theory that as far as service personnel were concerned, movie stars were expendable, and that if all three men got killed, the civilian population would know that we were in a war. Public Relations hoped that if anyone got killed it would not be Stewart or Gable.

They sent Rod on enough missions to qualify him for his Air Medal, and then kept him on the ground. Having visited London before the war, he was not a stranger to the West End, and he found his way back to the countess. Angela was fatigued by the war, the hazards and the austerity program, and one night Rod Fulton found that he had asked her to marry him and had been accepted. He was never quite sure how it happened; he had no James Francis in London whom he could turn to for advice, and who could think up a way to get him off the hook. So the marriage took place, with Sybil as matron of honor and Angela's brother as best man. The union was generally regarded as propitious, a sweeping away of class distinctions and a more than symbolic alliance of two typical representatives of Britain and America. Public Relations could not complain about that, and did not. At the earliest opportunity Angela was given a fairly high priority to fly to Los Angeles, there to do splendid work for the Red Cross and the U.S.O. while, in the words of her fellow-Briton Ivor Novello, keeping the home fires burning.

An early visitor was James Francis Hatter, who welcomed her with black market steaks, cigarettes, and nylons. "I don't know *when* I've had steak," she said. "You *are* a dear, Hatter."

"Yes, ma'am," he said. "Will there be anything else, ma'am?"

"Why are you imitating a film butler? That *is* what you're doing, isn't it?"

"Very good, ma'am. Yes, it is, you got it," he said. "Why I guess because I'm not used to having a woman call me by my last name."

"What shall I call you?"

"Jimmy. Or Mr. Hatter. Or Svengali. Baby, I don't care what you call me. If you want anything, I'll try to get it for you. Rod asked me to. But let's not you and me kid ourselves or each other."

"All right," said Angela. "In other words, if I need anything, you'll get it as a favor to Rod, not to me. I'm for that. Have you any influence with the airline people?"

"Some. Not as much as the studio transportation department. Why?"

"I know about the studio transportation people. Rod told me. But if I could go to New York next week without having to ask the studio's help, I'd be ever so."

"I might be able to fix it," said James Francis.

"And no questions asked?"

"Would I get a truthful answer?"

"This time you might, but I shouldn't count on it every time," she said. "It's rather relaxing not to have to pretend, don't you find it so?"

"Very. It was my idea. I couldn't see putting on an act with you. Life's too short for that, old girl."

"If I promise not to call you Hatter, will you agree not to call me old girl?"

"It's a deal."

"I'm two years older than Rod, if you must know. But I'm not twenty years older, or ten or even five. On the other hand, I'm not so young as to not mind being called old girl. I didn't object when you called me baby, although that's slightly disrespectful as you say it."

"Slightly," said James Francis.

"By the way, I know there's never been anything naughty between you and Rod. You hate me because I thought there had been. But I promise you, it wouldn't have made the slightest difference to me."

"Well, why should it? You've had girl friends, and it won't be long before you have some here, judging by the group you latched onto."

"I much prefer boy friends, but Rod wouldn't take kindly to that. How do you know so much about me, Jimmy? Rod doesn't know that."

"Rod doesn't know anything."

"He doesn't, does he?" said Angela.

"Maybe he will by the time you get through with him, but I doubt it."

"That may be a long ways off. I adore this climate."

"It can get monotonous."

"Oh, but I hope not," she said. "I love my England, but there's not much to be said for our weather. I could soak in this sunshine forever. This is only my third week here, but there's only a tiny bit of me that's my original color. Imagine. In February. You're quite brown, too. You must come and have a swim with me. I won't try to seduce you."

"Why not?"

"Well, if you put it that way, I will. Rod told me you were quite a swordsman, and we don't have to like each other, you know. I don't suppose you and I ever will like each other, but you brought me those nylons, and the cigarettes, and the steak, without liking me. I think I'll sit on your lap. May I?"

"Sure."

"Shall I just close this door so that we won't have any untimely interruptions?"

"I was going to suggest that," said James Francis.

"You see, we think alike in some respects." She got up and turned the latch in the door. On the way back she shed her pajamas. "I know I'm going to like this, and you are too," she said. "How much do you think I weigh?"

"Eight stone," he said.

"Extraordinary! One pound off. And you must be sixteen stone."

"Just about," he said.

"How too perfectly matched we are. You're *very* obliging, Jimmy. I was rather hoping this would happen, but you were awfully forbidding at first, with that chip on your shoulder. And now you've got a chippie on your lap. I'd never call myself a chippie to Rod." The frivolity disappeared. "He *doesn't* know anything, *does* he? He's a crashingly dull man."

"The hell with him, baby."

"I say so too, the hell with him," she said, and stopped talking.

Later she said, "Wouldn't it be better if I went to your house? Hereafter? You could never possibly spend the night here. I adored having a quickie with you, but that's not the real fun, is it?"

"No, and if you lock the sitting-room door you might just as well hang a sign out and tell the servants what you're doing. My house is much better. A taxi is better than your own car, too. You don't leave a taxi standing out all night, where everybody can see it. Not to mention gas rationing."

"Do you like me any better? A smidgeon better?"

"Well, I feel more kindly toward you."

"Me too. I can hardly wait to get into an enormous bed with you. You have one, I'm sure."

"Yes."

"There's so much of you—and there really is, you know. More than sixteen stone."

"Closer to seventeen. I don't watch my weight. It always goes up, never goes down."

"Oh, what an opening for a funny. Two funnies. I'm full of funnies today. Most likely because Rod told me years ago that you kept the whores laughing with your jokes. 'It always goes up, never goes down.' Unlimited possibilities there. Do you adore puns? My father adored puns, and I was the only other member of the family that did. Adore them. And of course the filthier they are, the more I treasure them. After I was married Daddy felt free to tell me some of the *mildly* filthy ones. In limericks, mostly. I've always adored talking dirty, and obscene picture postcards. I was sent down from my school, not for having them but for drawing them. I've never really had any inhibitions, you know."

"Who were you married to?"

"Oh, a chap. A stinker. Died ten years ago, but he was a stinker."

"How would a guy qualify as a stinker in your book?"

"He ruined my father, or very nearly. Money. He was a stockbroker. The title wasn't very old, but old enough to get him his job in the City. He persuaded Daddy to buy shares in a mining something or other in Rhodesia. Actually not to buy them but to give him the money to buy them. Never did buy them. Then when he got found out he shot himself, and a fat lot of good that did anyone. Only added to the mess he'd already created. Oh, he *was* a stinker."

"Were you in love with him?"

"Was I in love with him? Yes, I suppose I was, in the beginning. He was much older, and I was much younger. All the naughty things I was curious about were right in his line. He had me get girls for him. That sort of thing. I complied willingly enough. But he sent me to bed with a friend of his and then blackmailed him. Threatened to divorce me and name his friend, which would have been fatal to his friend's career. Then for the first time I realized that it wasn't all fun and games. If you ever want to write a scenario about a real stinker, I can supply you with quantities of material. Quantities of it. Piled high and very malodorous."

"They might have trouble with the casting."

"I quite see what you mean."

"And the last picture I worked on was for Nelson Eddy. Nelson Eddy and Jeannette MacDonald."

"I rather think she'd balk at playing me. Have you ever spoken to her? Had conversation with her?"

"Sure, why?"

"Does she speak, or does she sing? Lalalala lala. How do you do do do?"

"Not a bad dame," said James Francis. "Not the worst in this town."

"Who *is* the worst?"

"You've met her. She's in that group you've latched onto."

"Oh, tell me. Don't be a stick," said Angela.

"No, you find out for yourself. And you will," he said.

"Indeed I shall. Does everyone know she's the worst?" said Angela. "I mean to say, is she someone notorious?"

"No, you wouldn't call her notorious. As a matter of fact, she has quite a good reputation."

"Quite a good reputation? Then she's in the films? Not one of the wives? You can tell me that much."

"She's in the films."

"Ah, then I think I know which one you have in mind. Dining at her house Friday week. Will you be there, by any chance?"

"Hell, no. I'm not a member of that set," said James Francis. "You'll find out all about the Hollywood caste system as you go along."

"But you make pots of money."

"For a writer, I do all right. But it isn't all money, in that set. Gene Autry makes more than most of them, but he's not a member."

"Is that the cowboy that sings?"

"Yes. He sings all the way to the bank, as they say out here. There are a couple of actors in your set that don't make as much money as I do, and one producer that's in hock for the rest of his life. No, money's important, but it isn't the whole story. You'll find out."

"Would you *like* to be in that set?"

"Well, truthfully, nobody likes to be kept out of anything. I've never turned down one of their invitations. They used to invite me, at the last minute, out of desperation. You know, they'd go through their lists and see my name. Jimmy Hatter. Fat writer. Single. Salary, twenty-five hundred. Has Tux, will travel."

"Oh, now really!"

"Just about," he said. "I'd always go, and we'd all pretend I went there all the time. But gradually even the last-minute invitations got scarcer and scarcer."

"Do you know why?"

"Yes, I think I do. The women. They want *chic,* and I was never *chic.* It's the only word I can think of to explain it, and who can explain *chic?* You knew I didn't have it the first time you met me, that time Rod and I were in London. Rod didn't have it then, either, but he's acquired it since then. And as a dame you had a hunch that potentially he had it."

"Yes, he had it. The potential. He was so gauche, and he's frightfully dull, you know. I'm not sure that it's *chic* that he has, and yet I know exactly what you mean. It's true in London, too. That stinker I was married to had it, loads of it, although he had practically no chin and a figger like a scarecrow's. In spite of which, girls were mad for him. Just as they're mad for Rod, who *does* have a chin and a wedge-shaped figger. I have another explanation that isn't *chic.* It's the thing that goes on in a woman's mind, or elsewhere, her response when she sees a man, or a woman, or a thing. Does she want to possess it, to have it around, so to speak? No, I don't suppose that is a very good explanation. *Chic* is better. Not quite it, but better. Whatever name you give it, I know I have it, while much prettier women haven't. That ladies' luncheon I went to the other day, that got into the papers and supplied you with your information about my set—Louise Parsons's column, isn't it?"

"Louella. Yes, that's where I read it."

"There were four or at most five women that had it, this thing you're trying to define. And it's a dead cert that they'll be my pals. Birds of a feather, you know. Not because we're all naughty. After all, everyone's naughty when the door is closed, don't you agree?"

"Probably."

"Definitely. At all events, I have found my pals and they have found me, and so I propose to stop in this lovely California sunshine.

When this ugly war is over, and Rod comes back and takes up his wonderfully lucrative career again, I shall be the one who says what's *chic* and what isn't. And I'll see to it that you're *chic,* Jimmy."

"Baby, it isn't going to be that easy."

"Easy? I didn't say it was going to be easy. But you didn't come here with any intention of committing adultery with your best friend's wife. And I certainly had no intention of seducing you. But these things happen."

"Hollywood isn't going to be a pushover."

"No, but when I go after something, I get it. Rod, for instance. Wasn't a woman in London that would have said no to him. But I got him. Two years older, no money to speak of, no steaks or whiskey to lure him with, and he's never yet told me that he loves me. Nor I him. But here I am. And here we are. Shall I come see you tonight?"

"Sure."

"After the eleven o'clock news. I'll just pop in, and if you're asleep I won't disturb you. Ha ha. The hell I won't. Isn't it nice, though, how things have turned out?"

"Damn nice," said James Francis.

"And you mustn't have a guilty conscience, Jimmy. I seduced you, you didn't seduce me. Rod wouldn't like it either way, but I'm not going to tell him, and you're not, certainly."

"It's an interesting stalemate."

"Now don't imply that I planned it that way. I didn't. When Rod comes home and starts asking those dreary questions, I'm not going to mention you at all. If there's anyone else, I'll tell him, because I can hardly expect those London bitches to stay away from him, and he'll have to answer my dreary questions, too. But I'll keep you out. Of course it occurs to me that he won't believe me if I say there wasn't anyone. I'm afraid he knows me too well for that. Whom would he mind the least?"

"He knows you go for girls."

"Oh, brilliant, Jimmy! Of course. Think of a girl that he had an affair with and still rather likes. Are there any in my set?"

"Oh, yes."

"Be rather fun, you know. Writing and telling him that I'm seeing a lot of Susie Ramsbottom, his old girl friend, and then having him *force* the admission out of me that, yes, Susie and I did have a *little, tiny* whatchamacallit. He won't believe it was a little-tiny, but he'd rather believe that than have me tell him about some man."

"You know, Angela, I think you must be the worst woman I ever knew."

She paused in the midst of lighting a cigarette. "That would be more of a distinction if I knew more about your women. I only know about your whores, and they were *paid* for being naughty."

"I wasn't thinking of the whores."

She shook the matchstick long after the flame had gone out. "I'd also have to know who you considered the *best* woman you've ever known. Your mother, no doubt."

"My mother was somewhere in between the worst and the best. She had the morals of a reformed hooker. A whore that got religion late in life, but went right on stealing junk off the counters in the five-and-dime."

"Your mother was actually a whore?"

"No, I didn't say that. My father was a linotyper, a printer in a newspaper plant in Chicago and elsewhere. My mother was a bookkeeper. She was married once before she married my father, and her first husband died. My old man was a periodic drunk, but he made pretty good money when he was working. Men used to come to the house when my old gent was on a toot, and I've always assumed that she was putting out. Laying them. For money or not, I don't know. Maybe the old boy got drunk because she was putting out. That I don't know either. But they sent me to college for two years, and during my second year she went back to the Catholic Church. My old man wasn't a Catholic and I never was, but she was brought up one. The old man died, and she went back to work, and I quit college and got a job as a reporter. She earned her own living and I earned mine. She used to try to get me to turn Catholic, but I didn't want any of that. She was at me all the time, trying to convert me, until finally I had to move out."

Her interest was diminishing. "Then she wasn't the best woman you've ever known nor yet among the worst, down here with me. Is it sex things that make a woman naughty?"

"Not always, but often."

"But it's what you had in mind when you decided I must be the worst. Weren't you thinking that I have no morals?"

"Well, have you?"

"Yes, oddly enough I have. But not where sex is concerned. We have this business between our legs—you have yours, and I have mine—and obviously they were intended to fit together. Animals and Eskimos are born knowing that. But I've never considered myself an animal, or an Eskimo. I've always enjoyed tinkering with other people and letting them tinker with me, for pleasure. What does it matter if you get the pleasure from a man or a woman? Who *said* it has to be one way and not the other? A woman tinkering with another woman is not going to produce a child, nor a man tinkering with another man. But you see I believe that this thing is so strong within us that procreation is only a small part of the story. I produced one child. I never knew for certain whether it came from my husband or someone else. More than likely, my husband. I haven't seen it since it was two years old. It wasn't something you'd proudly display to the uncles and aunts. It died in a nursing home when it was eleven. I of course had jolly well seen to it that I'd never have another. But I'm not any worse off than a great many of my friends who've produced healthy, so-called normal offspring. Some of them turned out to be little stinkers. Some were killed in the war. And *all* of them were demanding, selfish, and rather ungrateful, even those with the good manners to pretend otherwise. I suppose all this adds fuel to your fire, your belief that I'm the worst woman you've ever known. If it does, I assure you I couldn't care less."

"That I'm sure of," said James Francis.

"What shocked you was my flight of fancy concerning Susie Ramsbottom. That I could be so—calculating. No more calculating than I was in marrying Rod Fulton. I wasn't calculating when I took off my pajamas and sat on your lap, though you may find that hard to believe. That was impulse, and being hard up. However, you could be forgiven for suspecting me of something else. Whatever I may have had in mind, you and I have cuckolded Mr. Fulton, and you're far more likely to feel guilty about it than I. My only suggestion is that as you're going to feel guilty anyhow, you might as well hang yourself for a sheep as a goat. You and I may as well keep the home fires burning till our boy comes home. Agreed?"

"I've already agreed. You're coming to my house at eleven."

"After the news broadcast," she said. "Don't try to lock me out. I'll climb in through a window."

Major Rod Fulton's predicted inquisition did no harm to his pride. "You probably knew this," he said to James Francis. "But you know who she cheated on me with? Melina Waltham. The two of them got talking about me one time, and before they knew it they were in the hay together. All the time I was banging Mellie I never knew there was any dike there. Did you?"

"How would I know?" said James Francis. "I don't move in that set."

"It's a funny thing now, to go to dinner at Mellie's and look at her and Angela, putting on this act as if they were like two Pasadena housewives."

"I don't even move in that set—the Pasadena housewives. Or the Santa Ana housewives. Don't complain. You're lucky she didn't fall for some filling-station attendant."

"Complain? Who's complaining? I just think it's funny. I couldn't complain. There was plenty of gash in London, and I admitted that I got some of it, but I didn't tell her how much. Do you remember me telling you about one named Sybil, that time you and I were there?"

"Yes."

"She was my Number 1 Priority. I went up in the world, from a countess to a duchess."

"Well, you went in as a captain and came out a major. You were entitled to a promotion."

"Yeah, son of a bitch, I got browned off on that. I thought I should have got bird-colonel. I think of some of these bastards that rank me. Not even lieutenant-colonel. Major. Wait till they want something from me."

"Did you get into any trouble? Is that why?"

"Well—there was a buck general after Sybil. He didn't help me any, I guess," said Rod. "He as much as told me that the R.A.F. boys were taking a *deem veeiew* of the duchess and I. And I said to him, 'General, is it the R.A.F. or something closer to home?' Meaning him, of course. He got it. And I got my travel orders to a dump in Northern Ireland. The same as Siberia. So I came out a major. I must owe you a pisspotful of dough."

"Not a nickel."

"I mean for all that black-market stuff. Angela says you really took care of her—in a nice way, of course. Steaks, nylons, and butter and all."

"It came to exactly seventy-five thousand eight hundred and twenty-four dollars and fifteen cents."

"No, seriously, Jimmy."

"Oh, for Christ's sake," said James Francis.

"It'd be funny if Mellie Waltham got some of those nylons."

"I hope not," said James Francis.

"She has a nice pair of gams," said Rod. "Well, now it's back to the old grind. And you know who's going to be in my first picture? If you don't know, you can guess."

"Miss Melina Waltham."

"You knew?"

"No, I guessed."

"I wonder how that's gonna be? The real acting won't get on film. It'll be Mellie and I between takes."

"Why kid around? It'll come out the first time you give her a jump."

"I wasn't sure I *would* give her a jump."

"Now you're kidding yourself."

"Maybe you're right. You usually are."

"It doesn't take much to be right about you and Mellie."

"Jimmy, I think you knew she was a dike and you knew it all along."

"As far as I'm concerned, personally, she's a virgin. If she ever wants to prove otherwise, you can give her my number. Whatever she is, it's nice pussy, and you're not going to pass that up."

"When you think of it, why should I? We're gonna be three weeks in the High Sierras, and Angela wants to go to Palm Springs. She's nuts about that sunshine. She says she's never going back to England. I'm not either, if I don't have to. Korda wants me for a picture there, but the studio wants me to do at least three for them before they loan me out. Did you know I was big in England?"

"Sure, didn't you?"

"Oh, not like when we were there. I mean really big."

"How are you in Northern Ireland?"

"You son of a bitch, the same old Jimmy. I tell you, guy, it's good to be back," said Rod. "Wuddia say you come up to the High Sierras with me? You can just fart around, do some writing. Maybe make a score with Mellie."

"No, I was thinking of going to the desert."

"The Springs?"

"Or Indio. Twenty-nine Palms. It'll probably be The Springs. The Racquet Club and the Chee-Chee Bar. I'm a creature of habit."

"Why don't you plan your trip the same tune as Angela's going to be there?"

"Oh, she's probably seen enough of me to last her for a while."

"Nuts. She's thinking of taking Ed and Mary Veloz's house. There'd be plenty of room for you, and you'd save a few bob on the rent."

"A few what?"

"A few bob. All right, that's limey talk. Anyway, that'd be a good chance for me to pay you back for some of those steaks and stuff."

"You'd better talk to Angela first."

"All right, I will," said Rod.

In due course Rod departed for the High Sierras, and Angela and James Francis settled down in the Veloz house in Palm Springs. "I'm beginning to think you're married to the All-American chump," said James Francis.

"I never thought otherwise," said Angela. "And this is the end, the living end. Very uncomplimentary to you and to me. Especially as Mellie promised to let me know the moment he comes creeping into her tent."

"You should see that tent. It's what you English call a caravan. Electric lights. Shower. Flush can. All the comforts of home. Rod gets one, too. They'll use his, because her maid sleeps in hers."

"There's nothing her maid doesn't know about her," said Angela. "I sometimes wonder about all this. Do you?"

"Yes, I do. We're all outsmarting each other, and the pay-off has to come sooner or later," said James Francis. "In some form or another. Is that what you meant?"

"Yes. I adore this life—the sunshine, and never having to worry about money and so on. But lately I've begun to realize how difficult life was before I married the film star. There was always something, you know. Money. My father growing feeble-minded. My mother giving me dark looks. My stinker of a husband. My child. The bloody war. But here I have nothing to worry about."

"Then don't worry."

"It isn't as easy as all that. The English weather makes us appreciate a few sunny days. By the same token, my troubles made me enjoy my fun. You see what I mean, of course?"

"I see that you're a restless dame that always will be restless," he said.

"I adore having you as my lover. But if I should bring home one of those tennis players, you wouldn't mind a bit."

"Are you thinking of bringing home one of the tennis players?"

"I did, yesterday. I wasn't going to tell you, but it belongs in this conversation."

"While I was playing dominoes at the club," said James Francis.

"I'll never have him here again. I'll never *have* him again. He was crude. And to top it all, he walked off with two hundred and thirty-four dollars out of my purse."

"I'm not sure which made you sore. The crudeness or the theft."

"Both. I've never had to actually pay money, you know. If anything, it's been the other way round. I've been given some awfully nice presents in my time. But this creature *expected* me to reward him. He put on his flannels and his blazer. I was still lying in bed. He picked up my purse and reached inside it and said, 'I'll just take this, lady. I'll be back next weekend, if you care to look me up.' Then it began to dawn on me that he'd always expected to be paid, and that at last I was one of those women. That if I'd been ugly and fat and unattractive, he'd still have come home with me. A gigolo in a Wimbledon blazer is a gigolo nonetheless. And a woman that he *expects* payment from is—one of those women. Am I one of those women, Jimmy? Have I reached that stage?"

"He's about twenty-two or -three, and you obviously picked him up."

"We'd been introduced, quite properly introduced. He should have known that I wasn't one of those women. I was much the most attractive *lady* at the club. You always tell Rod the truth—"

"Not always."

"You know what I mean. You're candid with him. Be candid with me. We're friends."

"What is there to be candid about, Angela? You know how old you are. You got hot pants for a tall young kid that you'd been watching playing tennis, where he's at his best. You invited him here, and both of you knew what you wanted him for. He must be used to that by this time, and if you're over twenty-five, he expects to get paid in some way or another. At least you got off without promising him a Lincoln Continental."

"I had a lovely affair with an Italian tennis player. Davis Cup. *Years* ago. This creature yesterday had never heard of him."

"There you are," said James Francis.

"But you? You're not cross with me?"

"If you mean, am I jealous? No. Would you be jealous if I brought someone home with me?"

"No. *Yes!* If you brought her here, yes. Unless you were bringing her here for both of us."

"That's different," said James Francis. "I am a little cross with you, though. This quick lay with your tennis player may get back to Rod, and if it does he's going to be sore at me *and* you."

"Why?"

"Because he's gotten really big, especially in the head, and out here he's royalty. He's not going to like having his princess get in the sack with a lowly tennis player. They're a dime a dozen in California."

"And why will he be cross with you?"

"Because I'm here to keep an eye on you. I am your duenna, while he's up there screwing Mellie Waltham, getting even with you and her for cheating on him during the war."

"He didn't mind that a bit. It rather amused him."

"That's what *you* think. That head has gotten so big that he wants to run all our lives."

"We could shrink that head, you and I. Shall we?"

"I don't want to. He'd be so bewildered if we told him about us, when he finally got around to believing it he'd be left with nothing. Nothing."

"You really love him, don't you?"

"Yes, I do."

"Why? Is it something in him, or something in you?"

"In me, I guess. When I first knew him he was pathetic, but at the same time I was sure he was going to get there. Whatever he has, I saw it in him, and I was the first to see it. I've never been an envious man, not even of other writers. I know my limitations there. I'm not as good a writer as Hemingway, but I doubt if year in and year out he makes as much money as I do, and your own Dr. Johnson said that a writer who didn't write for money was a damn fool, or words to that effect. I'm doing all right. Whenever I'm tempted to worry about the future, I tell myself that this is the future. I make so much money writing for pictures that I actually can't afford to write any more *Saturday Evening Post* stories."

"But your future that isn't writing—what about that?"

"I have none. One of these days the ticker will give out. Rich food, and booze, and mattress calisthenics—"

"Mattress caliswhat? Oh, mattress calisthenics. I see. I get it."

"When that happens, I'll give up writing and devote my remaining energy to loose living. At present, half of my energy goes into my work. But once I've had a stroke or something like that, I'll just keep sticking my finger down my throat, and some morning I won't wake up."

"I've never really, *really* thought of doing away with myself."

"Well, you have something to live for," said James Francis.

"Oh? What?"

"Pleasure. All-out, selfish pleasure," he said.

"Yes. I never thought of it that way, but it's quite true."

"Don't weaken, just because some jerk tennis player wounded your pride. You've been honest with yourself so far. You've never given much of a thought to anyone else, I'd hate to think you were going to spoil that record just because you're afraid of getting old. Some people do, you know. They reform, out of fear. But don't you."

"Are you being sardonic?"

"Not a bit," said James Francis.

"What you say about me is perfectly true, but it sounds so awful when put into words."

"I've known some women in their sixties that still get a great kick out of being wicked."

"I'm not wicked. I'm naughty, but not wicked."

"You can graduate to wicked."

"A wicked old woman. I'm not so sure I'd care to be that. What do they *do?*"

"Nothing very different from what they've always done, but the fact that they're doing it at sixty-five makes it wicked and therefore exciting. All their contemporaries are behaving like professional grandmothers, but they still get a bang out of seducing a willing bellboy."

"Or a tennis player."

"Or a tennis player. Or a young doctor. Or a clergyman. If they can't do it on the grand scale, with Lincoln Continentals, they do it with candy for the neighbors' children."

"Were you ever given candy by a wicked old woman?"

"I wasn't, but one of my chums was. He not only got the candy, but he used to tell me how the old lady made him *feel* good."

"Oh, yes," said Angela. "We had some of that at home, come to think of it."

"I'm sure it wasn't confined to my neighborhood in Chicago."

"And so you suggest that I save the little boys for my old age?"

"If that happens to please you. Mind you, it doesn't have to be sex. Some of them abandon sex for other pastimes. As in the case of my mother trying to convert me to her religion. Or those old women who louse up their children's marriages. Or go around bullying people by threatening to leave them out of their wills."

"But in my case it's more apt to be sex?"

"That's where you've operated mostly," said James Francis.

"It has been my speciality."

"Why do you say speciality? The word is specialty."

"No, the word is speciality. *Specialité.* I refer you to the French."

"You know, you're kind of wonderful. You're practically

illiterate, but you'll argue with a writer over the pronunciation of a word. The arrogance. I'm not going to worry much about you."

"It just happens that I was right and you were wrong."

"There's something else about you. A couple of times in my life I've lived with various dames. Shacked up with them for fairly long periods of time. But those ersatz marriages—to put it another way, I've come closer to the real thing with you than with anyone else in my whole life."

"That's rather nice. I like you, too. You're not like anyone I've ever known before. I've come to completely trust you, and that's a new experience for me. Even my father, sweet as he was, was rather ineffectual and not the tower of strength one hopes a father will be. He never cared much what I did, and you do. You tell me to go on being naughty, and give little boys candy to let me tinker with them. But that's you showing off, to prove to me how frightfully sophisticated you are. Actually, you're as sound as the Bank of England, and what *I* like is that you make *me* feel warm. Comfy. Protected. Are you by nature protective, Jimmy? You were with Rod, and now you are with me. I like it, and I've never known it before. Some night you may roll over on me and squash me to death, but with my dying breath I'll forgive you because I'll know you could never be cruel. It's the blind cruelty of men that I like the least about them. The tennis player. Rod. My other stinker of a husband. But never you. I really love you, and I almost wish I could say it without saying *really*."

"I know that," said James Francis. "I'd do anything for you, baby."

They were impulsively silent, the busyness of their thoughts for once dominated by the nearness of an emotion.

"Odd that we haven't heard anything from the High High Sierras," she said. "The High C's in the High Sierras. What made me think of that was Miss Waltham. At certain moments of ecstasy she hits high-C. She's a noisy piece. Rather common."

"Common to you and your husband, at least."

"Oh, shut up," she said.

"Mind your manners," he said. "What do you want to do tonight? Do you want some Chinese food? And then the Chee-Chee Bar?"

"Yes, let's be out when they telephone. They'll be so disappointed, whichever one it is. She'll be dying to break the news to me, and I think I'd like to take some of the fun out of it for her."

"He's getting under your skin, baby."

"Yes, as dear Cole Porter says, 'Don't you know, you fool, you never can win.'"

"I will take you out and get you slightly intoxicated."

"And when we come home I'll turn off the telephone, and sleep, sleep, sleep. Don't let me take any cognac. My heart thumps and keeps me awake. I've never really cared for spirits. My saving grace, that I never became a dipso. I may get tight as a nun's cunt on wine, but don't make me have those liqueurs with you."

"All right," he said. "Anything you say."

"Dear man," she said. "Dear friend Jimmy."

"Whom you really love."

"Whom I really love. It isn't quite the same, is it? If I say, 'I really love you,' it means not quite. But if I say, 'Whom I really love,' it means very nearly."

"And the French say *specialité.* Go take your bath, baby. Let's be ready in an hour," he said. "I have to eat an awful lot of Chinese food before the temple bells start ringing."

"The temple—"

"Before my stomach gets the message," said James Francis.

They returned from their night out shortly after one o'clock in the morning. "What time is it in the High-C Sierras?" said Angela.

"The same as here. Same time zone. But they'll have gone to bed hours ago, separately or together. They have to get up at half past four or five. We won't be hearing from them tonight, but I advise you to turn your phone off anyhow. They might decide to call you at nine o'clock in the morning. How do you feel?"

"Terribly sleepy. Not a bit tight, but terribly sleepy."

"Well, then I'll not foist my attentions on you," he said.

"I don't think I'd be much good," she said.

"I could use the sleep, too," said James Francis.

She was taking off her rings and bracelets as she spoke, and she opened the dressing-table drawer. "Someone's been here!" she said. "My jewel box is empty!"

"Uh-oh. What did they take?"

"I know exactly. The best things are at home, thank heaven. But my star sapphire's gone. My star sapphire. Gold wristwatch. A little pearl necklace. Five or six gold pins, costume jewelry. My small gold cigarette case that holds six. That sunburst I wear with a beret."

"Not exactly junk. What was the star sapphire worth?"

"For insurance purposes, a thousand pounds."

"Well, let's say six thousand dollars. Wristwatch?"

"Oh—probably a thousand dollars. The pins were worth at least a hundred apiece, dollars. The cigarette case can't be replaced. It once belonged to a grand duke and had his crest on it. I adored it. I bought it from a man in the Ritz Bar, in Paris. At least it was bought for me. Actually it was bought for Sybil, and she gave it to me for my birthday. How infuriating! Weren't we told that we didn't have to lock up?"

"Yes, but you don't leave ten thousand dollars' worth of jewelry lying around," said James Francis. "You make a list, and I'll call the cops."

"Do we want to do that? Call the police?"

"If you ever want to get any of it back."

"You know, of course, who I suspect," she said.

"Sure. The tennis player. He probably dropped in for a retake with you, and when you weren't here, he helped himself."

"At least he didn't find me *too* repulsive, did he?"

"Always look on the bright side, Angela. That's my girl. I suggest that we call the cops right now and lay it on the line with them."

"Tell them who we suspect?"

"Yes. This town doesn't like bad publicity, and if you play ball with them, they'll play ball with you."

"It's on your head," said Angela. "I wash my hands of it. Frankly, I think you'll be making a most awful mistake, but I'm a foreigner here."

The police car arrived in ten minutes. James Francis greeted the two patrolmen, identified himself and Angela, and gave an account of the burglary as he knew it. The sergeant, a man named Wittenberg, had dealt with Hollywood people before, but James Francis, a former newspaper man, had likewise dealt with police. "Here's the situation, Sergeant," he said. "Mrs. Fulton rented the house from Mr. and Mrs. Edmund Veloz—"

"We know that, all right," said Wittenberg.

"They're great friends of Mr. and Mrs. Fulton."

"We know that, too. Mr. Veloz told us all that," said Wittenberg. "And we know who you are, too, Mr. Hatter."

"Good. Now I'm going to level with you, because Mrs. Fulton is a foreigner. English. The wife of my best friend. She hasn't been over here very long, and her husband would want me to go to bat for her, so to speak. Yesterday she was followed home from the tennis club by a young fellow named Glenn Slaymaker—"

"The tennis player," said Wittenberg.

"Right," said James Francis. "Apparently Mrs. Fulton had said to him something about coming to see her sometime, in a polite English way. And he took her literally. In any case, she came home and five minutes later, Mr. Glenn Slaymaker appeared, and made some advances to Mrs. Fulton. She repulsed him and sent him on his way, but before he left he helped himself to all her cash, amounting to over two hundred dollars. He made no bones about it. He opened her purse and took out the money. She of course was only too glad to get rid of him. As you can see, Mrs. Fulton would be no match for Slaymaker in a real struggle, and two hundred dollars was a small price to pay, possibly for her life.

She was still nervous and overwrought when I came home, and I had a hard time getting the whole story out of her. Naturally, I wanted to notify the police immediately, but Mrs. Fulton didn't want any publicity that might adversely affect her husband. She hadn't been harmed physically, and it was only a couple of hundred dollars."

"Sure," said Wittenberg.

"However, there's one thing that might interest you gentlemen. It seems that Slaymaker told Mrs. Fulton that he was going away, but that he'd be back next week, and told her or *threatened* her with another visit. That's interesting to me, because he wanted her to think he wouldn't be here last night. In other words, my theory is—for what it's worth—Slaymaker was preparing a sort of alibi."

"Yeah, that could be," said Wittenberg.

"At the *same* time, warning her that he was coming back."

"Uh-huh."

"Now of course all this is pure speculation on my part. It may be absolutely worthless if it turns out that Slaymaker did go away, and didn't steal this jewelry. But he's my prime suspect."

"Use your phone?" said Wittenberg.

"Go right ahead," said James Francis. "This one, or there are others if you'd rather."

"This'll be all right," said Wittenberg. He dialed a number and spoke. "Norm? It's Frank Wittenberg, out at the Veloz house on that burglary. Find out if Glenn Slaymaker, the tennis player, is anywhere around. I just want to make sure if he's in town. No, don't pick him up just yet. I'll be back to you in ten minutes. Okay, Norm. Over."

"Could we offer you gentlemen a cup of coffee?" said James Francis.

"No thanks," said Wittenberg. "Itta been better if you notified us when he took that money yesterday. Guys like that, you know, they count on people being afraid of publicity. If we picked him up yesterday, he probably would of told an altogether different story. Like inferring that Mrs. Fulton gave him the money, and didn't force his attentions on her. We'd like to put this fellow away for a while, but if we don't get the right cooperation there isn't much we can do."

"You have a sheet on him?" said James Francis.

"No, we don't have a sheet on him. Well, we have a sheet on him, but it's unofficial. Not even an arrest. Were you ever a cop?"

"No, but I was a police reporter, back East."

"Oh. Well, if we could hit him with a grand-theft rap, we could put him away for a while. His kind of a guy will go right on as long as you people let him get away with it."

"Only too true," said James Francis. "But you know what the press would make of this. And there's that other angle. The Palm Springs angle."

"What angle is that, Mr. Hatter?" said Wittenberg.

"Oh—I've been coming here a long time, so I know a little bit about The Springs. How they don't like to have any bad publicity any more than a big star like Rod Fulton. The motion picture industry has always been sort of the mainstay of Palm Springs, from the very beginning. Looking at it realistically, it's always been a case of you scratch my back and I'll scratch yours. You know what I mean, Sergeant."

"Yeah, but I'd still like to put that fellow away for a while. We won't have any trouble getting him to leave town. But I'd like to see him in Q."

"The sergeant is referring to San Quentin. That's one of our prisons," said James Francis. "Well, I'll tell you, Sergeant. Both Mr. and Mrs. Rod Fulton usually listen to my advice. If you hang it on this guy Slaymaker, so that you have a real open-and-shut case against him, I'll advise Mrs. Fulton to cooperate completely. All you care about is sending him away. You don't care whether he cops a plea or not, do you?"

"He'll get a shorter sentence that way."

"What do you care, and what does Palm Springs care? As long as you hang it on him, it's not going to make any difference to you or to Palm Springs if he goes away for a year or five years. He'll be marked as a jailbird, and he won't be coming around here again."

"Well, we may be jumping pretty far ahead. We're not sure he did it."

"No, you couldn't go into court with what you know now. But as man to man, as an experienced police officer to an old-time reporter, I'll bet that's the way it turns out. Slaymaker's your man."

"I'm inclined to think so, but I'm a cop, not a lawyer."

"Bring him in for questioning. You'll know inside of ten minutes whether he did it or not. Just forget about the legal technicalities. Go by your experience with criminals. I think this guy'll scare pretty easily, too. He's used to frightening women, but he hasn't had to face experienced police officers."

"Uh-huh," said Wittenberg. "Mrs. Fulton, we'll want a detailed description of the stolen articles. The more detailed the better, like if you can give us little sketches of the design. Where the stuff came from. Any initials or other engraving."

"I should be delighted," said Angela. She was back at being a countess, on the side of law and order and gentility. She gave a performance that could not have been imitated by a mere actress. The cops, James Francis could see, were impressed. "There we are, Sergeant," said Angela when she had completed her list. "The money value may be high on some and low on others. The sapphire ring is the most valuable single piece, and the cigarette case has the greatest sentimental value. It once belonged to a grand duke, who was assassinated in the Revolution. It was given me by a friend of his. Actually she was a cousin, not a friend. I never knew the grand duke, but my late husband knew him. They were in the war together."

"Yes, ma'am," said Wittenberg. "Well, I hope we get it back for you, and the other articles. The drawings will be a lot of help."

"Thank you. You sound as if you went in for sketching. Do you?"

"Well, not any more, but I used to," said Wittenberg. "You folks won't be hearing any more from us tonight, but I'll call you first thing in the morning if we have anything."

The cops departed. "Another five minutes and you'd have had his fly open," said James Francis.

"Less than that, if you hadn't been here. You and the other policeman. Actually, I didn't flirt with him. I was being my most garden-party-and-parasol, slightly unbending."

"You gave a performance worthy of Norma Shearer, with a touch of Dame May Whitty. Knowing something about police procedure, I imagine this place will be under surveillance for a while. So for the next few days don't walk around without any clothes on."

"Thank you for taking charge, Jimmy. You were marvelous, really you were."

"We were both pretty good. That crap about the grand duke's cigarette case, that convinced the sergeant that he wasn't dealing with some Hollywood broad."

"I *had* to convince him that anything Slaymaker told him was a lie. About me, that is."

"He was partly convinced by the fact that I phoned him right away. If you'd have been afraid of what Slaymaker'd say, you wouldn't have let me phone. And that's why I phoned. It's Slaymaker's word against yours, and they won't want to believe Slaymaker. If he had any sense he'd be in Tia Juana by now, but I'll bet you he's still in Palm Springs. He's greedy."

"Do you think he might come back here?"

"Yes, and if he does he's on his way to San Quentin."

"Why would he come back here? He's taken all the jewelry I have with me."

"He didn't take what you wore tonight. That ring is worth more than all the rest of the stuff put together."

"Rod's wedding present," she said. "Yes, that's much the most valuable thing I own. I know he paid ten thousand guineas for it. I'm never without it."

"And charm-boy saw it yesterday," said James Francis. He got up and wandered about, opening and closing drawers. He left the room and came back with a snub-nosed revolver in his hand. "This is what I was looking for. I was sure Ed Veloz would have one somewhere."

"Please put it away. I hate them."

"Listen, I don't want to tangle with a trained athlete. Slaymaker would knock me out cold with one punch."

"But you said the police would be nearby."

"And they probably will be, but just in case," said James Francis.

"Do you know how to shoot it?"

"Christ, yes. I'm not Dead-Eye Dick, but I've fired plenty of them."

"Then please put it away, Jimmy. I'm really most awfully frightened of them."

"Just forget about it. I'll keep it in my room. Now you go to bed. Take a sleeping pill, and I'll see you in the morning."

"I haven't got any. Have you?"

"No, I don't use them," said James Francis. "Take a hot bath and I'll heat you some milk."

"Do you really think he might be back tonight?"

"I'm not ruling out the possibility," said James Francis. "If he does come, he won't stay when he sees this. As I told the sergeant, Slaymaker is used to threatening women, not a man with a .38 in his hand."

"I hope they catch him before he gets here."

"Devoutly, so do I," said James Francis.

She took her warm bath and he brought her a glass of warm milk. "I put a little nutmeg on top, and a teaspoon of sugar. It'll go down more easily."

"I really love you, Jimmy," she said.

"I know. Really. How many men have put you to bed with a glass of warm milk?"

"Not one. That's why I really love you," she said.

"Goodnight, baby."

"Are you staying up?"

"For a while. I have all the magazines to catch up on," he said.

He left her as she was slowly sipping the milk, her bedside lamp still burning. He got some magazines from the sitting-room and took them to his bedroom, undressed, propped up some pillows and sat in bed, reading. It was not long before drowsiness set in, and from force of habit he turned off his light. In two minutes he was asleep.

It was not a sound that made him come awake. He was awake, his eyes open in the dark, and *then* listening for a sound. But his instinct cautioned him to be as quiet as the quiet house. He reached under his pillow for the .38, and even the barely audible rustling of his hand on the bedlinen was still the loudest noise in the house. Angela's room was on the other side of the sitting-room, and he tuned his hearing for sounds from there. He got out of bed in the dark and in his bare feet. His vision was adjusting to the light in the sky and he began to discern the outlines of furniture. In the sitting-room he paused, and he saw that the light from Angela's room spilled out onto the turf beside the house.

He went out through the sitting-room door and walked on the turf until he was standing just outside the door of Angela's room. She was sitting upright in bed, and fear had made her modest; she was holding the bedclothes neck-high and watching Slaymaker go through a drawerful of lingerie, throwing it piece by piece to the floor. "You've got everything, I tell you," she said. "Take the ring and please go."

"I want to know where the other stuff is," said Slaymaker.

"I tell you it's in Beverly Hills, I swear it."

"Don't talk so loud, you'll wake that fag creep," said Slaymaker.

James Francis pushed the door open. "All right, I'm a fag creep," he said. "Back up against the wall. Angela, phone the cops."

Slaymaker rushed toward him, and James Francis fired the .38. Slaymaker was momentarily stopped, but momentum carried him forward and James Francis fired again. This time the impact of the bullet on his chest—higher than the first shot—knocked Slaymaker back and he fell over. "Jesus, I am Dead-Eye," said James Francis. Slaymaker looked up at him from the floor, and then the life went out of his eyes. "Never mind, I'll call the cops," said James Francis. Angela was weeping and muttering to herself, unintelligibly and childishly, like a little girl who has just been snatched out of the path of a nasty boy on a bike.

Sergeant Wittenberg found a .25 automatic in a side pocket of Slaymaker's blazer, and Angela's wedding-present ring in the breast pocket. "We were here till about an hour ago," said Wittenberg. "Then we got a call to the other end of town. Is that your revolver?"

"No, it belongs to Ed Veloz," said James Francis.

"I'll take it, please," said Wittenberg. He looked down at Slaymaker's body. "He sure takes up a lot of room here, doesn't he?"

"He was a big one, all right," said James Francis.

"He had enough stuff stashed away in his room to start a small jewelry store. All of your stuff, Mrs. Fulton, plus a lot of things were reported stolen. His wife came in while our men were having a look. One more day and she'd have had it over the border. Acapulco."

"He had a wife, eh?" said James Francis.

"And a kid on the way, judging by her appearance. A nice little doll, aged about eighteen maybe. Now the kid gets born in Tehachapi, most likely. 'I was born in Tehachapi, and my father was a famous tennis player.' That's what the kid'll be saying all its life. Well, we got things to do here."

"Let me brew some coffee," said Angela.

"Yeah, there'll be no more sleep here the rest of the night," said Wittenberg. "You know, the worst of it is, he had every opportunity. My kid idolized this bum. Idolized him."

"Can we go back to Los Angeles today?" said James Francis.

"Today? I don't know why not, as soon as you get the word from the Riverside County authorities. There won't be any charge against you, but they'll want to know where they can get in touch with you."

"Till the coroner's jury returns a verdict, as I recall it," said James Francis.

"That's about it. A couple weeks, then you're free to go anywhere in the world."

"In line of duty, did you ever have to kill a man?"

"Yes, I did."

"I was just wondering when it would begin to hit me, and how long it stays with you."

"Well, with me it's different, Mr. Hatter. I have a gun on my hip most of the *time.* I was a cop six years before I ever fired it at anybody. I winged him. I guess I felt worse about that than the one that died. Ask Merle. Merle had to kill a guy the second week he was a cop."

"Part of the job," said the other cop. "It was him or me. Crazy drunken wet-back come at me with a machete. There was his wife lying on the floor with her head half cut off. I gave him five slugs and he still nicked me just below the elbow. Twenty-four stitches. They were afraid I was gonna lose the arm through infection. You know they don't exactly sterilize those machetes. The arm was out like this."

"The second week he was a cop," said Wittenberg.

"It's part of the job," said Merle. "With this bum, it was him or you, Mr. Hatter. He had that jealous wife in his pocket."

"Our name for the .25 automatic," said Wittenberg. "They never seem to miss, either. A little old woman that never had a gun in her hand before, she'll point it at a guy and get him right through the heart. One slug."

"I'd like to get out of here, if you don't mind," said James Francis. "Let's go in the other room."

"You stay here, will you, Merle?" said Wittenberg. He lowered his voice. "You want to be sick, Mr. Hatter?"

"No, I just want to get out of this room. I have a feeling he's listening to us. Slaymaker."

"Right," said Wittenberg. "The fellow'll be here to take the necessary photographs, and then the body can be removed."

"The sooner the better," said James Francis.

"Right," said Wittenberg. They sat in the sitting-room, and Wittenberg lit a cigarette, first offering his pack to James Francis. "You didn't know Slaymaker, did you?"

"Only to see. I watched him play tennis a few times. He was good. Jesus! Now it's beginning to get me. I just thought of the thousands of people that paid to see him play, and now he never will again. Thanks to me."

"Wait a minute. Thanks to himself. Think of how many women he was blackmailing. You don't know it, but there's going to be plenty of them will heave a sigh of relief when they read the papers today. All over the country. Over in Europe, too. Mexico. This bum started a long time ago. First with a prominent business man in L.A., till the older guy had a stroke. Slaymaker was around seventeen then. Then there was a movie actress that I won't mention her name. You'd probably know her. But you see none of these people would ever sign a complaint. That's the kind of people he always picked on. He had a regular gift for—oh, thanks very much, Mrs. Fulton. Just sugar, no cream, thanks. Hard to get used to having sugar whenever you want it."

"Did you have *any* sleep, Jimmy?" said Angela.

"I had some."

"It couldn't have been much. Sergeant, don't you think Mr. Hatter ought to get some more sleep before—can't you *order* him to rest before they all descend upon us? The press, and the authorities and so on?"

"Well, he *looks* pretty peak-ed, but I can't order him to do anything. Our people will be here any minute, and then maybe you could go to some friend's house. Those reporters'll track you down, that's for sure, but if you had some friend's house you could go to, that'd be all right with us."

"I say let's get it over with and then I'll call the studio and they'll do what they can for you, Angela. The old Hollywood slogan. The studio can do anything. I'm free-lancing at the moment, but I have my car and I know my way around."

Thus, eventually, it was arranged. A chartered airplane took Angela to Santa Barbara, where she obtained a hotel room under an alias. James Francis left his own car at the Veloz house and rented a Chevrolet. He eluded the reporters and established his temporary headquarters in the bordello on Crescent Heights Boulevard. The madam was out shopping when he got there, but the colored maid let him in. "Early in the day for you, Mr. Hatter," said the maid. "Miss Bonnie is over to the Farmers Market, and all the girls is either asleep or out."

"That's all right, Lily. All I want now is a room with a telephone."

"With a telephone? Let me think. Yes sir, I guess Room 9 there's a phone in there."

"Didn't you hear about me, Lily? I'm hot."

"There's something I should hear about you, Mr. Hatter? I don't only seldom read the nespapers, and my little radio is on the blink. Wud you do now, Mr. Hatter?"

"I killed a man," said James Francis.

"That's serious—if you're serious. You done killed one, for sure? You always kidding around."

"Don't worry, Lily. I'm not really hot, but I don't want to be bothered with newspaper reporters."

"Then you come to the right place, that's for sure. I take you up to Room 9. You care for liquid refreshment? A sandwich?"

"If you have any cold beer, and a ham sandwich, maybe. Anything you can rustle up. I'll leave it to you."

Now began a couple of hours of revelation and frustration, unlike any he had ever known. He telephoned eight men—other writers, a producer friend, a saloonkeeper, his agent. The agent was playing golf. All the others wanted to talk about the shooting in Palm Springs. But not one of them would offer or even agree to put him up for a few days. Each of them had a sound excuse, some of which may have been true, but no one would stretch a point for him. "Every son of a bitch I called owes me a favor," he said to the madam on her return. "I'm just as hot as if I were guilty of a crime."

"I don't know, Jimmy," said Bonnie. "I just don't know."

"What don't you know?"

"Well, anybody gets in a jam—"

"But who's in a jam? Didn't you see the papers? I'm not a lammister. I wasn't even put under technical arrest. The cops actually helped me dodge the newspaper guys."

"I read all the papers and I been listening to the radio. The guy you shot was a bum, that's for sure. He never come in here, but you hear talk. All the same, though, Jimmy, I kind of understand what they're all thinking."

"Do you want me to get out of here?"

"No, no, no. You can stay. You *can* do *me* a favor. Tonight, when the customers start dropping in, I just as soon you didn't sit around the bar. You can stay a week if you feel like it, but they come here for a good time, you know. You ought to know."

"Oh, big deal. Big deal. How much do I owe you for the use of the room and the phone calls?"

"I wouldn't charge you if you stayed a week. I'd let you stay if you *were* hot. All I'm asking is if you keep out of the bar, that's all."

"My home away from home," said James Francis. "They were all local calls, so maybe I owe you a buck for the telephone. Two bottles of beer, that's two bucks. The sandwich, another two bucks. The use of the room, I don't know how to figure that when you didn't supply any entertainment. What do you figure it, Bonnie? I never came out of here for under fifty bucks, but this time you and Lily were the only females I talked to. Here's twenty bucks."

"I won't take your money. I only asked you one small favor and right away you get a fig up your rear end."

"Yes, I have a fig up my rear end. I shouldn't have come here in the first place. But I promise you this, Bonnie. I'll never set foot in your palace of joy again. The years I've *been* coming here I probably blew around fifty gees, but that, as they say, is water under the bridge."

He dropped a twenty-dollar bill on the table and left the house. He drove out to the Strip, up the hill to the vicinity of his house. But from a block away he saw a small group of bored men and women, some of them with camera kits slung over their shoulders, clustered across the street from his driveway entrance. He continued on his way, without being sure what that was. He was a marked man, and the mark was Cain's.

IT WAS OFTEN said in later years that Rod Fulton, whether you liked him or not, had stood by James Francis Hatter when Jimmy got in that jam in Palm Springs. That was the jam where Jimmy Hatter shot and killed a guy. There were a lot of stories at the time about how Jimmy happened to shoot him. The official version, of course, was that the guy was a thief, who had come to steal some jewelry from Rod Fulton's wife, the former English countess that Rod was then married to. Angela Somebody. Rod divorced her a couple of years later, and there were a lot of stories about that, too. She went completely Lesbo, according to one story, and Rod gave her a bundle and sent her back to England. There was another version that she had been banging the guy that stole the jewelry, and that he and Jimmy had a fight in the course of which Jimmy shot him. There were all sorts of rumors and the story never did get straightened out. One of the cops on the case ended up as the head of the security department at Rod's studio. Fellow named Wittenberg. Well liked. The other cop on the case, Merle Billings, was murdered in cold blood by his own wife, who shot him with a .25 automatic. The only reason people remembered that was because the wife's defense was said to have been based on her insane jealousy of Angela Fulton, but there was no testimony to that effect in court. If anybody should have been jealous of Angela Fulton, according to the Palm Springs gossip, it was Mrs. Wittenberg.

After Rod Fulton married Melina Waltham, and they became the first husband-and-wife team to win the Academy Award as co-stars in the same picture, Rod really settled down to serious acting. There was that one bomb, in which he played Plato, but he and Melina appeared in a string of successes. They had a tiny theater on their ranch in The Valley, where they gave Sunday night readings of Shakespeare and Molière and Sheridan, and whatnot, for a few invited friends who shared their intense interest in the drama. They were coached by Olga Chapman-Lang, formerly of the Royal Academy, who was a close friend of Melina Waltham's. Their ultimate aim was a New York production of *Macbeth,* which was announced prematurely and, of course, canceled forever by the tragic death of Melina by lung cancer. Rod was inconsolable. He asked for, and obtained, the postponement of the film he had hoped to do with Melina and which, they both knew, was to be their last co-starring vehicle.

He had seen very little of James Francis Hatter during his marriage to Melina. Olga Chapman-Lang had been frank to say that she considered Hatter a gross voluptuary, whose influence on Rod was disruptive and destructive to his serious preparations for the next phase of his career. "We cannot work, we cannot think, when that man is near," said Olga Chapman-Lang. "He must be kept away or I cannot go on working with you. He has no respect for anything he does not understand." As she had a strong ally in Melina Waltham, her wish prevailed; James Francis was not invited to the Rod Fulton house until after Melina's death. But he came as soon as he was asked, and Olga Chapman-Lang was seen no more at the Fulton ranch.

"How about going away with me for a while?" said Rod.

"Where to?" said James Francis.

"Up to Oregon, for the steelheads. I'll have to buy all new tackle. I gave mine all away."

"I can't do it, Rod," said James Francis. "No more roughing it for me. The old bones won't take it."

"Then let's go someplace else, just so we get out of here."

"Well, we could take an apartment in New York, and you could let the word get out that you're looking for a play."

"That'd be no more different than staying here," said Rod.

"Have you given up the idea of conquering the legitimate?"

"You know something? I wouldn't walk out in front of a Broadway audience for a million dollars cash. Those critics would tear me to pieces."

"Yes, in Shakespeare they would. You *and* Mellie. But you were safe. That Chapman-Lang dike knew better than to let you play *Macbeth.* She had a good thing going for her as long as you did your acting in the back yard."

"I used to wonder about that, but Mellie had her heart set on it. Olga had us both hypnotized. Mesmerized. Something."

"She sure did," said James Francis. "To convince Mellie Waltham that she could play Lady Macbeth. One of the greatest con acts I ever saw. Mellie, with her cute little nose and those gams, believing she could be Judith Anderson. And you. You went for it, too."

"Well, we used to enjoy those Sunday evenings. Those readings."

"I heard about those readings, Rod," said James Francis. "Nobody got in that Chapman-Lang didn't approve of. Her own hand-picked stooges. They'd come out here and stuff themselves with your food and your booze, and then go to your little jewel-box of a theater and applaud on cue."

"It wasn't always as bad as that."

"Yes it was. Sometimes it was worse than other times, that's all. I used to hear about it from some of the stooges. They delighted in telling me, because they figured you and I were on the outs. Just out of curiosity, what did you pay Olga?"

"Oh—maybe a couple of hundred dollars a week."

"Like five hundred a week?"

"I guess it was about five. She charges ten dollars an hour, you know."

"Well, that's less than a Powers model, which she certainly ain't. And much less than a head-shrinker. Which in a way she was. But five hundred a week isn't bad at all, considering that you supplied her with a car and most of her meals. Did she have totin' privileges?"

"What's that?"

"You never heard of totin'? That's a time-honored custom, by which the servants are allowed to take home as much as they can carry. Sugar. Butter. Meat."

"You don't have to put the blast on Olga," said Rod.

"I think I do," said James Francis.

"All right, but lay off Mellie."

"No, I won't lay off of Mellie, either."

"She had a very hard time there towards the end."

"She gave a lot of other people a hard time all her life."

"But not me, Jimmy. That you'll never understand. You didn't see us together, so you don't know how it was with she and I. We were right for each other."

"Well, maybe you were," said James Francis.

"It took a while, but after we were married about a year or so we began to level with each other. Angela was the big aristocrat, and she never let me forget that I wasn't. But Mellie was from the same kind of people I came from. Mildred Walsh, from Valley Stream, Long Island. Her old man a car inspector on the Long Island Rail Road, and she was knocked up by a booking agent when she was seventeen years old. She was a straight woman for a magician and God knows what else before she got in pictures. But once she was in pictures, boy, she was in her element. She played it their way, as tough as they come, and fighting all the way."

"Oh, so you fell in love with her? That must have been a surprise."

"Yes, I fell in love with her, and she fell in love with me. Not right away, mind you. But gradually it was there, and I didn't care if I never saw anybody else. I *did.* Once in a while I'd give a little screw to somebody or other. I laid Angela the night before she went back to England, and I told Mellie I did. But Mellie was so much smarter than I was, she would have guessed it. And she didn't give a damn. Mellie was a pro, a real pro. More than I ever was or ever will be. Angela was a bum. She had nothing going for her but being a bum. Well, Mellie was no angel. But she had something else going for her. Acting. Being a movie star. That's not supposed to be much, is it? Making faces in front of a camera. But for over twenty years people all over the world paid to see her make faces, and she was bigger at the end than she ever was. What the hell difference did it make if she didn't have any morals? She was Mellie, Melina Waltham. Over in Japan—*Japan,* mind you—three fans of hers committed suicide when she died. You ought to see some of the letters I got. Over eighteen thousand letters. I don't know how it is with a writer. But with Mellie, and to a certain extent with me, you get a feeling that you're with those people every minute of the time. They know who you are, you're in their thoughts, and you multiply that by two hundred million people—two—hundred—million—people—and there gets to be some kind of a thing in the air. We never knew about radio till a few years ago. Well, it's that kind of a thing. It goes back and forth between you and those people. Only it doesn't exactly go back and forth. It stays there. It's there. Yes, and Mellie had it, whatever it is. I had it, too, without knowing I had it till I married Mellie. The two of us had it together, and with all those people. Back and forth, but at the same time just staying there. It would take a writer to explain it, but I don't know if writers ever feel it, and if you don't feel it you can't explain it. I feel it, and I can't explain it. I had a letter from a young girl fan of mine, which she was embarrassed to sign only her initials. She asked me if I went to the toilet. Well, I used to wonder the same thing about George Washington, and here was a kid asking me. So I wrote on the bottom of her letter and said, 'Just like everyone else, signed, Rod Fulton,' I don't answer much mail, but I answered that one. With Mellie this thing was as close as she came to a religion. She was a Catholic when she was little, but she lost it on the road, when she was getting kicked around in vawdaville. For a while she tried Science. Christian Science. They had those booklets backstage. I remember them, in a tin box nailed to the wall. Help yourself. She tried that for a while. No go. Then she came out here and got to be a star, and instead of a regular religion she got this feeling towards the public. Towards picture business and the public, the two of them combined. They kid around about 'I belong to my public,' but by Christ there's something to it. There's positively something to it, and radio is the closest I can come to describing it. But explain radio! The ether. The airwaves. The oscillation. I got some of that in the service, but it was too deep for me. The Norden I could understand. The bomb-sight. They wanted you to understand that in case the bombardier and the navigator got hit, and there wasn't much to it. But the whole air full of guys talking from one airplane to another, and once in a while you'd get one kraut talking to another. That's too much for me. I can put out my hand here, now, and make a fist. You know what I'm doing when I make a fist? I'm squeezing the hell out of a lot of human voices and music, all in the air. This I never would have thought of but for the fact that I married Mellie and we used to exchange ideas. She was way ahead of me. I guess nobody else ever knew that side of her." He had come to the end of his soliloquy, and the subsequent silence was a part of it that James Francis respected by his own silence.

"Well, what are you thinking, Jimmy?"

"I'm thinking that you've begun to grow up," said James Francis.

"Well, wasn't it about time?" said Rod. "How would you like

to come and live here. You could have the guest cottage all to yourself."

"Nope. This place belongs to Mellie."

"You're right," said Rod. "I think I'll put it up for sale. You and I go abroad, and when I come back I'll live in a hotel. You're absolutely right, it belongs to Mellie, and if I stayed here I'd start talking to myself."

"That can get to be very dull conversation, I can assure you from experience. I've often tried to explain to a tennis player that I didn't mean to kill him. They don't listen. They're not tuned in."

"You know, I never even think about that, the Palm Springs thing. But I guess you do. Does it bother you?"

"No worse than if I'd killed somebody," said James Francis.

"But you did—oh, I get it. Well, we both need a trip. You be my guest."

"No."

"Then how about if I get the studio to buy some story of yours? Some old story you never could sell any place else?"

"That would be different. That, I'll go for," said James Francis. "The old saying is that the studio can do anything. My version of it is, the studio can do anything—and damn well should."

They were companionable again, each knowing that the conditions of the relationship had been changed, had been compelled to change during their separation. The circumstances of Rod's coming under the influence of Melina Waltham, and of James Francis's guilt neurosis, affected each man individually; as a pair of individuals they could function as friends if there were a tacit understanding that the once dominant James Francis was now the dominated. Perhaps the subtle difference was most evident in the fact that where James Francis had once made all the arrangements to suit his own convenience and pleasure, he now continued making the arrangements but to gratify the wishes of his friend. Rod frankly used him, almost to the point of abuse.

Rod was taken up by Society, the Society of the post-war gyrations in Florida, Long Island, and the ski runs. He got into some famous houses and some well-known beds, and James Francis became accustomed to being left behind. On only one occasion did he protest—when Rod went to Sun Valley. Sun Valley implied skiing, and Rod simply announced to James Francis that he was off to Sun Valley for a week. Before the week was up there were pictures in the newspapers of Rod Fulton and Ernest Hemingway in shooting clothes. "Why didn't you tell me you were going shooting with Hemingway—the one guy I wanted to meet?" said James Francis.

"I didn't think of it. You don't like to shoot," said Rod. Then realizing the tactlessness of the remark, he made it worse. "I mean, I thought you wouldn't want to be around guns."

"One way or the other, you're a liar," said James Francis.

"Well, the next time I'm going to see him I'll take you along. But don't call me a liar."

"You are a liar, and now I don't want to meet him. If he can stand your gibberish for a week, he's fallen pretty low in my estimation." James Francis stormed out of Rod's apartment in the Beverly-Wilshire. It was five or six days before Rod—as though nothing had happened—invited him to accompany him to the races at Santa Anita. James Francis, as though nothing had happened, accepted.

But something had happened, and things like it were happening rather frequently. "One of the papers called me," said James Francis one day. "They wanted to know if it was true you were going back to work."

"What did you tell them?"

"I said there was nothing to it," said James Francis.

"Good. They're going to make the announcement Friday, for release in the Monday papers."

"You *are* going back to work?" said James Francis.

"Yes. It was all very hush-hush. We didn't want to make any announcement till it was all set."

"You have a story?"

"A great story! An original written by some refugee. He used to be a playwright in Vienna. Or maybe it was Budapest. I can never remember his name. Vlas-loss or something like that. Nagly Vlas-loss. You probably know who I mean."

"Not from your description. What about my story?"

"Oh, don't worry. They're going to pay you for it. But they don't want it for me."

"You mean you don't want it for you."

"Hell, what do you care? You're getting your money. A hundred and twenty-five gees, I understand."

"I wanted the credit on your first picture back at work."

"Well, they might be able to work you in somehow. Split the credit on the screenplay."

"I don't split credits. My name goes up there by itself."

"Not always."

"Damn near always. What did he write it in? Hungarian?"

"I guess originally. I read it in English."

"That's for sure," said James Francis.

"No use getting a fig up your ass about this, Jimmy. This is a story you couldn't have written anyway. It's about a guy in the Resistance Movement."

"Where was your Hungarian resisting? In Malibu?" said James Francis.

But The Star, as James Francis sometimes called him, was as unpredictably considerate as he was carelessly tactless. On James Francis's fiftieth birthday Rod said, "I have a present for you, if you'll have dinner with me tonight."

"Sure. We were going to have dinner anyway," said James Francis.

"Well, I wanted to make sure. What size Cadillac do you wear?"

"You're kidding," said James Francis.

"I'm just throwing you off. Now you won't expect a Cadillac."

They met at Romanoff's, their usual table. The proprietor

came and sat with them for a moment. "Old boy, Rod tells me it's your birthday," said Romanoff.

"Yes, Mike. Don't tell me you're going to break down and buy a drink?"

"I have no such intention. However, I may take it under advisement. See you later, old boy."

Rod and James Francis had a couple of drinks. "Well, God damn it, where's my present?" said James Francis.

"It'll be along," said Rod.

"Then let's order."

"No hurry," said Rod.

They had another drink, and then Romanoff came back to the table. "I believe all is in readiness," he said to Rod.

"Come on, fat writer," said Rod. "Upstairs."

They went to the large room on the second floor, and as they made their entrance an orchestra played the birthday ditty. The words were sung by the highest-priced chorus in the land—every major star from every studio in Hollywood, producers and their wives, writers, some directors, starlets, cameramen, old-timers from all occupations, faces, and faces. James Francis lost his breath. He turned to Rod. "You son of a bitch. *You* did this?"

"Mike helped," said Rod.

It was one of the great parties. Everyone there had known James Francis at some time or other, in varying degrees of past intimacy and contemporary indifference, but they had known him. He was the common denominator, no cause of envy, and a recognized—just now recognized—veteran of picture business. They all wanted to speak to him. "Rosemary Theby, for God's sake. How's Harry? . . . Regis Toomey. Read this to me, Regis Toomey. I always have to say that. . . . Vilma. How's your golf, Vilma? . . . C. Aubrey, bless my soul. . . ." He had special whispered thanks for those who had written to him during the Palm Springs mess, and he refrained from embarrassing those who should not have been invited and those who should not have come. The party began to thin out at ten o'clock—early calls—and again at midnight, and at three o'clock they called it quits.

James Francis and Rod walked the few steps to Rod's hotel apartment. "You going to be able to make it home all right?" said Rod.

"What do you mean? I never made the load. Not many did, come to think of it."

"I was ribbing you. I meant, now that you're fifty going on fifty-one," said Rod.

"Oh, that's another story. By the way, I never got my present."

"Your present? I'll send you the receipted bill for the party," said Rod. "It's not deductible, either."

"You know, I wondered about that."

"My tax man said I'd have a hell of a hard time explaining a deduction for a birthday party for a fat writer. If you were Sidney Skolsky, I might be able to get away with it. But you're not, not by a half a ton."

"I'd still like a birthday present."

"All right, you son of a bitch, if it'll make you sleep better, you're getting one."

"What?"

"It's a book. A kind of guest-book. It was signed by everybody that was there tonight."

"Where is it now?"

"It's locked up in Mike's safe, overnight. I didn't want anything to happen to it."

They were in Rod's apartment. "You know that guest-book is going to be like my Oscar, only more so. I got my Oscar for a picture I didn't think much of. The studio spent a lot of money getting Oscars for the stars and the director, and I got a free ride on their publicity."

"Where was I when you got an Oscar? I never knew you had one."

"You were in England, in the service. I was kind of pissed off that I never heard from you, but then I remembered they weren't accepting congratulatory telegrams. You never knew I got an Oscar?"

"Never till this minute. It must have been for that Pearl Harbor picture, that I never saw."

"It was."

"Where do you keep it?"

"In my study, over the fireplace."

"Jesus, is it that long since I've been in your house?" said Rod. "I used to empty the ash trays in that house. I even washed your car."

"You remember that?"

"Well, why the hell do you think I threw this party tonight? I been working on this party for over a month. You should have seen the time we had tracking down some of those people. Some of those old-timers, not even Casting knew where to reach them. And swearing them all to secrecy, in *this* town."

"How did you do that?"

Rod considered. "That part you won't like."

"Go ahead, tell me."

"We told them that ever since the Palm Springs thing you were adverse to publicity."

"Yes, I'll bet that's exactly what you told them. Adverse. The word is averse."

"Well, that's what we told them. That if any word of it leaked out, you wouldn't show. You'd leave town."

"I probably would have, too," said James Francis. "When I killed Slaymaker I developed a passion for anonymity. You do."

"Well, after tonight you don't have anything to worry about. You have more friends in this town than you think you have."

"Yes, as a matter of fact it's going to be hard to adjust myself to it. All these years thinking I was a friendless soul."

"Except for me, I hope."

"Except for you."

"I don't have many friends. I never did have. The people that pay to see my pictures, that has nothing to do with friendship. Dwight D. Eisenhower."

"Is he a friend of yours?"

"Hell, no. I never got higher than major. I met him, in London, and he used to look at me and I knew he was thinking, 'Where do I know this guy from?' No, what I mentioned his name for, there was another guy that everybody in the world knew him, but how many friends can you have in that spot? When they were planning the invasion, he couldn't even be friends with Churchill. Friendly, but not friends. I'm no Eisenhower. But take for instance, Churchill had *his* ideas about the invasion, and Eisenhower had his. If they got to be too good friends, Eisenhower would start giving in to Churchill. The thing is, they all want something from you."

"Well, I never want anything else from you. After tonight, we're all square. I never did want anything from you, but it always bugged you that I helped you get started. Now you're in the clear."

"That's not why I did it, but if you want to think so, all right," said Rod Fulton. He stood up. "You want to shack up here instead of going home?"

"Thanks, but I think I'll go home and cry a little. All by myself. Do you realize that we ended up this evening without a couple of broads? And the worst of it is, I didn't even think about it till now. That's really being fifty."

"I don't know," said Rod. "It's kind of nice to just be able to hit the sack when you want to. I can get laid any time. And any*where.* That's the worst of it."

"Boy! We're getting there."

"Well, once in a while I get tired of women looking at me and saying—not in words but by the way they look at you—they say, '*I* will, honey, *I* will.' As if I couldn't get it any time and any place, whenever I felt like it."

"You need a month in Death Valley, without any women. As soon as your guide, or the burros, begin to look good—come home."

"I need more than that, but what it is I don't know," said Rod. "In the service I used to think all I wanted was to get the damn war over with and come back here. Life would be simple. It *was* kind of simple, with Mellie. But I'm not looking for another Mellie. I don't know what the hell I *am* looking for, and that's just the trouble. I just for Christ's sake don't know."

"Well, at four o'clock in the morning, after a great party, I'm not going to try to tell you. If you find out, maybe *you'll* tell *me,*" said James Francis.

Now that Rod was, as James Francis said, in the clear, he made rather a point of limiting their times together. Frequently a week would go by with no communication between them. Rod had achieved that degree of importance at which the studio no longer dared urge him to romance a co-star for the publicity; James Francis therefore assumed that the gossip items which coupled Rod's name with that of his current leading woman were accurate. She was, in the classic Hollywood phrase, a "New York actress," meaning a stage actress who had not acquired a motion picture reputation. Her name was Gwen Hickman, and the studio was unable to persuade her to change it, or her nose, or her indifference toward the Hollywood press. Her posture in relation to Hollywood was only her variant of the attitude of Garbo, Hepburn, and Margaret Sullavan, but she was affecting it twenty years later than they. She was rather dirty-looking, and the money she might have spent on clothes found its way into funds for liberal causes and through them into activities more sinister. But she had a keen sense of publicity values, particularly of the value of the Rod Fulton association. When he refused to take her to a movie premiere unless she changed into an evening dress, she put on an evening dress; when he refused to give any money to one of her causes, she did not press the point. When she asked him to marry her, he told her he was too old to get married to a woman not yet thirty. When she heard that he had a very large piece of the picture in which they were appearing, she accused him of romancing her for the exploitation. "Well, it hasn't done you any harm, has it?" he said. It was her first experience of the Hollywood *droit de seigneur,* and when the picture was completed she went back to New York and in a series of articles for an afternoon paper she allowed herself to be described as an escapee from the Rod Fulton harem. "Never again!" she said. And she was correct.

"What about that cunt?" said James Francis.

Rod Fulton snorted. "I read one of the articles," he said. "So I sent her a present. A dozen bars of soap, with my card. Just my card. Nothing written on it. But I'll say this for her, she helps the picture. She's supposed to have been gang-raped by a bunch of Nazis, and you don't have a hard time believing it. *On* the screen, that is. Off-screen, she was never raped by anybody."

"You gave her a lot of your time," said James Francis.

"I guess I did," said Rod. "But I got a guarantee of six hundred thousand dollars and a percentage of the producer's gross. If I went broke today, I'd still have a nice start for the future. This picture's gonna be big everywhere, and I wouldn't be surprised if she got an Oscar. If you don't vote for *her,* it'd be the same as voting *for* the Nazis. I'm thinking of becoming a star-maker. Get these unknowns for my leading lady, and meanwhile I get the cash."

"It worked with Barthelmess," said James Francis.

"It'll work with me. What have you been up to lately?"

"History is repeating itself," said James Francis. "A young actor came to me with a letter from Joe Shapiro, a guy I used to know in New York. Joe's retired now, but this young guy is a nephew of Joe's sister."

"This is where I came in," said Rod.

"Well, not quite. The kid came to see me, with the letter. I gave him a meal. Studied him. He had all the mannerisms of Julie Garfield, but none of the charm. The laugh. The toughtalk. It was like watching Julie with the Lane Sisters, before he made *The Postman.*"

"In other words, he had nothing," said Rod Fulton.

"Maybe it's me," said James Francis. "But when you showed up, I was sure you had it. This guy—no."

"What *did* I have, Jimmy?"

"I've often wondered," said James Francis. "I've come up with seventy-five different answers. The obvious answer is that I was queer for you. I don't rule that out entirely, but that only explains me. It doesn't explain what you had."

"You were never a queer, were you?"

"Very queer. And afraid of it, hence the broads."

"I had my hat blown a few times, when I was a chorus boy. But they were swish fags. I was never sure about you, but do you know who was? I mean sure that you weren't?"

"Angela."

"Who?"

"Oh, Angela," said James Francis.

"She told me you killed that guy because you were jealous of him."

"Is that what she told you? Well, maybe she was right."

"You were banging Angela, and I never knew it. But she told me before she went away."

"That was nice of her," said James Francis.

"She laid it all on the line because I was generous to her. You were in love with her, for God's sake."

"Well, not for God's sake. We can leave God out of it. But she's the only woman that—if I wasn't in love with her, she obsessed me. And she still does."

"I know that, and she knew it. That was her argument. That you were a one-woman man, and she was the woman."

"That's true. I don't care if I never see her again, but that's probably because I killed a guy on account of her. If I think of her, immediately I start thinking of him. Him, and his pregnant wife, and their kids. So I only think of her every day of my life. Every God damn day of my miserable fucking life."

"Oh?"

"Sometimes I'll be somewhere and somebody will be staring at me. 'What the hell are *you* staring at?' Only a couple of weeks ago, in the studio commissary. I called a guy that I thought was staring at me. A dress extra, he was. All through lunch I thought he was staring at me, and finally I went over and called him on it. What was he staring at? The woman with him burst out laughing. Staring? He couldn't see that far without his contact lenses. He wasn't staring at anybody, just giving his eyes a rest, she said. So then I had to apologize, and I never apologize, and I'm not very good at it. You'd know the guy. I think he's been a dress extra since Griffith made *Hearts of the World.* He has pure white hair."

"Oh, sure. I think I know which one it is. He gets work in every picture that Harry Hawthorne directs."

"That's the guy, all right. Well, if you want to know how he rests his eyes, he rests them by staring at me. Do you know anybody that rests their eyes by staring at you?"

"Plenty," said Rod.

"Yeah, but they're car-hops that say, '*I* will, *I* will.' "

"Christ, you never forget anything, do you?"

"Nothing worth forgetting," said James Francis.

"Well, I guess I won't be seeing you for a while," said Rod. "Starting the first of February I'm doing a picture in Italy. Venice."

"I saw you were," said James Francis.

"Then when we wind that up, I get a vacation in Norway, for some fishing. Then starting around the first of October I'll be in Ireland on an independent production of my own."

"You going in for the three-year tax dodge?"

"I'm going to try to," said Rod. "It's a long time to be out of the country, but I have nothing to keep me here. So why not make four or five or six million dollars that I can hold onto? I've been talking to an architect about building a new house."

"Where?"

"Here, somewhere. First we have to find out where they're going to build new super-highways. No use buying the land and getting a house halfway up and they come along and condemn it. So we'll have to wait and see. But we're going ahead with the plans for the house. Something to look forward to when I get back."

"You figure it'll be three years from now?"

"Three years from February, if I work the tax dodge."

"When you get back, I'll give a party for you. If I'm still around."

"All right, it's a deal. By that time you'll know all the new people and I won't know any."

"Will I see you before you go?" said James Francis.

"Oh, hell yes. I won't be leaving till the middle of January."

"That's not so far off," said James Francis.

"No, but we'll keep in touch," said Rod Fulton.

The day before he took off for Venice, Italy, he telephoned James Francis. "Well, guy, I'm off tomorrow," he said.

"Yes, I saw that," said James Francis.

"I'm sorry everything got so jammed up at the last minute," said Rod. "Is there any chance of your coming abroad?"

"So little you could stick it under your eyelid," said James Francis.

"Well, you know where I'll be."

"I'll just ask any gondolier," said James Francis.

"Right. Just ask any gondolier. Well, keep punching, and let me know what gives."

"Right," said James Francis. "Oh, say, Rod. Before you go?"

"What?"

"You wouldn't have time to wash my car?"

"Oh, very funny! *Verr*-ry *fah*-nee!" said The Star.

Natica Jackson

ONE AFTERNOON ON her way home from the studio in her cream-yellow Packard 120 convertible coupe Natica Jackson took a wrong turn, deliberately. Every working day for the three years that she had been under contract at Metro she had followed the same route between Culver City and her house in Bel-Air: Motor Avenue, Pico Boulevard, Beverly Glen, Sunset Boulevard, Bel-Air. In the morning it was Bel-Air, Sunset Boulevard, Beverly Glen, Pico Boulevard, Motor Avenue, Culver City, the studio. She was fond of saying that she knew the way in her sleep, because many mornings she might as well have been asleep as the way she was. In the afternoons and early evenings, tired though she was, it was not quite the same. The reason it was not the same was that when she got through working it was like being let out of school. In those days she was still close enough to high school to have that feeling. It had not been so long since a Warner talent scout saw her in a school play in Santa Ana and wafted her the fifty thousand miles from Santa Ana to Hollywood. They gave her a seven-year contract beginning at $75 a week, and in six months she was released, just before they would have had to pay her $125 a week. Then she got an agent who helped someone at Metro discover that she could sing and dance; and pretty soon the public discovered that there was something in the spacing between her eyes and the width of her upper lip that made her stand out, made them want to know who she was. Among beautiful women and cute girls she was the one that the public liked. She became everybody's favorite niece, and she also looked extremely well in black opera-lengths. The studio teamed her up with Eddie Driscoll in two dreadful musicals, the second so dreadful that it was scrapped halfway through, but Jerry B. Lockman saw enough of it to want her for a straight, non-musical comedy he was doing, and she walked away with the picture. Walked away with it. In the executives' diningroom they could not agree that Natica Jackson had star quality, but no one could deny that she was ready for stardom. Not Garbo stardom, not Myrna Loy stardom, but sure as hell Joan Blondell stardom, and maybe, in the right pictures she would develop into another Jean Arthur. The God damn public liked her. She couldn't carry a picture by herself, but whenever she was in a picture the people would come out of the theater saying how wonderful she was.

She bought the house in Bel-Air with money she had not yet earned, but her agent knew what he was doing when he helped her finance it. "I don't want you rattling around some apartment on Franklin," he said. "I'm thinking of ten years from now, when you ought to be making easily a couple hundred thousand dollars a year. Move your mother in with you and stay out of the night spots."

"And have no fun," said Natica.

"Depends on what you mean by fun. You have Jerry Lockman."

"He can't take me out anywhere," she said.

"I'll take you anywhere you ought to go. Anywhere I can't take you, you shouldn't be there."

"Don't try to make me into something I'm not," said Natica.

"How do you know what you're not? You know Marie Dresslier?"

"Tugboat Annie, you mean?"

"You know who she pals around with? Vanderbilts and Morgans, those kind of people. And you should make a year what she makes."

"Well, I hope she has more fun than I do."

"I hope you have as much fun when you're her age. Over sixty and making what she makes. Well loved throughout the entire civilized world. If all is not well with you and Jerry, get yourself a younger fellow. Only don't go for some trap drummer in a cheap night club. I'll look around and see if I find the right kind of a fellow for you. I coulda told you a few things about Jerry, but you didn't take me into your confidence till it was too late. But we can get rid of Jerry. You *graduated* from his type pictures. I got great confidence in your future, Natica. Not just next week or the week after. I'm talking about 1940, 1950, 1960!"

Natica had already been around Hollywood long enough to have respect for her agent, and she obeyed him in all things. Morris King was a rich man, an agent by choice, and not one of the artists' representatives who waited hopefully for a permanent connection with one of the studios. Morris had turned down offers of producer jobs. "I'll take L. B. Mayer's job, should they offer it to me, but not Eddie Mannix's or Benny Thau's," he would say. He had a big house in Beverly Hills, a 16-cylinder Cadillac limousine with a Negro chauffeur who wore breeches and puttees, and he had Ernestine, his wife, who according to other agents was the real brains of the Morris King Office. Ernestine would sit with Morris at the Beverly Derby, the Vine Street Derby, Al Levey's Tavern, the Vendome, Lyman's downtown, with her fat forearms resting flat on the table and her hands clasped, her eyes sparkling as she followed the men's conversation. She would wait, she would always wait, until Morris or one of the other men asked her what *she* thought, and her opinions were always so clever or so completely destructive that the men would nod silently even when they did not agree. She had opinions on everything; who was going to be the boss at Universal, who was going to win the main event at the Legion Stadium, why was Natica Jackson worth Morris King's personal attention. "Ernestine thinks like a man," said one rival agent. "I was having a discussion with her and Morris the other night. We happen to be talking about something, and in the mist of it I pulled a couple cigars outa my pocket and accidentally I offered one to Ernestine. I didn't mean anything by it. It was just like I said, she thinks like a man, and I done it like you offer a coupla men a cigar. Did she get sore? No, she didn't get sore. You know what she said? She said, 'The supreme compliment.' I don't say she's *all* the brains, but when it comes to thinking I give her credit for fifty-one percent. I give her the edge. Incidentally, she *took* the cigar. She don't smoke, but she wanted the cigar for a souvenir, a memento."

The Kings had no children, and at forty-four Ernestine was as reconciled to childlessness as at twenty-two she had been fearful of pregnancy. They loved Morris's business, going out every night, and each other. But Morris thought he saw through Ernestine's interest in Natica Jackson. "She's a little like you, Teeny," he said. "If you had a daughter that's what she'd be like. She even resembles you facially."

"You think you're smart, don't you?" said Ernestine.

"Maybe not smart, but not dumb either," said Morris. "It's all right if you don't want to tell me. I got my own two eyes."

"I know you have, honey," she said. "But I was never as pretty as Natica Jackson. That I can't claim."

"I only said she resembles you facially. I didn't say she was the exact duplicate."

"What if she was the exact duplicate? Would you go for her?"

He rubbed his chin as though he were stroking a Vandyke. "You know what I think? I think you're trying to find out if I *do* go for her. Like I saw the facial resemblance back there two-three years ago, and said to myself here was a modern-day version of Ernestine Schluter. Well, if that's what you're thinking, you're all wrong. The first time I saw her I took notice she had a pair of legs like Ruby Keeler and a kind of a face on the order of Claudette Colbert, only not as pretty."

"Claudette has a pair of legs on her."

"I'm telling you what *I* thought, not what you're thinking now, if you'll let me continue," said Morris. "So I did a little selling job at Metro. Then *you* liked her and the public liked her, and you more or less took her under your wing. As to me going for her like Jerry Lockman went for her, you got no cause to be suspicious."

"I know, Morris, I know. I was just kind of putting you on the pan," said Ernestine.

"Sure. But you got something on your mind, whatever it is," he said.

"It isn't much. The way some of you men buy a prizefighter and have him for a hobby, that's my interest in Natica."

"You wanta buy her from me? I'll sell you her contract and let you service her?"

"Not me. If there's anything I don't want to be it's a woman agent. But I'd like to have the say in her career, just for a hobby."

"All right."

"Starting with getting rid of Jerry Lockman."

"That's easy. She's fed up to here with Jerry."

"So am I, and she's been with him long enough. Everybody in town knows about Jerry and how he's peculiar, but if Natica keeps on being his girl they'll think the same of her. Get her a new fellow. An Englishman, or a writer, or I don't care if you get her an out-and-out pansy. But somebody that can be her escort."

"You want me to find a new girl for Jerry?"

"That shouldn't be hard. They're a dime a dozen in this town. The next new girl comes into your office, send her out to Jerry."

"Well, I guess I can do that," said Morris. "But you find a guy for Natica."

"All right," said Ernestine.

She found an Englishman who was also a writer and an out-and-out bisexual, who was more than willing to act as Natica's escort and lover. It was not the ideal arrangement for Natica, but they kept her busy at the studio, gave her bonuses for waiving vacations, and sent her home at night too tired to think. Alan Mildred, her English beau, sold the studio two original stories for Natica Jackson pictures, and one of them, *Uncles Are People,* was actually produced and did well. Twenty-five thousand dollars, less Morris King's ten percent, more than made up for the times when Natica did not wish to see him—or for the times when she did wish to see him. It became an understood thing that Alan Mildred was to make *some* money, as author of the original or collaborator on the screenplay, on every Natica Jackson picture. Natica's mother, who would have liked being a dress extra, was persuaded to take a job as saleslady in a florist's shop owned by Ernestine King. Natica's father, a brakeman on the Southern Pacific, went right on being a brakeman, but he had been separated from his wife for a good ten years. No one knew where Natica's brother was. Last heard from as a deckhand on one of the Dollar Line ships. But he was bound to turn up sometime and when he did he would have to be taken care of. Natica's maternal uncle, who had moved into the Jackson household when Natica's father left, was employed as a gardener at Warner Brothers. He had expected to move into the Bel-Air house, but there Natica put her foot down. "That dirty old son of a bitch can stay away from here," said Natica.

"That's no way to talk about your own flesh and blood," said her mother.

"Listen, Mom, there's no law says *you* have to live here either," said Natica. "You're making seventy-five a week."

"Yes, but for how long? My arthritis."

"Don't kid me, with your arthritis. If you have the arthritis I'll send you to the desert. Go see the doctor, and if he says you have the arthritis I'll get you a place to stay. But if Uncle Will thinks he's moving in here, you just tell Uncle Will it was Mr. King got him the job at Warners', and the same Mr. King can get him kicked out on his big fat can."

"I don't see why Mr. King can't get me a job as a dress extra. Then I wouldn't have to be in and out of that refrigerator all day."

"Well, I'll tell you why," said Natica. "They don't want you on the lot is why. And another reason is because they give those jobs to people that can act. Professionals. The only acting you ever do is putting on this act with the arthritis. Don't you exhaust my patience, Mom. Just don't you exhaust my patience."

"Sometimes I wish we never left Santa Ana."

"Here's fifty bucks," said Natica. "Go on back."

"Yes, you'd like to get rid of me, wouldn't you?"

"Oh, cut it out. I'm tired," said Natica. "I get up at five o'clock in the morning and get pushed around all day, and when I get home evenings I have to listen to your bellyaching."

It was a day or two later that Natica Jackson, on her way home from the studio in her little Packard, deviated from her customary route. There was a point on Motor Avenue where the road bore to the right. At the left there was a street—she didn't know its name—that formed the other arm of a Y. She had wondered sometimes what would happen if she turned in at that street. Not that anything would happen except that she would be a little later getting home and she would have seen a Southern California real estate development that she had never seen before. But at least she would have gone home by a different way. And so she turned left into a street called Marshall Place.

She had to slow down. Marshall Place was a winding road, S-shaped and only three-car width and a tight squeeze at that. The houses were quite close together and English-looking, and Natica wondered if the street had been named after Herbert Marshall, the English actor. The cars that were parked in Marshall Place were cars that were suitable to the neighborhood: Buicks,

Oldsmobiles, a Packard 120 like Natica's, a LaSalle coupe, an oldish foreign car with a name something like Delancey. It was a far superior neighborhood to the section of Santa Ana where Natica had lived, but she had so quickly become accustomed to Bel-Air that Marshall Place seemed almost dingy. She came to another turn in the road and now she could see Motor Avenue again, and she was not sorry to see it. Marshall Place was certainly nothing much, and whatever curiosity she had had about it was completely satisfied. Just another street where people who worked in offices lived. Fifty yards from Motor Avenue and farewell to Marshall Place—and then her car banged into a Pontiac.

The Pontiac was pulling out from the curb and she hit it almost broadside. It was a noisy collision in the quiet street. The driver of the Pontiac shouted, "What the hell?" and other things that she did not hear. She backed her car away and he reversed to the curbstone and got out. "What do you think you were doing?" he said. "Didn't you see my hand? I had my hand out, you know."

"I'm sorry," she said. "I didn't see your hand. It's kind of dark. I'm covered with every kind of insurance." She was wearing a silk scarf over her head and tied under her chin.

"Aren't you Natica Jackson, the actress?" he said.

"Yes," she said.

"I thought so," he said. "Well, my name is H. T. Graham, and I live in there, Number 8 Marshall Place. I suppose you have your driver's license and so forth? You'd better pull up to the curb or you'll be in the way of any cars that want to get through."

"Listen, Mr. Graham, don't start bossing me around like you were taking charge here. You say you had your hand out, but I don't have to take your word for it. The insurance company will pay for your damages, only don't start bossing me around. Here. Here's my driver's license and you can look on the steering if you want to copy down the registration."

"Don't pull any movie actress stuff on me," he said. "You were completely in the wrong and the condition of the two cars proves it. I didn't smack into you. You smacked into me." He took out a fountain pen and wrote down her name and address and various numbers in an appointment book. "Have you got a pencil?"

"No," she said.

"All right. Then I'll copy it all down for you." He did so, and tore a sheet out of his appointment book and handed it to her. "Some people would get a whole new car out of this, a crackup with a movie actress," he said. "But all I want is what I'm entitled to."

"Big-hearted Otis," she said.

"You movie people, you wonder why you're so unpopular with real people, but I'll tell you why. It's the way you're behaving now. Like a spoiled brat. You think a cheque from the insurance company is all that's necessary. This time you can drive your car home and tomorrow you can buy a new one. But the next time you may kill somebody. This is a narrow street, residential, small children. Luckily they're all home having their supper now, but a half an hour earlier this street would have been full of children. I read all about that drunken director that killed three people down in Santa Monica. He should have been put in the gas chamber."

"Listen, Mr. Graham, all I did was wrinkle your fender and put a few dents in your door."

"But if the window'd been up you could have blinded me with flying glass. Stop trying to make this seem like nothing."

"You stop trying to make it seem like a train wreck."

"Oh, go on home," he said. "And try and get home without killing anybody. Go on, beat it."

"I can't," she said.

"Naturally, your motor isn't running? Step on the starter."

"It isn't that," she said.

"Are you hurt?"

"No, not that either. I just don't want to drive. Would you

mind going in your house and calling a taxi? Suddenly I lost my nerve or something. I don't know what it is."

"Are you sure you didn't bang your head on the windshield?" He looked at her closely.

"I'm not hurt. Please, will you just call me a taxi and I'll send somebody to pick up my car."

"No, no, I'll drive you home. You feeling faint or anything? Come on in and I'll get you a glass of water. Or maybe a brandy is what you need."

"Honestly, all I want is if you'll get me a taxi and I'll be all right. I'm doing a delayed take, I guess, but I positively couldn't drive home if you paid me."

He got in her car and drove it to Bel-Air. She spoke only to give him directions in the final stage of the ride. "Now I'll get *you* a taxi," she said, when they reached her house. "Can I offer you a drink?"

"No thanks," he said.

"I guess you expected me to have a big car with a chauffeur."

"It'd go with this house, all right," he said.

"It's too big for just my mother and I."

"Aren't you married?"

"No." She telephoned the taxi company. "There'll be a cab in five minutes," she said. "I'm sorry I was such a jerk back there."

"I was pretty rough on you."

"Oughtn't you to tell your wife where you are?"

"She's away. She and the kids are down at Newport."

"Oh, then I guess you were on your way out to dinner when I bumped into you."

"I was going over to Ralphs in Westwood. I usually go there when I'm batching it."

"How about a steak here? I have dinner by myself and go to bed around nine. My mother doesn't wait for me. She eats early and then goes to the show."

"So I'm all alone with a movie star. This is the first time that ever happened to me. I have a confession to make, though. I've never seen you on the screen. I recognized you from the ads, I guess. I don't go to the movies very much."

"Well, what do *you* do for a living? Maybe I don't buy what you sell, either."

"No, I don't guess you do. I'm a chemist with the Signal Oil Company."

"I buy oil," she said.

"Well, my job isn't the kind of oil you use. I'm supposed to be developing certain by-products."

"Whatever that means. Wouldn't you like to make a pass at me?"

"You mean it?" he said.

"Yes. If you don't, I'm liable to make a pass at you," she said. "Come on over and sit next to me."

"I don't get it," he said.

"Neither do I, but I don't care. I don't even care what you think of me. I'll never see you again, so it won't matter. But when the taxi comes, here, you give him this five-dollar bill and tell him you won't need him. That's him now. They're very prompt."

"You sure you want to go through with this?"

"Well, not if we start talking about it. Will you send the cab away?"

"Sure," he said. He went to the door and dismissed the taxi. "What about your mother?"

"My room's in a different part of the house. We can go back there now." She stood up and he embraced her, and they knew quite simply that they wanted each other. "See? You did want to make a pass at me."

"Sure I did, but I wouldn't have," he said.

"Well, I would have," she said. "Come on."

They went to her room and he stayed until eleven o'clock. "I wish you didn't have to go, but I have to be up at five o'clock. And I guess you'll probably want to phone your wife. Do you phone her every night?"

"Just about."

"Well, tell her you didn't phone her earlier because you were in bed with a movie star."

"Shall I say who?"

"No, maybe you better not. You're going to have to tell her about the accident, and that's the first thing she'll think of, is what happened after the accident. Do you realize something?"

"What?"

"You're never going to be able to mention my name again without her thinking you did go to bed with me. That's always going to be in the back of her mind."

"No."

"Yes. Believe me. That's what I'd think, and that's what she's going to think. That maybe, *maybe* that night you had the accident and didn't phone her, *maybe* you spent the night with that Natica Jackson."

"I don't know but that you could be right," he said. "You have her figured out pretty well, for somebody that never saw her."

"That's because I think I know the kind of a girl you'd be married to. Did she ever know you were untrue to her?"

"Well, there was only one other time and that was in Houston, Texas."

"But I'll bet she watches you like a hawk."

"Yes, she's inclined to be jealous."

"And so are you."

"Yes, I guess I am," he said.

"Well, Hal Graham, I guess it's time you went home," she said. "I'll call you another cab." She did so.

"Where is your mother now?" he said.

"My mother? I guess she's in her room. Why?"

"I just wondered," he said. "You know, she'd think it was strange if she was sitting out there in the livingroom and I walked by."

"Well, she might," said Natica. "It doesn't happen all the time."

"That's what I meant."

"Don't get me wrong. It does happen. But not all the time," said Natica. "That is, I don't have a strange man here every night."

"I could tell that," he said.

"How?"

"Oh—it's hard to say. But you know these things. This house is so quiet, I got the impression that it's always quiet, and you're lonesome. Lonely, I guess is the better word. I get an altogether different impression than I had before."

"Of how a movie star lives?"

"Yes."

"Yes. Well, of course some of them are married. Most of them are," she said. "But I never got that lonely, that I wanted to marry the kind of a guy that wanted to marry me. I wouldn't marry an actor, even if I was in love with him. But if I didn't marry an actor, who else would I marry? Regular people don't understand the way we have to live. The only person for me to marry is a director. Then I wouldn't be always wondering whether he married me because I was a movie star, because I made a lot of money. I'd be willing to marry a big director, but they all have somebody. A wife or a girl friend. Or both. Or they're queer."

"You wouldn't marry a queer," he said.

"No, I guess not. Of course some of them are double-gaited, and some of the double-gaited ones are just as masculine as anybody."

"Do you speak from experience? You sound it," he said.

"Don't start asking me about my experiences. By tomorrow morning you'll be one of my experiences. And I'll be one of yours."

"The big one. Practically the only one. I don't know whether I'll be able to take it so casually."

"Yes you will. You will because you have to. Maybe not casually, offhand. But don't look at the dark side. Look on the bright side. From now on you'll be able to say to yourself, these movie stars are just like anyone else."

"The only trouble with that argument is I didn't think of you as a movie star. I never would have made a play for a movie star."

"You didn't have to. The movie star made a play for you."

"I had other girls make a play for me."

"But you didn't go to bed with them."

"Before I was married I did, but not after I was married. Except for the girl in Houston, Texas."

"And she was a whore," said Natica.

"No. She was the wife of a friend of mine."

"Oh, I thought she was some girl you met at one of those conventions."

"It was a convention, but I knew her before. She and her husband live there in Houston. He's another chemist. I went to Cal with him, and she was there at the same time, a couple classes behind us."

"Was she your girl at Cal?"

"No. I didn't have a girl at Cal, till senior year. The girl I married."

"Oh, so the one in Houston—"

"Was never my girl. But when I showed up at the convention and we all had a lot of drinks, that's all it was. Her husband passed out completely, and she said we ought to make up for lost time."

"Was he your best friend?" said Natica.

"No, just a friend. A fraternity brother. He was never my best friend. I don't have a *best* friend. I have guys I like to go fishing with, and others I work with at the lab, and there's two or three of us that play tennis together. But for instance I don't have anybody that I could tell what happened tonight, even if I thought they'd believe me. You're the first person I ever told about the girl in Houston."

"Then maybe I'm your best friend," she said.

He smiled. "Well, at least temporarily," he said.

"Did you ever stop to think that maybe we're both kidding ourselves?"

"How so?"

"About never seeing each other again," she said.

"Well, we oughtn't to," he said.

"You're weakening," she said.

He stared at the empty fireplace. "Possibly," he said.

"I've weakened already," she said. "I go by your house every day, twice a day, only a half a block away. Today I just happened to feel like turning off Motor Avenue into Marshall Road."

"Place. Marshall Place. Yes, you told me," he said.

"Why?" she said.

"Because you were tired of taking the same route every day. You told me."

"But I didn't say why, because I don't *know* why," she said. "Why did I turn off today instead of last week, when your wife was home? Why did you happen to be starting your car just at the same exact moment that I came along? Why did you feel like going to Ralphs at just that exact moment? If you stopped to tie your shoe or change your necktie, you wouldn't have been in your car when I hit it. It would have been sitting there at the curbstone, and I would have driven right by your house."

"The laws of probability."

"I don't know what that means," she said.

"Oh, I was just thinking of probability and chance, in mathematics. There wouldn't be any way to work it out mathematically, that I know of. So it comes down to luck, which is beyond our comprehension. Good luck or bad luck, or a little of both."

"Mathe-*matics?*"

"I use mathematics in my work, quite a lot."

"I thought you were a chemist, with test tubes full of oil."

"Actually I'm a chemical engineer, in research. It saves time to say I'm a chemist, since nobody knows or cares what kind of work I'm doing. Not even my wife. She was an English major, and if I told her what I did at the lab on any given day, she wouldn't understand it any more than you would. Plus the fact that it's a team operation, with five other men working on it."

"You have five men working under you?"

"As a matter of fact, I have," he said. "But how did you know I was in charge?"

"Just guessed," she said. "Then you must be pretty important."

"I'll be pretty important if I get the right results."

"And rich?"

"Rich? Well, no, not rich, but I'll be set for life. I probably am anyway. That is, I'll always make a pretty good living."

"What do they pay you now?"

He laughed. "Well, if you must know, eighteen thousand a year."

"I guess that's a lot in your business," she said.

"It's a lot in any business except yours, and I don't consider movies a business."

"Money is money," she said. "They don't look at a ten-dollar bill and say, 'Oh, this is Signal Oil Company money. That's worth twice as much as Metro money.' "

"No, they don't. But what will you be earning twenty years from now?"

"Two hundred thousand dollars a year," she said.

"What?"

"That's what Morris King says."

"Who the hell is Morris King?"

"My agent, and a multye-millionaire."

"Well, I hope he's right, for your sake," he said.

"He usually is. He advanced my career from seventy-five a week to seventy-five thousand a year, and next year I get more, and the year after that and the year after that."

"A young girl like you making that much money."

"Shirley Temple makes more, and she's a lot younger," said Natica. "But I'm getting started, according to Morris."

"Is that what you want most? Money?"

"I know God damn well I never want to be without it," she said.

"What about love? A home? Children?"

"Yeah, what *about* love? And a home and children. You picked a fine time to ask."

"Yes, I did, didn't I?"

"You have a home and children, and I suppose you love your wife, but you're still not satisfied."

"No, I guess I'm not," he said.

"Well? What do *you* want most?" she said. "Not money."

"No, not money for its own sake. I want to do certain things in my work, and I guess that's uppermost. And have a nice home and educate my children."

"And every once in a while somebody like me," said Natica.

"Yes."

"But not too often," she said. "You'd like to have your home and children and someone like me, off to one side, and your work uppermost. That's funny, me in the same category with your wife and kids. That would get a laugh in Culver City. But I guess that's the way most men would like to have it, and that's why I don't get married. I'm too independent, I guess."

"Maybe," he said.

"But I'm not independent," she said. "I have to get up at five o'clock in the morning and drive to Culver City. I'll toot my horn when I'm passing your house."

"You'd better have them check your alignment. You hit my car just hard enough to knock yours out of line."

"No, I think I'll just trade mine in on a new LaSalle. So the next time I run into you I'll have a new car. How early do you have to get up?"

"Oh, generally around seven," he said.

"You'll sleep soundly tonight," she said.

"I'll say I will."

"So will I," she said. "Be funny if all we got out of this experience was a good night's sleep for both of us. But don't count on it."

"I won't. What you started to say about if I stopped to tie my shoe, or put on a different necktie. We got sidetracked, but there's something in it."

She scribbled on a piece of paper. "Here. This is the number of my dressing-room. It's private, doesn't go through the Metro switchboard. If I don't answer it'll be my maid, but don't tell her anything. She gossips plenty about other girls she worked for, so she's sure to gossip about me. Tell her Mr. Marshall called, and I'll know who it was."

"I'll give you my number at the office," he said.

"No, I don't want to know it. You think it over, and if you want to see me again, call me up. But think it over first. You have the most to lose. Besides, *I* may not want to see *you*. But don't count on that, either."

"What's a good time to phone you?" he said.

"You have to keep trying. I never know when I'll be in my dressing-room or on the set." She looked at him, standing with his hand on the doorknob.

"What are you thinking?" he said.

"Wondering," she said. "But not really wondering. I know."

"So do I," he said.

"Left, and then straight down the hall," she said.

She heard the taxi pulling away. She reached out her hand to the table beside her bed and picked up a typescript, opened it to the next day's scene. "No," she said aloud and replaced the script and turned out the light.

At half past five the next morning she left her house, went down Sunset Boulevard, turned in at Beverly Glen and across to Pico and from Pico to Motor Avenue. She slowed down when she came to Marshall Place. She turned right and moved along in second gear. His car was at the curb. The left door and the running board had been given quite a banging. She looked up at the second-story windows. Two of them were wide open. His bedroom, without a doubt. He was sleeping there, and without a doubt he was sleeping heavily. If she tooted her horn she would wake up the whole neighborhood. She did not mind waking up the whole neighborhood, but it would be cruel mean to wake him. And so she kept going, through Marshall Place to the other end where it led into Motor Avenue, and ten minutes later she was on the Metro lot.

The early workers were already at their tasks and Natica Jackson was soon at hers, which began with the arrival of the young man from Makeup. "Somebody didn't get enough sleep last night," he said.

"You're so clever," said Natica.

"Oh, it's not bad," he said. "Not hopelessly bad. You're young. Not like some of these hags I have to bring to life again. Actually I love to work on you, Miss Jackson, especially around your eyes. But get your eight hours, always try to get your eight hours. And here's some of those drops for when you start shooting. Remember now, don't put them in your eyes till you're ready to shoot, and use them sparingly. They're very strong, and I don't want you to get used to them." He prattled on, and his prattling and professional ministrations returned her to her movie-actress world, and she stayed there all day. Lunch was brought to her in her dressing-room. She read the gossip columns in the newspapers and the trade papers. She was visited by a man who owned a chain of theaters in New England, who was being given a tour of the studio. He wanted her *personal* autograph and not just one of those printed things that meant nothing. She asked him if he would care for a sandwich or something, but he thanked her and said he was having lunch with William Powell and Myrna Loy. She resumed eating her lunch and was interrupted by a girl from Publicity who wanted her to give an interview to the Hollywood correspondent of some paper in Madrid. "Don't do it if you don't feel like it," said the publicity girl. "But if you do, make sure you don't get alone with him. He's a knee-grabber." A stout man with a cigar tapped twice on her screendoor and pushed it open. "May I come in? Jason Margold, from New York City. I see you're eating gyour lunch," he said. "Would you rather I came back in ten-fifteen minutes?"

"Who did you say you were?"

"Jason Margold, from New York City. But I don' wanna disturb you while you're—I see you got a preference for cottage cheese. You know what's good with cottage cheese? Try a little Major Gray's chutney."

"What's this all about? Who are you?"

"My card," he said. "My business card."

She read it aloud. "Jason Margold, vice-president, Novelty Creations, New York, London, Paris. So what?"

He removed the day's newspapers from a folding chair, placed them on the floor, and seated himself. "You mind the cigah?"

"Quit stalling around, will you?" she said.

"I won't take but a minute of your time, Miss Jackson," he said. "It jus' happened I said to Jerry Lockman, I said who in his opinion was the real coming star on the Metro-Goldwyn lot."

"Oh, you know Jerry Lockman?"

"Jerry jus' happens to be my brother-in-law, once-removed. His sister, the former Sylvia Lockman, is married to George Stern. George used to be married to my sister Evie till she passed away of heart trouble several years ago."

"And?"

"So I asked Jerry, who was the young star that they were banking on the most here at Metro-Goldwyn. And without a moment's hesitation he named you. Miss Natica Jackson. So I said right away I wanted to have this talk with you for the purpose of sounding you out on this excellent proposition whereby, whereby we could work this out to our mutual advantage and profit."

"Is this a tie-in?"

"Well, you might call it a tie-in, but tie-in usually means a product gets tied in to a certain motion picture and like they run your picture in the ads and the actress never gets a nickel out of it, only the publicity for the motion picture. We'd be willing to pay you a royalty on every item we sold bearing your name."

"What is the item? A pessary?"

"Huh?"

"You're so God damn mysterious, I thought you didn't want to come out and say what it was."

"Well, it isn't anything like what you mentioned, Miss Jackson. It's an item of hand luggage that we expect to sell up in the millions."

"If I got five cents on every pessary I'd make a lot of money, too. The Natica Jackson pessary."

"You got a sense of humor, I'll give you that," he said.

"I need it, in this business," said Natica. "Just a sec'." She dialed a number on the intra-studio telephone. "Me speak to Mr. Lockman. It's Natica Jackson."

"You checking on me?" said Margold.

"Hello, Jerry? This is my lunch-hour and I'm supposed to get some rest. What the hell do you mean sending some jerk relation of yours to my dressing-room? Come and get him out of here before I call the studio cops. That's *all.*" She hung up daintily.

"Now*way* da minute. Why did you have to go and do that?" said Margold.

"Miss Garbo's dressing-room is down the way. Try *her,*" said Natica Jackson.

"You din even listen to my proposition," said Margold.

"Screw, bum," she said. "Take a powder."

Margold left. It was fun to have Jerry Lockman in such an embarrassed position. She could imagine how he was stewing now, for fear that she would tell other executives about his brother-in-law once-removed. Let him stew. Let him roast in hell.

"The car's downstairs," said her maid.

It was an elderly Cadillac limousine, to take her to the back lot. "You ready to go? You got everything?" said Natica.

"I think I got everything," said the maid. "Two packs of Philip Morris, makeup box, your mules, two packs of Beech-Nut gum."

"Do you have the eye drops?"

"In the makeup box."

"We're off," said Natica. She was in a bathing suit and a

bathrobe, ready for the scene on the back lot, in which she was to drive a motorboat a distance of forty feet. The scene had originally been written to take place in a diner, but it had been changed to give her an opportunity to wear the bathing suit. They had shot the scene five times that morning and it had never been right. They were afraid to expose her to the sun for more than a few minutes at a time. The last thing they wanted was for her to acquire a natural sunburn that would not match her body makeup. The shooting schedule called for a ballroom scene the next day, and two hundred extras had been hired for it, but if the fair skin of Natica Jackson was reddened by the sun in the motorboat scene, they would have to shoot around her. Moreover, the natural light changed at three o'clock in the afternoon, and if they didn't get the motorboat scene right before three they would have to come back and shoot it again sometime. The complications had nothing to do with acting, but Natica was used to that. Acting was the last thing you did after everything else was ready, and you did that for two minutes at a time. Then they glued those two minuteses together until they had eighty minutes that made sense—and then they put you in another picture. She could not understand how people got an impression of you from this collection of two-minute, one-minute, thirty-second snatches, but they did, and if they liked you that was all that mattered. Of all the girls she had known in Santa Ana she was the only one who could say, "I'm going to get a new LaSalle," at eleven o'clock at night and be sure that it would be delivered to her the next afternoon. She was certainly the only Santa Ana girl who had been kissed by Robert Taylor, and Garbo had smiled at her. Life was funny.

They did the motorboat scene three times while the light was still right. The director rode back to Natica's dressing-room with her. "I think the second take'll be the one, but I won't know till I see the dailies," said the director. "Let me have a look at your nose."

"It feels all right," said Natica.

"Yeah, it looks all right," said the director. His name was Reggie Broderick and he had grown up in the business. He spoke the jargons of the camera and lighting crews, he knew or could improvise sight gags that were not in the script, and he loved to direct motion pictures. He was not quite an artist, but his pictures always displayed ironic touches that other directors admired. "You got a new fellow, Natica?" he said.

"Maybe," she said. "Why?"

"Maybe, meaning you're not sure he's going to be your fellow?" said Reggie Broderick.

"Something like that," she said.

"Well, that's all right," said Reggie. "But send him home early, in time to get your eight hours. It's a good thing we didn't have any close-ups today, or you'd have been a total loss."

"I'm sorry," she said.

"No harm done, but tonight go to bed early."

"Was it my eyes?" she said.

"It wasn't only your eyes. You went around all day with your buttons showing."

"My buttons? In a bathing suit?"

"Your nipples, dear," he said. "You were a woman fulfilled, today. You can hardly wait to get back to this guy, whoever he is. Which is all right, as long as you get your sleep."

"I never even thought about him, all day," she said.

"Subconsciously you never thought of anything else," he said.

"Well, maybe you have something there," she said.

"We only have twelve more days on this picture, kid. As a favor to me will you postpone any emotional crisis? Only twelve more days."

"You know what I said to him last night?" she said.

"No, I can't even *guess* what you said to him last night."

"We were talking about marriage—he's married. And I said the only kind of a guy that I ought to marry is a director. I wouldn't think of marrying an actor, and the only person I could think of marrying was a director."

"Well, I tell you what you do. You finish this picture for me and I'll marry you. Unless you had some other director in mind."

"I didn't even have *you* in mind," she said.

"I must be losing my grip," he said.

"You never showed any interest, that way," she said.

"That's because this is our first picture together," he said. "The next time we do one, I'll see to it that we have a couple weeks on location. Where would you like to go? Don't say Catalina. That's too near. How about the High Sierras?"

"Why does it have to be on location?"

"Because I have to go home at night otherwise," he said.

"Oh, this wasn't going to be marriage," she said.

"I thought we got away from marriage," he said.

"I'm back to it," she said. "I think you ought to marry me and see that I get to bed early."

"Or vice versa. But meanwhile what about this guy that kept you up last night? What do we do about him?"

"That's going to be a problem," she said.

"Who is he? Can you tell me? I'm not butting in, but you went serious on me all of a sudden. How is he going to be a problem?"

"I guess I *was* thinking about him all day, subconsciously. I expected him to phone me, and he didn't," she said.

"He might have phoned while there was nobody here," he said.

She shook her head. "I expected him to keep trying. I was here all during the lunch break, and my phone never rang. And we've been sitting here over half an hour."

"And there's some reason why you can't phone him," he said.

"I told him I wouldn't. That he had to phone me. I don't even know his number. I know where to reach him, but I told him I wasn't going to try, that it was up to him."

"Are you going to sit here all evening in case he does phone? I don't think that's such a good idea."

"No, if he hasn't phoned me by this time, he isn't going to," she said.

"How would you like to come home and take pot-luck with the Brodericks? Mona's a great fan of yours. If you don't mind eating dinner with two small boys, aged seven and ten."

"I can't figure you, Reggie," she said. "Are you a family man, or aren't you?"

"I'm a family man," he said.

"And a Catholic, I guess, with that name."

"A family man and a Catholic," he said. "But I've had some things to tell in confession. And not just eating meat on Friday."

"Then why didn't you go for me?"

"I don't always go for the girls in my pictures. Not even most of the time. Very seldom, in fact. It interferes with the work, and this is my job."

"But you like me. I can tell that. You've been nicer to me than any director I ever worked with," she said.

"Yes, I like you. I asked to do this picture, you know. They had me down for something else, but I wanted to work with you."

"Who was in the other picture?" she said.

"A prima donna. Somebody I never worked with, but I heard all about her from another director. And *she* wanted *me.* The studio got a little tough when I said I wanted to do this picture and not hers. They would have put me on suspension if they hadn't been afraid of the bad publicity. Not the bad publicity for me. They didn't give a damn about that. But it would have got out that I preferred working with you, and that would have given her a black eye. So they told her I was off on one of my benders and wouldn't be in shape by the starting date of her picture."

"Were you off on a bender?"

"No, but I'd have gone on one," he said.

"Why did you want to work with me?"

"Because so far all they've done is photograph you. I looked at every picture you ever made, including one dog you made at Warner's."

"And was that ever a dog!" she said.

"Then I saw you in a dumb musical they made here, and a comedy Jerry Lockman produced. You used to be his girl."

"Yes."

"I can well understand why you gave him the air. They've never known what to do with you around here. This picture we're doing now. It isn't the greatest thing in the world for you, but I've made a good try with it. It's a common-ordinary program picture that'll make some money, but the pleasure I get out of it is what it'll do for you, and therefore for me. You're going to be surprised when you see this picture. How much have you seen?"

"Most of the footage that I'm in, but that's all," she said.

"Well, there's a lot more to the picture than that. By this time I can pretty well visualize the whole thing, the final cut. From now on you can figure to be in pictures the rest of your life. You have a career."

"I thought I *had* a career," she said.

"Two years? Three years? You'd be surprised how many women had two or three years at a big studio, and then disappeared. I don't mean disappeared to Republic. I mean disappeared entirely. And you never quite know why. They brought a girl out from New York. She was beautiful, she could act. She'd been a hit in two big plays on Broadway, and they signed her to a contract that was something fantastic. Five thousand a week. They gave her a deal that was absolutely unheard of for somebody that'd never been before a camera, but they wanted her. Do you know where she is now? She's back in New York, living in a hotel and waiting for Hollywood to come to their senses. She was in exactly two pictures. The first one was one of the most expensive pictures they ever made here. The story costs alone amounted to over two hundred thousand dollars. A top director. An expensive cast. The works. And it wasn't bad. It really wasn't a bad picture. But nobody went to see it. The people didn't care whether this girl had a Broadway reputation, or how many writers worked on the picture. They couldn't knock her looks. She photographed beautifully, and she had a good voice. *I* couldn't figure out why the picture laid such an egg. Then I happened to be in New York about a year ago and I was having lunch at the Algonquin and this girl came in. I never knew her when she was in pictures, and I asked the guy I was having lunch with what she was doing. The guy was a playwright, knew all the Broadway crowd, and when I asked him about this dame he said—as if I was supposed to know—he said she had a new girl friend. She was a Lez. I'd never known that, and I don't think most people in Hollywood knew it. But do you know who did know it? Those people that pay to go to see movies. Most of them have never heard of the word Lesbian. Wouldn't know what I was talking about if I said some actress was a Lez. But they knew something was wrong, something was missing. Some warmth that wasn't there. As soon as I got back to the Coast I ran that picture, and there it was. But only after I'd been told. I called up the director, a friend of mine, and asked him about this dame. I put it to him straight. Did he know she was a Lez when he was working with her? He said no, never suspected it for one minute. He knew there was something lacking, but he blamed himself. He never knew about her till after she washed up in pictures, and then some New York actress told him."

"You should have asked me," said Natica.

"You know who I'm talking about?"

"Sure. Elysia Tisbury."

"Now how did you know? A high school kid from Santa Ana?"

"My feminine instinct," said Natica.

"No, I won't buy that. No."

"Well, I was given a hint," said Natica. "She used to go out with Alan Hildred."

"Oh, your English boy friend. So she did. So she did."

"But that doesn't mean I'm that way," said Natica.

"You know, if I ever found out that you were, I think I'd start wondering about myself," he said. "You're about the last person in the world I'd ever think that about."

"Ooh, but when I get to be a big star," she said.

"You're planning to turn Lez?"

"I'm thinking of it," she said. "Alan says I'm terribly unsophisticated."

"Well, he's not."

"I know. He tries to sophisticate me."

"A guy like that could sophisticate you right out of pictures. Or would, if you didn't have so much common sense."

"Well, I'll say this for Alan. He's fun to *be* with. Not all the time. But I never knew anybody like him in Santa Ana. There *isn't* anybody like him in Santa Ana."

"There aren't very many like him in Hollywood," he said.

"You don't like him, but you're not a woman. If I was just one of those girls I went to high school with, I never would have understood a person like Alan. All they ever wanted was to marry a boy that had a father that owned a bank or something. That wasn't what I wanted. I wasn't even sure what I did want till I got this offer from Hollywood. Then I knew what I wanted, all right."

"What?"

"To have every big star know who I was," she said. "Not for me to know every big star. But every big star to know me."

"Well, they just about do," he said.

"G.G. spoke to me one day. Not exactly spoke to me, but nodded her head and smiled. I think she knows me now."

"All right. What's next?"

"To have my name in lights on the Statue of Liberty."

"That seems reasonable enough," he said. "Then what?"

"After that? Well, maybe a statue of me there."

"That'll probably happen. The Goddess of Liberty doesn't look very American, and you do. After that, what?"

"You know Joan of Arc?"

"Not personally."

"I'd like to be something like her," she said.

"You don't want to be barbecued."

"No, I guess I wouldn't go for that part. Who were some of the other famous women?"

"Cleopatra, but she got a snake to bite her right on the teat."

"No. Who else? Queen Elizabeth."

"Too late. She was known as the virgin queen."

"Do you think she really was? How old was she?"

"You can forget her. She wasn't very pretty. Mata Hari, but she got shot."

"It'd be fun to be a spy, but if I was famous I couldn't be a very good spy. They all seem to get in some jam. Martha Washington, but they only know about her through George."

"And Lincoln's wife went off her rocker," he said.

"My big trouble is, I'm not very glamorous. You can be famous without being glamorous. I'm pretty famous now, I guess, but people think they know all about me. America's niece, is what Alan calls me."

"You'll be more than that when we finish this picture."

"But not glamorous."

"No, but not all sweetness and light, for a change. The sexiest shot of you, you're wearing that housedress. I hope it gets by."

"I know which one that is. That was what you had the wind-machine for. Where I'm standing on the roof."

"That's the one. Better than a skin-tight bathing suit. You should have heard them in the projection room when they saw that shot."

"What did they say?"

"They said, 'Wow!' And they meant every word of it," he said. "Tomorrow they'll see you in a bathing suit and it won't mean a thing. But in that housedress, with the wind against you, you might as well have been soaking wet. But at the Hays Office they watch out for dames in soaking-wet dresses. This way I may sneak it by them."

"Was Jerry Lockman at the rushes?"

"Jerry Lockman? Jerry Lockman, the way he stands now,

couldn't get in a projection room if he paid admission. You don't keep up with your old boy friends. I hear they offered him the job of producing travelogs, and if he's smart he'll take it. They've gone sour on him."

"Oh, dear. Why?"

"You never know the real reason."

"Maybe the public found out that he's a Lez," she said.

"You may be kidding, but the things that turn the big shots against a man make just about as much sense. You and I, what they call the talent people, we tend to overlook the fact that our jealousies are nothing compared to what goes on among the big shots. Now Jerry Lockman, for instance. He more or less discovered you, with a little help from Morris King. So Jerry was instrumental in helping your career. Fine. But there are fifteen other supervisors on the lot that *didn't* discover you. Every single one of them thinks that's a black mark against *him.* So there are fifteen supervisors, or associate producers, or whatever they want to call themselves, that automatically hate Jerry. One of them happens to be Joe Gelber, the man that's producing our picture. He particularly hates Jerry because you were Jerry's discovery, so Joe has to go after Jerry hammer and tongs. Joe absolutely has to see to it that Jerry gets none of the credit if our picture turns out well. Which it will, don't worry about that. It'll make nice money. But Jerry Lockman mustn't be able to claim that he had even a tiny pinch of the credit for you. For the last six months, ever since Joe Gelber was assigned to this picture, he's had to put the knock on Jerry Lockman. Not only where you're concerned, but in every direction you can think of. I've heard him. He'll make fun of his clothes. Drops little jokes about his sex life. I heard him say it was very odd, very strange that Jerry went abroad on the *Europa* a couple years ago."

"What's wrong with that? I remember that," said Natica.

"The *Europa?* That's one of Hitler's boats. In case you're thinking of taking a trip abroad, young lady, don't book passage on the

Europa or the *Bremen*. Not while you're under contract here. Hitler isn't very popular in Hollywood."

"Oh, *Hitler*. He's against the Jews," said Natica.

"Hitler's against the Jews, that's right."

"But Jerry's a Jew," she said.

"Sure he is. But what kind of a Jew will travel in a boat owned by Hitler? Every opportunity Joe gets, he puts the rap on Jerry. And when a guy like Joe Gelber goes to work on somebody, he never loses his temper or says things that aren't true. He'll point out a hundred little faults that nobody ever noticed before, or that never bothered anybody. Jerry Lockman's neckties are no worse than L. B. Mayer's. But if you keep hammering away, calling attention to any man's shortcomings, you can finally get somewhere. And Joe Gelber has finally done a job on Jerry Lockman."

"Isn't it childish?"

"Yes. Childish and vicious. And it's exactly what Jerry would have done to Joe Gelber if he'd had the chance."

"You bet he would," said Natica. "A phony intellectual is what Jerry used to call him."

"If there's anything intellectual about Joe Gelber, it sure is phony."

"I wouldn't know," she said. "He has all those books in his office. I wondered when he got time to read them, but I didn't say anything."

"Well, he's on my side now. And yours. By the way, why did you ask me if Jerry was at the rushes?"

"I was wondering what he'd say when they all said 'Wow.' He would have been the only one that knew what was underneath that dress."

"Would you care what he said?"

She hesitated. "I guess I wouldn't," she said. "Not any more. A few years ago I would have. But you know I discovered something. When a man and a woman have something peculiar about their sex life, people always laugh at the man. They make fun of the man, but not of the woman. Have you ever noticed that?"

"I never thought of it before, but you may be right."

"Do you know why that is?" she said.

"No. I'd have to think about it."

"It's because men aren't supposed to be that much interested in sex. They should be more busy with their work and stuff. Sex is all right for women, but men ought to have it and forget about it."

"To rise supremely above it?" he said.

"I'm serious! A man that thinks about sex all the time, like Jerry, or Alan Hildred, I think he ought to have something else to think about."

"You're just restating an old poetic theory. 'Man's love is of his life a thing apart, 'tis woman's whole existence.' "

"Yes, we had that in high school," she said. "But look at the way a woman is constructed. She's built for sex. And a man—well, a man only partly. You never saw anybody put a brazeer on a man. Except at a drag. And even a drag! What do they do at a drag? They dress up like women."

"Do you really like sex, Natica?"

"I love it, but I'm a woman. I don't think men ought to like it so much. And yet every man I ever slept with does. Except that son of a bitch that didn't call me all day. Never gave me a jingle. And I know why. I was the one that made the first pass."

"Make a pass at *me,* dear heart, and *I'll* phone you tomorrow," he said.

"You know, I almost would. If we were at my house I would, but not here. Even in Jerry's office, when he'd lock the door and shut off the phone, I never felt right about it." She looked around her dressing-room, and shook her head. "Just a lousy chaise-lounge."

"For purity," he said. "Well, how about coming home and having dinner with us?"

"I just remembered. I'm supposed to have a brand-new LaSalle waiting for me." She dialed a studio number. "This is Miss Jackson. Natica Jackson. Do you have a car there for me? You have? How does it look? Does it have white-walls? Fine. Thank you. Okey-doke." She hung up.

"It's there?" he said.

"It's been there since early this afternoon. I'm glad. I loved my Packard, but I'm glad I don't have to see it again. Once I make up my mind to get rid of a thing, I don't care to see it any more. I wish I could be the same way about people."

"Who says you're not?" he said.

"It's not as easy with people," she said. "I'll give you the first ride in my new car."

"And have dinner with us?"

"I'd love to," she said.

"Let me call Transportation and I'll have somebody drive my car home, and maybe I ought to tell Mona you're coming. She won't want to have her hair up in curlers when you arrive."

"I won't mind."

"A figure of speech. I've never seen her hair up in curlers."

On the walk to the parking lot she was always half a step ahead of him. They admired the new car from all sides, and the parking attendant showed her the starting and lighting controls.

"Well, off we go," she said. Darkness had come.

She was a good driver and was taking pleasure in her new car. "Your new pony cart," he said.

"I never had one," she said.

"Hey! Straight ahead," he said. "Pico is straight ahead."

"This is Marshall Place, where I had my accident yesterday," she said. She had slowed down.

"Oh."

"He lives at Number 88. There, on the right. And there's his car. See the door, where I hit him? House all lit up. Maybe his wife came home unexpectedly. And maybe I'm just making excuses for him." She blew her horn, held her hand on the button, and drove away. "Well, so long to you, Mr. Hal Graham."

"He isn't one of our people," said Reggie Broderick. "Don't lose any sleep over him."

"Oh, you just don't want me to lose any sleep," she said.

They went to Broderick's house in Beverly Hills, and she was affable. The Broderick sons were delighted with her, the Broderick wife—after one hard look—was friendly. Natica gave the boys a ride in her new car (they chose to sit in the rumble seat), and when she brought them home again she did not get out of the car. She said goodnight to all the Brodericks and went home to Bel-Air. She lay in her warm, perfumed bath and wondered what the hell.

They finished the picture a day ahead of schedule, and Natica went away with Alan Hildred, to a borrowed cottage at a place called San Juan Capistrano. The water was too cold for her to swim in but Alan went in three or four times a day. They observed silences. He would take a pipe and a book and be self-sufficient until mealtime, sitting in the sand close enough to hear her if she called him. She slept late every morning, had breakfast of orange juice, toast and coffee; read the newspapers until lunchtime. After lunch she would read magazines and detective stories until sleep overtook her. She would nap for an hour, have coffee, and do some telephoning and letter-writing, and then it would be time for cocktails. He would have five, she would have two Martinis, and then dinner. The owners of the house, California friends of Alan's, had left behind an assortment of phonograph records as heterogeneous as the books on the shelves. Some good, some bad, and some cracked. At eleven o'clock, never later, she would go to bed and Alan would come in and make love to her, and for her it was a combination of sensation and detached remote observation. So it went for four days, as pleasant a stretch of time as she had ever known. On the fifth afternoon she went out and lay, belly-down, on the sand beside him. "Do you want to go home?" she said.

He took the pipe out of his mouth. "I suppose it's time we were thinking about it. Are you getting restless?"

"I could stay here forever, just like this," she said.

"Oh, really? I know *I* couldn't. I've got to think about making some money. So have you, for that matter. Don't they expect you for fittings next week?"

"Tuesday," she said. "Oh, I'm not kidding myself. I'm not rich enough to stop working, and wouldn't want to anyhow. But I've been so relaxed, Alan. That was you. I never knew anybody that was so relaxing. You can just sit and read, and smoke your pipe, off by yourself, and be perfectly content."

"You didn't know that side of me," he said.

"How would I? I guess I never knew you till now," she said. "Were you ever married, Alan?"

"Oh, yes."

"You never mentioned your wife. I just took for granted you were always a bachelor."

"Oh, no, I had a wife. Would you like to hear about it?"

"I'm dying to," she said.

"Well, it isn't much of a story, actually," he said. He sat cross-legged, tailor-fashion, and ran sand through his hands. "I'm older than you think."

"I was sure you were older than you look."

"Mm, thanks. I'm thirty-seven."

"You had to be, to've been to all the places you've been to," she said.

"Well, in some of them I didn't stop very long." He laughed. "In one place they wouldn't even let me land. Apparently my reputation had preceded me."

"What were you then? Were you a writer then, too?"

"Not, uh, recognized as such. I'd written a very bad novel, but I believe it stopped selling at two hundred copies. It was reviewed in a Yorkshire paper, and a pal of mine mentioned it in *Sketch.* No, I wasn't a writer. Various other things, but not a writer. Odd jobs, some of them very odd indeed."

"How did you meet your wife?"

"That was just after the war. I'd been in it, and I was still wearing His Majesty's uniform. I had a week or two to go before I was required to get back into cits, and I took every advantage of that situation. There were a great many parties in London, and crashing them wasn't at all difficult. I was, let me see, twenty-two. Been to a *fairly* good public school. Had two pips on my shoulder straps, and I'd acquired the M.C., the Military Cross. By purchase. It made all the difference, you know. No one asked how I got it, but they'd look at the ribbon and nod approvingly and *compel* me to drink some more champagne. It was too good to last, and I was only too well aware of that fact. Consequently, when I was introduced to Miss Nellie Ridgeway, the soubrette, who'd just been divorced from one of our more solvent bookmakers, I confessed to an undying devotion to her. There was some truth to that. I'd seen her in one or two shows, and I remembered one of her best songs. 'You and I in Love,' it was called. She was forty. Or she may have been forty-two. Perhaps a trifle thick through the middle, and not too firm up above, but the legs were good. Well, she consented to be my bride. Her money was unfortunately tied up in real estate holdings, not easily converted to cash, and I had one hell of a time getting my hands on any of it. She gave me ten quid a week, pocket money, but out of that I had to pay her cab fares and odds and ends, and she was extremely disagreeable because she didn't have a show that season and was having to spend her non-theatrical income. Actually, she was quite a chiseler, as so many actresses are apt to be. Always economizing on food and drink unless it was for show. A great one for professional discounts, too, and my tailor didn't give professional discounts."

"Was she good in the hay?"

"In a word, no. But insatiable. Stingy women are apt to be, I've found."

"So you divorced her."

"I left her. I took a few things. Her best gewgaws were locked up in a safe to which I didn't have the combination, but I realized about a thousand pounds on cigarette cases and vanities and that sort of thing, and off I went. I left a note, saying I was going to

Scotland to try to think things out and do some writing, and she'd hear from me soon. That gave me time to board a rusty old tub that was bound for South Africa. Very astute of me. Naturally she didn't quite believe the Scotland story, but expected me to head straight for the French Riviera. I wasn't the tramp steamer type, and certainly not the South Africa type. I was one of the Mayfair boys, or so she thought. I'd never given her any reason to think otherwise."

"How long were you married?"

"How long did we live together? Less than a year. We were never divorced. She died while I was on tour with the Miller Brothers-101 Ranch Circus. I read about it in the newspapers."

"What were you doing with the circus?"

"I was a Cossack."

"Could you ride?"

"Of course I could ride. I could do all those things. My father was a very keen sportsman, and as I was the only son amongst five daughters, I had a vigorous boyhood. Riding. Boxing. Shooting. Fishing. Not to mention the defense of my chastity against the onslaughts of the elder sisters. A nasty pair, they were. The English public school has a lot to answer for, but the upper middle-class English home such as mine, with five daughters and one rather pretty son—between the two I'll take the public school. It's possible to buy off an older boy with money or sweets, but two predatory older sisters are unbribable."

"Oh, well that's not just England. There was a girl on our street that had her little brother a nervous wreck, and her parents never caught on. Did you ever get married again?"

"No. The other side of me, that you've seen these past few days, has kept me from marriage or any similar involvement. I must have my privacy."

"Is that the way you pronounce it? You make it sound like an outdoor toilet. A Chic Sales. I say pry-vacy."

"Very well."

"What would you think of marrying me?" she said.

"Is that a proposal of marriage? I'd like you to state it more unequivocally."

"You mean lay it on the line? All right. Would you marry me?"

"Thank you very much, but no," he said. "I only wanted you to say it so it could go in my memoirs. October the somethingth, 1934. Received proposal of a marriage from lovely young movie star. Why would you want to marry me, Natica? You know I've pimped and buggered my way around the world all these years. I know you're a lonesome kid, dissatisfied. But don't for heaven's sake get yourself into anything like that."

"If I didn't like it, I could get out of it," she said.

He lit a cigarette. "May I offer two bits' worth of advice?"

"Sure," she said.

"Don't marry before you're fifty," he said.

"Fifty?"

"Take lovers, and make a lot of money, but don't marry. It'll only complicate your life, and it isn't as if you had to prove something by getting a husband. That presents no problem."

"You're wrong. No one ever asked me to marry him."

"Well, that's a quibble, isn't it? You could have a husband if you liked. These few days down here have been very pleasant for both of us. But they're only a holiday, and you can take a holiday when you feel like. Not always in such charming company, it's true, but the charming company can also be very difficult." He looked away. "I might bring a friend home with me. And he might be hard to get rid of. That *has* happened, you know."

"Oh."

"I can't help it, Natica," he said. "I seem to have a limited capacity for feminine companionship, and then I turn to someone of my own sex. Isn't that putting it delicately?"

"You get tired of girls, and then you go for the boys," she said.

"I was afraid you might have put it more crudely, but I should have known better," he said. "You don't seem to mind."

"I never said I didn't mind, but it was sort of none of my business."

"Well, of course it wasn't, was it?" he said. "The Kings, or at least Ernestine King, made it worth my while to officiate as your gentleman-in-waiting. Unhappily, as I made more money, I spent more. Old friends turned up that I hadn't seen in years. One of them came to stay, or so he thought."

"How did you get rid of him? How do you get rid of people like that?"

"In this case, I took him for a ride. A modification of the Chicago gangster method. We drove up beyond Oxnard and I stopped the car on the roadside. It was late evening, and I daresay I'd given him the impression that I had romantic notions. But I got out of the car and pulled him out, and my old boxing lessons stood me in good stead."

"You beat him?"

"Unmercifully," he said. "A boy for whom I'd once had a feeling of real tenderness. I couldn't stop punishing him. When he could no longer stand up, I gave him my boot. I left him there. What ugliness."

"Well, I guess he asked for it," she said.

"Oh, yes," he said. "He was no rose."

"That's another side of you I never saw," she said.

"And I hope you never do." He got to his feet and peeled off his sweatshirt. He was a slender man, with overdeveloped biceps and forearms that seemed to have been attached to the wrong torso. He walked slowly to the water and stood at knee depth, and when he was good and ready he dived in and swam out a long distance. She had seen him do that before, and the first time she was frightened, but when he returned, and she told him he had scared her, he had only smiled and said, "That's one thing I *can* do, my dear." Now she could see him, doing the dead man's float, and she was not worried about his ability to get back. But she knew with sudden clarity that one day—and it could be soon—he would not want to come back. He was—what was he? Thirty-seven—and ageless. He got older, because we all get older by the day, but he already spoke of his life, the events of his life, as though they had no relation to the present. An end had been put to his life, and the thing that had put an end to it was not an occurrence, a nasty event or a tragic occurrence, but simply the exhaustion of his will to live. She had never known anyone who caused her to think such thoughts. Everyone else spoke of things to come, for them, for her. But for Alan Hildred she had always been dimly aware that it was all over, and that she had forced or demanded the continuation of his existence. She had often put him aside, but she had always picked up with him again, and during this stretch of peace she had reached a state that she wanted to prolong by a marriage that could only be prolonged under precisely the conditions of these five days. If, this minute, he came out of the water and said he would marry her, she would go through with it. But the man floating in the troughs of the waves was going to stay there. He had tried to tell her that he was empty of desire for her, and it did not really matter now where he went next. She would let him go, and she would not ask him to come back.

She rose from the sand and returned to the house and took a bath. She put on a suit of lounging pajamas and went to the sitting-room, and presently he appeared, dressed in his blue blazer and slacks and rope-soled espadrilles. He had a scarf at his neck.

"Martini time?" he said.

"Sure," she said.

"It's a bit early, but the gin may warm me up," he said. "Besides, I have a rather important announcement to make."

"What's that?" she said.

"I'm leaving Hollywood," he said. He stirred the drinks and poured them.

"For good?"

"If you mean permanently, yes." He sipped his drink and obviously he was in a good mood. "I arrived here, in Hollywood, with something under two hundred dollars. I'm leaving with just under twenty thousand. I call that a successful sojourn, especially as the money was paid me for services rendered. Nothing illegal about it. They gave me twenty-five thousand apiece for the stories they bought for you, and they paid me to work on the scenarios. But it isn't going to last forever, is it? I imagine I could find someone a great deal less attractive than you to squire about, but you've spoiled me for the Nellie Ridgeway types. And I'm afraid the time has come when you're ready to give me my walking papers."

"What made you think that?"

"Your proposal of marriage, oddly enough. As I was lying out there in the deep blue sea, I asked myself what was behind your proposal. The good time we've had this week, obviously. But you've got to be back in town Tuesday next, and this relationship will never again seem as pleasant to you as it's been here. You had a premonition of that, too. I'm very happy to've made you at all happy, Natica, and in these four or five days I have given you some happiness, if that's not too big a word."

"Yes, you have," she said.

"Then forgive me if I desert you before you give me the air," he said.

"All right," she said. "You're under no obligations to me."

"Sensible girl," he said. "Extraordinarily sensible girl."

"Where will you go?"

"Sensible girl, asks the sensible question, too. I'm going home to England. I've been naughty, but my peccadillos have been committed in far-off lands. There's no one back home who's apt to turn me in for stealing Miss Ridgeway's gold lighters and ivory cigarette holders."

"And what will you do there?"

"Oh, we have a film industry in England, too, you know. And I have several imposing screen credits on Natica Jackson pictures. I shouldn't have too much trouble finding gainful, legitimate employment. And it's fifteen years since I've been home."

"Have you missed it?"

"Not in the beginning. But I don't want to die out here."

"Are you planning to die in England?" she said.

"Yes," he said. "And planning to is the word. My father cut me off when I married Miss Ridgeway, and all I'll have is the money I take back with me. I can live on that reasonably comfortably for four years without working in the films, without doing a tap. But I'm not going home to scrounge around or work as a dustman. I shall live at a certain scale, and when my money runs out, I'll shoot myself. Nothing terribly dramatic about that. Life isn't very dear to me anyhow. Look at mine. Look at me. Look what it's always been, and now I'm thirty-seven. Life has had its chance to be attractive to me, and I say it's failed dismally."

"I don't know whether you're joking or not," she said.

"I believe you know I'm *not* joking," he said. "I wish I could make love to you now, Natica, and have it mean much more than it ever has. But unfortunately all passion's spent. Will you accept that rather tired bouquet?"

"I accept it," she said.

"Will you also forgive me if I nip off first thing in the morning?"

"In whose car? You can't have mine."

"I'll hire one."

"I guess I might as well go too," she said. "I wouldn't want to stay here by myself."

"Splendid. Then let's get an early start, shall we?"

"Okay by me," she said.

They had dinner, and he drank more than usual. He finished the batch of Martinis, had sherry with his soup, and a Mexican red wine with his steak. He put a bottle of cognac at his side while he had coffee, and she saw that he was determined to get drunk. "I'm going to bed if we're getting up early," she said. "Did you tell Manuel we were leaving in the morning?"

"He's heartbroken," said Alan. "Rita's heartbroken, too, but not as much so as Manuel. He hopes we will come back many times and stay longer."

"Will you tip them in the morning?"

"Whatever you wish, my dear. I suggest twenty dollars, ten apiece."

"I'll give it to you in the morning," she said. "Goodnight."

In the morning her car was gone. Alan was gone, but his clothes had not been packed. She telephoned Morris King and had him send a Tanner Cadillac for her. When she arrived at Bel-Air her brand-new LaSalle was parked in her driveway, without a scratch on it. But she never knew what Alan did with her car in the meanwhile. She never heard another word from him, ever, and neither did anyone else in picture business.

"I could fix it so he'd never get work at Gaumont-British," said Morris King.

"Why would you want to do that?" said Natica.

"I thought maybe you'd want me to," said Morris.

"What did he do to me? I wouldn't want to keep anyone out of a job."

"Well, he sort of humiliated you," said Morris.

"I think you got that idea from Ernestine," said Natica. "He sort of humiliated her, because he didn't turn out right. But I have nothing against him."

"Then okay, we'll forget about him," said Morris. "You go in Tuesday for fittings, right?"

"Right," she said.

"I worked them for a $5,000 bonus," said Morris.

"You did? Good for you, Morris."

"And it's all yours. No commission. That make you feel better?"

"Five hundred dollars better," she said.

"Buy yourself something nice with it, with my compliments. You can consider it my bonus for being a good girl. However, Natica, you gotta be ready to go on suspension after the next picture."

"I do? Why?"

"Because when this one's in the can, then I'm going after a new ticket. Tear up the present contract and write a new one for you. This they will not do without some cries of anguish, including they'll put you on suspension. They gotta do that, Natica. The suspension gimmick is something a studio gotta do to keep people in line. Not you, so much as other people. They'll make it look like it's costing you a lot of money to turn down your next picture, but you'll get the money back in the long grun. That'll be taken care of. But I'm just forewarning gyou now, that this picture you work as hard as you ever worked in your whole life. Give them no cause for complaint, you see what I mean. Then they come around with a picture to follow this one and down we turn it. Flat. They turn around and say you don't work anywheres else, and so forth. Well, *we* know that. You're under contract to Metro, and you'll still owe them a couple more pictures under that contract. You can't work anywheres else. We know that. But in this business you strike while the iron is hot. I'm not waiting till they offer you a new contract, two pictures from now. I'm hitting them as soon as you finish this next one. They moan and wail, and they hit you with a suspension. But when they get done crying and threatening, I go in and talk to them and say who's the loser? And they know who's the loser. They are. You lose a few thousand dollars' salary on suspension, but it's big money if your suspension holds up a picture, and that's when New York starts calling gup. Straighten out that Jackson contract and quit futzing around, New York says."

"Well, I hope you're right," she said.

"Natalie, you're on the verge of—"

"Natica."

"Yeah, Natica. A slip of the tongue, when I get all enthused. Anyway, dear, we're gonna get you a contract that frankly you're not entitled to yet. Frankly, you're not. But we're only getting you what you'll be entitled to two or three years from now. I'm gonna fight to get you the kind of money they pay bigger stars than you are, but I'm doing git for a reason. You want to know what that reason is?"

"Sure."

"That reason is because your whole life is gonna be in pictures. Don't ever come to me and say get you out of a contract so you can do a Broadway play. If you do, you're gonna have to look for representation elsewhere. To me you are motion pictures and no place else. I don't want you to as much as walk on a Broadway stage. I don't want you monking around with Broadway."

"I'm not a stage actress. I know that," she said.

"You know it now, but these Broadway managers come out here and put the con on picture people. Art. The Theater. And all they do is stir up trouble. I got clients I *want* to go back and do a Broadway play every once in a while. *Let* them go back and take fifteen hundred a week or less. But that's for the actors and actresses that started on Broadway. I got all the confidence in the world in you, Natica, but I never want to see some Broadway critic take a crack at you because you're a movie star. You know why? Because I'll tell you why. Because I been going through the reviews of all your pictures since you were at Metro, and I never came across one single review that was a rap. Here and there they rap the picture, but never you. Everybody likes you. You. But some hundred-a-week guy on a New York paper is just liable to rap you because he don't like picture people."

"Well, that wouldn't kill me."

"Kill you, no. But out here they never saw a bad notice for you. They never *saw* one. And I don't want them to ever see one. But if some hundred-and-a-quarter critic on a New York paper raps you, the spell is broken, Natica. And we got a fortune at stake. Human nature is human nature, and once somebody takes a rap at you, others will follow suit. It's human nature, and I won't allow it. I got actors on my list that they go back to Broadway, and if they get one good notice in some New York paper, it keeps them alive for a year. They come back here and work in pictures, make some money, and they start itching for Broadway again. So all right. They're not picture stars. They're Broadway people. You are a film star, and you stay that way."

"Morris?"

"What?"

"Is somebody trying to get me for Broadway?"

"Huh? What makes you ask that question at this particular time?"

"Are they?"

"Hell, there's always some manager wishing to capitalize on a picture reputation."

"What is it? A musical comedy, or a play without music?"

"You know, for a young girl that was never outside of the State of California, I have to hand it to you," he said. "Ernestine often said to me, she said one of these days you'd surprise me with how sharp you were."

"I learned it all from you, and Ernestine. You still haven't said what the offer was."

"A musical comedy," he said. "I told them to get lost. They wanted to pay you a thousand a week and no guarantee of any kind whatsoever. They wouldn't even guarantee me they'd open in New York. You could spend all that time in rehearsal, anywheres from three weeks to a couple months out of town, and they could close the show in Baltimore. I told them to get lost. Imagine you coming back here after closing a show on the road, and I go into L. B. Mayer's office and start telling him why you ought to have a new contract. It makes me positively sick to think of it."

"What did Ernestine say?"

"She was positively nauseous, the gall they have coming out here and making an offer like that. The guy said it was a chance to prove what you could really do. And Ernestine said to him right to his face, 'Fifty million people go to the movies every week, and they're all that much farther ahead of you, Mister.' "

"Mr. What?" said Natica.

"You want to know his name? It's a fellow named Jay Chase. If that name don't appeal to you he used to have another one when I knew him in the old days. But what the hell, I had a different name then myself, and Natica Jackson used to be Anna Jacobs if I'm not mistaken."

"Getting me off the subject of Jay Chase, Morris," she said.

"Yeah, I was. But I'll get you back on the subject I wanted to talk about. You and pictures. Natica, I see you—do you know what I see you as? I see you as like Garbo. Gable. Lionel Barrymore. Crawford. I see you as much a part of the Metro organization as Mr. Schenck. L. B. Mayer. The lion. Wally Beery. Them. Some of my clients I can never hope for such an arrangement, whereby they got a home lot and it's a regular second home to them. You think of Metro and automatically you think of Natica Jackson. You think of Natica Jackson and automatically you think of Metro. That's the way I want it to be, because that way you're set for life. I want that for you before you start getting married and maybe you marry a fellow that gets you all discontented. But if you got a permanent home lot, that much of your life is all taken care of."

"You want me to marry Metro."

"Exactly. Or Metro to marry you. I don't care how you put it."

"Some people say a star is better off independent," she said.

"Yeah, that's what they say. You hear that all the time, from actors that it don't look so good for their next option. You hear it from actors that the studio only wants them for one picture. You hear it from agents that can't land a contract for more than one picture. Yeah, a star is better off independent, once he got about two million stashed away and don't care if he never works. But that won't be you for another ten years or so. You're a working girl, Natica."

"That's the only thing you said so far that makes any sense to me. I'm a working girl," she said. "Morris, you and Ernestine stop filling me up with big talk. All of a sudden I'm not a kid any more. I was eighteen and got into pictures, and almost got out. Then you and Jerry Lockman and Joe Gelber and a half a dozen pictures, and this guy and that guy. And my folks sponging off of me, and I get overcharged in the stores. And nearly all the girls I went to high school with are married and started a family. And I'm nearly twenty-four years old. A woman. Not a girl any more. Sixty million girls would like to trade places with me, and I'd be one of them if I wasn't Natica Jackson. I'm lucky, and I know it. But one of these days don't be surprised if I blow my lid."

"You're entitled," he said.

"Just don't be surprised, that's all," she said.

"What are you thinking of doing?"

"I've been thinking of going after something *I* wanted, for a change."

"A fellow?"

"What else? I can buy nearly anything else," she said. "This one I couldn't buy."

"Oh, you got him picked out. Well, you talk to Ernestine and next week we'll take him to the fights. Is he—"

"Oh, no, Morris. You and Ernestine have to stay out of this."

"Who is the fellow? How did you conceal him from us?"

"You put your finger right on it," she said. "You and Ernestine and the studio have to know everything I do. But this was one time I got away with something. Imagine. I slept with a fellow, and you and Ernestine didn't know about it."

"When did you have time to?" he said.

"I get a kick out of this," she said. "I got you puzzled."

"Just don't get yourself into any trouble."

"I know. A fortune's at stake."

"And you want to be sure he's worth it. Don't do nothing you'll be sorry for."

"I sure will," she said. "I am already, but I didn't know how good that can feel. The only thing I *have* felt, these last couple of years."

"Married, this fellow?"

"The works. Married. A good job. Respectable."

"What does he get out of it? What good's it gonna do him?"

"Him? It may not do him any good at all," she said.

The new picture went into production and Natica Jackson was a dream to work with. Everybody said she was a dream to work with: the director, the other actors and actresses, the producer, the unit man from the publicity department, the script girl, the assistant director, the little people from Wardrobe and Makeup, the little people from Central Casting, the little people from Transportation. She had always been easy to work with, but now she was a dream. She was cooperative, tractable, patient, and cheerful; and she was punctual and always knew her lines. She was also good. There is in Hollywood a legendary tribute to a scene well played. It is that moment when a performer finishes a scene and the grips and the juicers burst out in spontaneous applause. It is a phony. It does not happen. But there is the real thing, which happens no more than once or twice in a dozen pictures. It is that moment when a performer has finished playing a scene, and for perhaps a count of three seconds no one on the set speaks. There is complete silence on the part of everyone who has been watching the scene. The silence is usually broken by the director, who says—and does not need to say—"We'll print that." Then all the people on the set go about their business once again, the better for having witnessed a minute-and-a-half of unrecapturable artistry. Natica had two such moments in the new picture. One was during the scene in which she hears shots that she knows will kill her brother. The other was in a church pew, kneeling beside the gangster who she knows has killed him. In the one she blinks her eyes as though she were receiving the shots in her own body. In the other she is full of fear and loathing of her brother's murderer. Both were routine bits of screen writing, but they were redeemed by her potentially explosive underplaying. "This girl can go," said the director. "She can really go."

"Oh, she can go, all right," said Joe Gelber.

"Reggie Broderick told me she could go," said the director. "But you know how it is, Joe. One director can get it out of an actor, and the next director can't."

"You're getting it out of her, Andy," said Gelber.

"I know I am, but it had to be there in the first place," said Andrew Shipman. "What was she doing with that English fag?"

Gelber shrugged his shoulders. "What was she doing with Jerry Lockman?"

"That's true," said Shipman. "And who else did she have?"

"I don't know. Reggie Broderick, maybe."

"No, he said no," said Shipman. "He said she'll talk about it, but that's about as far as it gets."

"Well, you have over a month to find out."

"She may be what I call a cucumber," said Shipman. "Show business is full of cucumbers, but particularly in our business. They look good as hell, the answer to all your wildest dreams. But you get in bed with them and that's when you discover the cucumber. No steam. No blood. It's all an accident of how they photograph. Either that, or they save it for their acting. This girl may be a cucumber, but I hate to think so."

"She may be. Jerry Lockman, and the English fag. That's all we got to go on."

"Pending further investigation," said Shipman. "You're sure you never looked into the matter, Joe?"

"Listen, I'd tell you in a minute," said Gelber.

"Yes, I guess you would," said Shipman.

"I'd tell you quicker than you'd tell me. You held out on me before this."

"Only temporarily," said Shipman.

"Well, you want to know the truth, Andy," said Gelber. "I like them prettier than her. Either they gotta be prettier or so God damn perverted I don't want to be seen in public with them."

"You're as bad as Jerry Lockman," said Shipman.

"Maybe worse, but everybody found out about Jerry. I operate different. One big-mouthed dame spread it around about Jerry, because she was a star. Who would of listened to her if she wasn't a star? My motto is—well, I don't know. I guess I don't have any motto."

"I have. My motto is, if at first you don't succeed, you're wasting your time. I'll give you a report on Miss Jackson later on. But meanwhile, the kind of report the studio's interested in is all good. She can really go."

Every shooting day the girl who could really go drove her LaSalle past the Marshall Place intersections of Motor Avenue and was pleased with herself. Now the temptation to reenter Marshall Place and Hal Graham's life was completely controlled. Her mind was made up, she would call the shots. Early in the morning, on her way to the studio, as she came to the Marshall Place entrance she would call out, "Sleep well, get your beauty sleep, Mr. Graham. I'll be with you in a little while." First she must finish this picture, working hard and well and cheerfully. Then Morris King would make his demands, suspension would follow, and her time would be free. Homeward bound in the evenings, she would call out, as she came to Marshall Place, "Another day, another dollar, Mr. Graham. See you soon, Mr. Graham." She was happy. They were wonderful to her at the studio, they let her know they were pleased with her, and Morris King confided to her that he was planning to adjust his demands upward, so that her suspension might be longer than his original guesses of four to six weeks.

"The things I been hearing about your performance," said Morris. "If they were just a little smarter, the studio, they'd come to me and they'd offer to voluntarily tear up your contract. Imagine how good that would make them look? But the studio mind ain't constituted that way, so what'll happen is naturally I'll go in some day and they'll be able to tell by the look on my face that I didn't come in for any social call. But wouldn't they be so much smarter if they anticipated me?"

"And you say to them, you have all your other clients that will never work for Metro unless they give me a new contract," said Natica.

"You *think* it, and you get the thought across so *they* think it. But with Metro you don't threaten. RKO you can threaten. Universal you can threaten. Republic you don't even answer your phone. But Metro, the lion is the king of beasts, you know. You threaten without saying ganything. Jack Warner you can threaten, Harry Warner you don't. Harry Cohn threatens you first, and bars you from the lot. Sam Goldwyn don't use enough people, so when he wants somebody you let him come to you. He'll scream at your price, irregardless of what it is, but when he wants somebody he wants them, so you wait till he calms down and you knock off a few dollars and you got a deal. Agenting is a great business as long as they can't bully you. Nobody can bully me any more, and even Metro knows it, but all the same I'm careful who I threaten. None of these guys are using their own money, and I am."

"You're using my money if I get put on suspension," she said. "I'm the one that's not getting paid."

"You'll get it all back in the long grun. Just don't lose your confidence in yourself. And don't lose your confidence in me."

"I'm kidding," she said. "I've never been so confident in my whole life."

"Yeah, and it makes me wonder," said Morris. "Also it worries Ernestine. If you got one real friend in this business, it's Ernestine. So don't go antagonizing her too far. Everybody has to have one real friend in this business."

"Morris, you handle the studio, and let me ruin my own life," she said.

"I'll let you run your own life, but it sounded as if you said *ruin* your own life, by accident."

"Ruin is what I said," she said.

"All right, have it your own way," he said.

She invented, and rejected, a dozen ruses which would bring about her next encounter with Hal Graham. Some of them were neat and logical, and some relied on sloppy coincidence. They were all pleasant time-killers, anticipating the actual event, which she was willing to postpone because the postponement was in her hands. She was on the final week of the picture and beginning seriously to consider her plans for Graham and herself, and one afternoon Andrew Shipman told her she might as well go home early, that there was nothing more for her to do that day. "I'll need you in the morning," said the director. "Made up and on the set at eight-thirty."

"Eight-thirty? That's practically the afternoon," she said.

"Well, this won't take long. It's a retake of the long shots in front of the church. You might as well get used to loafing again."

"Thanks," she said. She did not point out to him that it would be close to five-thirty by the time she left the studio. Five-thirty was still better than seven-thirty.

She took off her makeup and changed into her slack suit and left the studio. It was still daylight as she drove up Motor Avenue, and as she proceeded she noticed that a pest was following her in a black Buick convertible. She was familiar with the type. They hung around the studio parking lots until they saw an actress leaving by herself. Sometimes they were impossible to shake until she got to the gate at Bel-Air, but once there she could stop and ask the watchman to intervene.

This one was the playful type. He began blowing his horn, and made no pretense whatever of not following her. She stepped on the gas, hoping to lose him, but he kept the same distance, and at Pico he even drove through the stop signal to keep up with her. Instead of turning in at Beverly Glen she kept on to Westwood Boulevard, hoping that the added distance would enable her to lose him in the Pico traffic. The strategy did not work. She was driving through the university campus, with Sunset Boulevard in sight, when he drew up beside her and maintained her speed.

"Do you want me to call a cop?" she shouted at him.

"No," he said.

Then she recognized him. He was grinning. "How do you like my new car?" he called to her.

She pulled over and stopped her car, and he did likewise. He got out and came to her car. "So it was you," she said. "I thought it was some high-school goon."

He put one foot on her running board and his elbows on the right-hand door. "How've you been?" he said.

"Oh, eating my heart out because you never called," she said. "You know, I've forgotten your name."

"Hal Graham," he said. "I've been reading a lot of compliments about you."

"You have? I thought you didn't like picture people."

"I don't, but you're the one I knew," he said. "This is *your* new car, eh?"

"Not so new. I got it the day after you ran into me."

"I ran into you," he said. "Well, we'll skip that. How do you like my chariot? I just took delivery on it last week. I almost got a LaSalle, but the resale value is better on a Buick. Of course you don't have to worry about that angle."

"Do you want to get in and sit down, or would you rather follow me home?"

"Whatever you want me to do."

"If we stay here the autograph hounds will start collecting," she said.

"Yeah, these kids are UCLA. Up at Cal we have more sense."

"If you're going to be unpleasant—"

"No, just joking." He went back to his car, and when she pulled away his followed her to her house.

"Is your mother home?" he said.

"Why?"

"I don't know. I just asked," he said.

"No. She's down at Santa Ana at some funeral. Would you like a drink?"

"Are you having one?"

"No."

"Then I won't."

"The last time you were here, your wife was down in Balboa or some place. Did she ever get back?"

"The next day. One of the kids took sick and she came home."

"And that's why you decided not to call me?" she said.

"Partly. Not entirely," he said.

"You were ashamed of yourself."

"Yes, I guess so. There was no percentage for you or me."

"Then why did you follow me today, blowing your horn like a God damn idiot kid? Going through that light at Pico. All those people from the Fox lot. You could have killed a dozen."

"I just wanted to see you, that's all. To talk to you," he said.

"What about, for God's sake?"

"Listen, don't be so stupid. In the first place, you're not that stupid. As soon as I saw you I would have followed you to Santa Barbara."

"Why not make it San Francisco? Santa Barbara isn't very far. Well, what shall we talk about, Mr. Graham?"

"Nothing, if you're not more friendly."

"Don't expect me to be as friendly as the last time. I learned *my* lesson. You should have learned yours, too."

"Well, I didn't. I thought I did, but I didn't," he said.

"I guess not. Not if you were willing to follow me all the way to Santa Barbara. That must be a hundred miles. You *are* romantic."

"No, it isn't a hundred miles," he said. "It's closer to sixty."

"I have no sense of distance," she said.

"You're sore at me because I didn't phone you that time. I'll make it worse. The kid didn't get sick. I made that up. The fact of the matter is, if I would have seen you the next day I never would have stopped seeing you."

"Is that so?"

"Well, as far as I was concerned."

"So you went back and worked on your invention," she said. "You had some kind of an invention you were working on. How did it come out?"

"It's coming along. It isn't an invention. It's a process."

"Tell me all about it, but some other time. So you went back to your process, and the wife and kiddies. Have you had any more kiddies?"

He hesitated.

"Don't *tell* me," she said.

"There's one on the way," he said. "I got a raise, and my wife decided we could afford another child."

"Oh, it wasn't that you were so ashamed of yourself that you had a guilty conscience, and became attentive to her?" she said.

"I wonder."

"You're stupid, aren't you?" she said.

"In some things, I guess I am," he said. "I don't pretend to be very good about people. I remember telling you I didn't have any close friends. My wife says I'm too wrapped up in my work, but why shouldn't I be? I know I'm good and I'm headed for somewhere. They gave me a raise, and next year the company's doubled my appropriation. My work is showing results two years ahead of time."

"Why, it's just like bringing a picture in ahead of schedule," she said. "You're stupid enough to be an actor, and you're almost good-looking enough to rate a screen test. You know you're good-looking, don't you?"

"So I've been told."

"Well, you are."

"Looks don't mean anything in my job. I never think about my looks, one way or the other. And it sure as hell wasn't my looks that you went for. You're with those movie actors all day."

"I want to ask you something. Is your wife pretty?"

"Oh, yes."

"Has she got a good shape?"

"Terrific. Beginning to get big now, with the kid on the way, but she has a great figure."

"Then why don't you get in your new Buick and dash home and jump right in the hay with her?"

"Because I don't feel like it."

"And why don't you feel like it?"

"Because I never got over you," he said.

"Oh, nuts," she said.

"That's true. And you never got over me. I told you, maybe you forgot, but I remember telling you I had plenty of girls before I was married."

"And then you quit, except for one girl in Dallas."

"Well, it was Houston, but I see you remember," he said. "I remember everything, too. I can tell you every word you said to me. I could draw you a sketch of the headboard on your bed. I am stupid about some things, because I don't care. But I remember everything about you."

"Well, do you want to refresh your memory?"

"If I do, Natica, this time we're starting something that may be hard to finish. I'm not going to just think about you all the time. So send me home now if you don't believe me."

"I believe you," she said.

"My wife's going to catch on, and she's going to make trouble."

"I know that. She would."

"Bad trouble, for you *and* me."

"Oh, stop talking about it. *Bad* trouble. What other kind is there?"

"Well, if I didn't love you it wouldn't be so bad. But I do."

"Do you? I never even thought about that," she said. "Well, maybe I did. Maybe I never thought about anything else."

"Why are you smiling?"

"Something a director said. It was about my buttons," she said. "I'll tell you later."

"Order me the hamburger and baked potato," said Morris King. "I want to go over and talk to Leo McCarey a minute."

"It'll get cold," said Ernestine.

"Well, order me one anyway and tell the girl to save it for me," he said.

"All right," said Ernestine. She turned to Natica. "What do you feel like having, Natica?"

"I think I'll have the avocado with the Russian dressing, to start with. Then I'll have the hamburger too."

Ernestine shook her head. "Where does it all go to? If I had the avocado—well, I'll have it anyhow." She waved the menu to summon the waitress.

"Good evening, Mrs. King. You decided?"

"Hello, Maxine. Yes, there'll be two avocados with the Russian dressing, and two hamburgers with the baked potato. Then also I want you to hold a hamburger and baked potato for my husband. He's over with Mr. McCarey."

"And coffee with?" said Maxine.

"Yes, I'll have coffee," said Natica. "How are you, Maxine?"

"I'm fine, thanks. I was home last Tuesday. They were all asking me did I ever see you. I said you come in once in a while."

"I didn't know you two knew one another," said Ernestine.

"We went to high school together," said Natica.

"Yeah, but what a difference," said Maxine. "I end up in a balloon skirt and look where she is today. Well, we're all proud of her. Nobody begrudges her success."

"Thank you," said Natica.

Maxine left. "She's cute," said Ernestine.

"Yes. She took a fellow away from me or maybe I would have married him."

"How could she take a fellow away from *you?*"

"By being cute. She married him, too, but I guess it only lasted a little while. Joe Boalsby. As dumb as they come, but awful pretty. Blond curly hair and built like a Greek god."

Ernestine put her elbows on the table, and looked at Natica. "I had a visit from your mother, Natica. She's fit to be tied."

"Well, get a rope and tie her."

"Is it true what she said? She said you put her out of the house."

"It's true," said Natica. "I got her an apartment on Spaulding. Eighty-five a month, furnished, and a colored woman to come in five days a week."

"Yes, well, Morris and I are kind of worried about that. You remember when we helped you with the house in Bel-Air, it was the understanding that your mother was to live there."

"I know," said Natica. "And I owe money on the house. But if my mother stays, I go. I'll take the apartment on Spaulding."

"She's in the way. Is that it?"

"That's part of it. I don't care where I live, but it's got to be alone. No member of my family is going to live with me. I can be out of the Bel-Air house tomorrow. Morris can sell it, and give me what I put into it."

"You're too big a star now to have a dingy little apartment on Spaulding."

"It isn't a dingy little apartment. It's a duplex with plenty of room, and the furniture is better than what my mother bought for the Bel-Air house. Listen, Ernestine. Let's quit beating about the bush. I have a new fellow. He's married, and has a job and all like that. He has no intention of marrying me, and I have no intention of marrying him. So far his wife hasn't gotten wise to it, but she will sooner or later, and then I don't know what'll happen. But the way I feel now, I'll trade places with Maxine if necessary. You can take Metro-Goldwyn-Mayer and stick it. I'm crazy mad for this fellow, and I never was that way for anybody. You have Morris, that you were married to for twenty years, but all I ever had was Joe Boalsby, that ditched me for Maxine, and Jerry Lockman, and Alan Hildred, and this one and that one in between. Do you want me to shock you? Or maybe it won't. Maybe it won't shock you at all. But to show you how hard up you can get, I asked Alan Hildred to marry me. I think that's what frightened him off, the poor bastard."

"Yes, it would," said Ernestine. "Not because he's a fag. But because he's a snob. You knew he married that English actress, older than he was."

"He finally told me, but I had to ask him," said Natica.

"He was ashamed of it. He's ashamed of his whole life, because he's a snob. Everything about his life he's ashamed of. You know who seduced him, don't you? His older sisters. And he turned fairy when he went away to prep school."

"You had the same conversation with him I had."

"Uh-huh."

"You're not trying to tell me he was *your* boy friend," said Natica.

"The only one," said Ernestine.

"Why? Did Morris cheat on you?"

"Not that I know of. Maybe he did. But that wasn't my excuse. I didn't have any excuse, except that I wanted to have a lover, and Alan showed up at the right time. Maybe I would have gone for him no matter when he showed up. I know for a while there I had Alan Hildred on the brain. Brain, nothing. I was like any silly middle-aged dame that gets stuck on a younger man."

"How did you get to know him?" said Natica.

"Oh, he came in the office one day, trying to get Morris to handle him. About four years ago, this was. He had a copy of some book he wrote, and he gave it to Morris and said he didn't think there was a picture sale in it, but he understood the movies were looking for new writers. Morris never reads anything, so he took the book and said he'd have someone in the office look at it. Meaning me, of course, only he didn't say so. Well, you know how Alan could be, when he wasn't having one of his homo spells. Charming. And I was having a hard time keeping from making passes at elevator boys. So we walked out of the office together and we went to a speakeasy, and he began sizing me up, and the first thing I knew I was lending him a hundred dollars. Me! I never lend anybody a nickel, without a promissory note, but here I was giving this total stranger a hundred dollars that I knew I'd never get back. But it wasn't only the hundred dollars. Morris and I were worth well over a million and I could afford it. But that Alan, he knew my psychology. 'Wouldn't you like to see where I live? It's only a few steps from here,' he said. And I went. One room in a little bungalow just off Vine. So I had my lover. He never asked for too much. I told Morris to get him a job polishing English dialog. They were doing a lot of English plays that they got American writers to adapt, but the dialog was too American. So that's how Alan got in pictures. Two hundred a week. Three hundred. Never any screen credit, but a living, and learning a little about writing for pictures."

"And then you palmed him off on me," said Natica.

"Well, later. I got a little afraid that he'd tell one of his boy friends about Mrs. Morris King. I wasn't afraid of Alan. I always trusted him. He was a gentleman. But some of his boy friends were real scum. Male whores. And I was afraid I might get a disease, and give it to Morris. That frightened me as much as blackmail, so I gave him up."

"I could have got a disease," said Natica.

"You were old enough to look out for yourself," said Ernestine.

"Then *let* me look out for myself," said Natica. "If I was old enough then, I'm that much older now."

"You're right, you are," said Ernestine. "Well, I had to talk to you, though. Morris wanted me to, and I'll always do what he says. Tomorrow's the day he goes to Metro and hits them for a new contract, and he wanted me to talk to you."

"And you did," said Natica.

"And I didn't get you to change your mind."

"You didn't want me to, did you?"

"I'd like to been able to tell Morris I got you to change your mind. But in a thing like this, one woman trying to change another woman's mind is only wasting her breath. I just hope you come out of this no worse off than I did with Alan Hildred. I could of got myself into a lot of bad trouble, but instead of that I only made a fool of myself in my own eyes."

"Bad trouble. That's what he says we have to be ready for," said Natica.

"Well, if he knows that maybe he'll have some sense, or at least be a little more careful," said Ernestine. She patted the back of Natica's hand. "I'm with you, if you need anybody."

"Thanks, Ernestine. I guess all you can do is pacify my mother. Keep her out of my way."

"If it was all as easy as that," said Ernestine. "Three days' work as a dress extra and she'll be glad to go back to the flower shop. Your mother is one of the dumbest dumbbells I ever knew."

"And one of the meanest."

"Yes, I'll bet she is," said Ernestine. "There's Bing Crosby sitting down at McCarey's table. I better get Morris away from there or he won't have sense enough to leave them alone. *Maxine, will you tell my husband we want him back?*"

THEY SNEAK-PREVIEWED THE new picture in Long Beach and Van Nuys and the comments were so good that the studio was in an awkward position, torn between the urgency to spread the word in the industry and the wisdom of postponing the happy news until Natica's contract was renegotiated. "They're playing it very smart," said Morris. "They can't suspend you till you turn down the next picture, so they don't seem like they're gonna show you a script. So you're still on salary. They may keep you on salary a long time without sending you a script. They can afford that. But on the other hand they want to be able to announce you in a new picture for next season. Sometimes they're smarter than I give them credit for."

"Well, what do you want me to do?"

"Keep out of trouble," he said. He was firmer, closer to anger, than she had ever seen him. "Get yourself in a scandal and all my work goes for nought. This fellow you're sleeping with, he's just about the perfect example of what a movie actress should lay off of. A young professional man, with a wife and kids and an excellent reputation. The All-American ideal husband, with the All-American ideal home. Broken up by a movie actress."

"Oh, you found out who he is," she said.

"You wouldn't tell me yourself, so I got someone else to find out for me. Yeah, a detective. The license number of his car, parked in your driveway. I got his credit rating, how much he earns, what he's working on. I guess you knew his father-in-law is a Presbyterian minister in Oakland."

"No, I didn't know that," she said.

"His uncle that he's named after, the same identical name, is the superintendent of schools in Whittier. Oh, I got it all, believe me. Your boy friend Graham, as far as I've been able to find out, there isn't a member of his family on either side that got so much as a parking ticket."

"Well, you don't want me getting mixed up with some saxophone player."

"You can lay off the sarcasm, too," said Morris. "You ever meet his wife?"

"No."

"Well, I got pictures of her when they were married and a trip they took the year before last. You know what type woman she is? The Irene Dunne type. In other words, he don't have the excuse of being married to some homely broad. This is a good-looking woman, and to cap the climax, she's having another kid. Oh, you picked good this time. What ever made you give up that English fag?"

"Graham."

"Well, what'll make you give up Graham?"

"Nothing. Nothing except Graham," she said.

"I wonder what'd make him give you up?"

"Right now, nothing. I don't say it's going to last, but we want it to."

"You just won't listen to anybody, will you?"

"I'll listen. I'm listening now," she said.

"This guy has a clean record, Natica. I spent over two thousand dollars checking, and outside of some college-boy dates, the only woman he ever got mixed up with was his wife."

"That may be," she said.

"You can count on it. Also, her record is even cleaner. She was a studious type and didn't have dates till she started going out with him. She wrote poems. She got some prize for writing a poem. People like that, you know, they're not like people in our business. They take things big. I'm trying to warn you."

"I've been warned. By Graham. I'll take the consequences."

"Big talk. What consequences? How much sleep are you gonna lose if you break up a home with three children?"

"Don't try that argument, Morris. I had to grow up without both my parents. I'm in love with this guy, and I don't want to think about anything else."

"All right. I give up."

"That's good. Don't try any fast ones," she said.

"When the roof falls in, I'll get you a good lawyer. That's all I can do now."

BERYL GRAHAM'S POETRY prize was a certificate, eight inches by ten, made of a simulated parchment stock, and matted and framed. It rested, rather out of sight, on top of the built-in bookshelves of the den at 88 Marshall Place. The text of the document stated that the eighth annual first prize for poetry of the San Luis Obispo County Poetry Society was awarded to Miss Beryl Judson Yawkey for her sonnet, "If I at Dawning." The certificate shared space atop the bookshelves with Beryl's Bachelor of Arts degree, Hal Graham's Bachelor of Science degree, his commission as second lieutenant in the Army Reserve, and the Grahams' high school diplomas.

It should have been a comfortable room. The chairs were chosen for comfort; well cushioned and with pillows. An effort had been made, too, to create a comfortable relaxed atmosphere, with a sampler that said "God Bless Our Home," and the coats of arms of the Sigma Nu fraternity and the Pi Beta Phi sorority on the walls; a portable phonograph, a small radio, a portable typewriter, a magazine rack filled with recent copies of *Time* and *The Saturday Evening Post,* three silver-plated tennis trophies, half a dozen framed photographs of the Graham family. But everything in the room had been given its carefully selected place, and once given its place had never been put anywhere else. The room had acquired a stiffness that was the opposite of the intended effect. It was just like all the other rooms in the house, from kitchen to bedroom. The nubbly counterpanes had to be where they belonged at ten o'clock every morning, and at one P.M. the Venetian blinds on the west windows were closed against the strong afternoon sun.

Beryl Graham could not have lived any other way, no more than she could have permitted herself the fifteenth line of a sonnet. Sometime in the first year of her marriage she had arrived at a personal ritual of lovemaking, with limits beyond which she would not go, and the ritual remained constant throughout the succeeding years. She did not wish to hear of other women's and other men's variations. She accepted Hal's admiration of her body as a proper compliment not only to herself but to all womankind, and she would speak generously of another woman's "lovely" figure without going into detail that might cause her husband to dwell upon the individual woman as an individual. Beryl made herself the guardian of all women's mysteries. Being a woman was something that no man could ever understand, and he must be prevented from violating women's secrets. It was quite enough for him to be a partner to her climax. He must be satisfied with that intimacy, and he must then go to sleep, gratefully.

She was happiest in the company of other women. It was always a clouding conclusion to a pleasant afternoon when a husband would appear to call for his wife after a bridge game. It was a male intrusion into a feminine world, an end for that day to the pleasing gentleness of women's voices and the pretty sight of feminine things. Beryl loved her kitchen and her bathroom, the tapestries in her hall, the chinaware in her diningroom, and the husband and children that so admirably completed her establishment, *her* establishment among the establishments of other women. She had a son as well as a daughter, but a son was a boy and a boy was a child that was not a girl and children belonged to the mother, a woman. A boy was not a man, and even when he became a man he would become the husband of a woman. It would be nice if her boy went into the ministry. There was still time to direct his steps. He worshiped her, even if he did understand the terms of his father's profession. Howard in a pulpit was an inspiring dream. The Reverend Howard Yawkey Graham. She could see his name in white letters under glass on the sign on a church lawn up North. Sacramento. Fresno. Oakland. San Francisco. The Reverend Howard Yawkey Graham will preach on "Woman's Role Today."

Jean, of course, was already so much like her mother that Hal sometimes would jokingly refer to her as little Beryl. He could just as well have referred to Beryl as big Jean, for with the exception of the overt sexual relationship there was little difference in his treatment of the one and the other. Correspondingly, their treatment of him was tolerantly maternal. The daughter had learned fast.

Howard was nine years old, Jean was seven, and they had been told to expect a new little brother or sister. The age gap between Jean and the unborn child worried Beryl not at all. She fully expected the older children to assume a proper responsibility toward the child that she had tentatively named Emily, after Emily Dickinson. The difference in ages between Emily and the older children was perfectly calculated, she felt. One of the women in her group (whom she did not like very much) had introduced her to the term, sibling jealousy, which turned out to be a name for the hitherto nameless concern that Beryl had disposed of before undertaking her third pregnancy. She disposed of it by deciding firmly that Howard and Jean must learn to love "Emily" before she was born. In this she was succeeding nicely, and for a little while she had no unnecessary worries. In spite of the obstetrician's reassurances Beryl discontinued conventional lovemaking with Hal and they went back to the "heavy necking" that was as much as she would allow in the weeks before the formal announcement of their engagement and the wedding ceremony. Hal's protests were mild, and then he told her that he had decided to stay away from her until after the baby was born. He would sleep in the guest room.

It was such a sensible idea that she playfully accused Hal of suddenly acquiring the ability to read her mind. No man on earth could read her mind, she was certain, but she had so strongly wished that Hal would come to just that decision that she wondered if she did not possess some extra-sensory powers that could be as effective as the spoken word. In many marriages the husband and wife often found themselves thinking the same thought simultaneously, and Hal's decision might only be an extension of this common coincidence. The power of her wish had been undeniable, and if it had not been such an intimate matter, she would have mentioned it to her father as bearing a close relation to the power of prayer. It was too bad, in a way, that she had never discussed those things with her father. But then she had never discussed them with her mother either. She had never really discussed them with anyone, not excepting Hal. She was much too proud of being a woman to relax her own reserve. The same pride had often served her well when Hal made love to her; it was unthinkable that she would ever let him know that *he* could leave *her* unsatisfied. No woman should be that dependent on a man.

But nearly seven years had intervened since Hal had slept in the guest room, and in all those years not a single week had gone by without his getting in bed with her. It was healthy for him. Five years ago, when she had her appendix out, he had slept alone for five or six weeks, but that did not count. She remembered it, though, because he had been so nervous and irritable in spite of himself and his good intentions; and there had been a remarkable demonstration of men's dependence on sex when the doctor said it was completely safe for her to allow Hal to make love to her again. Overnight he became cheerful and relaxed and his old sweet self. Now that he had once again betaken himself to the guest room she began to look for indications of a return of his nervous irritability. At the end of the second week of his celibacy—a fair test—she could see no bad effects, physically or spiritually. He was neither constipated nor petulant. She kept track of his bowel movements and she watched his manner with herself and the children. He was normal. And then she knew, for a fact beyond the suspicion stage, that Hal Graham was having sexual relations with another woman.

She did not need proof. She did not want proof, in the usual sense of the word. Hal Graham was all the proof she needed. She knew him like a book, a man who did complicated equations in a laboratory and could speak for an hour on problems so abstruse that not a hundred men in the entire State of California could follow him for five minutes. That was all there was to him, really, all that set him apart from the race of men. Otherwise he was a vapid, uninspiring person who drove a certain kind of car, played certain games, wore certain clothes, said certain things, and was now indulging certain animal instincts with a certain inferior type of female. Beryl Graham's contempt for her husband had never had occasion to be expressed. The feminine woman, to avoid being a freak, required a husband, a male to fertilize her and to signify his responsibility to her by giving her his name. The inconveniences attendant upon this convention were bearable so long as the relationship was not cheapened by disrespect. But sexual infidelity was disrespect of the most grievous kind. It placed the wife on equal terms of messy intimacy with the husband's mistress. The unfaithful husband sought in his mistress the thrilling shudder that was the proud woman's weakest moment. The cheap and traitorous woman gave him what he sought, and while she was a pitiable and contemptible person, she must be punished for her disloyalty to her sex.

The punishment, however, must be carefully thought out. It need not be visited directly upon the traitorous woman. It should unquestionably be administered indirectly through the offending, disrespectful man. And under no circumstances should it be of a character that would further lower the dignity of the offended wife. Beryl Graham almost automatically discarded the notion of divorce. There was no dignity in becoming the self-proclaimed victim of Hal Graham's disrespect. She next ruled out financial punishment. She could impose upon him a financial burden that he would carry all his life, but two factors decided her against that: fundamentally he cared very little about money, and, secondly, he was so indispensable to his company that they would make some arrangement to help him. It was quite possible, too, that the woman, whoever she was, had money of her own. She was certainly not costing Hal any money now. Beryl knew where every penny went.

No, the usual forms of punishment and revenge were not acceptable to Beryl Graham. They were insufficient, inadequate to the offense, and they were *unsubtle, unfeminine.* They were the thinking of men, the thinking of lawyers, and most lawyers were men.

In her present condition Beryl had plenty of opportunity for calm reflection. Her pregnancy gave her an excuse to give up tennis with the women of Marshall Place, and now that she was convinced of Hal's disrespect to her she used her pregnancy as an excuse to give up the enjoyment of her afternoon bridge games. After she sent the children off to school in the mornings she did her housework and was left with the entire day in which to be alone with her thoughts. When Marshall Place neighbors dropped in she would let them stay only a little while, and she soon discouraged their casual visits. It was not long before she had almost the whole day to herself, and she went through her household duties mechanically while occupying her mind with the problem of dealing with Hal and his unknown woman. It was not a problem that could be solved as he would solve one of his chemical formulae, if he solved chemical formulae. It was not a mathematical thing or a test tube thing; it was not a materialistic matter. It was a problem for a poet.

"How are you getting along?' he said to her one night, when the dishes were put away and the children had been put to bed.

"Me? Fine, thanks. Why?" said Beryl.

"I just wondered," he said. "You have any trouble with little Emily?"

"Not a bit," said Beryl.

"Do you feel life?"

"Of course I feel life," she said. "Men don't understand those things."

"I guess not," he said. "Well, I guess I'll say goodnight."

"Goodnight," she said. She gave him her cheek to kiss.

"Are you sure everything's all right?" he said.

"Why shouldn't it be?"

"I don't know," he said.

"If there's something bothering you, for heaven's sake tell me."

"Well, something is," he said.

"Oh? What?"

"The children. Well, not both children. But Howard said he hoped you'd have the baby soon."

"Why?" said Beryl.

"Because you're acting strangely. He didn't say that, but he thinks it."

"What *did* he say?"

"He said you talk to the baby as if it was alive."

"Well, it is alive."

"I know, but he doesn't understand that."

"And what did you tell him?"

"Well, I tried to explain that the baby's alive, and that it had to grow a little more before it was ready to be born."

"He knows that. I've told them that."

"But he doesn't understand why you'd talk to it now."

"Well, do *you?*"

"I do, because you used to talk to *him* before he was born, and Jean, too."

"I suppose I did," said Beryl. "I believe mothers *should* talk to their babies."

"They don't usually, before they're born," he said.

"Don't they? How would you know? There we are again, you see. A man is so different from a woman that it's just hopeless for him to try to understand us."

"All the same, Beryl, you have to admit it's kind of confusing to a young boy Howard's age, to overhear his mother talking to someone and you can't even see who she's talking to."

"I don't admit anything of the kind. It may be confusing to Howard, because he's a boy. But I'm sure it isn't confusing to Jean."

"I don't know," he said. "She hasn't mentioned it, but she wouldn't anyway. She doesn't confide in me, and never has."

"Naturally. If she had anything to say, she'd say it to me."

"I guess so," he said.

"Oh, I know so," said Beryl. "And there's nothing else on your mind?"

"No."

"Nothing out of the ordinary at the lab?"

"Not a thing," he said. "The usual slow progress. We try one thing, and if it doesn't work, we start all over again and try something else. But we know we're in the right direction."

"That must be such a great satisfaction, knowing you're at least in the right direction," she said. "But what if you found out some day that you were going in the wrong direction?"

"What do you mean by that?"

"Just what I say. Suppose you discovered that these last five years' work was all wasted? That you were completely wrong?"

He smiled. "That would be impossible, now. This is scientific work, you know. Every step is experimental, yes, but when we've proved something by one experiment, that's scientific fact. Then we take up the next experiment. Step by step, experiment by experiment, we accumulate our scientific facts. Those are things you can't deny. Certain elements behave certain ways under certain conditions. Those aren't laws that man made. Man only discovers them."

"But what if something new comes along and proves you were wrong?" she said.

"Nothing new comes along. It was always there, but we hadn't discovered it. Where we can go wrong is through ignorance. But the things we've proved, scientifically, are never wrong."

"You're all so conceited. So sure you're right."

"Not for one minute," he said. "We're sure that the laws are right. The laws of physics, I mean. But the man that's sure *he's* right, disregarding those laws, doesn't belong in the lab. He *is* conceited, and we don't want him around."

"How interesting," she said.

"You're getting bored. I'll let you go to bed," he said. "Goodnight."

"Goodnight," she said.

He closed the door of her bedroom and she sat with the pillows propped up behind her and a limp-leather volume of Wordsworth's poems lying open at her side. She had a feeling that she was getting closer to the solution of her problem. Whatever it was, it would certainly involve his destruction. This blindly conceited man, with his prattle about laws, must be rendered harmless. There must be a castration of his egotism, so that he could never again take that superior tone. How he had gloated over her and her unconscious, innocent habit of talking to the child in her womb! Did *he—he—*presume to judge her strange?

ON THE MORNING of the second Friday after the preceding conversation Beryl waited until Hal had left the house and then announced to the children that she had a surprise for them. They were not to go to school that day, but instead she was taking them to Newport a day early. Daddy, she said, would join them the next day.

She drove them to their cottage, had them get into their bathing suits, and informed them that as a special treat she was taking them for a ride in a motorboat. They went to Red Barry's pier, where the Grahams customarily hired boats, and Red gave them a new Chris-Craft because he trusted Beryl's ability to handle it.

They took off into the San Pedro Channel, which was calm, and when they were about five miles from shore, Beryl stopped the boat and told Howard he could go for a swim. The boy dived in, and Beryl then told Jean that she could go in too. The girl was somewhat reluctant, but she lowered herself into the water. Beryl then started the motor and pulled away. She made a wide circle until she saw first the boy and then the girl disappear beneath the surface. She circled again several times before turning back to shore.

In the words of Red Barry: "She brought the boat in all right, and tied it up herself. And then I thought to myself, 'Hey, wait a minute,' and I asked her. I said where were the two kids? And she looked at me like I was asking some kind of a dumb question, and said, 'They're out there somewhere.' And I said to her what did she mean by out there somewhere, and did she mean she had some kind of an accident? You know, I thought she was out of her mind from shock. But she was just as calm as if nothing happened, and I took notice her dress wasn't wet. Her hair was dry. In other words, she hadn't been in the water. And I thought, Jesus Christ, what *is* this? So I right away went to my shack and phoned the police. I didn't know what the hell else to do. Now there's a woman I been dealing with, her and Graham, five or six years at least. I would of trusted her with my own kids. And it isn't as if she wasn't a great swimmer. Pregnant, yes, but maybe that's the cause of it. You know, when a woman's expecting, and it's six or seven years since she had a child, it's hard to say. In fact, if you ask me, it's hard to tell about them anyway. Like I thought, well the first thing I better do is repaint that boat a different color, but I'm a son of a bitch if there wasn't a party of four wanted to take it out the following Sunday. They asked specially for it. I couldn't let them have it, though. The police impounded it. And how would you like to be Graham the rest of your life? He wasn't even here, but how do you live that down? Because right away people began saying he must of had something to do with it. A guy is married to a crazy woman, a real monster, but they try to shift the blame on him. Well, I guess if I didn't know him I'd probably think the same thing."

MORRIS AND ERNESTINE King came out of the Beverly Derby, the one-legged newsboy handed Morris the folded morning papers and was handed a fifty-cent piece. "You want to go to the Troc for a little while?" said Morris.

"I don't know. For a little while," said Ernestine.

"Yeah, we might as well go for a little while. It's early."

Their car was crossing from the parking lot.

"What's the headline? There's a big headline," said Ernestine.

"There's always a big headline," said Morris. " 'Mother Held in Tots' Drowning.' Now that's nice. To practically accuse a mother of drowning her kids."

"Let me see it," said Ernestine.

He handed her the *Examiner,* and she read the big story. "If I live to be a hundred, I'll never get used to Newport being in California. To me, Newport—wait a minute. Oh, *wait* a *minute.* Morris. What's the name of Natica's boy friend?"

"The name of Natica Jackson's boy friend? Some name like Hamilton. One of those names. Why?"

"Hamilton," said Ernestine. "You're sure it isn't Graham?"

"Graham is what it is," said Morris King.

"Harold T. Graham?"

"Yeah, why?" said Morris.

"Get in the car," said Ernestine. She spoke to the chauffeur. "Eddie, take us out to Miss Jackson's house."

"Natica Jackson, in Bel-Air?" said the chauffeur.

"Yes, and I'm sorry, Eddie, but don't figure on getting home at a decent hour tonight," she said.

"That's all right, ma'am, as long as I can have tomorrow off," said Eddie.

"Don't even count on that," she said.

Morris was reading the newspaper under the dome light of the town car as they proceeded out Wilshire Boulevard. He finished the *Examiner* and read the *Times*. Before they had got as far as Beverly Glen he refolded both papers and put out the light. "You got any ideas?" he said.

"First we have to find Natica," said Ernestine.

"Yeah, first we find her, then what?"

"What's the use of ideas till we had a chance to talk to her?"

"I guess so," said Morris. "I was thinking we ought to secrete her someplace. I hope we can secrete her before she finds out about this."

"We don't know anything, where she is or what she knows. Have a cigar to steady your nerves."

"A good stiff hooker of brandy is what my soul cries out for at this particular moment," said Morris.

"You're behaving admirably, Morris," said Ernestine. "Considering what's going on inside. When the chips are down, I have to hand it to you."

"And a hell of a lot of chips are down right now. A matter of two hundred thousand dollars, our end. A million-eight for Miss Natica Jackson. And from the studio's point of view, *you* guess. Now when we get there, I'm gonna let you handle the situation. One woman to another, till we find out where we are. But I want to be in the room all the time."

"If she's there," said Ernestine.

"If she ain't there, I want to go somewhere and get pissy-assed drunk."

"No, you don't want to do that," said Ernestine.

"There you're wrong. I won't do it, but I'll want to. I want to now. If I wasn't afraid of you thinking I was a kyoodle, I'd quit the business tonight."

"Never would I think that, Morris," she said.

The car halted at Natica's door and they got out. Morris pushed the doorbell button, and after a pause the door was swung open by Natica, who closed it quickly behind them. "I had to be sure who it was," she said. "I apologize for making you wait."

"You got a peephole?" said Morris.

"Yes. It isn't in the door. It's off to one side so it won't show the light. It's in the lavatory."

"Oh, good idea," said Morris. "You had any other visitors?"

"No," said Natica. "I phoned you, but they said you were out for the evening."

"We came out of the Beverly Derby and Ernestine happen to take a glance at the morning papers."

"Oh, you found out that way," said Natica. "Can I get you both a drink?"

"You wouldn't have any celery tonic?" said Morris.

"What's that?" said Natica.

"If you have a Coke or some ginger ale," said Ernestine. "Morris'll get it. Dearie, bring me a ginger ale with maybe a little twist of lemon peel."

"What do you want, Natica?" said Morris.

"A big slug of brandy, but I guess I better stick to Coke," said Natica. "Thanks, both of you, for showing up like this."

"Yeah. Well, you two talk while I get the drinks," said Morris.

Natica sat down and lit a cigarette. They were in a small room which contained a portable bar, and ordinary conversational tones sufficed. "He was supposed to come here around five," she said.

"This is Graham, you're talking about?" said Morris.

"Uh-huh. I had a hair appointment for three o'clock, but I decided the hell with it and lucky I did or I wouldn't of been here when he phoned. He was phoning from some gas station on the way to Newport. The police down there notified him what happened and told him he better get there right away. That was after he got back from lunch. He usually has lunch with some fellows on LaCienega every Friday, and then he goes back to the lab. The laboratory. So the police finally got in touch with him around ha' past two. He told me what they told him. That the two children met with an accident and his wife was at the police station. He asked them to put her on, but they said she was in custody. The poor guy, he asked them what they meant by that and all they'd say was he better get down there as soon as he could. They wouldn't even tell him if the kids were alive or dead. They said they didn't know for sure. And he started to tell them he thought his wife and the kids were still home. They weren't supposed to leave till tomorrow. But the cop said he didn't want to talk any more on the phone, and for Hal to get there as soon as possible. The rest I got by listening to the radio."

"We have the morning papers," said Ernestine. Morris served the drinks and took a chair. "And naturally you haven't heard any more from Graham?" said Ernestine.

"No. And he said for me not to try and get in touch with him. He said it looked very bad, and he didn't want me to get mixed up in it. God, I don't want to get mixed up in it either, but I'd like to help him."

"And the way to help him is to stay the hell out of it," said Morris. "The only way."

"Oh, sure. I know that," said Natica. "There isn't any doubt about it, is there? I mean, she did drown the two kids?"

"Wait till you read the papers and you'll be convinced of that," said Morris. "They're holding her on an open charge, but the whole thing is there for anybody to read. They got him quoted saying he didn't know why she'd do it. The grief-stricken husband and father, it says. The pregnant mother showed no signs of remorse or even awareness of the tragedy. The father went out on a Coast Guard boat to join in the search, which already attracted more than fifty small craft containing volunteers and curiosity-seekers. The *Times* has an aerial photograph of the boats, and there's a statement here from a veteran fishing captain who says it may be days before the children's bodies are found. A man named Barry rented her the boat and he's the one that reported it to the police. He refused to talk to reporters, but it was learned that he observed her return to his pier and questioned her as to the whereabouts of the children, and she is alleged to have told Barry that he would find the children 'out there.' He then telephoned the police. Mrs. Graham was taken into custody while returning on foot to the attractive cottage which the family had rented annually for the past five years. And so forth. I'd say the woman was what they call criminally insane."

"She talked to herself," said Natica.

"She did?" said Ernestine.

"And not to herself, really. She talked to the baby in her womb. She worried the poor kids, according to Hal. But he wasn't as worried as they were, because he remembered she did the same thing when she was carrying the boy *and* the girl."

"She'll get off," said Morris.

"They'll put her away somewhere," said Ernestine. "It's too bad they didn't a long time ago."

"Yes, you're right," said Morris. "But now let's talk about you, Natica. First, who knows you were sleeping with Graham?"

"Well, you two do. She didn't. That I know for a fact. She never accused Hal of sleeping with anybody. Not once, and she wasn't the kind that would let him get away with it."

"She wasn't the kind that would murder her two children, either. That's how well Graham knew her," said Morris. "So we don't know what she knew. Who else?"

"Nobody, unless Hal told some friend of his, and he said he didn't."

"It'd be pretty hard for a guy like that to not brag about getting in the hay with Natica Jackson," said Morris.

"He wasn't the bragging kind," said Natica.

"And he had something to lose," said Ernestine. "How about you? Who did *you* tell?"

"A long time ago, Reggie Broderick, but I never told him who the guy was," said Natica.

"What about your servants? Your mother?" said Ernestine.

"My mother doesn't know a damn thing about him. The cook and the maid, if he gets his picture in the paper—"

"Which you can be damn sure he will, tomorrow," said Morris.

"Let me finish. The cook never saw him. The maid could have, if she hid somewhere and watched him leave, a long time ago. Lately he never came in the front door, or left by it. I have a door in my bedroom that opens out into the garden and then through the back gate. I'm not worried about the maid. And if he had to phone me he used the name of Mr. Marshall. There's one person that does know, Morris."

"Who's that?"

"Your detective," said Natica.

"God damn it, that's the thing that's been plaguing me. I knew there was somebody. I knew it, God damn it."

"He has his name. License number. Address. Every damn thing about him and his wife," said Natica. "So, it's up to you, I guess."

"It's absolutely up to me," said Morris.

"Who was it? Rosoff?" said Ernestine.

"Yeah."

"Well, how much can you trust him? He never popped off before."

"No, but he never had anything as big as this," said Morris.

"How much do you think he'd settle for?" said Ernestine.

Morris shook his head. "Who knows? A pension, the rest of his life."

"Well, he wouldn't be the first in this town to get that kind of a pension," said Ernestine. "Do you have his number?"

"Yes, I guess so. You mean with me? Yes. Why?"

"I have an idea," said Ernestine. "Get him on the phone, tonight. Right away. Tell him you have a big job for him, but don't say right away what it is. Find out if he connects up this Graham with the one he investigated."

"He will."

"All right, suppose he does. I have to think a minute," said Ernestine. They were all three silent, until Ernestine tapped her kneecap. "This is what you do. The minute he thinks you're buying him off, you're in for it. He'll bleed you, he'll bleed Natica. I wouldn't even be surprised if he tried to take the studio."

"That he better not try, if he wants to walk around on two legs," said Morris. "Me and Natica he can take, but the studio won't fool around with a small-time operator like Rosoff."

"So you don't want him thinking you're buying him off. Instead of that, you want him thinking you want him to do a little dirty work. You're in it together. You pretend you're taking him into your confidence. 'Rosie,' you say—now let me think." She paused. "I got it. You tell him you're worried about Natica getting mixed up in this thing. Be frank, like. And you say you got a tip that Mrs. Graham, Beryl, went to Europe several years ago and had a child by somebody that wasn't her husband. You aren't sure whether it was Paris, London, or Monte Carlo. But you want him to go abroad right away, as quick as he can, and check the hospital records of all the private hospitals in Paris and London. You'll pay all expenses and fifty dollars a day, or whatever he charges. But he has to do it right away or you'll have to get someone else."

"It won't work," said Morris.

"I guarantee you it will, Morris. Fifty dollars a day and all expenses? I know Rosie well enough to know he won't pass up a chance like that. That's, uh, for two months that's three thousand dollars plus his living, plus a little larceny on the expense account. And a nice de luxe trip to Europe."

"You're spending my money, Teeny, but what for? What do I get out of it?"

"Jesus Christ! The one thing you want right now. Time. *Time.* You get this goniff out of the way for the next five, six, seven weeks. He won't find anything, but he won't be around here making trouble. By the time he gets back to L.A., Mrs. Graham will be put away somewhere. And by that time there'll be five other scandals for the newspapers to occupy their attention. If Rosie wants to blackmail us then, we laugh in his face. But I wouldn't laugh in his face tonight, or next week. Tonight I'm afraid of him. Tomorrow I'm afraid of him. I'm afraid of him till he gets on board The Chief and I'm still afraid of him till he gets on board the *Ile de France.* Then I begin to rest easy."

"It'll work," said Morris. "It'll positively work. Natica, where's your phone?"

"Right there where you're sitting," said Natica.

Within an hour Morris had tracked down Rosoff at a gambling house on the Sunset Strip. "Rosie? You winning, gor losing? Well, can you meet me at the Vine Street Derby in three-quarters of an hour? I need your very urgent help in a matter, and it won't keep till tomorrow. Right, Rosie. If you get there first you tell Chilios I'm on my way, and if I'm there first I'll wait there. But be a good boy now, Rosie, and don't you keep me waiting." Morris hung up. "He says he's winning. I say he's losing or he wouldn't answer the phone. You couldn't get him away from that blackjack game if he was winning. I seen him on two or three occasions blow a couple months' pay inside of an hour. So did you, Teeny."

"Yes I did," said Ernestine. "He's a chump from the word go. You want me to come with you?"

"This time, no. If you were there, he'd smell a rat. No offense, sweetheart. But you know. He'd be looking for an angle. With just me there, he don't get suspicious. You ladies wish to sit and talk, keep one another company till I phone you?"

"If Natica wants my company," said Ernestine.

"Of course I do, you silly," said Natica.

"All right. Then get going, Morris. And good luck," said Ernestine.

"Too bad Natica's not a hunchback. I could rub it for luck. Why wouldn't it be just as lucky to give you a little rub in front?" said Morris. "Wuddia say, Natica?"

"Get out of here," said Ernestine.

"Ah, she knows I'm only kidding."

"Yeah, but do *you* know it?" said Ernestine.

He left.

"There goes a nice little fellow," said Ernestine. "Tough. Shrewd. He'll murder you in a business deal. He'll have the gold out of your teeth before you open your mouth. But if he likes you, once he gets to liking you, you never saw such real, genuine loyalty. And he likes you, Natica."

"I'm positive of that," said Natica.

"How do you feel?" said Ernestine.

"I feel all right. I felt panicky till you and Morris got here. I couldn't think who to turn to. The only person I could think of was Reggie Broderick. All the people I know in Hollywood, and the only ones I had to turn to were you and Morris and Reggie. I would of phoned Alan Hildred if I knew where he was."

"Yes, in a spot like this you could count on Alan. A no-good English fag, but you could count on him in this kind of a situation. Well, that's four people. That's not so bad."

"I ought to feel worse about those two little children, but I don't. He was crazy about them, Hal. But the mother never let him get very close to them."

"What do you know about her?" said Ernestine.

"Hardly anything, it turns out. I thought I knew a lot, mostly from knowing him. But he didn't know much about her either. Married all that time and that's as well as they ever got to know each other. You'd think a married couple would know each other better, but they didn't. I know one thing about her he told me."

"What?"

"She never wanted to look at his private parts. He could look at her, but she wouldn't look at him. She wasn't modest about herself, but he always had to keep covered up till they turned out the lights. She wasn't a Lez, but she hated men."

"She was a Lez," said Ernestine.

"That's what I said, but he said no. She liked to be laid, but she didn't care what happened to him. It was all for her. I don't know, Ernestine. I often felt the same way with Alan. Maybe I'm like her."

"I doubt that," said Ernestine.

"I was with Alan."

"But not with Graham," said Ernestine.

"No, not with Graham."

"Well, you see I was just the opposite with Alan," said Ernestine. "If he told me to—one time he did tell me to do something terrible in front of one of his boy friends, and I did. That was the last time I had anything to do with him, but he had that power over me. That was why I had to stop seeing him. But he had no power over you, and Graham did."

"I would have done anything Graham wanted me to, anywhere, any time. And I would now."

"Well, with me it was Alan. Starting with the first time I ever met him, when I lent him a hundred dollars."

"How did you have the strength to break it off?" said Natica.

"I don't know. Fear, I guess. Not strength. If he could make me do that in front of his boy friend, what next? Those kind of people, people like Alan, that have that much power over a person, maybe the good Lord only gives them so much power. If they had a little more power—but they don't. And that's how the good Lord protects us. You see what I mean?"

"Yes, but how do we protect ourselves from ourselves?"

"Search me. I guess we don't, till we get frightened."

"You think I'm gonna get frightened?"

"Yes, I do," said Ernestine.

"You're right. I am frightened. I'm frightened of that crazy woman with the child in her womb."

"Of what she'll do, or what she'll say?"

"Neither one. I don't think she can do anything, locked up in an institution. And nobody'll pay much attention to what she says."

"Then what are you frightened of?" said Ernestine.

"Her. I never even saw her, and I probably never will. But I'll be afraid of her for the rest of my life, like she was some kind of a ghost. Her and those two children, but mostly her. I want to talk to Reggie Broderick."

"What the hell for, Natica?"

"He's a Catholic."

"I'm Jewish. You can talk to me."

"No, I remember those Catholic girls I grew up with. They'd get into trouble—not just knocked up, but other kinds of trouble—and they weren't as afraid as the rest of us."

"It only seemed that way. They were just as afraid, if not more so. And anyway, is Reggie Broderick going to get rid of your ghost? I doubt that, Natica. Him *or* his religion. Think it over before you start spilling everything to Reggie."

"Well, maybe you're right," said Natica. "Right now I don't know my ass from first base. I wish to hell I could get drunk. I wish Hal Graham would walk in this room. Only I don't. A terrible thing is I don't want to see him and maybe I never will want to again, with that damn crazy murderess looking over his shoulder at me. That's my ghost, Ernestine."

"Yes, I see what you mean," said Ernestine.

"What happens to her baby when it's born?"

"I don't know what the law says about that."

"I wasn't thinking about the law. I was wondering about the child's future."

"I imagine the father will be given custody, and I suppose he'll move away. Maybe change his name. Get a new job and so forth."

"Do you know something, Ernestine? As sure as we're sitting here, he's never going to see me again. He'll want to, maybe, but the kind of man he is, he'll have a ghost, too. Not only his wife locked up in an institution, but a child to raise. And he'll never try to see me. And all of a sudden I'm beginning to realize that that crazy woman knew what she was doing."

"What?"

"Just as if she called me on the phone and told me. Maybe she doesn't know my name, even, but I get it inside me, Ernestine. She's telling me."

"Telling you what, dear?" said Ernestine.

"She's saying, 'This is what you have to live with. Ann Jacobs or

Natica Jackson, or whatever you call yourself, this is what you have to look forward to.' "

"I wish I didn't believe that," said Ernestine.

"But you do," said Natica.

"I won't lie to you. It's the only thing to believe that makes any sense," said Ernestine.

They were silent for a moment, then Natica spoke. "I told him once, if he hadn't stopped to put on a necktie I never would have smacked into his car."

"I don't get it," said Ernestine.

"Oh, I'll tell you sometime, but not now," said Natica.

"We ought to be hearing from Morris," said Ernestine.

"No hurry. I can wait," said Natica. "I have complete confidence in Morris."

The Way to Majorca

SHE HAD STARRED in eight pictures; program pictures; nothing very big, nothing to invite a second or third look by the people who searched for hidden meanings in popular entertainment. The parts she played were within a certain range, *her* range, as an actress and as a credible woman for the type-casting. She had played a nurse, a newspaper reporter, a telephone operator, the wife of a navy petty officer, a night-club singer, another night-club singer, the wife of a private eye, and a gangster's moll. When the dialog had her slangy, she was unhesitatingly convincing and unhesitatingly acceptable to audiences. Her figure was faultless, and they dressed her in clothes that were suitable to the role and in their simplicity (and scantiness) showed her figure to advantage.

In the parts she played she was always loyal and trustworthy, always at some point in danger or distress. Her growing public could "identify" with her, even though they might never in their own lives find themselves in quite the same predicaments. But they felt strongly that if they ever got in such predicaments, they would have the same fears and hopes as Sally Standish. In a great many of her fan letters her admirers expressed the thought that if they were ever in trouble, they felt they could go to her. In point of fact, several of her friends and acquaintances in the industry *had* gone to her for help and comfort, and she had always come through. The movie hacks who worked on her scripts agreed that she was easy to write for. All you had to do was think of her, and forget about the dames who fought to play a different character every time they made a film.

She was always somebody's girl. She was married at eighteen to a vaudeville actor who had already been married three times. She was a chorus girl in a Broadway show; he was playing the Palace. He met her one night in Dave's Blue Room, told her she was a juicy little thing, and married her three days later. She stuck it out for two months, accompanying him to the cities where he was appearing in the stage shows of the big movie theaters. But she got tired of sitting in his dressing-room, and he got tired of seeing her there, and she said she was going back to New York. "No hard feelings," he said. She wanted to say, "That's what *you* think," but she had no money and was hopeful of getting some of his. He gave her eight hundred dollars. He said it ought to take care of her for a while.

"What about a divorce?" she said.

"No divorce, honey," he said. "*You're* leaving *me,* aren't you? Divorces run into a lot of moola, take it from one who knows. You go back to New York and get yourself a job. Then when some guy wants to marry you, he can pay for the divorce as a wedding present. Right?"

It was no use arguing with him, and truthfully she was getting away from him because he made her feel that the novelty of her had worn off. Already some of the stories she had heard about him were confirmed in her relations with him, and from the yet unconfirmed stories she knew what to expect. At eighteen she was not ready for first-hand experience of the things she had heard about from her chorus girl friends.

He apologized for not being able to take her to the train, as he was playing five shows a day and could not leave the theater, but he told her to get in touch with his agent, who would be helpful in getting her a job. As it turned out, his prediction was accurate. The agent got her a bit in a musical comedy, which led to her screen test and a bathing-suit contract in Hollywood: seven years, starting at $100 a week, with six-month options. During the first period of the contract she spent the usual time on the beach at Santa Monica, posing for fan magazine art. One photograph, however, was the break she had waited for: for the Hallowe'en issue of a fan magazine she posed in a cat costume of black opera-lengths and a black leotard and skullcap. She looked saucy, and the studio got two hundred letters from college boys and prison inmates, among others, asking for glossy prints of the photograph. She was thereupon discovered by an assistant casting director and recommended for a cigarette-girl bit in a motion picture. The female star of the film helped her career by demanding retakes of two scenes in which the unknown cigarette girl shared the frame with her. "Who the hell is going to look at anything else when that shape is on the screen?" said the star, and the answer was so obvious that the retakes were shot and Sally Standish was out of that film but given more to do in her next.

Nurse. Newspaper reporter. Telephone operator. Petty officer's wife. Night-club singers. Private eye's wife. Gangster's moll. The original contract torn up. The assistant casting director succeeded by a cameraman. The cameraman succeeded by a leading man. The leading man succeeded by a more prominent but happily married leading man. And the prominent leading man succeeded by a Los Angeles playboy, whose father owned a chain of supermarkets. She very nearly eloped with the playboy, but remembered in time that she was still married to the vaudeville actor. She telephoned him.

"Give me twenty-five big bills and I'll bow out gracefully," said the vaudevillian. "You probably don't have it, but your delicatessen man has."

"I wouldn't ask him," said Sally Standish. "You ought to have some decency, you jerk."

"Decency, honey? Why, the boys at the Lambs club tell me you almost broke up good old George Bedford and his wife. They been married longer than the Lunts. Rumor hath it that George is still stuck on you. So am I, for that matter. Don't you ever miss your ever-loving spouse?"

"Oh, drop dead, you creep," she said. She hung up the phone, and about a week later he obligingly did drop dead in the bar of the Lambs club. The wire services asked her for a statement on his sudden passing, and with the assistance of a man in the publicity department she issued a tribute to a great artist for whose help in the early stages of her career she would be unceasingly grateful. Not a word of her statement appeared anywhere except as a shirttail to the great artist's brief obituaries in the Hollywood trade papers, and even there he was identified as "Sally Standish's Ex." The supermarket heir eloped with someone else.

She did not mourn the loss of the playboy or of her husband, and she had no conscience pangs concerning the readiness with which her broken-down ex had obeyed her last command. Nevertheless—and possibly because she had some free time on her hands—the coincidence of the one man's death and the other's capriciousness gave her a small jolt. She would be twenty-seven on her next birthday, and although she possessed much more than the $25,000 that her husband had hoped to extract from her, she had never made the kind of money that builds to a fortune and independence. She was a star, but a star in what? She was in one low-budget picture after another, the bread-and-butter pictures, the studio called them. They were usually brought in for less than $500,000 apiece, never played the big New York theaters, nearly always were shown as half of a double-feature. For the first time since they had given her top billing she was not completely confident that they would take up her next option.

She thought of the other girls who had had careers very much like hers, and she had no difficulty in counting to eight before the game became too depressing. They too had starred in money-making, low-budget pictures, playing the wisecracking, heart-of-gold night-club singers and newspaper reporters; and not one of them had lasted beyond thirty. Before they reached thirty they were cut loose, and as free-lances they were glad to be given two or three weeks' work. The next step from there was hazardous. A girl could get work in character parts, but if she was still pretty and photographed young, the leading women did not want her. If, on the other hand, a girl was willing to play a prison matron or an aging actress or the wife of a cattle rancher, she was renouncing youth and ambition. She was giving up the hope of remaining a star and staying up there like an Ethel Barrymore or a Gladys Cooper. No one in her right mind expected to stay young forever, but it was possible to mature by degrees by fighting for the right parts.

And now she was approaching, if only approaching, a decision. She was rather out of practice in making decisions; the studio and her agents had been telling her what to do for so long that she had not made an important decision since she walked out on her husband. That one had been a decision arrived at through disenchantment and the instinct of self-preservation; this one was based on the instinct of self-preservation and panic. But before she could come to any decision at all she would have to yield to her fears, and she did so in a day of weeping. She had never before pitied herself, and fear, self-pity, loneliness, the absence of anyone to love and the state of being unloved all combined to give her an extremely bad twenty-four hours.

But she had not played those courageous nurses and spunky young wives for nothing. Forgotten situations and lines came back to her. Movie scripts were all she had ever read, and as they had been written directly for her, they had formed the character she was in real life. Until now she had never given much thought to the men and women who had written her scripts; in most cases she had never even met them. They were, so to speak, gypsies, who went from studio to studio on one-picture deals, and as a rule they were nowhere on the lot when she was ready to start shooting a film. But there was one writer who had worked on two of her scripts and had recently sold the studio an original story for a future Sally Standish picture. His name was Meredith Manners and he looked the way a writer should look. He was a fairly tall, rather stout man, who always wore cashmere or tweed jackets, slacks and sleeveless sweater, carried a cane, and smoked a pipe. He was in his forties or certainly in his late thirties, tanned, with a small moustache and horn-rim glasses. He had fallen arches and he moved slowly. Sally Standish had often seen him in the studio commissary and wondered who he was. He looked out of place in the commissary, not so much because there was anything unusual about his appearance—his costume was a screenwriter's uniform—but because he seemed to *feel* out of place. He seldom sat at the writers' table. He preferred to have his lunch alone or with a visitor to the lot, not always the same visitor, but nearly always someone who was definitely not picture-people. Sally Standish was introduced to him by a producer, who muttered something about their getting to know each other since they were both part of his unit. Thenceforth Mr. Manners made a point of bowing to her, and once at the end of the working day he walked with her to the parking lot, and she was surprised to see that he had his name painted on his space, an indication that he was under long-term contract. He had a large foreign car, a green convertible coupe. She was not surprised to hear him speak with a *sort* of an English accent, but he quickly denied that he was English. He came, he said, from Minnesota, and spoke that way because his mother was an elocution teacher and his father a clergyman. One thing sure was that he was a fag.

He was a *sad* fag, probably because he was older than those she had known among the chorus boys of her Broadway days. He had a burden, as older fags often had. Sometimes when she walked with him to the parking lot she could see in his face the vestiges of a youthful prettiness, and she was pleased with her discernment when he told her that he had begun his show business career not as a writer but as an actor. "In stock," he said. "I never quite got to Broadway. At least as an actor. I had to write a play to scale those heights." He sent her a copy of his play, and she read it with great interest. It was a comedy, very nearly a farce, and it showed her that he could not always have been so sad. But of much more interest to her was the female lead. "*I* could have played that part," she told him.

"I know you could," he said.

"Did you ever sell it to pictures?"

"They bought it and made a musical of it," he said. "It was one of the first big musicals. Made a potful of money for the Warner frères. Of course they changed it completely, to fit Ruby Keeler."

"Then I guess I must have seen it. I love Ruby Keeler," said Sally Standish. "But they would have to change it, you're right. I started out in the chorus, but I've never been in a musical. It's funny, you know, you writing this play. It's as if you knew me beforehand."

"I anticipated you, by about fifteen years."

"Just about," she said. "Funny."

They never met off the lot. He lived somewhere in the hills above Franklin Avenue and so did she, but they did not know that until her day of weeping, when those parts she had played came back to her and gave her courage of a sort. If it was courage, it was not her own courage but that of the girl she had played in eight films. She was not so sure about her own courage, but the Sally Standish character—those gutsy nurses and night-club singers—was always plucky, able to make decisions. It came to her that twenty-five percent of her—two pictures out of eight—had been created by Meredith Manners, whom she had learned to trust. On the morning after she had wept away much of her misery and fear she telephoned Meredith Manners at the studio and asked him to come to her house that afternoon.

She dressed carefully for his visit, a plain suit and black turtleneck sweater, as much like Katharine Hepburn as her wardrobe could supply. Already she was at least tentatively beginning to change her type, and she did not wish to alarm Meredith Manners with a threat of seduction. He noticed right away. "I never saw you in an Eddie Schmidt before," he said.

"It's the only one I own," she said. "I ordered it for traveling, but I don't hardly ever travel. I've been stuck here so long, and they don't give me much time off between pictures."

"Well, you make a lot of money for them," he said.

"Help yourself to a drink. You know what you want," she said.

"I'll have myself a Scotch and splash. Can I get you anything?"

"I'll take a 7-Up, if it's there," she said. "I don't go for the hard stuff."

"You're very wise," he said.

"I learned the hard way. My mother was a lush. They took me away from her when I was twelve years of age and I was raised with an aunt till I went in show business."

"What happened to your mother?" he said.

"She died in Bellevue."

"What about your father?"

"He was a section-hand on the Sixth Avenue L. He paid for my board and room, but he liked the stuff too. He got my mother to drinking, only she couldn't take it. When she got put away he boarded me with his sister, my aunt, but she paid for my dancing lessons."

"What happened to your father?"

"He slipped on the ice and fell and broke his neck. Right there at the corner of Fiftieth and Sixth, where the Music Hall is. It would have been funny if I turned out to be a Rockette, but I didn't."

"No, you certainly didn't," he said.

"That cues me in to what I wanted to discuss with you—can I call you Meredith?"

"Call me George. That's my real first name. The last name is Mantz, but I got rid of that as soon as I could. George Meredith Mantz, son of the Reverend and Mrs. Karl W. Mantz. There, now you see me with my mask off."

"Well, what the hell? Sally Standish? Sara Sullivan, if you want to know the truth. Sara Veronica Sullivan, but nobody called me Sara since I was sixteen years of age. I was Sally Sullivan till I got in pictures, but in pictures you have to be Sullavan with an *a,* like Margaret Sullavan. Or with an 'O' in front, like Maureen O'Sullivan. Now I want to change it to something else and change my whole personity."

"Oh, really? I can hear screams from the studio," he said.

"That's what I wanted to ask you," she said. "I consider you a friend of mine, George. I have an agent, and a lawyer, and a lot of people I know in pictures, but they all have an angle."

"I have an angle, too, Sally. I just sold an original for one of your pictures and I got a pretty good price for it. I got twenty-five thousand dollars and I get to work on the screenplay. Figure six weeks' work on the script, that's nine thousand, and twenty-five for the original is thirty-four thousand dollars. That's my angle. I'm one of the few writers on a yearly contract. They make me work, but if I can sell an original now and then, I'm doing pretty well."

"Yes, you can make more than I do," she said. "And you don't have to run up the bills I have to."

"Well, I have certain commitments."

"Who doesn't?" she said. "Well, maybe you'd rather not hear about my problems. I don't want to put you on any spot."

"I'll help you if I can," he said.

"Advice, that's what I need. Somebody that I can honestly trust to give me the right advice."

"Me? You think of me that way? Why would you trust me?"

"I don't know. I just do," she said.

He looked at her, and she looked away. "I suppose I know why—and so do you."

"Well—" she said.

"Be frank, Sally. You mean we're not apt to wind up in the hay together."

"Well, I wouldn't have any objections to that. I like you more than some I did end up in the hay with."

"Thank you," he said. "That's—friendly. And flattering. But you're just as safe with me as I am with you. It's six of one and half a dozen of the other, to coin a phrase. I have a friend that's dying to meet you, by the way."

"Who is he?"

"It's not a he, it's a she," he said.

"Oh." She shook her head.

"I didn't think so," he said. "I guess what made me think of it was seeing you in that suit. The suit, and the turtleneck. I've never seen you in that kind of a combination before. And you said you wanted to change your personality. You see, I'm being absolutely frank with you, Sally, and I still don't know what your problem is. Some girls out here, they get so fed up with being chased by the wolves that they go completely the other way."

"Well, I haven't reached that stage yet. Not saying I never will. I can get pretty disgusted with men sometimes. But so far I never had anything to do with a dike."

"The girl that wants to meet you isn't a dike," he said. "She has men, too."

Sally smiled. "Well, maybe I ought to take her name for future reference."

"Can I tell her that?"

"No, let's wait a while," she said.

"All right," he said.

"What did she say about me?" she said.

"Well, she thinks you have one of the great shapes of all time, and that's no news to anybody. But she also thinks you're a much better actress than you've been given credit for."

"Oh, I like this girl. Maybe we ought to call her up right away," she said.

"You're not serious," he said.

"No. But I'm glad you said that, because that's getting close to my problem. What do you think of me as an actress? Level with me."

"Level with you? All right," he said. He took a sip of his drink. "Frankly, I've never had much occasion to think of your acting ability, beyond a certain point. You only have to do certain things, and you do them well. I understand you're a quick study, and you take direction well. I'm being absolutely frank with you, Sally."

"That's what I want," she said.

"Well, you know as well as I do that you go from one picture to another, and the only difference from one part to the next is you wear different costumes. I worked on two of your pictures, and in the first one you were a night-club singer and the second you were a kind of a poor man's Myrna Loy, in one of the Thin Man series. This new one I just sold them, you'll be the wife of a test pilot. But you'll be doing the same things you've done in all your pictures and playing just about the same part."

"The hell I will," she said.

"The hell you won't," he said. "As long as you stay in action pictures, you're going to be the girl friend or the wife of the test pilot or the gangster or the orchestra leader or whatever it is. Nobody's going to fool around with a tried and true formula."

"I know. And how much longer do you think I'll last?"

"Oh, I see," he said. "Well, to be brutally frank, as soon as you show signs of wear, they'll get another girl. And *she'll* do the Sally Standish pictures."

"And where will I be?" she said.

"Yes, you have to think about that."

"If you want to know, I'll be twenty-seven on my next birthday."

"I was wondering. You could be good for about three years more, as long as you take care of the chin-line, and don't let the lard accumulate on your tokus. After thirty, though, they simply can't make you look twenty, no matter how good your shape is."

"I don't expect to last that long, frankly. Playing those same parts."

"Your problem is how to grow old gracefully, is that it?"

"It sure is," she said. "Practically overnight. If I was born with a lot of sense I would have realized that earlier and started to do something about it."

"Like taking acting lessons?"

"Yes, that's one thing," she said. "I could still do that, I guess."

"Yes. Madame Ouspenskaya. Constance Collier. They give private lessons. Would you care to have me talk to them?"

"Later, maybe," she said. "But what I should have done was be more independent. When I was a few years younger I should have told the studio to give me different parts."

"They would have told you to go to hell."

"Probably," she said. "But then I should have told *them* to go to hell. And *then* I could have."

"No. They had you sewed up in a contract that you couldn't break."

"But what if I refused to work?" she said.

"Is that what you're thinking of doing now?"

"What I'm thinking of doing now is retire," she said.

"You must have saved your money," he said.

"No, unfortunately, I didn't," she said. "But I could retire for maybe a couple of years. I'd have to sell this place, and some jewelry, and live on that for a couple of years."

"Why do you want to retire?"

"Temporarily. I'd come out of retirement when I got the right part," she said.

"That takes guts, dearie," he said.

"Well, Sally Standish has guts. I don't know about Sara Sullivan, but I ought to know about Sally Standish. So ought you. You helped to invent her."

"It's too bad you haven't got a rich husband," he said.

"You don't have to tell me that," she said. "What I want you to tell me is, what are my chances? How about writing a story for me that isn't a Sally Standish?"

He shook his head. "Too late for that. If I'd had the guts to retire ten years ago, and write the play that I wanted to write, or the novel, I wouldn't be writing Sally Standishes today. Or maybe I would. Maybe I'd have written a flop play or a flop novel and be glad to have the Sally Standishes to write. But I didn't take that chance, and now I have to play it safe. In four more years, I ought to have enough to retire on."

"How much is that?"

"In my case, a half a million. I'd have an income of twenty to twenty-five thousand for life, and I'd be all set. I'd move to the South of France, or Majorca, or some such place."

"I thought you were rich," she said.

"I am—as long as I keep working. The minute I quit, I go from fifteen hundred a week to five hundred. That is, after I have my half-million. But if I had five hundred a week in a place like Majorca, I'd live three times as well as I do here. That's why I don't mind being a Hollywood hack for four more years. You see, I have no desire to spend my declining years in genteel poverty. I expect to live it up, but good. Servants. Wine with my meals. Friends to visit me. I could quit with what I have now, but the shock of doing without a lot of things I have now would be too much for my nervous system." He hesitated. "Not to mention the fact that an old queen like me has to have money. I don't get anywhere on my looks any more."

"If you stop to think of it, we're both more or less in the same boat."

"Why yes, we are. That's a very trenchant observation, Sally. What a very trenchant observation!"

"How much more do you need for your half a million?"

"Oh, roughly a hundred thousand," he said. "Perhaps a little more. I figure to save about $25,000 a year for the next four years."

"I have a hundred thousand."

"You hinting that we ought to pool our resources? It would be fun, in a way. But of course it would never work out. Financially, it might. But otherwise, I'm afraid not. If you and I were living under the same roof in a place like Majorca, my friends would make life miserable for you. They can be very cruel, especially to someone as female as you are. That would get you down in no time. Were you thinking of a marriage of convenience, or living in so-called sin?"

"Marriage."

"Why marriage?"

"Well, we wouldn't be fooling anybody, but it's better to be married."

"From your point of view, but not necessarily mine," he said.

"I have more than a hundred thousand, George. I don't have four hundred thousand, but I have more than one. With what I have and what you have, we could leave this town tomorrow. But supposing I put a hundred and fifty thousand into it and you died? I wouldn't get anything. It'd all go to your relatives."

"Not so fast," he said. "You're taking an awful lot for granted, dearie. This was your idea, not mine. However, I ought to examine it. Goodness knows, I'd just as soon leave now as four years from now."

"Take all the time you want," she said.

He put down his glass with a vehemence that nearly shattered it. "Oh, let's do it!" he said. "Why not?"

"You mean get married?"

"Of course. We'll get right in my car and drive to Las Vegas. Are you game?"

"Sure, I'm game."

"A lot of people will be furious, but we don't care, do we?"

"I don't know anybody that'll be furious," she said.

"I was thinking of my friends. Some of them will be absolutely livid. But I love doing things on the spur of the moment, don't you? I used to, all the time, but I've gotten so hidebound. It's rather a long drive. What are you going to wear?"

"What I have on."

"Perfect. And you'll need a warm coat. You must have a mink."

"Yes, I do," she said.

"You don't want any attendants, do you? A maid of honor? Fanny Brice had a boy I know for her maid of honor that time she married Billy Rose. But I always thought that was a bit much. Let's not tell a soul till after the deed is done. And if I start camping during the ceremony, you just give me a good kick."

"Don't worry, I will."

"And I want you to promise me one thing. One thing. You must promise me not to sneak off and phone Louella."

"I don't owe her any favors," said Sally.

"I'm really quite excited about this, aren't you? You don't seem as excited as I am."

"I was married before," she said.

"Oh, yes. To that What's His Name, the vaudeville man. He went bye-bye, though, didn't he?"

"Yes."

"I thought I remembered reading something. This is *fun,* Sally. It really is. There are hundreds of things we ought to talk about. The sensible things. But if we stop and do that, we won't go through with it. And somehow I really feel that we're doing the right thing for both of us. I do, honestly. And anyway, what have we got to lose?"

"I don't know of anything," she said.

The film industry was stunned—and that was the word most frequently used—at the news of the elopement. The press went as far as it could within the libel laws to explain that Meredith

Manners was a confirmed bachelor, whose name had never been linked with that of any of the Hollywood beauties. Miss Standish, on the other hand, had had numerous romantic attachments (listing them), including one with a prominent actor who was rumored to have offered his wife $1,000,000 for his freedom in order to marry Miss Standish. The photographic layouts of Sally's career, from her lucky Hallowe'en cat picture to some stills from her current movies, provided a telling contrast with a group picture of Meredith Manners and friends. The knowledgeable Los Angeles newspaper readers could read between the lines of the caption, which gave the names of Mr. Manners's friends: a costume designer, a hair stylist, an elderly tennis player, an interior decorator, a songwriter, and a cowboy-actor-turned-art-dealer.

"I think they got it across," said George to his bride.

"Well, so what?" said Sally.

"Nothing, just as long as you don't mind," said George.

"Whose idea was it? It was my idea," she said.

"I know, but you didn't know you were going to get this kind of publicity. They all but come out and say it, that you married a fairy."

"I wish they would say it. Then you could sue them," she said.

"I wouldn't collect," he said.

They were in her house, and the worst of the two-day notoriety was over. They could open closet doors without fear of having a reporter pop out. "Tomorrow we go to the studio and hear what *they* have to say," said George. "It may not be nice. It *won't* be nice."

"We're married," said Sally. "We didn't commit any murder."

"My dear, we have flown in the face of public opinion. We have outraged the sanctity of marriage, et cetera. Did you ever sleep with Sol Hamper?"

"No."

"Well, it wouldn't make any difference if you had. It might have made some difference if *I* had, but he's always been too busy with girls. When we get in there, in his office, you let me handle it. I know him pretty well."

There were smiles but no felicitations to the bride and groom on their way past Sol Hamper's assistants and secretaries. "Now remember, don't you say anything. Not even hello," George whispered. "We make him speak first."

Sol Hamper, vice-president in charge of production, was pretending to be busy with a piece of paper as they entered his office. He had a fresh cigar between his fingers, and he did not immediately look up. Sally and George stood side by side in front of Hamper's bastion of a desk.

"Ah, there you are," said Sol Hamper. "Well, take a seat. Have a chair. Make yourself comfortable." He clicked a key of the intercom box. "No calls, Irene. Nobody," he said. He leaned back in his chair, put the unlighted cigar in his mouth, and touched his fingertips together. He looked from Sally to George, smiled, and said, "So what's new?"

"You tell us," said George Meredith Mantz-Manners.

"Yeah, I'll tell you all right. What's the big idea?"

"What had to be, had to be, Sol," said George. "I'm pregnant."

"Listen here, Meredith. I don't want any of your fag sense of humor. We got our bellyful of that these last couple days. You take this young lady off to Vegas and make a laughingstock. Not only out of her, but the studio, matrimony, the entire motion picture industry."

"Have you had any cancellations?"

"Cancellations? Cancellations of what?"

"Bookings. My pictures. Sally's pictures."

"That ain't the way we do business. This is picture business, not vaudeville. But that ain't saying it won't be next to impossible to sell next season's product. Next to impossible. We got two Sally Standish pictures lined up for next season, and what you two done yesterday, the day before yesterday. All them small-town bookings, there'll be pickets in every theater from here to Bangor, Maine."

"Very well. We'll get a divorce," said George.

"Jee-zuz Christ, man! Are you out of your mind? We got enough trouble with this marriage."

"Then I don't see what you want us to do. We don't have to get a real divorce. Sally can get an annulment. On grounds that the marriage was never consummated."

"You lousy fag son of a bitch. Do you want to ruin us?"

"No, dear," said George. "I'm forever grateful to pictures and to this studio. I adore pictures, and the studio, and you, Sol. You just tell us what's on your mind. Or have you got anything on your mind? Aside from wanting to give us hell."

"You got a fag way of thinking. It's a regular fag way of thinking, till you twist everything around."

"Of course," said George. "When you're ready to cool down a bit, I have a suggestion or two."

"Yeah? Who wants any suggestions from you?"

"No one, I guess," said George. "I've tried to tell you that the Utrillo would look better over there than there. The light's—"

"Cut the crap, cut the crap. Let's hear it," said Sol.

"Well, Solly, it's only a suggestion."

"You bet your sweet ass it is."

"My what? I didn't know you cared," said George. "All right, Sol. Down to business. Down to brass tacks. In the first place, you know damn well you can't do a thing to us. We did the most respectable thing you can do—get married. No matter what you think of our marriage, dear boy, it *is* a *marriage.* Therefore we don't come under the morality clause or anything like it. Show him your ring, Sally."

"I don't want to see no ring. You keep talking," said Sol.

"A few nasty-minded people in Hollywood may think this marriage wasn't made in heaven, but nobody cares what they think."

"They don't, eh? I was talking to New York this morning. You ought to see a line they got in Kilgallen's column."

"Does it mention my name?" said George.

"It don't come out with your name, but everybody knows who it's about."

"Well, maybe I can sue her. In any event, Sol, you can't do anything to two people who go to Las Vegas and have a legal marriage ceremony. So you mustn't make any threats of reprisal against us. I'm sure Rosenbloom in Legal would tell you that if you made one move in that direction, he'd tell you you were out of your mind. Wouldn't that make a nice story in the newspapers? A studio invoking the morals clause because a man and woman veil up. Legal and Publicity would soon talk you out of that, Sol. So what is there left for you to do?"

"You tell me. You got something up your sleeve."

"A handkerchief," said George. "I'll tell you what you can do. And I mean this quite sincerely. Get Rosenbloom in here so he can hear what I have to say."

"Forget about Rosenbloom. Tell me first."

"Very well. I just thought it would save time if Rosenbloom were here. The truth of the matter is, Sol, both Sally and I are quite fed up with making pictures. We want to quit."

"That don't break my heart," said Sol.

"Sally's contract has fifteen more weeks to run. Mine has a little longer, but it's roughly the same. All we want is for you to agree to keep us on salary for the remainder of our contracts, and we'll leave Hollywood today. Or the day after tomorrow, actually."

Sol laughed. "Now who's out of their mind?"

"Oh, you say no to everything, automatically. But this makes a lot of sense from your point of view. Sally and I want to go away, to Europe. We want to get out of the Hollywood rat-race. And we can. We don't need your permission, Sol. You can say we'll never work in Hollywood again, and that would be perfectly true. You could keep us from ever working in pictures anywhere. But you can't make us stay here. If Sally were in the midst of shooting a picture and walked out on you, you might be able to take some legal action, but she happens to be on vacation. And I am assigned to her next picture, the one based on the original I sold you. Actually, not her next picture, but the one after that. So there's nothing to keep us from packing up and leaving tomorrow, because the only threat you can hold over our heads is that we'll never get another job in pictures. But we don't care a hoot about that."

"I like to think about it," said Sol.

Meredith Manners shook his head. "No. We want your answer now. You called us in here to bully us, but you didn't have a leg to stand on. You should have been nice and wished us happiness, but instead you said a lot of very nasty things to my wife and me."

"I just got to thinking. If you're so fed up with pictures, why did you come back to Hollywood?"

"The money, Sol. You'd understand that," said Meredith Manners. "We'd like you to keep us on the payroll for that little extra. Fifteen weeks in Sally's case, and just about that in mine."

"Only a mere trifle of around forty-five thousand dollars for the two of you. Some wedding present."

"I'm not going to beg you for it, but if you don't think Sally's entitled to it. She made eight pictures for you, all good money-makers. You could think of it as a bonus of six thousand for each of her pictures, and never mind about me. Never mind about the stories I called to your attention that made good pictures for you. I looked upon that as part of my job, although strictly speaking it was the story editor's job."

Sol looked at Sally. "What do you think about all this, Sally? You never opened your mouth the whole conversation."

She looked at her husband and shrugged her shoulders.

"You got her like she was hypnotized," said Sol.

"She is," said George. "Aren't you, Sally?"

Sally nodded.

"She looks prettier than I ever saw her," said Sol.

"That's what marriage does to some girls," said George.

"You think you're kidding, but do you know something? This

young lady, I had her in eight pictures. Eight pictures. But I never had the slightest interest. I never even offered her a cup of coffee, and you know why? I tell you why. Because she was always too frisky. Too excitable. I like a dame that's quiet. Reserved, if you know what I mean. Ever since I knew this young lady she always looked like she was ready to break into a Charleston. Hey-hey. Charleston. They come in here and wave their keester at me, and I'm supposed to start breathing heavy like a hard-up kid. *She* used to come in here like that. They all think Sol Hamper can be had as easy as that. But not me. She can tell you herself, I never made a pass at her. But I would now. Sally, we get rid of this handkerchief-up-his-sleeve and take a trip somewhere."

She shook her head.

"He won't mind. Why should he mind?"

She looked at her husband.

"You don't have to ask him," said Sol. "Make up your own mind."

"She won't, though, Sol."

"I want to hear her say it. Will you go, or won't you?"

"No," said Sally.

"But if you told her to say yes, would she say yes?" said Sol.

"Academic. Because I'm not going to tell her to say yes. So why don't you stop bothering her? Let's get on with our discussion, if there is anything to discuss. If not, we bid you adieu."

"You go out of here when I tell you to."

"Would you like to bet?" George stood up. "Come on, Sally." She stood up.

"I warn you, Manners. You walk out that door and you'll never get another nickel out of pictures. Her either."

"You're getting tiresome, Sol. Say goodbye to the man, Sally."

"Good-bye," said Sally. She took the arm her husband offered, and they left the office. "Keep walking and don't say a word," he whispered to her. "And don't look around."

They proceeded to the elevator and pushed the button. "Don't look around," said George. "There's somebody coming down the hall, but don't look."

It was Sol Hamper, a little out of breath. "I decided to walk down to the car with you. There's no use parting bad friends."

"That's terribly nice of you," said George. The elevator door glided open and they got in.

"You're actually leaving town?"

"As soon as possible," said George.

"Whereabouts do you think you'll go?" said Sol.

"Most likely to an island called Majorca. It's in the Mediterranean."

"Well, I'll be over in Europe the latter part of October," said Sol.

"Then you must come and see us, if you're anywhere near."

"What kind of a place is this you're going to?"

"Rather picturesque. A sizable artists' colony. Writers."

"Like Carmel?"

"Well, more or less."

"What's *she* gonna do there—Sally?"

"Study."

"Study what? Art?"

"Humanity."

"What kind of an answer's that? You can study humanity anywhere."

"Except here."

"Is it cheap to live there?"

"Very."

"How cheap?"

"Oh, I have friends living there, that do very well on two thousand a year."

"I make better than that a week," said Sol.

"Of course you do."

"I'd like to have a look at the place, for when I retire," said Sol. "Who owns it?"

"Spain."

"How are they towards Jews, do you happen to know?"

"No, I don't, but I can find out for you."

"What's the name of the place you're staying?"

"Palma is the largest city, but I'll have to let you know when we get there."

"You promise me that?"

"Yes, if you promise me something."

"What?"

"That you won't come there and start your own little picture company."

"Meredith, once I retire I hope I never see another foot of film. That's where I envy you. That, and her. A woman that don't have to talk, talk, talk. I don't get it, why she wanted to marry you. But I don't know why you'd want to marry any woman."

"Sol, I'm afraid you're not very consistent. The thing that you think is most important in marriage is also something that you can have any time you want to. But you're very particular about the kind of woman you enjoy it with. Therefore, it isn't absolutely essential to your relationship with women. The same is true for me. I happen to want it even less than you do."

"Are you trying to make me out a fag?"

"Maybe a half fag."

"Well, don't try to make me out more than half. Because the half I got that *ain't* fag, that gives me plenty of trouble. Plenty. Where you got your car parked?"

"My regular place."

"Tomorrow they'll paint somebody else's name there. We got a shortage of parking space."

"You can paint Sally's name out too."

"Yeah, and I wished I could paint my own out. The times I have to drag myself out of bed and come here."

"Give it up."

"For what? I ain't so sure you won't be back, either. So I decided to give the both of you the wedding present. You're on the payroll till your next options come up."

"There's a gimmick, Sol. What is it?"

"I don't know. I'll let Rosenbloom figure out something. Look at her. Tell her it's all right to smile, will you?"

"Smile for the man, Sally."

She smiled.

The Sun Room

THE BUTLER WHO came to the door was English and correct, down to the black four-in-hand tie and gold watch-chain. "Good afternoon, sir," he said. "Mr. and Mrs. Barlow?"

"Yes, we're expected," said Henry Barlow.

"Yes, if you'll just follow me, please," said the butler.

"We're a little early," said Barlow. "We thought we'd have more trouble finding it."

"Very good, sir. If you'll just have a seat in here," said the butler, and bowed in the direction of a small room. Henry and Wilma Barlow sat down and the butler disappeared.

"A butler, yet," said Wilma Barlow.

"Yes," said her husband. "His name is Kenneth Kingsley. Didn't you recognize him?"

"Why should I?" said Wilma Barlow.

"Well, maybe you shouldn't. He's been in seventy-five thousand pictures."

"You know him?" said Wilma.

"No, but I recognized him," said Henry. "He never got to be a Leo G. Carroll or Arthur Treacher, but he worked."

"I guess I didn't notice butlers," said Wilma.

"That's why he worked. He wasn't supposed to be noticed. But he probably went right on year after year, making his fifteen or twenty thousand—and saving it. He probably owns some nice real estate."

"Then why would he be doing this?" said Wilma.

"Because Eileen asked him to, and because he couldn't say no to the money she offered him. How the hell should I know?"

"Funny he didn't recognize you," said Wilma.

"Why should he? He probably never saw me before, and believe me, movie butlers were never impressed by movie writers. I just happen to have an extraordinarily good memory for bit players and dress extras. I should have had a job at Central Casting."

"It worked out better this way," said Wilma.

"The pay was better this way," said Henry.

The butler returned. "Miss Elliott will see you in the sun room," he said. "This way, please." He now led the Barlows through corridors on varying levels and finally to a large, glass-inclosed porch. "Mr. and Mrs. Barlow," he announced.

"Of course, Henry and Wilma, you're so prompt," said Eileen Elliott. She gave them both hands and presented her cheek to be kissed. "What delicious intoxicant can I offer you?"

"A very light Scotch and water for me," said Henry Barlow.

"Oh—a vodka and tonic, if I may," said his wife.

"You may anything," said Eileen. "Let me bartend, I *want* to." She thus dismissed the butler, who bowed and vanished.

"Didn't he used to work for someone else?" said Henry.

"Some very old families named Fox and Goldwyn and Warner. Also the Paramounts and the Metros, and no doubt the Republics. His name is Kenneth Kingsley, and he's an old dear. I've been in any number of pictures with him. He won't come if I'm having a director friend or one of the old-time stars. It would embarrass him and embarrass them. But a writer is different. Didn't you recognize him, Henry?"

"Well, as a matter of fact, I did," said Henry.

"It was nice of you not to let on. He comes because he adores me. He doesn't need the money, the old fox. He owns a motel out in the Valley. He's as queer as a jaybird, but there was always a certain type of pansy that watched every single penny. If you were nice to them, you could always go to them for money, if they had any reason to think you'd pay them back. Kenneth lent me the money for my first abortion, that's how long I've known him. I couldn't go to the father, because he was a star and I was very much on the make for him, and he'd have dropped me like the proverbial hotcake. He did anyway, the stupid bastard. Why stupid? Because I kept him out of a picture when I became a star. And there you have the story of my first three years in Hollywood. I'm dying to know why you wanted to come to see me."

"I said in my note, I wanted Wilma to meet some of the real people," said Henry.

"That's subject to several interpretations," said Eileen. "I'm sure you know, Mrs. Barlow, that your husband and I had a torrid romance lasting two months."

"Three," said Henry.

"Was it three?" said Eileen.

"Yes, I knew," said Wilma.

"We were both very young, of course," said Eileen. "I was practically a virgin, having had only one abortion. And Henry was an innocent young writer who tried to lay every girl in Hollywood, and very nearly succeeded."

"I missed out on a few," said Henry.

"But we always stayed friends," said Eileen. "You could, you know. More than once, as I've gotten older, I've found myself admiring some middle-aged man and had to remind myself that there was a *time,* there was a *time.* We were so full of sex, and so active, that it left no impression whatever. Anyway, you'd go out of your mind re-living all your old romances. If a man wasn't an out-and-out fairy, and you weren't too tired, you'd say, 'All right, come on over,' and who cared whether you went to bed with him or didn't? If you didn't, he was almost sure to say you did. And if he was a big enough star, *you'd* say you did. I was married four times. I had a son by my first marriage, and he's over forty. He and his father live in my home town back in Ohio. Both married, have families of their own, and the only time I ever hear from them is when some friends of theirs wants to visit a studio. My son was brought up by his stepmother, and she and his father have managed to convince him that I abandoned him for a career in pictures. The fact is that my first husband used to beat hell out of me whenever he got tight, and I did run off to Detroit with a band leader. My husband kidnaped my son and left me with the band leader, and I came to Hollywood with him. I could sing a little, but what made the difference was that I had a shape. A lot of girls had shapes, but that was during the flat-chested look, the tight bras. Not for me. I had them, and I showed them, and boy did the women hate me! But not the younger ones, and they were the ones that were going to the movies. In droves. The men liked me, and the young girls liked me, and I got paid ten thousand dollars a week. Five for the right one, and five for the left one."

"Oh, the face helped a little," said Henry.

"Thank you, dear," said Eileen. "You see why we had our mad romance, lasting three months? He remembered that I had a face too."

"It was a nice face. It had real sweetness," said Wilma.

"You must have been one of the younger ones," said Eileen.

"Well, not much younger."

"Did you belong to one of my fan clubs?"

"No. But I was a fan," said Wilma.

"You never wrote me for a picture, enclosing twenty-five cents to cover cost of mailing?"

"No, I didn't."

"The odd thing was that girls used to send me pictures of themselves, to prove that their bust development was as good as mine. Needless to say, I never rushed into a producer's office with one of those pictures. Right into the wastebasket they went. And the better the bosom the quicker the wastebasket. What kind of a damn fool did they think I was? Ten thousand a week. I wonder what ever happened to it—as if I didn't know."

"Are you broke, Eileen?"

"Make me an offer. No, I'm not broke. I have a nice income. It's no ten thousand a week, and it isn't as much as they pay the President of the United States. But Honest Andy Anderson—do you remember Honest Andy?"

"Sure. The agent," said Henry Barlow.

"Honest Andy made me go into the studio retirement plan, and it's paying off now. Also, I go back every summer and do the straw hat circuit for ten weeks, and that pays very well. And once a year I go to Vegas for two or three weeks. I'm not filthy rich any more, but I live nicely and I pay the taxes on this house. One of these days this house is going to make a lot of money for Eileen."

"It's beautiful, isn't it?" said Wilma.

"And I'd sell it at the drop of a hat, but I have to get my price. Would you like to buy it?"

"No, we're settled in Vermont," said Henry Barlow. "Wilma writes, too."

"Not really. I'm a teacher," said Wilma.

"She teaches creative writing, and so do I."

"And your books make money, don't they?"

"They do pretty well. We don't need much," said Henry. "I never got up to ten thousand a week."

"But you got two," said Eileen.

"No, fifteen hundred was my top. But I used to get as much as twenty-five for an original, and a six-weeks' guarantee for working on the screen play. For a man of limited talent I did all right."

"Are you and Wilma going to write about me?"

"I hadn't thought of it," said Henry.

"Oh, what a liar," said Eileen. "Every writer that comes here goes away and writes something."

"Some of them have, there's no doubt about that," said Henry. "That's why I wanted Wilma to see for herself. But we're not going to write about you, so relax."

"Well, why *don't* you write about me? What you don't know, I'd be willing to tell you. And I wouldn't sue."

"I don't think people care that much any more," said Henry.

"Maybe you're right. There's practically nothing left to the imagination on the screen, so why should they want to read about it? Do you remember when we used to look at dirty movies at parties?"

"Yes," said Henry,

"I used to love them, frankly. But I saw a feature picture a week ago, two big present-day stars that got a half a million apiece for this picture. In our day they'd have got fifty dollars for just about the same thing. I mean, what they left out of this picture the other night I'm sure is on film. Because what they started, they had to finish, you know? We did one on 16-millimetre at Malibu. The works. It was practically suicidal to let that get around. The studio sent for me and I went to J.B.'s office and of course denied everything. The only trouble was, he had a print right there, and it was a dirty movie all right. So I broke down and admitted it, and waited for the ax to fall. The morals clause. Well, it was the morals clause that saved us. How the hell were they going to tell the American public that they were firing four of their biggest stars for being in a dirty movie?"

"What finally happened?" said Wilma.

"They got rid of one girl that they were going to get rid of anyway. They simply didn't renew her option. The rest of us got away with it, although it cost the studio a fortune to buy up the prints and the negative. I understand they're planning a remake of the picture."

"Oh, come on," said Henry.

"Oh, not with the original cast," said Eileen. "Actually, when I was in England shortly after the war I met a duke, who told me he had seen me in a film that not many people had seen. It was the dirty movie we made in Malibu, and the studio had shown it to a select few V.I.P.'s in New York. 'How was my makeup?' I said. I wasn't going to take any crap from him, duke or no duke."

"How *was* your makeup?" said Henry.

" 'Outdoor Number 7,' I think I used," said Eileen. "Not taking any crap from you either, Henry."

"I'd forgotten Outdoor Number 7," said Henry. "There's so much I don't remember about picture business. But I did remember Kenneth Kingsley. Why did you have him here today? Not to impress us."

"Not exactly impress you, but yes, to impress you if you were going to be condescending."

"We're not in the least condescending, and anyway, how could we be? You're still Eileen Elliott."

"You can bet your sweet ass I am. Anybody that thinks they can tear that up and thereby make me into nobody—they soon find out. They can laugh at the scrapbooks and the souvenirs, but I have them. Some little jerk pretends to pity me, with my memories and my mementoes, but I can always say, 'And how many kings did you know, mister? How many presidents did *you* have *your* picture taken with?' And I'm not talking about college presidents. I'm talking about presidents of the United States. Coolidge, Hoover, F.D.R., Truman. Eisenhower, when he was a general but not when he was President. By that time I wasn't getting top billing, a hundred percent of the main title. I had some pushy little woman come and ask me to donate some money to some charity she was heading up out here. She said Mr. Eisenhower was honorary chairman and gave a strong hint that the major contributors would get an autographed picture. 'You mean *this* Eisenhower?' I said, and showed her a picture of Eisenhower and me during the war. Any autograph I don't have, I don't want. How many Lyndon B. Johnsons will you trade me for my Wallace Reid?"

"Wasn't he a little before your time?" said Henry.

"In his heyday, he was, but the poor junkie, I asked him for one anyway," said Eileen. "Tell me about your job, teaching at the University of Vermont."

"Anticlimax department," said Henry. "Well, it isn't the University of Vermont. It's a smaller college called Whitefield, privately endowed."

"That sounds rich," said Eileen. "Or are you here to put the bite on me?"

"We didn't have that in mind, but I'm sure a large donation would be gratefully accepted," said Henry. "No, it was started a few years ago by the Whitefield Foundation, mostly the heirs of the late Benjamin Whitefield and his brothers. They were in the textile business, and the Foundation started with twenty million but became worth a lot more. We have about five hundred and fifty students. Small, by present-day standards, but our entrance requirements are fairly high."

"You mean they don't let in any Jews, Henry?"

"I wouldn't say that. No restrictions based on race, creed, color, or national origin. Only on the individual's potential."

"I was wondering," said Eileen. "And Wilma teaches creative writing there?"

"I give a course in creative writing," said Wilma. "I don't like to say I *teach* creative writing."

"I guess if it's creative, it can't be taught. Is that what you mean?" said Eileen.

"Exactly," said Wilma.

"They wanted me to give a course in acting at one of the local universities. I thought about it. One week I'd lecture on bust development, which was such a great help in my career. The next week I'd demonstrate the technique of the casting couch, which was also a great help in my career. I could spend several weeks on that. Then of course the art of reading contracts. The man that came to see me about it was inclined to think I wasn't taking the thing seriously enough, but I assured him that I was. If he was talking about acting for the movies, it was a damned sight more important to know how to handle producers than it was to give out with the pear-shaped tones. But he wasn't talking about movies. He was talking about *films.* He called them films, and I called them movies. I never learned to call them anything else, try as I might. Always movies. Never films. And never, never cinema. Those people that call them films, and cinema, they're the kind of people that talk about the art of some little broad that makes a sexy mouth and every man, woman and child in the world gets the message. That's art? Who's kidding who? The poor little broad begins to believe it, and the next thing you know she's late on the set, and fighting with the director, and coming out against poverty. She ought to be in favor of poverty. If it wasn't for poverty, who'd want to go to the movies? They used to say it was Mr. DeMille that popularized the bathtub. Nuts. It was the ordinary set dressers with ordinary tubs, not Mr. DeMille and a pool full of slaves. You might as well say Mr. DeMille popularized slavery. People who worked for him wouldn't give you an argument there. But I don't know that that was more true of Mr. DeMille than a lot of other directors. Give anybody too much authority and you have a slave-driver. I'll bet you can be a son of a bitch with your pupils, Henry."

"Students. I don't call them pupils," said Henry.

"*I* don't call them *students,*" said Wilma.

"Well, you have to have some name for them," said Henry.

"Enrollees," said Wilma. "Time-passers. Excuse-makers."

"You gather she hates her work," said Henry.

"I really do," said Wilma. "But I'd never say so in Vermont."

"All work is disgusting," said Eileen. "Ten thousand dollars a week doesn't make it any the less so. But it's nicer to be paid ten thousand a week for doing something you don't like than fifty dollars a week for something you don't like. My idea of heaven was getting full salary for doing nothing. The home office used to call from New York and raise hell. 'When is that Eileen Elliott picture starting shooting?' And the supervisor, as we used to call them then, would say we were having script trouble. It almost never occurred to them to have the script ready ahead of time. And as far as I was concerned, it didn't make any difference. I was getting paid anyway. *Then.* When I began to slip a little and wasn't getting ten thousand fifty-two weeks a year, I began to feel the pinch. Only the pinch didn't come from the big producers. The pinch, or the feel, came from elderly English actors. I could always tell when I was beginning to slip. That was when the English actors began to make up for lost time. They wanted to be able to put it in their memoirs that they had put it in me. And I may say that one or two of them did. They weren't much different from the cloak-and-suiters, but they could make adultery seem high class. Adultery! What a word! What a fancy word! I don't think I ever stopped to think that I was committing adultery. The only time I was conscious of committing adultery was when I ran away with the band leader, and I wouldn't have thought of it then if my husband's lawyer hadn't reminded me. Legal language can take the fun out of anything. I'm still not sure what sodomy is. Is that when—well, never mind. I'd rather not know."

"Oh, you know, Eileen," said Henry.

"As a matter of fact I do," said Eileen. "But I have to stop and think. When I was a girl back in Ohio I thought it was one thing, and then I found out it was something else. Sodom and gonorrhea was the way I associated them. Does this remind you two of your conversations back on the old campus?"

"You should hear the conversations back at the old campus," said Wilma. "Those kids all know what sodomy is."

"Well, I should hope so," said Eileen. "They're supposed to be educated, aren't they? My son is a college graduate, and if he doesn't know what sodomy is, I wasted a lot of money. Oh, yes, I was allowed to pay for his education. His stepmother and his father didn't want me to abandon him *that* much. They thought it would embarrass me to come to his graduation, but I wouldn't have been a bit embarrassed. I could have brought the bills along to show I had a right to be there. Do I sound bitter? I don't mean to. If you want to know the truth, I'm confused. I haven't been able to figure out why you came to see me. Why did you?"

"No angle, no hidden motive," said Henry. "As I said before, I wanted Wilma to meet one of the real ones."

"The real what, Henry?" said Eileen. "The old-time movie star, waiting for the phone to ring? The broken-down glamor girl with a pansy actor for a butler? You have plenty of curiosity, or you wouldn't be here. So I'm entitled to some curiosity of my own. You say no angle, no hidden motive, but that's only what you *say*. Wilma, did you think it would be sort of fun to make love to me, or me to make love to you? That would be a good one to tell back in Vermont."

"I never thought of it," said Wilma. "Why did you?"

"Why did I? Because I always think that women that dress like you, those black blouses and tan cotton skirts, and those ballet slippers—they all look as if they spent a lot of time with the head-shrinker."

"I was in analysis," said Wilma.

"I was sure of it," said Eileen.

"Weren't you ever?"

"Of course I was, when it was the thing to do," said Eileen. "You either bought a Picasso, or you were psychoanalyzed. Sometimes both, but if you were making two thousand a week you did at least one. You *had* to. You were nothing if you didn't. I didn't know anything about art, so I settled for the couch. Well, now, I want to tell you, I went to that guy for two months, and what I didn't know about him at the end of two months simply wasn't worth knowing. But then we all got interested in the Hollywood Canteen, war work. Have your picture taken washing dishes and doing the Lambeth Walk with the service men. Loddy da-da loddy da, loddy da-da loddy da. I was just getting around to the interesting part, how I fell in love with the iceman's horse when I was ten years old, and I had to tell the head-shrinker that they wanted me in the war effort. So he slapped me with a nice fat bill for professional services and I guess no one will ever know about me and the iceman's horse. I go back to the day when there *were* icemen and they had *horses*. I cover a lot of American history. My father-in-law had a Haynes. Do you know what a Haynes is? Or was? It was a big car that people bought in Ohio. My father-in-law had one that he drove us to church in on Sunday. My husband washed it every Saturday so it'd be nice and shiny on Sunday, for church, and it was just about the only God damn time we ever got a ride in the God damn thing. My father-in-law was the meanest old bastard in the State of Ohio, and the only thing he ever loved was that Haynes car. He'd sit there on the side porch and watch my husband washing it. 'Don't get any water on the upholstery. It's bad for the leather,' he used to say. He was Presbyterian and I was brought up Lutheran, on top of which my father worked with his hands, and wore overalls. No trade, no steady job. Anything he could get. He played the cornet in the town band, and that was his way of getting free beer. Hard liquor he liked better, but beer was free for the men in the band. You see I had a musical background, what with my father and the man I ran away with. He also preferred hard liquor. In fact I never saw him take a glass of beer, not even to be sociable. But he was sweet. He really was. When he got tired of me and wanted to get rid of me for good and all, he did his best to pass me on to his tenor sax player, the highest paid man in the band. That's what I call sweet, don't you? If you don't, you don't know musicians."

"You were never much of a drinker, were you?" said Henry.

"Not then, and not now," said Eileen. "You'll see me put away a few scoops of vodka, or gin, or tequila as the day wears on. But it has very little effect on me except it makes me drunk. No, I wouldn't call myself a drinker. What the hell do you mean, I was never much of a drinker? I started hitting it when I was in my early twenties, and the only reason I'm alive now is because I never stopped. Some women, most women put on weight when they drink. It just so happens that I don't. We all have a different chemistry, and I don't put on weight. I may get disagreeable, or I may wake up and wonder who that is I'm in bed with, but I don't get fat. I weigh now just about what I weighed when they were paying me ten thousand a week, a hundred and twenty-eight pounds. I never diet, I never go on the wagon, I've never given up smoking, I don't take any exercise. They ask me what the secret is, and I tell them. Do what you please, and keep out of jail. I said that in an interview once and the studio had a hemorrhage. I was denounced from every pulpit, a man made a speech in Congress, and the women's clubs threatened to march on Hollywood. I was going to be boycotted all over the world. But it had the opposite effect. The grosses on my next picture were bigger than ever and it was a lousy picture, but my little announcement of my personal philosophy saved it. It isn't the public that cares whether a movie actress is having an affair with a married man. It's the studios. They have some idea that if they put the pressure on you morally, they can keep putting it on when option time comes up. As far as morals are concerned, I'd still be making ten thousand a week. But the one thing you can't beat is youth. Not age. Youth. Youth is another word for new faces. Not new figures. New faces. We all know how a woman is constructed, and why. But about once a year a new face comes along, and there's no way to fight it, and I can prove it. I could go out now and round up a dozen car-hops with figures as good as mine ever was. But I can't turn them into movie stars by just photographing their shapes. The kisser, the face is what counts. But they get hired for their shapes, the way I was. Why? Because they're hired by men, and men see the shape first. I've come to the conclusion that every studio should have a committee of Lesbians and fairies to pass judgment on the new talent, because they actually look at the faces. The only trouble with my idea is that the committee would be hiring all their little chums, and the queers go for some very strange mutts. The queers only go for people they can feel sorry for, feel superior to, masculine, feminine, or neuter. They can spot a weakness right away, and that makes *them* feel good. If you want to be popular with the queers, you'd better have a weakness. In my case, they liked me because they could make jokes about my shape, which they turned into a land of a weakness. Fortunately, the normals didn't see it that way, and I became a big star. But I stayed popular with the queers because my morals were bad and I was always getting into trouble with the studio. You want to know, if I was popular with the queers, were the queers popular with me? Well, if you mean was I one of them—no. Did I play around with them? Maybe a little around the edges. A little. You go through phases in this town, and I guess I went through most of them, but my queer phase didn't last very long. A jealous man I can understand, but a jealous Lez is sort of ridiculous, as if she were carrying the masculine bit too far. At least that was what happened to me. I had a Lesbian girl friend—and believe me, when they take over, they take over. She ran my house for me, and gave me financial advice, and got rid of some of the people that were sponging off of me. She was the same as a husband, except of course in the one department. And that was the whole trouble. I like an occasional man—a habit I got into when I was about fifteen and was never able to break myself of. Nature invented the male sex, and I refused to deprive myself of them. But my girl friend was very jealous and she finally said it was either them or her. Out of politeness I gave the matter some serious thought, like counting up to two, and came to my decision. She spread some nice stories about me, but how can you top the fact that for about a year she was living here with me and everybody knew it? How do you ruin a reputation like mine?"

"I never thought of your reputation as being especially notorious," said Henry.

"You take that back or I'll sue you!" said Eileen. "The only thing I was never accused of was murder, and I came pretty close to that. Not that I ever killed anybody, but I was on a party where a silly broad shot herself and everybody there was questioned. Do you remember Dolly Duval?"

"I do, but I don't think Wilma would," said Henry.

"She was—let's face it—one of those dime-a-dozen not-quite stars that had to shoot herself to get publicity. That may sound heartless and cruel, but it's the truth, and she'd have shot someone else, anyone else, if it would have done her any good. There've always been girls in picture business that would do anything for the publicity, but no matter what they'd do, the newspaper people wouldn't print it. Dolly was one of those. Another thing about them, they're always publicly in love with guys that aren't in love with *them*. They're what used to be called professional torch-carriers. Some guys would go to bed with them, thinking it was a one-night stand, and a couple of days later she'd be on the phone to the columnists saying that this was it, this was the only guy she ever loved, et cetera. Meanwhile the poor chump was in blissful ignorance of any romance, and the first thing he'd know about it was if one of the columnists called up to check. 'What's this about you and Dolly Duval?' they'd say. 'Dolly *Duval?*' he'd say. 'Come on, pal, you've got to do better than that.' But you'd be surprised at some of the big names that she got mixed up with. It finally got so that guys avoided her like Typhoid Mary, although she wasn't bad-looking and she had a nice little shape. She'd come to press parties alone, uninvited, and usually she'd go home with one of those correspondents for the foreign papers, the great free-loaders of all time. Even they were wise to her, but she was buying the dinner, also providing the other entertainment, and some of those creeps were hard to please."

"She was pretty. I remember her," said Henry.

"How well?" said his wife.

"Not *that* well," he said.

"No, Henry wasn't a star, and he was never one of those free-loaders. Dolly Duval wouldn't have gone for Henry—lucky for Henry," said Eileen. "This one night, there was a big opening, a world pre-meer at the Cathay Circle. Searchlights. Radio interviews. All the hired limousines. The bleacher seats for the fans. This one Dolly was invited to, because she had a small part in the picture, and her studio saw to it that she had an escort. He was a creature named Rod Something. Rod was a New York actor who usually played gangster parts, and hung around the Vine Street Derby. Rod Rainsford, he called himself, and he also had a part in the picture. Well, what do you know but he damn near stole the picture, and on the way out they were all talking about a new Cagney, a new Tracy, a new George Raft. And nobody was talking about Dolly Duval. Nobody. In those days everybody went to the Troc after every opening, and Dolly had reserved a table to make sure she got one. But when she and Rainsford arrived at the Troc he was whisked away by the studio big shots, and given a seat at their table between the head of the studio and Marlene Dietrich. I've never known anyone for being there at the right time like Marlene, and of course she was a bigger star than Dolly Duval. And where was Dolly? Dolly was at her own table, with a couple of bit players. In fact, one of them was Kenneth Kingsley, my temporary butler today. Kenneth looked well in tails, and he never got drunk, but he wasn't the lion of the hour. The lion of the hour was at the big shots' table with Marlene. After the Troc there was a party at somebody's house in Beverly, to which all the cast were invited, and Dolly couldn't keep away. She arrived alone, having sent Kenneth and the other person home, and she then proceeded to drink it up. Up to that time she'd stayed sober and on her good conduct, but she had a few things to say to Mr. Rainsford and she was going to get them off her pretty little chest."

"I remember. It was a pretty little chest," said Henry.

"It seems to me you remember too well," said Wilma.

"Go on with your story, Eileen," said Henry.

"Try and stop me," said Eileen. "One thing about our Mr. Rainsford, some of the people he hung out with at the Vine Street Derby were genuine hoods, and one of them was called Al Cummings. He was a gambler, a bookmaker, mixed up in the rackets, and altogether a very bad boy. I imagine Rainsford owed him money, because Rainsford was the kind of guy that owed everybody money, including hoods. It was easier to borrow money from hoods, because they charged high interest, and they liked to have people like Rainsford in hock to them. Cummings always carried a large bankroll, and he always carried a medium-large revolver. They were sitting there when Dolly arrived, and she had a big double bourbon and went over and sat beside Cummings. 'Hello, Al,' she said. 'What are you doing wasting your time with this small-time hambo? I thought you had better taste.' Something like that. She was really burned up at Rainsford, and began making passes at Cummings, in the course of which she came across his revolver. 'What's this?' she said, and took if out of his pocket. 'Give it back,' said Cummings. 'No, let her play with it,' said Rainsford. 'Let her blow her silly brains out.' And now I want to tell you something, because I was there, and only about from here to you away from them. That girl put the revolver to her ear and did just that. She pulled the trigger and blew her brains out. Ugh. Ugh. The whole half of her head, the whole left side was scattered all over. The yelling and screaming that went on, and at the same time the laughing, because the room was half full of people that didn't realize what had happened."

"She just put the gun to her head and shot herself?" said Henry. "Because Rainsford told her to? That seems incredible. Why would she want to do that?"

"There you start going into something that there's no real answer to," said Eileen. "How did she get into that state of mind?

It goes 'way back, I guess. She didn't do it because Rainsford told her to, but that's exactly why she did it. Rainsford was nothing to her, but who was? It came out later that Al Cummings was one of her many boy friends, but only one of many, and never anything big. The procession of guys that had to go to the district attorney's office was a parade of actors and agents and cheating husbands and chiselers and wolves and some nice guys that happened to be in Dolly's little book. Girls like Dolly Duval always keep a little book. Never fail. Alongside of some guy she's been sleeping with will be the name of the Japanese gardener or her foot doctor, but they're all in there. It would save a lot of trouble if they said who was what. I used to keep a diary, pretty hot stuff it was, too. But that was separate from the names of my foot doctor and the man that cleaned out my swimming-pool. Although one fellow that repaired my pool filter was in both. *There's* one I haven't thought of in years. He was absolutely beautiful, so consequently I was always having something the matter with my filter. You can take that any way you like, I don't care. You can knock California and I won't object, but where else could you call up the swimming-pool repairman at ten o'clock in the morning and at half past ten a beautiful blond Swede arrives to spend the day? He was an Olympic swimmer, or maybe a diver. Olympic I'm sure of. He's probably nothing now, but I suddenly remember him with great tenderness. He took my mind off Dolly Duval, and Kenneth Kingsley was never able to do that."

"Probably not," said Henry.

"They're always saying we had too much sex in Hollywood. But on the contrary, we never had enough," said Eileen.

"Do you mean on the screen, or off?" said Henry.

"Either. Both. On the screen the best they could do was once in a while in a mob scene they could sneak in a long shot of a man and a woman going at it, but that was always in some Roman orgy and you couldn't even be sure unless you had them rerun the footage. Even then you couldn't be positive. What they should have done back in the Thirties was show a couple of big stars going to bed together, the whole works. Close-ups. Two-shots. They'd have got a lot better acting, I can tell you, because it was all some of them could do. As a matter of fact they did get some good acting out of some of the men, who had no more desire to kiss a woman than I have to kiss a pig. Some of those male stars were so queer they'd come off the set after a love scene and be shaking with fright, afraid they were going to murder the girl. One of them told me once, 'Eileen, it isn't against *you* personally. It's because I can't stand to have a woman touch me.' But the director knew that, and he made us do our love scenes over and over again because he'd get one scene that he could print, and the actor would look like the most passionate lover in the history of the world. Why? Because real hate and real love are hard to tell apart. Dolly Duval loved herself and hated herself, which is why she blew her silly brains out. Or why any of us would. I never reached that stage, but I may yet. I'd hate to think my feelings weren't as deep as Dolly Duval's, but maybe that's why I'm still alive. If I were more sensitive, and more passionate, I could give myself a pretty good argument for knocking myself off. But I was never really passionate. Hot, but not passionate. You're my witness, Henry. Was I really passionate?"

"I thought you were, but maybe you were only hot," said Henry.

"I'm passionate, and not very hot," said Wilma.

"I was hoping you'd say that," said Eileen. "It was the way I had you figured. Henry wouldn't know the difference."

"There isn't any difference," said Henry. "You two just like to think there is."

"That's how much you know," said Eileen. "You've stayed married to a passionate woman, whereas the hot number that *I* was lasted a couple of months. Henry, you were more passionate than hot."

"That's not the way I remember it," he said, "But I could argue either way."

"And would, just for the sake of argument," said his wife. "The blond that came to fix your swimming pool—what was he?"

"Passionate," said Eileen.

"Because he'd stay all day?" said Henry.

"You're damn right," said Eileen.

"That wasn't passion, that was vitality, or virility," said Henry.

"You're damn right it was," said Eileen. "He could have stayed a week. Wilma, it was a pity you and he never got together, two passionate people."

"I probably would have taken an instant dislike to him. He probably looked too Nordic for me," said Wilma.

"He looked Nordic, all right. But you wouldn't have been the first Jewess I knew to go for a Nazi," said Eileen.

"Oh, he *was* a Nazi?" said Wilma.

"I don't know what the hell he was. Nordic, Nazi. When you say one you mean both, don't you?" said Eileen.

"Pretty much, I guess," said Wilma.

"Wilma could never have fallen in love with a Nazi," said Henry.

"Who said anything about love?" said Eileen.

"Have you got a picture of him anywhere around?" said Wilma.

"A *picture* of him?" said Eileen. "The man that took care of my swimming pool?"

"It wasn't all he took care of," said Henry.

"Why, I haven't even got a picture of *you,*" said Eileen.

"That doesn't surprise me," said Henry. "But I was never Olympic, at anything."

"Don't be *too* modest, Henry. I don't want to have to boast about you in front of your own wife."

"Go right ahead. I might learn something," said Wilma.

"So might I," said Henry.

"Yes, we all might," said Eileen. "I could put myself into some kind of a trance and remember every man I ever had any kind of relations with. And sometimes I do. But I'm probably wrong half the time. Did you ever have your appendix out, Henry?"

"Yes, when I was in high school."

"Did I?" said Eileen.

"Well, I don't remember," said Henry.

"You see?" said Eileen.

"Yes, but we weren't looking for appendectomy scars," said Henry.

"I remember some," said Eileen. "My swimming pool man had a beaut."

"Yes, I guess there's not much about him you don't remember," said Henry.

"You sound just a trifle jealous. How nice," said Eileen. "But don't be. He was all body. Tight blond curls. Big shoulders. No hips. Wilma, you really should have seen him. I'd have lent him to you. I was never stingy about that, and you must have had a nice little figure."

"Would that have made any difference?" said Wilma. "He sounds like he'd have done anything you told him to."

"That was more or less true," said Eileen. "More or less."

"I wish you wouldn't try to get my wife all steamed up about some stud horse you had an affair with thirty years ago," said Henry. "It isn't good for her."

"I've really taken a tremendous dislike to this man," said Wilma. "In fact, I'm not even sure he ever existed. Are you sure he isn't all your fantasies rolled into one?"

"I never had much time for fantasies, Wilma," said Eileen. "I was much too busy with action."

"A fantasy doesn't take long. You can have one while the action is going on," said Wilma.

"You shouldn't have said that," said Eileen. "I know it, and you know it, but Henry won't like it."

"Men have fantasies," said Henry.

"We know that too, but you don't like us to have them," said Eileen.

"How old-fashioned can you get?" said Henry. "Wilma has

been having an affair with Benjamin Disraeli since she was in high school."

"George Arliss must have spoiled it for her," said Eileen. "If there was ever a stuffed shirt it was George Arliss. I used to see him on the Warner lot. But I don't know who I'd have gone for in history. I can't think of anybody. Daniel Boone. He was a sort of Tarzan if you stop to think of it. Lafayette might have been fun, but I don't know much about him. Franklin—wasn't he quite a chaser?"

"I loved Disraeli, and he would have loved me," said Wilma.

"She really means that, too," said Henry.

"Arliss. That's all he is to me," said Eileen.

"Do you ever talk about anything but sex?" said Wilma.

"I guess I never get very far off the subject," said Eileen. "Maybe you'd rather talk about politics, but how long would it be before you got back on sex? Was Hitler a fairy, or wasn't he? He always seemed to be having a good time with that doll he was shacked up with but out here everybody insisted he was a queen. On the other hand, if it was so bad for him to be a fag, what about Marcel Proust?"

"Marcel *Proust?*" said Wilma.

"Yes, I heard of him, Wilma."

"You don't speak of him in the same breath," said Wilma.

"I do. I just did. I'm sitting right here with the first person that ever tried to get me to read Marcel Proust. Your husband."

"You tried to make her read Proust?" said Wilma.

"Yes, I tried," said Henry.

"And what's more, I did," said Eileen.

"And how did you like him?" said Wilma.

"Don't look down your schnoz at me, pal," said Eileen. "I didn't like him, but I didn't say so till after I read him. I know plenty of people that said they liked him, and hadn't read as much of him as I did. Don't look down your schnoz at me. Did you read him in French?"

"No, did you?"

"No, but I made ten thousand dollars a week. What did your father do for a living?"

"My father? He was in the textile business. And he *didn't* make ten thousand a week," said Wilma.

"Why not? That's what he was in it for, wasn't he? He wasn't in it because he liked the feel of cotton ginghams, was he? Or maybe he liked the feel of a size-ten model. Maybe we'd better get back on sex."

"Were we ever off it?" said Wilma.

"Not while I'm around," said Eileen. "I'm trying to be a good hostess, because I know damn well you and Henry came to see a sex freak. You came to the right place, all right. Now I think it's time you went back to Vermont and talked about Marcel Proust. But don't forget how I got my introduction to him. In a triple-size bed, with Mr. Henry Barlow, who wanted to improve my mind."

"We're being asked to leave, Henry," said Wilma.

"Oh, Henry can stay if he wants to," said Eileen.

"You bitch," said Wilma.

Malibu from the Sky

IN THE HILLS above Malibu she stopped her car for a look at the not too distant sea, her first real look at the waters of the Pacific. And though she had driven out from Hollywood with no other purpose than to be able to say she had seen the Pacific, it seemed a waste of time not to stay a few minutes and find out what thoughts came to her on this occasion. The thoughts began to come, and she did not like them much. She was here, she had come all the way, with too many stops along the way, and now that she was here, what the hell of it?

Down there was Malibu Beach, where the big shots had their beach houses, which they pretended were mere cottages, nothing at all, really. But she knew enough about those big shots to know that they had not started life with anything so grand as those mere cottages. Back where she had started her own life the biggest house in the whole town could not hold a candle to most of those beach cottages, in size or luxury. She knew. She had been to the biggest house in her old home town, and she had been to a couple of those beach cottages, so-called. In her home town the biggest house was owned by a rich Irish doctor, Dr. Kelly, who practically owned the local hospital and was said to own most of the stock in the larger of the two town banks, and out in the country he owned a farm where he had four or five trotting horses. She had never been to the farm, but she had been invited often to children's parties at the house in town—until, that is, she stopped being a child and started wearing high heels and a brassiere. Then the invitations stopped, although for a while there she was seeing more of Dr. Kelly's eldest son when he was home on vacations from Georgetown Prep. She well knew who had stopped the invitations to the Kelly house—Mrs. Kelly, Kevin's mother. "It's funny I never get invited to your house any more," she said to Kevin one night. She did not think it was very funny, but she wanted to see what Kevin would say. He fooled her. "You want to know why you're not invited any more?" he said. "I can give you two reasons." And he pressed his hand over each of her breasts. He was a wild one, not safe for a decent girl to go out with, everyone said. More money than was good for him, they said. Started drinking too early, others said. Spoiled by both his parents and chased after by everything in skirts, including a couple of married women who had husbands working in the mines. She had had some very anxious moments because of Kevin, especially those first two weeks after he was killed in an auto accident and she thought she might be having a baby. She would never have been able to go to Dr. and Mrs. Kelly for help, help of any kind. But after that narrow escape she left town, with sixty-five dollars her father gave her and thirty-five dollars from her mother. "Get work quick," said her father. "That's the last you can expect from us."

"I'll pay you back, every cent," she said.

"All right, if you can. We'll accept your kind offer," said her father. "But don't send home for any more, because there's none to give you. You only got this much because we won't be supporting you and there'll be that much saved." Her father worked in the mines, made good money in good times, but ever since the big strike, work in the mines was anything but steady. The car went, the washing machine was repossessed, the food on the table was enough to live on but not a pleasure to eat. The only time she saw steak was when Kevin would take her out in his car and they would stop for a sandwich on the way home.

The work she got in Philadelphia was not hard, even if it did not pay well, but with only two years of high school she was lucky to get anything that was easy and in pleasant surroundings and did not take much brains. It was clerking in a candy store near the Reading Terminal, eighteen dollars a week. It did not take her long to figure out why they hired her. Philadelphians eat a lot of candy, and a lot of it is bought by men. The commuters who took the Chestnut Hill local every afternoon liked her looks, as well they might, and pretty soon they were asking her to go out with them. One of them began to get pretty serious. She had no intention of letting him give up his wife and two kids, but she took money from him so that she could dress better and attract men who did not offer matrimony but might help her on her way to Hollywood.

It had always been Hollywood, Hollywood for itself and because it was the great chance for girls like herself. Some of the biggest stars had never had any acting experience, could not sing or dance. The important thing was to get there under contract to some studio, not to go there in the hope of finding a pleasant job in a candy store. A girl would be making a big mistake to go to Hollywood without a contract, and that was one mistake she was not going to make. She had even read about one girl who was *born* in Hollywood and went to school there, but had been smart enough to go to New York to be discovered. They did not think much of you out there unless you had a contract. And so the idea of a contract had always been in her mind.

One of the men she attracted in Philadelphia had a connection with a big movie company. That is, he worked in an office that distributed films. He never got to the Coast, although he often went to the New York office and had met the big stars. He had a lot of inside gossip on the stars and their peculiarities. It was quite a letdown to learn from him that one of her favorites did not like girls at all. How did he mean he did not like girls? "He likes boys," said her friend, Sid. That was her first personal disillusionment about Hollywood, and she did not like Sid for telling her such a thing. However, she went out with Sid and a couple of times she went to New York with him, and through Sid she met the man who persuaded her to come to New York. New York was New York, and she did not feel so strongly that you could not go there without a contract. The new man did not offer her a contract or even a job, but he paid her rent in an apartment just off Fifth Avenue in the West Fifties, and she got work modeling lingerie and hosiery and managed to get along rather well. Arthur, the man who paid her rent, was more important in the film business than Sid. He was in the theater end, with a title that she never could get straight—eastern district something, advertising, publicity, and exploitation. When he took her out to restaurants and speakeasies he was always saying hello to the newspaper fellows, and more or less as a gag one of the fellows that wrote a column put her name in print for the first time: "Model Mary-Lou Lloyd being screen-tested?" The comparatively few people who knew her were very impressed and took the item very seriously. A couple of nights later she was actually introduced as Mary-Lou Lloyd, who was being screen-tested. "Who by?" said the man to whom she was being introduced.

"Oh, there's nothing to that," said Mary-Lou.

"Don't be cagey," said the man. "Give, *give.*"

"No, there isn't anything to it," she said.

"When are they making the test?" said the man.

"That was just something in one of the columns," she said.

"Listen, if you're not signed up, I might be able to arrange a test for you. If you're not signed up. If you already signed, skip it."

"I haven't signed a thing," she said.

"She really hasn't," said Arthur.

"Arthur, I wouldn't believe you under oath," said the man. "Young lady, come to my office eleven o'clock tomorrow morning and we'll have a conversation." The man's name was Lew Linger, and he had a job similar to Arthur's at another studio. "Will you be there? Eleven A.M.?"

"Tomorrow I can't, but thanks for the invitation," she said.

"Then when can you?" said Lew Linger. "The next day?"

"All right, the day after tomorrow," she said.

That night Arthur was greatly disturbed. "He means it, Lew Linger."

"Well, that's great," she said.

"Yeah, but where does it put me if *his* company makes a test of my girl? I'm making with the rent and Lew Linger steals her right out from under me. I'll be the laughingstock. I *could* lose my God damn job. Supposing Lew's company makes a test and they sign you? I heard of guys getting fired for a lot less than that."

"Well, you get me a test with your company."

"I don't have the authority. Those tests cost money, and anyway that's not my department. Who the hell does Lew Linger think he is?"

"I don't know, but he can get me a screen test, and if he's that inarrested. . . ."

"Oh, personally he is, all right. Lew Linger is a regular wolf."

"If he can get me a screen test he can take a bite out of me—where it won't show."

"Don't *say* that," said Arthur.

"I will say it. Sixty dollars a month rent doesn't mean you own me. You're getting off pretty light, considering. You don't think I don't get other offers? Listen, there isn't a day goes by without I get some kind of a proposition. And a lot better than sixty a month rent. As far as that goes I could pay my own rent."

"Sixty dollars? You think that's all you cost me? I'm always giving you presents. Who gave you the silver fox, two hundred and seventy-five dollars and worth twice that retail? How much do you think I spent taking you to the cafés?"

"Is it worth it, or isn't it? That's the main question. You're not doing it for charity, Arthur. You make me mad, throwing that up at me how much you spend on me. Big-hearted Otis, sure. Well, listen, Big-hearted Otis, go on back to that dumpy wife of yours in Fort Washington—"

"Port Washington, and I never said she was dumpy," said Arthur. "I said she was zaftig, which doesn't mean the same thing."

"That's your way. You always try to change the subject, but you're not getting away with it this time. I'm mad, see? So either you get me a screen test or don't call me up any more. You can go home right this minute, for all I care."

"At ha' past two in the morning?" said Arthur.

Before the night was over he had agreed to try to get her a screen test, and before the day was over he had persuaded the studio to give her one. His argument was based on the fact that Lew Linger, who was a wolf but a cagey one, had shown so much interest on his very first meeting with her.

The test was made in a studio in Brooklyn, without sound, and consisted largely of Mary-Lou walking around in a silk bathing suit. It was hardly more than some footage of a young girl with an exceptionally good figure, and such tests were as often as not put away and forgotten. But Mary-Lou, who was learning fast, telephoned the fellow who had put her name in his column and thanked him for the mention. He in turn thanked her for thanking him and two days later she was in his column again. "You saw it here," he wrote. "Lovely Model Mary-Lou Lloyd was slated for a screen test, we said. She made the test and execs of the Peerless Studio are readying an all-out campaign for their new discovery."

When the item appeared she telephoned Lew Linger. "Why you double-crossing little bitch," he said.

"Maybe I am," she said. "But it would of been worse to double-cross Arthur. You know how it is with Arthur and I. Almost a year now."

"Don't tell me you're in love with him," said Lew Linger.

"I didn't *say* that, Mr. Linger. But he's been awfully good to me."

"Are you leveling?"

"He has been. If it wasn't for Arthur I never would of got to know all these people."

"If you're leveling—you remind me of an old song. 'I Found a Rose in the Devil's Garden.' All right, no hard feelings. Maybe we have that talk some other time, wuddia say?"

"That's entirely up to you, Mr. Linger," she said.

"I get it. Well, how about this afternoon?"

"What time?" she said.

Lew Linger was a much more interesting man than Arthur, and not only because he was a wolf and Arthur was not. You went out with Lew Linger and people were always coming to *his* table, not a case of him always going to theirs as it was with Arthur. You never saw Arthur's name in the gossip columns, but Lew was in them all the time, either as the escort of some girl or as the originator of some wisecrack. To a certain extent he was a celebrity on his own, not the recognizable kind who was asked for his autograph, but a special kind that got a big hello from a lot of those who were asked for their autographs. More to the point was that when you went out with Lew Linger you often ended up at Reuben's in the company of some very famous people. Nothing had come of the screen test that Arthur got for her and Arthur naturally stopped speaking to her when he found out that she had dated Lew. It went without saying that Arthur would stop making with the rent money, but Mary-Lou, after an anxious week or two, adopted the habit of borrowing money. She would say to a man, "How would you like to lend me a hundred bucks?"

"What the hell for?" the man would say.

"Well, I might be able to pay you back *some* way," she would say.

"That's a new approach," the man would say. But it was remarkable how often it worked, and putting it on a loan basis made it a different transaction from that of a hustler and a john. She always paid the man back, and not in money, and usually within twenty-four hours. Some of the men were repeaters, and she had a pretty good winter, borrowing from some and going out with Lew Linger, but Lew said no more about a screen test for his company. One movie star invited her to accompany him on the train ride back to the Coast, but she told him she would never go to Hollywood without a contract. "You're not so dumb," said the movie star.

"Who said I was?" said Mary-Lou.

However, she was beginning to get a bit worried about the summer, when a lot of the men would be going away and things would be slack, as her father always said about work at the mines. Lew Linger was planning a trip to Europe with some company executives. "I wish you'd take me, but it'd be like carrying coals to Newcastle," she said.

"Yeah, or taking a broad to Hollywood," said Lew. "I understand a certain movie star offered you a ride out to the Coast."

"I wouldn't leave *you,* Lew," she said.

"The hell you wouldn't. Don't try to con me, baby. I went for that act once, but not twice."

"Well, you tried to con me, too, you know. That stuff about the screen test."

"You want to know something? That wasn't altogether a con," said Lew.

"Well, you can still get me one," said Mary-Lou.

"You don't want a screen test, you want a term contract."

"All right, so I do. So get me one."

"You want one of those seventy-five a week for the first six months and options up to seven years? You wouldn't want one of those. You're doing better right here in New York City, putting the arm on guys."

"I want to go to Hollywood," she said.

"Baby, you'll be out there six months and they won't take up your first option."

"I don't care, just so I have a contract. Let me worry about the option. Do this for me, Lew, and I'll never ask you for another thing."

"You wouldn't get another thing."

"Listen, I know if I go out there under contract I'll stay. Once I'm in pictures I'm all set. And even if I don't get to be a star, a *big* star, I'll manage all right. There's none of them are better built than I am, and who says you have to act?"

"Nobody," said Lew.

"I just want to be in pictures, Lew. I got a fixation on it, a real fixation. Since I was ten years old, going to the matinees on Saturday afternoon. That was where I wanted to be, up there on that screen."

"Yeah? Who was your favorite movie star?"

"I didn't have any. It was me I wanted to be up there. I didn't go around imitating other people, or wishing I was Clara Bow. I never saw a one of them that I didn't think I was prettier than, and better built."

"I was thinking more of the male stars. Who were your favorites among them?"

"You know the only one I ever sent away for his picture? Eric Von Stroheim. I never got it, either," she said, and paused.

"If I ever got in a picture with him I'd fall away in a dead faint," she went on. "The handsome ones never thrilled me, except one I found out later was queer."

"Who was that?"

"I'd be ashamed to tell you. Everybody knows he's queer, everybody in picture business. You'd laugh at me if I told you. The first time I ever heard it was in Philly, a fellow I knew in the distributing end. I wanted to hit him. But that's me. The only male stars I ever went for, the big heavy and a panseroo. *Get* me a contract, Lew. Even if it's only one of those seventy-five a week ones."

"That's all it would be, too," he said. "All right, I'll speak to Jack Marlborough."

"Who's he?"

"Nobody very big, I assure you. But big enough to get you that kind of a contract. You might say he's vice-president in charge of starlets, only he's not a vice-president. He's assistant to the casting director, and if *he* signs you it's the kiss of death, because everybody'll know he's doing somebody a favor. In this case, me."

They gave her a contract, and it was for seventy-five a week for six months, a hundred a week for the second six months, and so on for five years until she might be earning five hundred a week if all her options were taken up. They paid her fare to Los Angeles, in a lower berth on less famous trains, and she was not at the studio two weeks before she realized that she was never going to be a star in motion pictures. They had her posing for stills—fan magazine art—but the only time she appeared before a movie camera was as a cigarette girl in a gangster film. She was not given lines to read, not even "Cigars, cigarettes." She took a one-room apartment in the Rossmore section and bought a Ford V-8 roadster on the installment plan at a used car lot on Vine Street. She slept with the head cameraman who shot the gangster picture and he put her name in his little black book. Jack Marlborough introduced her to a couple of agents who showed no interest in furthering her professional career, but one of them invited her to a party at Malibu Beach which turned out to be a celebration of the twenty-first birthday of the son of a movie producer. She and the four other girls at the party were required to take off their clothes for the men at the party, who consisted of the birthday boy, the agent, and two college classmates of the birthday boy. It was the messiest party Mary-Lou had ever been to and it lasted two days. It came to an end when the birthday boy's uncle arrived and compelled the agent to take the girls back to Hollywood.

Her next visit to Malibu Beach was hardly more profitable but somewhat less messy. An English novelist, who had been singularly unsuccessful in his efforts to get the big stars to go to bed with him, was the house guest of an aging character actress who had a cottage at Malibu. He complained to her that he simply could not go back to England with his virtue intact, and she told him that he must lower his sights; that he might be a very popular author throughout the United Kingdom, but to the glamor girls of Hollywood he was just another Englishman with ants in his pants and no studio connection. "I'll see what I can do," she said, and Mary-Lou Lloyd got a surprise invitation to dinner from Cecilia Ranleigh, whom she had never met. Jack Marlborough, who had suggested Mary-Lou to the old lady, said that it would be a good chance for her to meet a different class of people.

"What's the gimmick? Why me?" said Mary-Lou.

"You'll find out when you get there. Miss Ranleigh is sending her car for you."

The car, a ten-year-old Rolls-Royce, was reassuring, but when Mary-Lou was greeted by her hostess and introduced to the other guests she knew immediately why she had been invited. The eager smile of the man with the missing molars gave him away. The dinner guests were ten in number, English writers with their husbands or wives, and with the exception of Cecilia Ranleigh, no one Mary-Lou had ever seen before. She had a hard time understanding what they said, but what got through was some juicy gossip about absent members of the British colony. The gossip was not particularly new, but they all enjoyed retelling it. The only man who did not join in was the writer on Mary-Lou's left, and he hung back because he was waiting to be asked to do his spessiality, his collection of Goldwynisms. On Mary-Lou's right was Geoffrey Graves, the man with the missing molars, who was so eager to be pleasing. He emphasized several conversational points with pats on Mary-Lou's knee under the table and she let him get away with it temporarily. Her mood, however, was not jovial. Jack Marlborough had practically ordered her to go to this party, despite the fact that he would not discuss her soon-due option. He was going to get all he could out of her before telling her that the ax was about to fall. In the second place, she was having a lousy time with these people, who managed to make her feel that they all knew she was there to entertain Geoffrey Graves. In the third place, she was not even repelled by Geoffrey Graves. He was a slightly lecherous schoolboy, and neither a Kevin Kelly, a Lew Linger nor an Eric Von Stroheim. In the fourth place, she did not like being made to feel like a foreigner when she was the only person there who was not one. Accordingly, at the dessert, when Mr. Graves let his hand linger on her knee, she looked deep into his eyes and smiled and burnt his hand with her cigarette. All present guessed what had happened, and laughed. But though they were laughing at him, they made it seem that the laugh was on her.

"Could have happened to anyone, you know," said the man who had done the Goldwynisms. "Imeantosay."

It was a great, great joke. "Serves you jolly well right, Geoffrey," one of the woman said, but without in the least being on Mary-Lou's side.

Furious, Mary-Lou got up and said, "If you don't mind, I'm going home."

"Oh, my dear, you've been embarrassed and you mustn't be," said Cecilia Ranleigh. "Really you mustn't."

"Puts old Geoffrey in the spot, I mustsay," said the Goldwynist.

"I'm most dreadfully sorry," said Geoffrey Graves, but he divided his apology between Mary-Lou and Cecilia Ranleigh.

"Skip it," said Mary-Lou. "If you don't want me to take your car, call me a taxi. But I'm getting out of here."

"Well—if you won't change your mind," said Cecilia Ranleigh. She spoke to the butler-chauffeur. "Bring the car around for Miss Lloyd, please."

Mary-Lou left the diningroom and waited in the hall. No one bothered to wait with her, and she could hear a lot of laughter from the diningroom. They were having a lot of fun at the expense of Geoffrey Graves, but at hers too. On the ride back to Hollywood the chauffeur said nothing until they got past Beverly Hills and were in the Sunset Strip with the lights of the Trocadero and other restaurants. It was not yet ten o'clock. "It's early, Miss," said the chauffeur. "Would you care to stop for a drink?"

"With you?"

"That's what I had in mind," he said.

"Don't you have to be back there right away?"

"They could do without me. I could have a flat tire."

"Well, why not?" said Mary-Lou. Without his chauffeur's cap his livery made him look like a middle-aged man in a dark suit. "Not the Troc, though. Let's go to some place quiet."

The place they picked was quiet in that it did not have an orchestra. Otherwise it was lively. The customers were finishing their dinner and settling down to their drinking. It was a youngish crowd, and Mary-Lou recognized some of them. "Strange people," said the chauffeur, when they were seated.

"Who? These?"

"I was thinking of those we left. The dinner party. By the way, my name is Jack."

"You're not a real butler, are you?"

"Not a real butler, but a real chauffeur. I buttle when I have to but only for the money. There aren't so many jobs for chauffeur only." He was bald and probably close to fifty, but the moment he lit a cigarette he abandoned the servant manner. "Welsh, aren't you? With the name Lloyd."

"My father was Welsh descent. My mother was Irish."

"Quite a combination, isn't it? Produce quite a temper. Well, he deserved it. I've watched him making his passes and getting nowhere, Mr. Geoffrey Graves. He's not a very personable chap, but I suppose at home he trades on his reputation. Here, so few ever heard of him." He talked on and they had two or three drinks until he looked at his watch. "Oh, dear. Time I fixed that flat tire. The bill, waiter, please."

They went back to the car. "I'm going to sit in front," said Mary-Lou.

"Very well," said Jack "I get Thursdays off and every other Sunday. Could I have your phone number? I'd like to take you to dinner."

"You would?"

"Yes. You like me, don't you?"

"Yes."

"Do you like flying?"

"You mean in an aeroplane? I've never been up in one," she said.

"Never? You must let me take you up. I was in the R.F.C., and I've kept up. Chap out in Glendale lets me fly his Moth. Will you go up with me one day soon?"

"Maybe I might. Not if I think about it, but I might."

"You'd love it. I know you would."

"How do you know?"

"Oh—one knows."

"What else does one know?"

"Well—one knows that you stood up to those hyenas single-handed. Miss Cecilia Ranleigh is a formidable woman, and the others are not bad individually. But en masse they can be very cruel."

"I hated them," said Mary-Lou.

"Of course you did. Then you'll let me take you up?"

"Yes," she said.

"You might like it enough to learn."

"Let's not rush things," she said.

He never telephoned her, but as it happened he had only two weeks left in which he might have. An item in a chatter column said: "British colony saddened to hear Cecilia Ranleigh's butler, John Motley, killed in plane crash at Glendale." That was all he got in the press, and it was probably too late to send flowers. . . .

Down there was Malibu Beach, and now Mary-Lou could honestly say, when she went back to New York, that she had seen the Pacific Ocean. She had almost been able to say she had seen it from the sky.

Hello Hollywood Good-bye

THE LAST TIME I had been in Palm Springs, only a few professional military men had ever heard of Dwight D. Eisenhower. That was in 1941, when everybody with any sense knew that we were going to have to tangle with Nazi Germany (and only a few fanatics in Washington and Tokyo were giving serious thought to the probability of a side-show war with Japan). Eisenhower had made a brilliant record at the Command and General Staff School, the War College and the Army Industrial College, but his national reputation came nowhere near that of Peter Lorre, Paul Lukas, Charlie Farrell, Gilbert Roland, Frank Morgan, Charlie Butterworth, Robert Benchley or any of the other friends with whom I sat around the Palm Springs Racquet Club pool. If anyone had mentioned the name Eisenhower I might have said that there were some Eisenhowers (Eisanhauers) in Elizabethville, Dauphin County, Pennsylvania, a town that was known to Pennsylvania farmers as the place where they built the Swab wagon. The Swab Wagon Works manufactured good, honest, sturdy vehicles that we

Pennsylvanians considered superior to the Studebaker, and the Swab family produced a girl named Carrie Swab who was very pretty and whom I called on whenever I visited my relatives in nearby Lykens. My father and my grandfather owned Swab wagons and swore by them, but in spite of the company's reputation it went out of business. Do you know what a chunk is? A chunk is a work horse of the kind that used to haul Swab wagons. Farmers stopped buying chunks and Swab wagons at the same time, and somewhat indirectly Dwight D. Eisenhower, whose family came from Elizabethville, had helped to put the horse and wagon out of business. During World War I young Eisenhower had been in charge of an Army tank school.

I sat and talked with General Eisenhower for a couple of hours not long ago in Palm Springs, and as far as I was concerned we could have talked for a couple of months. My wife and I had had lunch with Mr. and Mrs. Freeman Gosden and Mrs. Eisenhower at Eldorado Country Club in Palm Desert, near Palm Springs. We had never met the Eisenhowers, and it was also my wife's first meeting with the Gosdens. The luncheon could have been one of those pleasant social occasions where everyone is friendly and polite, and that leave no special impressions. But we liked Mrs. Eisenhower and she liked us, and when that had been established—two minutes after we met—the occasion became a special one. She invited us back to her house to meet her husband.

Sitting there alone, watching a golf tournament on TV with the sound turned off, was the man who had commanded the mightiest army in the history of the world and had twice been President of the United States. I was not there for an interview and I am not going to quote him, but I violate no Official Secrets Act by revealing that the TV was silent because my host is just as impatient with TV commercials as you or I. I shall also take the liberty of stating that the first Republican I ever supported for the Presidency is, like me, an armchair member of Arnie's Army. From then on, for two hours, we chatted—as I later told my daughter—like a couple of senior citizens at the Nassau Club. Mrs. Eisenhower was showing my wife around the house while her husband and I had our conversation, on sports, politics, history, current events, our ailments, Pennsylvania, in an atmosphere that was relaxed and reasonably sprinkled with helling and damning. When it came time to leave we signed the guest book and I neglected to write my name in a collection of my short stories that Mrs. Eisenhower had on her desk. I was in a fog of euphoria produced by the experience of wanting to like two people and finding that you would have liked them anyway.

We went back to the Palm Springs Racquet Club, where we were staying, and it was then that I began to wrestle with the meaningful thoughts about Life that seem to be particularly intrusive whenever I revisit California. It is all wrong to be that way in Lotus Land. Most writers go to California because they have been hired by Hollywood, expecting to hate it and doing so. Since 1934 I have gone there about fifteen times, for stretches as long as two years and as short as two days. For various reasons I was never very happy there, and sometimes I was miserable to the point of despair. But the scene of intense feelings, of love and failure and hope and envy and loneliness and frustration, becomes in time historical ground. It is not quite the remote cemetery that it becomes so long as you stay away from it. You have spent, expended, too much of your life there, and all the memories are revivified when you go back. So it is for me in Southern California, a place that I have known so well and for so long that half the citizens do not remember my old landmarks, and I find my way around by points of a compass rather than by names of highways and buildings. When I first arrived in California there were Jews who regarded Franklin D. Roosevelt as more dangerous than Adolf Hitler; the picture I was assigned to work on was for Richard Arlen and Carole Lombard; the band at the Coconut Grove was led by Gus Arnheim (with the Downey Sisters up front); the fashionable restaurant was the Vendome; the biggest automobile in town was a Lincoln town car, license number MW-1, owned by my neighbor, Mae West; it was against the zoning ordinances to put up a building more than fourteen stories high, Toby Win was a starlet at Paramount, Mary Pickford was still married to Douglas Fairbanks and Pickfair was a quasiofficial Blair House to which Will Hays would take visiting notables. Irving Thalberg was the reigning genius at Metro and they had not yet built the Iron Lung, as they called the main office in Culver City. Sound was here to stay, and along LaCienega and Fairfax and on the side streets of Hollywood, little bungalows had been converted into studios where veteran singers and Shakespearean troupers were giving lessons to people who wanted to learn to enunciate and project. Hedda Hopper was still an actress who played society bits, and Frank Sinatra was trying to get on the Major Bowes amateur hour. Olin Dutra won the U.S. Open back in Philadelphia, but the cash value was so small that he sold me a set of matched irons for half price at the Brentwood Club, where he was the pro. That was 1934 for you, when the Swabs of Elizabethville were much more famous than the Eisenhowers, and I was getting $300 a week at Paramount.

Every day I made some excuse to stop at a Sunset Boulevard garage owned by Eddie Pullen, the former racing driver, to have a look at a while Rolls-Royce phaeton he had for sale for $1,500. It was a beautiful thing, about ten years old, and I think the only reason I did not buy it was that I was making good money for the first time in my life and had developed a horror of going into debt. I spent every cent I made, of course, and my credit was getting good, but to go into hock for $1,500 for a Rolls-Royce would have been to deprive myself of the first real financial freedom I had ever had, and I was enjoying every minute of it. I was twenty-nine years old, divorced, not on good terms with my family, with no commitments or responsibilities, the author of a highly successful first novel, almost two years on the wagon, and as one girl said, a pullover. I spent about five months in Hollywood, and then suddenly I had had it. I am an Easterner and my favorite season is the autumn. Perhaps I had been reading in the week-late New York Papers about the Ivy League football prospects, and the plays that would soon be opening on Broadway, and I was beginning to be impatient to get to work on my second novel. At all events I had had enough sunshine and I asked for and got my release from Paramount and drove back to New York, determined to stay in the East but knowing that Hollywood would always be there. And it was, but not quite on my terms.

I wrote my second novel, saw it become a best-seller, and ratted around New York until I was sick of New York and New York was sick of me. Of all the places in the world that I could have gone to, I picked Hollywood. I had no movie contract, but I did not need movie money. I could have gone anywhere but Nazi Germany or Soviet Russia; I had made myself *persona non grata* to the governments of Hitler and Stalin, and General Franco probably would not have hung a medal around my neck, though oddly enough I did visit Italy and someone in Mussolini's headquarters offered to provide me with an Isotta-Fraschini. Perhaps Il Duce enjoyed the harsh things I was saying about Hitler and Stalin, or possibly thy got me mixed up with Archbishop John *F.* O'Hara, of Philadelphia, or Bishop Gerald O'Hara, of Savannah, Georgia; or maybe Mussolini had read *Gone with the Wind.* I'll never know. But I went to Hollywood, where no one offered me an Isotta-Fraschini, but I was given the opportunity to lead the schizophrenic existence that seemed right for me at the time. I played a lot of tennis in the daytime, saw a lot of stimulating people at night—James Cagney, Clifford Odets, Sidney Skolsky, Lewis Milestone, Oscar Levant, Mike Romanoff, Cedric Hardwicke, Lothar Mendes, Gilbert Roland, Robert Benchley and Peter Lorre were the men I saw nearly every day, except when an antisocial mood was upon me and I would sit for hours in a tiny study that had windows placed so high that I could not look out.

• • •

SOME NOT VERY good things had happened to me, and not the least of them was the bad critical reception of my book, which was a best-seller but gave the critics an opportunity to second-guess the favorable opinions of my first book. F. Scott Fitzgerald was a friend of mine, and I had seen what terrible shape he was in the year before in Baltimore and New York. I continually wondered about the parallel between his early career and mine that had just begun: a big success with *This Side of Paradise,* followed by unjustified chastisement for *The Beautiful and the Damned.* He had, so to speak, redeemed himself with *The Great Gatsby,* and I had begun work on a new novel that was to be about the same length. But after *The Great Gatsby* he had toiled and sweated over *Tender is the Night,* which I considered far and away his best novel. As a favor to Fitzgerald I had read proof on *Tender Is the Night,* galleys and page proofs, and I was shocked and probably frightened by what the critics and the public had done to it and to him. People from whom he had the right to expect respectful treatment were condescending or worse, and I was convinced that I had nothing better to look forward to. I was politically to the left of Fitzgerald, but it was no more in my nature to write a proletarian novel than it was for John Steinbeck to write a novel about Hobe Sound, or Fitzgerald to write a documentary about Pacific Grove. Because I was involved with the New Deal, I attempted a dramatization of *In Dubious Battle,* but I abandoned the project when I found that in those moments of truth when a writer must believe what he says, a thing is not finally true because another has said it is true. What was true for Steinbeck was not true for me. I had read Silone and Malraux as well as Steinbeck, and I was seeing Odets almost daily, giving money and lending my name to liberal causes, and I had worked with my hands and been miserably poor. Yet I could not, or stubbornly would not, write a novel that depicted all men in Brooks Brothers shirts as fascists and all men in overalls as crusaders for freedom, decency and truth. My memory of fascists in overalls and genuine liberals in button-down shirts was always getting in the way, whenever I was tempted to follow the trend of the proletarian propaganda novel, and thereby escape the fate of Fitzgerald. I was then thirty-one years old, just under half the age I am now.

We fade out here and stick in some stock shots of the Anschluss and Neville Chamberlain waving that Peace in Our Time appeasement paper and the invasion of Poland and the bombing of Rotterdam and of Pearl Harbor. These are followed by some more stock shots of atomic explosions in New Mexico and Japan, and General MacArthur accepting Japanese surrender, and we fade in with some footage of a terrible picture that was the first thing I worked on after the War, which I did with Jimmy Stewart, Hank Fonda and Burguess Meredith. That was 1946; Fitzgerald was dead, I was a new father, forty-one years old and beginning to feel that it was time I began to feel my responsibilities. At least I was growing up, and it may have been a sign of a new self-confidence that for the first time I insisted on a clause in my contract that permitted me to do most of my work at home, back East.

It also may have been something other than self-confidence. It could have been recognition of the fact that the Hollywood I had known and been a small part of was never again going to be the same. There was plenty of evidence that the War had changed nothing; that extravagance and bad taste and poor judgment had not vanished. But the picture business itself was no longer the spectacular enterprise it had been in the life of Southern California. The big conspicuous spenders, for instance, were the people who had made fortunes in the War, in everything from aviation to heavy metals, in oil and in real estate. There had always been rich Californians, but now there was a new breed. They were, in a sense, prospectors, but they had not come around the Horn or by way of the Donner Pass. They had already made their stake in the East and the Middle West and Texas and Oklahoma, and instead of digging for gold they were investing and speculating on a big scale. Most of them had acquired a working knowledge of the tax laws, and they had not come to California merely to avoid the blizzards and the blue northers.

The subtle effect on me was that I stopped thinking automatically of Hollywood as the place where the money was. The money was in California, all right, but it would do me no good to let my agent know that I was available for a three-month hitch with an oil company. If my friends who owned land in Orange County needed expert advice on how to convert a vast citrus acreage into a brand-new town, the last person they thought of was me. So I stopped thinking of Hollywood as a place where I could get a job to tide me over, and to a large extent I stopped thinking of Hollywood at all. From 1946 to 1955 the movie industry muddled along with no assistance from me, and since then I have spent little time there. I live only fifty miles from New York City, and I don't even go there as often as once a month. Indeed, in the last seven or eight years I have been to England more frequently than I have been to California.

MY MOST RECENT trip to California was inspired by the fact that my wife claims (undisputedly) that she goes stir-crazy after Christmas and loathes cold weather. As she had never been to Palm Springs, I suggested Palm Springs. Our widely traveled Philadelphia friends, Mr. and Mrs. Richardson Dilworth, told me that I wouldn't know the place, but they were wrong. I'd have known it anywhere. We drove there directly from the Los Angeles airport, checked in at the Palm Springs Racquet Club, and took a little ride around town. I was actually looking for a shooting gallery where Franchot Tone and I tied for second place in .22-rifle marksmanship in 1939. Not only was the shooting gallery gone; the entire block was gone, Palm Canyon drive was widened, and the big Los Angeles stores like Bullock's and Desmond's had built branches to help create the illusion that you were on an extension of Wilshire Boulevard. Those funny-looking American men with their plaid shorts and their anklet socks and their cameras and their golf caps and their energetic wives were window shopping, stopping to stare at the same nationally advertised merchandise that was for sale in the store back home. Why have I got such an unreasoning prejudice against those combination eyeglass-cases and pen holsters that men clip onto their shirt pockets? Somehow they make me think of civil servants who sit in Washington and draw plans for highways that bulldoze their way through our towns, without regard for character or beauty, knocking down houses that were built in Revolutionary times and uprooting trees that can never be replaced. There were hundreds of those men on Palm Canyon Drive, and in a few minutes I discovered where most of them were staying: in the giant motels and the trailer camps. May I add another unpatriotic note? On the way out to California I looked down at the ground, 30,000 feet below, and made a guess that we were flying over Oklahoma. The man sitting across the table from me was wearing a tie clip in the shape of a tiny slide rule, and in a playful mood I suggested that he use the slipstick to make a quick calculation of our whereabouts. "It don't work," he said.

Gadgetry has always been a form of self-expression in California, whether in slide-rule tie clips that don't work, in the worship of the Lord, in foods, clothes, optional equipment on automobiles, and everything. I was therefore less surprised than my wife when we paid a visit to a trailer camp that everyone said we must see. It was called Blue Skies or Blue Heaven or something blue, and it is owned by Bing Crosby (who now makes his home up north near San Francisco). You may think that the charm in owning a trailer is in its mobility, that you can wake up any morning, make the necessary attachments, and be on your way to new territory. In England trailers are called caravans, a name that connotes the gypsy spirit (in the movie business a trailer is what you nonprofessionals call a "coming attraction"). Well, we went and saw Blue Something, which is certainly the ultimate in trailer camps and is one of the ultimates in gadgetry.

Apparently what you do at Blue Something is to buy or lease the space for your trailer (or two trailers) and then get busy at fixing it up to look like anything but a trailer. As for mobility, forget it. Like the tie-clips slide rule, it don't work. It may not take an Act of Congress to move you out of there, but impulsive decisions to light out first thing after breakfast are simply out of the question. The Blue Something area is so vast that we lost our way on Jack Benny Drive, or maybe it was Burns and Allen Drive. However, the Blue Something is not for impulsive gypsies. Continentals and Imperials are a dime a dozen among the inhabitants, and of the two Rolls-Royces I saw, one was a 1967 and the other a 1965. Vaguely I was reminded of those marble palaces in Newport that the owners insistently called cottages. The reminder was fortified by glimpses of the interiors of the trailers as we drove by. We did not snoop; a good many of the trailers have large plate-glass windows to enable the passers-by to observe the furniture which made the interiors look like model homes decorated by a team from W. & F. Sloane and Gump's.

Only an old-time tennis bum or an orchestra leader can have had more experience of country clubs than I, beginning around 1910 with the Outdoor Club, Pottsville, Pennsylvania, and up to now I have visited the plain ones, the fancy ones, and those in between. The Berkshire, the Harrisburg, Fountain Springs, Whitemarsh, Whippoorwill, Allegheny, Fox Chapel, Longue Vue, the Creek, Sands Point, Jupiter Island, Midwick, Burlingame, Hurlingham, Gleneagles, Mainstone, Riviera, Lakeside, Bedens Brook, Niagara Falls—I have missed a few thousand, but I have seen the typical ones. Eldorado Country Club is not one of the typical ones; it is *sui generis,* and it is not what I would want in a country club. My preference runs to informal white buildings that do not make you feel you have to ask the name of the architect. I like a country club to be as unlike the Waldorf-Astoria as the Model A station wagon was unlike the Minerva town car. The Byzantine splendor of the Eldorado Club did not repel me, and as I was wearing a blazer with the patch of as good a golf club as there is in the world, all the luxury and service and food impressed me only to a degree that I am impressed by a deluxe restaurant. Eldorado is a private club, probably very hard and very costly to get into, but as they used to say in the 1920's, very dressy.

In Southern California, which is semitropical, the women always seem to be in a state of rebellion against the dictates of the climate. San Francisco is a city where the weather encourages the wearing of suits and furs the year round, and since women's fashions originated in cities with more or less similar weather—Paris, New York, Rome, London—the women of Los Angeles are, so to speak, left out in the warm. With oranges growing in the backyard, the Southern Californian women who can afford high style are compelled to dress, or overdress, for the North Temperate Zone. And they do. American women generally overdress and Southern California women lead the nation in this dubious distinction. The only clothes maker of real distinction that Southern Califinia women ever had was Eddie Schmidt, a man's tailor who made suits *and* slacks for Adolphe Menjoe *and* Marlene Dietrich, and Eddie Schmidt has long since gone out of business. Consequently the ladies of Beverley Hills and Holmby Hills, Pasadena and Santa Barbara, have gone right on wearing expensive merchandise that was intended for other, colder towns. I am speaking, naturally, of daytime clothes. Evening dresses do not count; they are uniformly so ugly that a Southern California woman and a London woman and a Bloomfield Hills woman are indistinguishable after dark. But in the daytime, on her native heath, the Southern Californian of means is a sartorial accident, victim of circumstances beyond her control, namely, the local climate and the distant designers' habit of making clothes for cooler weather. This is not very important except that it has been going on for so many years that it seems to be a permanent characteristic of the affluent Southern California women, and reveals a flaw in the indigenous culture. The Parisienne is famous for her tunic, and true or not, that legend has been established as a national trait. The essence of chic in Southern California is deplorable, and I deplore it. The men's clothes are even worse. They are gadgety, day and night, night and day, at the office, on the golf course, at a black-tie dinner party (where the black tie, if it's black, is likely to be half tucked under a white-on-white collar). I am reasonably sure that I would see the same vulgarity and lack of chic in Miami Beach, but I don't care anything about Miami Beach, and I do care something about California. As I said earlier, I have expended a considerable portion of my life in California, by choice, and in my personal history it is historic ground.

Men return to battlefields and beaches where they existed in a state of terror, and they go back to schools and scenes of their boyhood where the tedium and terror no longer threaten. There is a theory, too, that men return to the scenes of their crimes, though I have always questioned that theory. Nevertheless I concede (and maintain) that the temptation to revisit places where you have drunk the water, breathed the air, become familiar with the sounds and smells, and above all struggled with love and hate and turmoil and peace, is irresistible. You have paid rent on that ground, you own a piece of it, and it owns you. I don't think I'll ever go back to California again, until I have to. Nothing can make me go back again, unless I have to take another look at my property.

About the Editor

MATTHEW J. BRUCCOLI is the leading authority on John O'Hara. In addition to writing the standard biography, *The O'Hara Concern,* he has edited *The Letters of John O'Hara* and *Gibbsville, PA: The Classic Stories.* Bruccoli published *John O'Hara: A Documentary Volume* in 2006.